FREEFALL

www.kristenheitzmann.com

FREEFALL

KRISTEN HEITZMANN

BETHANYHOUSE
Minneapolis, Minnesota

Freefall
Copyright © 2006
Kristen Heitzmann

Cover photography by UpperCut Images, © 2005 Richard Radstone.
Cover design by Jennifer Parker

Published by Bethany House Publishers
11400 Hampshire Avenue South
Bloomington, Minnesota 55438

Bethany House Publishers is a division of
Baker Publishing Group, Grand Rapids, Michigan.

Printed in the United States of America

ISBN-13: 978-0-7642-2829-2
ISBN-10: 0-7642-2829-3

Library of Congress Cataloging-in-Publication Data

Heitzmann, Kristen.
    Freefall / Kristen Heitzmann.
        p.   cm.
    ISBN-13: 978-0-7642-2829-2 (pbk.)
ISBN-10: 0-7642-2829-3 (pbk.)
    1. Amnesiacs—Fiction. 2. Kauai (Hawaii)—Fiction. I. Title.
    PS3558.E468F74   2006
    813'.54—dc22   2006019505

To my dad, Richard Patrick Francis,
home with the Lord
and
to Alfred Otto Heitzmann,
my father-in-law,
friend and exhorter

The Spirit of the LORD will rest on him—
the Spirit of wisdom and of understanding,
the Spirit of counsel and power,
the Spirit of knowledge and of the fear of the LORD.

—Isaiah 11:2 NIV

ONE

The blow came like the torrent below, hard and swift and unexpected. Framed by jungle foliage, a face, the thrust of an arm. Her spine arched. She screamed, jerked, and pinwheeled, then splashed in and went under. Swept up in fluid momentum, her head broke the surface. A shout bounced off the canyon wall. She couldn't turn to place it, couldn't catch the words. Another shout, drowned by an ominous roar.

Realizing the danger, she kicked against the rabid current, but it surged, tipped, and flung her down, down to the pounding base. It drove her into the pool, tumbling and crushing, exploding in percussive blasts like war around her. She hit something hard. Pain seared her head. Her limbs slackened. Darkness.

Ears popping, lungs bursting, she woke with a single thought: *Fight!* She pulled and kicked, broke free of the tumultuous churn, and propelled herself to the surface, sucking air and choking. The hungry current dragged her from the pool into the rocky channel. She kicked and ducked—not thinking, just guarding herself as she rushed along until the cataract broadened and slowed.

Ahead, she glimpsed a promontory of dark rocks gilded with moss. She pushed toward them, grasped and slipped off the first but caught hold of the next. Pulling herself into the niche, she choked, then settled enough to draw air in through her nose, out through her

7

mouth. The fire in her chest subsided.

Head throbbing, she leaned against the rock and dragged her thick-tread hiking shoes onto the promontory one foot at a time. A haze of gnats wafted by her face, drifting over the water. Her vision blurred and cleared as she clung there in the pooling edge of the river. A brown bird called raucously. Ferns, broad-leafed trees, crescent-leafed trees, vines, and bushes surrounded her.

Something cut into her chest. She reached up and felt the stiff nylon straps of a hydration pack. Hardly thinking, she took hold of the mouthpiece at the end of the water bladder's hose, bit the release, and drew in warm, then icy water. But as she drank, panic gripped her throat. Where was she, and what was she doing there?

∾

As best he could tell, the waterfall had thrown him back into a sunken lava cave. The roar of the falls resounded inside the walls as he pulled himself over the lip and onto a ledge, using only his arms. Explosive pain shot down his battered and bloody legs. Pieces of his left shin ground together with each infinitesimal shift. His right ankle burned with a different but no less incapacitating throb. Teeth clenched, he rolled to his side, fitting himself into the curve of the cave wall. He lay still, stunned and weak, letting his body recoup, acquainting himself with the points of injury.

He squeezed his brow, rubbing the water from his eyes, and shivered. When Gentry toppled into the water, he'd shouted a warning, but already she was past the point of no return. Not even the strongest swimmer could resist the rushing cataract—as he'd learned. Maybe he shouldn't have gone in for her. There'd been no time to think, to consider, only to react. Seconds before he went over he'd seen her surface in the pool below, but his own plunge was less successful.

He reached down and probed his shin, found the break he'd suspected. Waves of pain kept him from exploring further. *Easy*, he told himself. *Easy.* He could only pray Gentry hadn't hit the same rocks. But then, like him, she'd have been channeled into the cave behind the falls, not carried out. Was she there still?

"Gentry!" No way she'd hear him over the echoing roar, but something in him had to cry out. His eardrums were shell-shocked from the din, but he yelled again. "Gentry!"

Sense returned. If Gentry was out there, he couldn't reach her. He'd never pull through the falls. He'd be smashed down again onto the rocks. And if she tried to reach him?

"No. Please, God." Cut and bleeding, pain escalating, he groaned. Her only chance—and his—was for her to get out, to get help. The trail, hardly more than a wild boar path over roots and rocks and clay, was so remote there was no telling how long until anyone might pass by. And it led to the top of the falls. People weren't supposed to go over.

He dropped his head back and expelled his breath. What had happened? Gentry was an experienced hiker, strong and surefooted. But he'd read enough survivor stories—and stories that didn't turn out as well—to know things could simply go wrong.

He closed his eyes. He needed to garner what energy he had, recover from the shock, rest. His bleeding had slowed, the wounds coagulating. The break in his bone could be bleeding into his leg, but he couldn't help that. At this point, he couldn't help anything. He drew a staggered breath and prayed.

✑

Clouds puffed past overhead, carried swiftly through the sky, but heat blanketed the deep-cut valley where the winds didn't penetrate. Moisture rose from the water and joined the graying gauze that erupted in showers, then passed.

Too woozy to think, she dragged herself ashore. She wanted to stay there, but an indistinct urgency moved her on. Following the water, she pressed her way through the palms and bushes, groping over tangled roots and rocks. She missed her footing and slid back into the river, then scraped her palms and bruised her hip climbing out. Her mind felt like sludge.

The cataract fanned out, plunging abruptly through jagged ridges, the nearest a rocky channel too steep and slippery to attempt. She splashed over and let herself down beside the next channel. Equally steep, the rocky edges of this one were possibly navigable—though not before resting. She drank from the water pack on her back and tried to stop shaking.

After less time than she'd have liked, she started down, turning almost immediately to work down the face like a rugged irregular ladder. Tucking her fingers into a crevice, she was startled by a sharp-faced chameleon-type lizard that skittered over her hand and into the vines that cloaked the ridge on her left. A short way down dangled a large black-and-yellow spider, whose legs went out in diagonal pairs. Again she heard the birds. Around her life teemed, but she felt unutterably alone.

Her arms shook as she stretched down for a hold. The cliff dropped away below. The water broke loose and fell, casting her in mist and slickening the rocks she clung to. Her breath came sharp and shallow as waves of dizziness took hold. She pressed herself to the wall, letting it pass, making it. Maybe there was a different way down, but she didn't have the strength to climb back up and find it.

She inched her foot down, dug in the toe of the hiker, then forced her other foot to release. The bad stretch wasn't too long. She could make it. She had to. She moved her hand, clawed a jut in the rock, then eased down. A slender white bird winged over the falls with a dipping motion that rolled her stomach.

She pressed her face to the stone and waited it out. Clouds parted and the sun caressed her. With her thigh quivering, she groped for a foothold, found a good-sized step, and lowered herself. She could do it. She would.

She reached level ground, staggered into a small clearing beside the stream, and dropped to her knees beside a boulder. Her head felt as though someone had opened it up and filled it with sand. She laid it on her arms. Maybe she'd just . . . rest. . . .

A sudden burst of birdsong penetrated her stupor. She drew in the scent of earth and water and rank foliage. Opening her eyes produced a grinding headache. She reached up and felt the top of her scalp, swollen, tender, and crusted under the hair. What. . . ?

Green folds of land rose steeply all around her, leaves and blooms just tinged with dawning light. She turned slowly, holding her head between her hands, and found the source of the mist wafting over her. A lacy spread of falls tumbled down a jagged cliff, forming streams that flowed past the rock where she'd hunched . . . all night?

In addition to scrapes and bruises, welts on her arms raised up and itched where something had fed on her. She groped up from her knees, brushed the wet, reddish brown leaves off her pants, and stood. Dizzy, she waited for the hazy vision to pass—or not. She rubbed her temples. Where was she? Why had she spent the night in a jungle?

Her parched throat grated. Automatically she reached for the water tube that dangled beside her cheek and took a cool drink. She squeezed the clasps and unfastened the straps across her chest and waist, then, grimacing, worked the pack off her shoulders. Every muscle griped.

She sat down on the rock and laid the pack across her legs. The main pocket held a stick of turkey jerky, a PowerBar, and a trail mix of mostly raw nuts and seeds with enough M&Ms to make it worth it. She found a packet of medicated Band-Aids in the small zippered pouch, and she used them on her left elbow and wrist and applied a layer of sunscreen to her arms and face from the tube in the side pocket. Whatever she was doing, she'd come prepared. But by the throbbing in her head, something had gone wrong.

She tore open the PowerBar and bit into the stiff, semisweet staple. Chewing made her temples throb and killed her hunger. She wanted to lie back down on the damp ground, but something told her she had to keep moving. She didn't know how long or how far. Or which direction for that matter.

She searched the steep slopes to the tops of their ridges, then dropped her gaze back to the valley floor, where the river's voice reminded her: Follow the water. Water runs down. Water leads out.

She slipped the pack back on, fitting it snugly enough to her back that in her daze she'd hardly noticed it was there. With the thin-stalked palms higher than her head, she decided to walk in the shallow edge of the stream. Her canvas hikers were made for water, but the going was slow on the slippery rocks. She gave it up and pressed through where the shorter, thigh-high ferns had taken over beneath the overarching branches of trees.

Ragged clouds overhead dropped misty rain, filling her nostrils with an ozone-rich scent. She kept moving, driven by a need beyond thought. Her vision grew wavy, her balance askew. She stumbled on, the water's voice her only constant. When fatigue demanded, she rested but moved again when she was able.

The sun came out and warmed the air to a mild sauna and brought a fresh chorus of birdsong. She tore a yellowish fruit from a branch, ripped open the peel and sucked out the juice and pulp. She nibbled from her pack. Sometime in the afternoon, she threw up.

The sun was setting when she staggered into a wide, lush, verdant-smelling expanse. She stumbled onto the level ground as at the unexpected end of a staircase. Thorns and branches had torn through her lightweight pants; scrapes and scratches stung her arms and legs. None of that mattered if this valley was what it looked like.

Righting herself, she started across ground patched with watery plots of a broad-leafed, red-stemmed plant. The paths between the paddies were raised and dry, but by the time she'd traversed the plots she was more crawling than walking. As twilight deepened, she staggered into a yard and grabbed hold of a low stone bench.

With the culmination of effort, she slumped to her knees. Her joints felt near to separating. She was aware of her skin. Fatigue weighted her head until it rested on the edge of the bench. Her ears thrummed like a hive, and she thought she might faint.

Then a golden light spread over the fragrant yard. The sound of a door opening. Footsteps on the soft, mossy ground and a voice, not unlike the birds whose conversations had filled the hidden spaces of the forest throughout the day. "Hello?"

No strength to answer.

"Hey." The hand on her shoulder was gentle. "Are you all right?"

Her sand-filled head refused to nod.

"Here, sit." The woman helped her onto the bench. "I'm Monica."

Raising her eyes, she searched Monica's heart-shaped face, looked into the dove gray eyes and registered nothing familiar.

"Can you tell me your name?"

Soaked and shaking, she parted her lips. Her mind groped, but with panic rising in her throat, she whispered, "I don't know."

TWO

Okelani held her hands inches from the stranger's face as though parting the air over her and stroking it down and away. "Plenny fear."

Monica swallowed. She'd recognized confusion, disorientation. But fear? The young woman lay unmoving in the daybed on fresh sheets hung just that day on the lines in the carport. They still smelled of the valley mist and the garden's blooms. She had probably lost her way on one of the trails through the preserved areas of the island. By the bruising on her limbs and head, it was clear she'd taken at least one fall. Okelani would provide something to treat the scratches and cuts, but beyond that, what should be done?

The old woman's sensitive hands glided over the air above the woman's throat and collarbone, breasts, and abdomen. "Malice," she murmured, "but it nevah start here." With thigh-length black hair streaked with gray, eyes nearly white with film, Okelani floated her hands down the woman's torso. She could have the cataracts removed, artificial lenses implanted to restore her sight, but she believed that as God clouded her eyes, he deepened her inner vision, gave her understanding she had been too distracted to attend before.

Monica watched in silence as Okelani listened with her hands. She loved the old woman. She trusted her. But through a tight throat, she asked, "Should I take her to a doctor?"

Okelani lowered her hands to her sides and turned, her body still graceful. "Doctor? Huh. Den why she come for you?"

That was the question she'd been trying to avoid. Of all the yards for this person to stumble into, why had this woman's feet brought her here? "What should I do?"

"What you always do. A pillow for her head. Shelter from da storm."

"Do you sense a storm?"

The old woman turned slowly. "Da Lord my light and my salvation. Who I 'fraid of?"

Monica knew the words like her own skin, but fear took many forms, and she knew that equally well. She trembled for this stranger, and for herself. She did not have the strength to go through it again. Okelani was telling her the woman had come for a reason. But then, they all did.

~

A rooster's crow woke her with a vague sense of unease. Before opening her eyes, she tried to gauge the sensation, to name it. Fear? Too strong. Urgency? Yes. But for what?

She opened her eyes to a preponderance of cacti, one like a heap of bristling snakes, another with folded, cabbage gray leaves like rippled brain tissue. Interspersed were pots and pots of delicate orchids; white, magenta, red speckled. Ferns dangled from the rafters, so that her next thought was of the tropical forest.

The room was the one she'd stumbled into the night before. She must have fallen asleep at once, because she recalled nothing after lying down on the rattan daybed and breathing the scent of freshly laundered sheets. She rose to one elbow. The bed was the color of milk caramel, the sheets frothy cream.

Outside the wide sliding doors, a sheet of gray mist passed. She shuddered. The sense of something pending intensified—but what?

A tap came at the door. The woman from the garden peeked in. "You're awake." Her eyes were almost the exact color of the rain outside. "Did you sleep well?"

The disconnect indicated sleep wasn't a problem. She nodded and winced. Verbal responses would hurt less.

"Last night you couldn't tell me what happened. Or even your name."

Her name . . . How could she not know? She pressed up to sit. "I must have hit my head."

"You still don't remember?"

Fear stirred. But was the fear that of not knowing? "I remember yours. It's Monica." She clung to that piece of information.

"Call me Nica." The women sat down on the edge of the daybed, concern etched on her face. "Maybe you should see a doctor. Okelani thinks you have a concussion."

"Okelani?"

"She examined you last night."

Dismay sank in. She had no memory of another person. Nothing.

"You were too deeply asleep to notice."

That was some relief, though not when she thought of lying utterly unaware. Anything could have happened. Something already had.

Nica said, "Don't worry. Okelani's son Clay, the pearl diver, once hit his head so hard he repeated the same things over and over for days."

"Am I repeating myself?"

Nica smiled. "No. You seem to have a gap in your memory."

"A gap . . ."

"Can you tell me anything?"

Fear spiraled up. "No, I . . . it's all gone." Maybe she should see a doctor, but an unaccountable hesitation kept her from saying so.

"Maybe the police—"

"No." The word was out before she knew why.

Nica tipped her head. "Are you in trouble?"

"I don't know. I said that without thinking."

"A reaction more instinctive than thought." Nica turned pensive.

"Maybe." Without recall, did she function on some primal level? She pressed her palm to her temple.

"Okelani thinks someone hurt you. She sensed malice."

Malice. Wouldn't she know? Maybe she should go to the police. Yet something stronger held her back. "I can't explain it. But I need to wait."

Nica nodded. "So what should I call you?"

She shook her head, fists clenched. How could everything be gone, as though she'd only begun yesterday?

Nica fingered a succulent plant with leaves like small polished stones. "How about Jade?"

She gave the room a quick glance. If she was going to be named for a plant that was better than Aloe Vera or Orchid. "Jade. Okay." She slipped the name like a thin garment over her nakedness.

"Would you like some fruit, Jade?"

"Maybe a little." She was still queasy, but a bump on the head couldn't last forever. She'd remember, and then she'd understand. "Could you tell me . . ." Her mind clogged with questions, all the things she didn't know. "Where am I?"

"Hanalei. On the island of Kauai."

"Kauai?"

Nica nodded.

Jade bit her lip. What was she doing on Kauai?

"Come and eat something." Nica stood and glanced over her shoulder. "It'll all work out." But her smile didn't hide the shadow on her face.

Nica looked out through the window to Jade sitting in the garden, and an ache settled in the pit of her stomach. Maybe this time would be different. But if it wasn't? How many damaged souls could she usher to the portal of death and let go? She still ached from Old Joe's passing. He'd reached her with his body so full of cancer she'd smelled him before seeing the heap of rags and bones at her steps. She recalled keenly how his fingers had clung to hers, unable to relinquish even the pain until she had banished his fear, giving him a peace she could hardly find herself.

She touched her fingers to the glass. Jade had come like an injured bird, her trouble locked in her mind. She might be nothing more than a clumsy tourist, but Okelani didn't think so. What storm could be brewing for the woman with no memory? Had someone hurt her, and would they try again?

Like Jade, most of those who came clung to their privacy and what little dignity they had left. She usually involved no one but Okelani, but now she picked up the phone. Jade had said no doctor, no police, so there was only one place to turn.

The rings ended in an abrupt, "Cameron Pierce."

"*Aloha*, Kai."

"Nica." He softened perceptibly, though she'd obviously interrupted. It was midmorning on the West Coast.

"Are you working on a case?"

"Shuffling a handful, why?"

"I have someone who might need your help."

"Another stray?" His tone communicated his frown.

"A woman came to me last night. She doesn't know who she is."

"Right." The word, clipped and skeptical, did not surprise her.

In light of the sorts of things he handled, she could imagine his wheels turning. But once he saw her, he'd realize Jade wasn't what he thought, that it was as Okelani said; if she was in trouble, the malice was bent on her. A shiver of fear shimmied down her back, though she tried to hide it in her voice and said simply, "It would be nice if you could come."

"Give it to me on the serious scale—one to ten."

"I'm calling, aren't I?"

He expelled a hard breath. "I'll see if Denny's flying over." His hanging up without saying good-bye was more an indication of his focus than his temperament. He didn't mean to be rude, but sometimes he trampled the niceties. Like the sea—Okelani had said—at high surf. Nica smiled.

⌐

In the dim recess of the cave, something bumped against the arm that had slipped into the cool water, something that felt different enough to stir him from sleep. He moved his hand and took hold of . . . his pack. Water streamed from his elbow as he hauled it up against his chest, hyperventilating with relief and groping it like a loved one.

Though it had been ripped from his back, leaving welts across his waist and chest, it didn't seem to be damaged. He'd carried the major portion of their provisions, but what he needed most was clean water. He'd avoided drinking from the dark, still pool, intending to hold out until help came, but now he bit the release at the end of the hose and drank.

Heaven.

He furtively rose to one elbow. He'd always bought the best equipment, believing it might matter someday. With fumbling fingers, he checked pocket after pocket. Knife, food, first-aid kit, all protected by the waterproof exterior. "Oh, Lord." The words slipped from his mouth with deepest gratitude.

For the first time since dragging himself onto the shelf, he felt true hope, not just wishful thinking. With what he had in the pack, he could hold on. Gentry would have climbed back the way they'd come and found her way out. *If* she was uninjured and able to hike.

He prayed again that she had not struck the rocks that had battered his legs. If she was out there, wounded . . . He couldn't think it. He'd seen her surface just before he went over. She'd been carried out and away. She had to be all right. But it bothered him that he'd heard nothing.

Was the cave visible from the other side? The mouth was low, admitting only a half-moon of light, the largest portion underwater, and the waterfall sheeted it. If not for the shelf, he'd be lost. Once again he offered thanks. It was going to be all right. Those details helped him see it. He wasn't young, but he wasn't that old either. And he was fit. Remarkably fit. He'd endure the pain. He'd be smart. He'd make it.

～

After sitting outside between misty showers in the garden, Jade had lain down to rest again in the little porch room in Nica's house. Sleep seemed to steal up and erase hours at a time, and now the day was waning. Her headache and dizziness had subsided, along with the nausea, though she was still stiff and sore. Her ears rang faintly, but her vision had cleared. And her mind?

She pressed her fingers to her temples and tried . . . but could not come up with the answer to Nica's most basic question. Sighing, she went upstairs and found a note saying, *I've gone out. Help yourself for dinner if you're hungry before I'm back.*

Amazingly trusting. A strange woman in her home who refused conventional help and offered no understandable explanation. Why, even she didn't know. And Nica treated her like a guest.

She wasn't hungry—only frustrated, discouraged, and a little afraid. For that she had to get outside and think . . . or whatever her brain was doing instead. *Taking a walk,* she jotted, *to the shore.* Nica had said the bay was within walking distance. Maybe it would trigger something.

She had a sense of having walked along a shore, wet sand, frothy water licking her ankles. She couldn't place herself, couldn't name the strip of beach where her feet had impressed their form, but she could almost feel the sand beneath her toes. Not a memory she could hang a date and location on, but something.

She went out the front door, through the front garden, teeming with a profuse and varied horticulture. She made her way to the road that led past the neighbors' houses and, with the broad valley and the mountains behind her, headed toward the ocean.

It was farther than she'd thought, but walking felt good, in spite of her aches. The damp evening was redolent with wet earth and vegetation, and she drew the aroma into her lungs. The white leather sandals Nica had lent her grew slippery from the wet ground. No rain fell, but moisture so infused the air that the borrowed cotton sundress, a grayish blue batik, grew thick and clingy.

Balmy winds caught her hair as she waited for a few cars, then crossed the two-lane highway. She passed elegant island estates and neared the grass and sand that stretched down to what Nica had told her was Hanalei Bay. Disappointingly fatigued, she took a seat on a low stone wall and watched a handful of distant surfers bob in the swells.

The setting sun broke through the clouds and spilled gold over the deepening blue of the sea. Whitecaps rolled in, catching the rays in their glassy turquoise arcs before tossing themselves on the sand. By the damp state of things, it must have rained most of the time she slept, but she was still surprised more people were not out enjoying the scene.

She supposed familiarity could leach the magic from anything—unless one was in the unique position of finding nothing familiar, not even oneself. A wave of panic rushed in like the breakers before her. Each time she had awakened, she'd expected it all to come back ... but found the same blank wall. She didn't like walls.

And how did she know that? She half smiled. On what did she base such self-awareness? Her smile faded.

Shifting her focus to the bay, she watched her drama played out in nature as the waves rushed in, forgot what they'd come for, and withdrew. She breathed deeply the salt tang of the sea and something smoky cooking nearby. She'd had fresh fruit for breakfast and a plate of rice with strips of grilled chicken for lunch. She might eat again when she returned to Nica's, but in the meantime, she accepted the gentle caress of the island in contrast to its previous rough handling.

There was no reason to take it personally. Nature was nature. The error would have been hers. A misstep, a wrong turn. If only she could remember.

A brown-and-white sparrow flitted to the path and hopped about at her feet. She watched him court her, darting in and tipping his head, pecking the ground to make his point.

"I'm sorry. I have nothing to give you."

The bird hopped along the beaten dirt path, turned his chest to the sun, and flew off for more promising beggary. Or maybe the approaching footsteps sent him off. She glanced at the round-shouldered man who approached from the right and paused.

"Hey, aren't you . . . nah." He shook his head. "Sorry. You looked like . . ." He gave a little laugh. "Name's Sam. What's yours?"

His question echoed in her void. In golf shirt and baggy, flowered shorts, he seemed anything but dangerous, but wariness crept in nonetheless.

"Jade."

"Sure. For your beautiful green eyes." The cliché floundered, but he didn't stop there. "What would you say to a fun night on the island?" Sam shook the thermos he carried. "Mango-passion mai tais." He wiggled eyebrows that, like the pale mustache over his fleshy red lips, bore an unfortunate likeness to mold.

"No, thanks. I can't drink."

He rubbed his cheek, mottled pink from too much sun. "A.A.?"

"Brain damage."

He half laughed before he realized she might be serious, then covered it with a cough. "How about a walk on the beach?"

She shook her head. "Sorry."

Undeterred, he perched himself about five feet from her on the rocky wall. A chunky gold and emerald ring jutted out from his index finger like a promontory when he poured himself a mai tai. He drank it heartily, then bestowed on her the conversational gem, "Ice melts quick here; have you noticed?"

THREE

She almost left the wall to Mai-Tai Sam and went back to Nica's, but even as she hoped he'd lose interest and, like the sparrow, leave her for better prospects, someone else approached from the direction she'd come. As he moved toward her without shifting his gaze, she strained to recognize him.

The closely trimmed beard outlined his mouth and jaw in a way she'd always found dramatic—She stopped with a jolt and replayed that thought. Yes. Ever since grade school. She had looked at the posters of the Spanish Conquistadors in their shining armor and crisp beards, and even though their conquests had been rough for the natives, she couldn't help the thrill that came over her at the sight. The sense of power, even danger.

Dressed in Teva sandals, worn cargo shorts, and a faded navy T-shirt, this man who looked more Hamlet than Cortez had elicited a real glimpse into her past. Could she know him? He stopped beside her perch and fixed her with a piercing indigo stare. No one would be so bold with a stranger. Hope flared.

"Jade?"

She deflated like a pricked balloon. "Yes?"

"I was told I'd find you here."

She studied his brows, the slight lump on his nose, the chestnut hair cropped and either gelled or naturally unruly in the damp air.

Apprehension touched her spine. "Who told you?"

"Nica."

Sam poured a second mai tai and reestablished his position on the wall. With his trusty thermos he'd gained confidence, mellowing into a better opinion of himself. Or maybe the appearance of a competitor awoke something fierce inside his soft shell. Should she be glad he was there?

"We need to talk."

"So talk."

He glanced at her companion. "I've got my truck. Let's take a drive."

"I don't think so." Her head spun. Her breath quickened. *"Malice,"* Nica had said. Was he there to see if she could identify him? He could claim to be anyone, and she wouldn't know.

"What's the matter?" His eyes glinted.

"Nothing." *Everything.* Why couldn't she think? Concussion. Brain injury. And if she'd been injured why hadn't she gone to the police? The resistance had been so strong, yet now it seemed foolish in the extreme.

He frowned. "Look, Nica's—"

"How do I know you know her? You could be anyone. You haven't even given me a name." Which at least Sam had done right off.

He took out his wallet and flipped it open. Pierce. His last name matched Nica's. Cameron Pierce. Great picture. Who took a good driver's license picture? That alone was suspicious. Except that the resemblance to his sister was striking, more obvious in the photo than in person, where his masculine presence superceded their similar features.

She looked up. "Even if that's real, I'm not leaving with you. We can talk here."

"You might find my questions sensitive." Again he glanced at Sam.

"At Nica's, then. I'll meet you—"

"No." He shook his head. "I don't want her upset."

"Do you plan to be upsetting?"

"Nica's way too trusting. She wouldn't see through the Invisible Man."

Under other circumstances she might enjoy his wit.

A couple of teenagers passed by them, toting their boards, and the breeze wafted their sea-soaked scent. Cameron must have seen her digging in her figurative heels, because he slipped his wallet into his pocket and said, "There's not really a choice here."

Au contraire. She shifted position on the wall, adjusting the drape of the dress over her legs and sending the silent message that this location suited her fine. If she'd been the victim of an attack and had no recollection of whom to blame, everyone was suspect. The way he got under her skin could be nothing more than his arrogance, or it could be an internal warning.

Add to that the frenetic way her mind kept processing every detail of his face, physique, and manner. . . . Frustration took hold, then aggravation. Before she could voice it, his cell phone rang. He checked the source and turned away to take the call.

She glanced to her side, wondering if she should bolt.

Sam had developed a glaze. "Walk on the beach?" He grinned.

She'd underestimated Mr. Mango-Passion. The more buzzed he got, the better his chances seemed.

"I'm sorry, no."

"You're tough." He nodded toward Nica's brother. "I don't feel so bad anymore."

"You will in the morning."

He laughed as though it was the funniest thing he'd ever heard. "That was good. Quick and snappy."

"'Brevity is the soul of wit.'" The instant rejoinder sent a quiver of familiarity. She'd used that phrase before. Not just in conversation, but what? Instruction?

Sam's mood shifted from amused to melancholy. He looked ready to beg, but Cameron finished his call and turned.

"Ready?"

Flanked by pathetic and pathological, she almost laughed. "For what?"

"I'm parked right over there." He splayed his fingers toward someplace behind her.

"Saves you wandering around."

He hung his thumbs from his cargo shorts. "Let me put it this way; I'm half owner of the house Nica calls home. I have eviction power."

"One for and one against."

His eyes took on the deepest ocean hue, the part where chance of survival would be negligible. "I'm persuasive."

A brown gecko skittered across the path as the sky grayed around them, silhouetting a fringe of coconut palms. Her beautiful evening was drawing to a close and had been anything but peaceful. "I don't know what you hope to accomplish. You can ask all the questions you want, but I can't tell you anything more than I told Nica. I wish I could." She countered the plaintive note with a square-shouldered pose that said back off. She had enough to deal with.

Cameron Pierce was spectacularly slow on the uptake. He motioned toward his truck, and this time she turned enough to see a black Tacoma parked with the bed toward them, sea turtle decals on the rear window. Hardly a symbol of malevolence, but still.

She didn't recognize the vehicle, but that meant nothing; she didn't recognize herself in the mirror. Even without her vague, sustained anxiety, common sense would keep her from accepting the ride. She shook her head.

"If I were a predator, I wouldn't have wasted time arguing."

"Maybe I know karate."

"Maybe you don't."

He didn't seem the predator type, but her senses were raw, her mind washed clean of any recollection that might identify him. She had nothing but her impressions to go by.

Sam burped discreetly, watching without interfering. While he didn't mind begging, she must not be worth fighting for. Maybe he'd assessed his chances in a clash with Cameron Pierce as nil. Nica's brother exuded a confidence one either respected or resented, but couldn't ignore.

So he took her by surprise when he heaved a sigh and said, "Okay. I'll walk you back to Nica's." She hadn't expected a concession from the conqueror god with the clipped beard and haughty countenance. But then, how accurate were her perceptions? Maybe Sam was the psychopath and Cameron—

"Walk, amble, before it gets dark. . . ." He swept his hand in the direction they should go.

By whatever means her mind currently operated, she decided to accept his graceless offer. If they stayed in the open, where she had room to run and scre—

She felt the vibration in her throat, chords stretched, tissue inflamed. Her fingers went to her throat. Something flickered like a minnow gleaming for a second in a sunlit stream. Another flick and it was gone. But it had been there and left a residue of fear.

She had expected to remember something by now, but there'd been nothing until Nica's brother triggered, if not memories, at least the sensation of memory. And even though the sensation seemed closest to fear, she clung to it—nature abhorring a vacuum. For that reason more than anything else, she got up and started back the way she'd come.

Cameron fell into step, slowing when they neared his truck, then picking it up when she stalked past. "Let me get this straight," he said. "You don't know who you are or how you got here."

"Yet."

"You have no ID, no money, nothing but a swelling on the brain."

"Are you saying I have a big head?"

He slid her a sidelong glance, acknowledging her attempt at humor without finding it humorous. Sam was a better audience. Again a sensation of déjà vu.

"You have no idea what happened?"

A pang squeezed her. "I must have had an accident."

"But you haven't reported it."

How could she explain her unease without raising his suspicions? "Getting lost isn't a crime."

"And yet no one's reported you missing."

She stopped. "How do you know?"

"I asked."

Her jaw fell slack. "You went to the police?"

His eyes turned flinty. "Is that a problem?"

Was it? She didn't know. She could have gone to the authorities herself, but hadn't. Nica had respected that. Her brother must not be so inclined. "My situation is not your business."

"Your situation involves my sister."

And that obviously gave him carte blanche.

"I asked the local authorities if there'd been any recent missing-person reports."

And there hadn't. She didn't know how to feel about that. "You told them about me?"

"Nica asked me not to."

She started walking again. Nica at least had sway with him, and he was possibly not as unreasonable as he seemed. "No report," she mused. "Then there must be no one here to miss me."

"I wouldn't lay long odds on that."

"Why not?"

"You're not the type to travel alone."

She turned. "And you would know this because . . ."

"It's my job."

"You're a fortune-teller?"

The corners of his mouth quirked. "I investigate fraud."

"What kind?"

"Insurance. Criminal schemes. False claims."

"You think I'm faking?"

"It's possible."

Honest. Direct. Irritating. Who could ask for anything more? "And how would I file a claim? What name would I use?" Her steps had quickened with her agitation. "What social security number?"

"You've considered the angles."

She shook her head. "You're like a hypochondriac physician. You see fraud in every face. But believe me, I'd rather know—" Would she? What if she'd blocked her memories because they were too painful, or too frightening? And why was she trying to explain? He was a man who uncloaked liars for a living.

"What are you after? Drugs?"

Something to kill the headache would be welcome.

"Nica doesn't have—"

"I don't use drugs."

"How do you know?"

"Because I . . . know." She felt it. His question insulted her. There was no lick of desire, no craving. Her body knew what her mind had forgotten.

"You think Nica's an easy mark?"

"What?"

"Who told you to go there?"

Nica must have told him what happened. If he didn't believe his sister, what explanation would convince him? She shut her mouth and walked in silence a few moments before glancing sideways. "Why don't you just save us both the hassle and tell me what you want."

And if he wanted her out? She felt suddenly weary. She'd spent one night at Nica's recuperating. For that she was thankful. But where would she go? Who else would show the kindness his sister had by not forcing her into actions that felt wrong—like getting help?

Cameron said, "I'll tell you what I don't want; Nica hurt. Or taken advantage of, or made a fool of."

"You don't have much faith in her."

He hadn't expected that, and by his frown didn't like it. But he also didn't refute it.

She considered the woman whose face was even now the first coherent memory she could conjure up—heart shaped, with a perfect point to her chin that must similarly give her brother's beard that protruding hauteur. Her eyes, in direct contrast to his, held a sincerity that, to Jade's traumatized mind, showed compassion and generosity. Maybe to Cameron it looked weak or gullible. Maybe it was.

"I appreciate everything Nica's done. And as soon as I remember, when I know anything about who I am . . ." She didn't know how to finish. *I'll go back to my life? I'll finish my vacation? I'll know what I was doing in the mountains of Kauai. . . ?*

In the deepening twilight, she kicked a bone-white lump of surf-tossed coral at the edge of the narrow highway, feeling as out of place as it looked on the pavement. They paused long enough to note a lack of traffic either way, then crossed.

"You remember nothing?" he prodded again.

Only the glimpses he'd provoked. "It's pretty much a void."

"And you've done nothing about it."

"It's only been a day. I'm sure the bump will heal." Right. No problem. She could wake tomorrow with everything restored.

"And if it doesn't heal?"

How could she answer that? With what could she predict a future when her past was wiped clean. Who would she call? Where would she go?

"You'll hide at Nica's until you're old and gray?"

She frowned. "Thank you for the grim prognosis."

"I don't pretend to understand your *injury*."

"Just my motives and character."

He sighed. "There are things you don't know."

She spread her hands. "Revelation."

They entered the dusky yard lit with tiki-style lanterns that shed a benevolent glow on the fronds and foliage of Nica's garden and the pathways in between. While the yards around hers were mostly moss-like lawns, Nica's dense, blooming plants created a heady aroma.

Cameron frowned. "Nica is . . ." But then he caught sight of her seated on a stone bench. Instantly his manner changed. "What's wrong, Nica?"

She looked down at her hands. "I found it in the street."

FOUR

Cameron turned to the woman called Jade. Though he'd alluded to Nica's temperament, he didn't want to play it out in front of a stranger. He hadn't learned enough on the walk back to make any kind of decision about her, so he said, "Go ahead in. We'll talk more later."

"If you don't mind, I'll go to bed. My head is splitting." The furrow in her brow punctuated the point.

That meant another night for her at Nica's, but he hadn't decided against that so he nodded, then squatted down beside his sister. The chick was hardly into its feathers. No blood. No telling what had ended its brief existence. He sighed. Telling her it was just a fowl, one of the multitudes that ran wild all over the island and died every day, would not ease her sorrow over this one.

She could get through it without him. He'd made sure of that before moving to the mainland. This was a tiny prick compared to some of the wounds she'd borne. Nica had absorbed more grief than anyone he knew, and she kept opening herself for more.

But he was there now, and his mode was to fix. "You want me to bury it?"

She shook her head.

"Sure?"

She looked up, her face illuminated by the flames. "I didn't ask you here to interrogate her."

"I know that."

"Does she?"

He glanced at the closed bamboo screen. "Hard to say what she knows, isn't it."

"Kai." She said his name like a sigh.

She must have known he wouldn't buy right in. Whether she'd thought it through or not, she'd called him for counterbalance. Why had she thought she needed help this time and not the others? "I don't like it."

Nica drew a hand spade from the box at the end of the bench and stood. "What don't you like?"

"Amnesia." He spread his hands. "It's too convenient. Too easy an alibi."

She stared. "Alibi?"

He hadn't sounded harsh, but there was no tone gentle enough if Nica didn't want to hear something. Jade had made an impression on her, and nothing short of showing her the smoking gun would shake her faith in another complete stranger who'd "happened" to find her door. He shook his head. "You don't need this."

"It's not about what I need." Her eyes were large and tender. "It never is."

"You have choices, Nica. Things don't have to just happen."

"But they do." She carried the chick to the base of an oleander, dropped to her knees and hollowed the earth.

He jammed his hands into the pockets of his cargo shorts. There was no point arguing. Where Nica was concerned, something constantly conspired. She was a vortex for heartbreak, and try as he might he could not find a way to stop it. Not that she ever asked him to. She poured herself out for the countless unfortunates who came to her. He suspected an organized pipeline: Broke, desperate, dying? See Monica Pierce. She never thought to guard her heart, or maybe she didn't know how. They took what she had to give and left her shattered.

She laid the chick in the ground. "I hoped you could help her."

Again he considered how unusual it was for her to include him when she knew how he felt about her openness to strangers. "How?"

She spread the red earth over the fallen fledgling. "Investigate. Find out what happened."

He hung his thumbs on the waist of his shorts. "She's not inclined to cooperate."

"You probably scared her half to death."

He scoffed. "If she's scared, it's because she's hiding something."

Nica's gaze soaked him like a secret tide pool. Okay, so he tended toward skepticism.

"I can't imagine what she's going through. To lose her past, her *self*."

Plenty of times he'd consider that an improvement, but no point getting Nica on that track. He sighed. "I'll look into it tomorrow. Unless she has a miraculous recovery tonight."

Nica frowned at the sarcasm. "Her memory could return at any time. You remember Clay. He walked around like a broken record for days; then suddenly he was fine."

"He knew who he was."

"So maybe she injured a different part of the brain."

"An MRI would determine that."

Nica sighed. "I offered to take her in for tests. She doesn't want it."

"Now, why might that be?" He planted his hands on his hips.

"Kai." She shook her head. "She trusts me, and I'm not going to betray that."

"Then why call me?"

"Because Okelani said—"

He expelled an exasperated breath. "Don't tell me this is some *kapukapu* nonsense." A gecko mocked him with a sharp *kekekekek* from the screen over the window.

"You wouldn't call it sacred nonsense if she were here."

As he took the time to form an inoffensive response, the trade winds blew clouds off the moon, but it quickly covered its face again. "I love Okelani. But that doesn't mean I buy in to everything she says."

Nica laid a hand on his arm. Her fingers were cool. "Jade's in trouble."

"No doubt." And she'd brought her trouble to the one person whose quota had been filled a long time ago.

"Okelani sensed malice but said it did not originate with her."

"Doesn't mean she isn't party to it. Malice has tentacles." Cameron crossed his arms.

"Don't," she whispered.

He unfolded his arms, accommodating her sensitivity to body language. "I wish you hadn't gotten involved."

She said nothing. They both knew she could no more ignore a person in need than such people could avoid seeking her out. From the time she was small, wounded creatures and other children had found in Nica a listening ear and healing kindness. She believed they were sent by God, but in recent years sojourners had come to Nica to die. If God thought she was prepared to handle that, he wasn't watching too closely.

Maybe this time Nica knew she'd reached her limit. It was why she'd called, and why he'd come immediately. But she wasn't ready to admit it, so until then he'd do the best he could. He stroked the line of beard that framed his mouth. "We'll see what the morning brings."

Her gratitude was deep and immediate. *"Mahalo."*

"A'ole pilikia." No trouble.

⌒

The sun's rays never penetrated the incessant flow, but when morning came, the churning water curtain lit up like a gauzy, white wall and brought some comfort to the hollow that had in the dark grown tomblike. When he opened his eyes this morning, the mist held a tiny rainbow. He cried.

Three nights he had spent on the ledge, as immobile as he could keep himself. If Gentry had retraced their path and found no one— likely since it was a local's trail not included in any guidebook he'd seen—she'd have had to walk. She didn't have the Jeep keys. They'd been in his pocket but were there no longer. The barely discernable track was six miles to the more passable, yet still obscure, four-wheel-drive road another eleven miles from the shore. How long would it take on foot?

Not three days. Something was wrong. Was she injured or lost? Maybe there was no passage back to the top of the falls. Maybe she'd tried a different way. Or been carried by the water. Where would it take her? He wished he'd studied that.

Gentry knew to head down away from the center of the island. Even so, much of the coastline was native, especially at the northwest end, the western Na Pali shore entirely so. If she hadn't hit a road or trail, there was no telling how long until she found help. He laid his head back and swallowed the pain.

As he'd done throughout the last three days, he prayed for Gentry to find her way, prayed for her safety, then broadened those prayers to encompass all she'd been through lately, and all that still might come at her. He had hoped this getaway would take her mind away from her trouble, not bring her more. He knew too well the forces arrayed against her, the power of lies, the voices of evil, even the voices of friends infected by the poison of doubt.

He'd seen her stunned disbelief, watched it eat away her confidence, the optimism that had been her nature. He had watched her faith get rocked, the radiant faith that had seemed so solid before she'd been cast into the furnace. He'd prayed she would emerge tempered, not scarred. He prayed it now, taking his mind from himself.

But then he shifted and pain shot through him. The leg had swollen, and some of the lacerations not only bled but oozed. He'd done what he could with the small first-aid kit, but the injuries were too many. His right knee and ankle had swollen, though the pain in that leg had a different tenor and he suspected sprained ligaments. If the injuries had all been to one leg, he might have attempted escape, but having both legs unable to kick and bear weight had made the battering beneath the falls an unwarranted risk he knew better than to consider—until now.

His original focus had been to deal with his condition until help came. But it had been three days, and he had to face the fact that help might not come. His only chance—and Gentry's—could be for him to make it out.

It wasn't fear that hollowed his insides at the thought. It was cold reality.

⌒

Jade made her way up to the kitchen where Cameron and Nica were seated at the round rattan-and-glass table. It had taken her a good part of the night to fall asleep, and it showed. Her eyes were hollowed and her head ached. Hour after hour chasing after sleep, she had felt so close to remembering things, but then they'd drift away like the mists outside, as insubstantial and impossible to grasp. Seriously discouraging.

Cameron looked up from the morning *Islander*, his smile as sincere as a salamander. "And who are we this morning?"

She glared at his rested and robust mien. "Who we've always been, regardless of recall."

Nica sliced a papaya and laid the coral-colored slivers next to the chunks of fresh golden pineapple on the plate. "Good morning, Jade. Did you sleep well?"

"Not really." She tenaciously held Cameron's stare. "I couldn't stop trying to remember."

He laid the newspaper down. "And?"

Her jaw tightened. "I'm not sure pressure helps."

"Wouldn't really know, though, without a professional opinion."

"Are you offering yours?"

"I'm suggesting a doctor."

A thin, gray-and-white cat circled the table, meowing with a raspy noise that sounded as though something had stomped its throat.

"I suppose you're paying since I have no money, no ID, no credit card or proof of insurance." She took a seat at the table and breathed the sweet, tangy aroma of the fruit. "I think we discussed that yesterday."

"A stop at the Hanalei precinct would take care of it."

"I can't risk the pub—" The word died in her throat. Aggravation with him had spurred another glimmer. But why would she be concerned with publicity?

He cocked his chin up. "What?"

"Nothing."

His gaze locked on like an arched and hooded king cobra's. "Can't risk publicity?" The mesmerizing stare laid siege to her defenses. "What don't you want publicized?"

Her mind fought for an answer. It was almost painful.

"Please," Nica murmured.

Cameron's combative attitude had challenged her complacent mind and triggered thoughts or at least impressions that slipped past her block. But sensitive to Nica, he sat back, palms resting on the table. "You need a medical opinion. Your memory could be blocked by a clot or tumor. We're only assuming a head injury, and none of us—" He glanced at Nica. "Not even Okelani is qualified to make a diagnosis."

Clot? Tumor? Her stress level was so much better now.

"Can we vouch for her?" Nica's soft voice broke through their standoff. "Say she's our guest from the mainland and . . ."

"Make up a name, a story?" Cameron's gaze was gentle on his sister, but it was obvious what he thought of the idea. "You want to falsify records?"

Jade tightened her jaw. "I'm not asking anyone to lie for me. And I'm not going to the hospital. There'll be too many questions. You can't keep something like this quiet." Again she had the need to shield herself, even if she couldn't tell him why.

He turned back and fixed her with a probing frown. "Should we recognize you?"

She glared back. "*America's Most Wanted*, maybe?"

"Why the aversion to publicity?"

"I'm not av—" Or was she? She turned away and chewed her lower lip.

"What if he's right, Jade?" Nica slid the fruit plate her way. "We should rule out something more serious." Her voice quavered. "Something life-threatening."

Jade sank back in her chair. "Life-threatening?"

For the first time Cameron's tone softened toward her. "I'll guarantee payment. You can pay me back when your insurance reimburses you."

Jade swallowed. "You think something's wrong. Really wrong."

He flicked a glance at his sister. "Nica's worried. I want to set her mind at ease."

"It's not about me." Nica squeezed her hands together.

It obviously was to him.

His tone was reasonable. "I think we should know what we're dealing with."

Jade almost snapped that he wasn't dealing with anything, but that would be untrue. He and Nica had both been dragged into her situation. And what if it was something serious, life-threatening? "What if I don't have insurance and can't reimburse you?"

"I don't think you're indigent."

"Your crystal ball again?"

"You were wearing Merrell Chameleon hikers when Nica found you, and your pack is top-of-the-line."

"Do you always pry into people's personal belongings?"

"When I'm asked to investigate."

Nica gasped. "I asked you to help, not . . ."

"It helps to gather everything I can from what I have to work with. People who vacation on Kauai with premier sporting gear are likely to have insurance."

Jade dropped her hands to her lap. "You make a lot of assumptions."

"My profession is mostly gut instinct."

"Then I'm certainly a dangerous criminal you want nothing to do with."

"An MRI might clear things up."

Was there a tumor in her brain, something malignant squeezing out the memories, making her paranoid? Had she wandered into the mountains in some kind of daze? She shivered. "All right. I'll see a doctor." It was probably the right thing anyway. "But no police. People listen to scanners."

He raised curious brows. She squeezed her temples, surprised herself by the things coming out of her mouth. She was sitting at a table with strangers, wearing a borrowed sundress, and wondering, wondering. Tears caught in the back of her throat.

Cameron's tumor comment scared her, even if he was just protecting his sister, who might very well need protecting. She had intruded on them. And her resistance to the obvious steps seemed ludicrous. "I'll get my—your sandals on."

"Jade." Nica touched her shoulder. "Only if you want this."

She sighed. "I want to remember." At least she thought she did.

Cameron crossed his ankles and watched her all the way to the glass door that opened to the lanai. She resisted glaring back at his cynical face. She had nothing to go on except her inner perception of self, but she didn't think he was right about her. Avoiding a spectacle didn't make her dishonest or criminal. He was probably right that she needed to be examined, but his suspicions infuriated her.

The outside stairs were the only way back to her little porch room. If only she could stay there. She had the strongest feeling that she was about to set things in motion that she had no power to control.

FIVE

Cameron sat with Nica and Jade in the cramped medical office as Dr. Yamaguchi explained the results of her tests. "A contusion to the central area of the brain can disrupt retrieval of retrograde memory while allowing normal formation and storage of new—exactly the type of amnesia you're experiencing." He seemed intrigued by Jade's case, but not overly concerned. "I would like to schedule an MRI for tomorrow to gauge the full extent of the injury."

Cameron nodded for her to agree to it. He'd cover that expense, as well, in order to lay Nica's mind at rest. He felt confident Jade had the resources to repay him, though it might be through ill-gotten gains—in which case a reward could cover her debt.

"But," the neurologist emphasized, "I'm doubtful we'll see any signs of hemorrhage or tumor."

From his vantage point, Jade's relief seemed sincere, Nica's transcendent. If the news had been bad, he would not have let her stay. He might have tried to find her another place, looked for family or friends. At the very least he'd have convinced her to rely on the authorities to assist her. Anything to save Nica the angst she would suffer watching another person come to her and die. That much, at least, was no longer a concern.

"So, I will remember." Jade's voice held a cautious expectancy.

The doctor shifted the thin wire rims up the narrow bridge of his nose. "This complete a loss for this duration is unusual, but every amnesia is different. Very likely things will return to normal within days, maybe even hours."

Hope bloomed in her face. If she was faking, she was good. And he'd run into plenty of consummate fakers, people who milked similar situations for all they were worth. He was singularly able to take them apart, but Jade's reluctance to seek medical help didn't fit his experience.

"It is also possible that some things may never return," the doctor told her. "Directly before and after the accident, for instance."

They had guessed she'd fallen while hiking one of the trails, and that was possibly true. Other scenarios were possible too. Like a blow to the head. Her initial paranoia might suggest an attack, and explain her insistence on remaining anonymous if she knew the attacker. He didn't want Nica caught between.

"Rest is essential," Dr. Yamaguchi said. "Let your body's energies realign."

Jade thanked him, then turned with a vindicated visage. Cameron paid the bill. Outside, he let them into his truck with Nica in the middle like the soft tissue of an inflamed joint, between two bones juxtaposed and out of sync. Nica didn't want Jade pushed further than she was ready to go, but it was his pushing that had gotten them this far. Besides, if Jade wanted to know who she was, why resist the step that could lead to answers? If she was in danger, that step was even more necessary.

He started the truck. "Now that we can assume you're not dying, we ought to work on figuring out who you are."

"The doctor said I'll remember."

"If you went to the police, they could circulate your picture, even put it on the news. Someone would recognize you."

She turned and gaped.

Still a hot button. He pushed it. "Doesn't that make sense?"

"I told you no."

Nica touched his arm, but her peacemaking was starting to grate.

If he could give her a perfect world, he would. But that wasn't reality. She might experience violence up close and personal if Jade was in real trouble.

Driving the winding road from the hospital, he divided his attention between it and Jade's face. Late twenties, he guessed, and more attractive in the whole than in her individual features. Except for her eyes. Memorable eyes, a vibrant shade between green and blue, and her hair; amber overlaid with gold. And her mouth— He shook himself. *Get a grip.* She enticingly filled out Nica's dress but had an athletic definition to her limbs, a combination of soft and strong that would once have drawn a powerful response.

The irritation of that thought made him caustic. "What are you trying to avoid?"

She jutted her chin. "My picture plastered all over the news? Cameras flashing every time I show my face, people ramming mics, demanding answers?" Brow pinched, she pressed her fingers to her temple.

Hard to imagine the sleepy Hanalei precinct managing anything of that scale. But her scenario sounded like experience, so he pressed harder. If she got mad enough, she might break through. "Sounds like gross exaggeration."

"You haven't been there."

Bingo. "Have you?"

She didn't answer, just stared out the window as he pulled onto Highway 50, the two lanes that circled the developed part of the island and led back to Hanalei. He wanted to push again, but Nica was pale with distress. He'd have to wait, get Jade alone. Before his mind took that and ran, he reminded himself she was under investigation. His.

Jade clenched her hands. Fear had made a burrow and hunkered down in the hollow of her stomach. Not fear for her physical condition anymore, but of what might lurk in her mind. Was the scene she'd imagined gross exaggeration? She'd felt the press of people, all of them wanting a piece of her. She'd felt judged and condemned. Wounded.

Had she been accused of something, found guilty? She didn't feel guilty. Just scared. And angry. Her anger wanted an object and, not recalling its source, settled on Cameron Pierce. What right did he have to force her into anything? She'd gotten answers, but was she any better off than before he'd started laying new fears on top of old?

She stared out the window. Her anger might be misdirected, but it was potent. She wanted to strike out—strike back? The thought caught her short. At whom? Or what?

She leaned her shoulder to the door. If she fell out, would another blow to the head restore her identity like a character in a zany cartoon, conked with a hammer twice her size? Tears stung. "Lord," she whispered, then startled with the revelation.

It had felt natural and right to call on God. Reflexive. Habitual. She must believe. She couldn't conjure an experience or practice of religion, but in that unguarded moment, she'd looked outside herself for strength. Did faith exist with nothing concrete to anchor it? And if memory never returned, would she still have such reflexes to live by?

The shoreline they wove through was lovely, forested with lush flowering trees that gave way to half-moon beaches of golden sand and turquoise water crashing white and retreating. Paradise found, but what had she lost?

As they approached the combined Hanalei fire and police building, did she imagine Cameron slowing? She kept her face to the window, refusing to react. Maybe he would leave, go back to wherever he came from and forget about her. *Hah.*

⌣

Back home, Nica slid out of the truck behind Jade, absorbing her weariness and confusion as she'd soaked up their tension. She felt battle weary, though the last part of the drive had been silent. Doubt and scrutiny, resistance and fear had tugged at her like the ocean she hadn't stepped foot in for years.

She was failing to bring peace to the person entrusted to her care. "The doctor said to rest, Jade. Do you feel like lying down?"

"Maybe I should."

"There are books in the cabinet next to the bed, if you like to read."

Jade shrugged. "Maybe I do."

Coming around the truck, Cameron didn't stop Jade from walking straight-backed into her room.

Nica said, "I want you to stop, Kai."

"Stop?"

She nodded. "Now that I know she's all right—"

"She's not all right."

"A full recovery, the doctor said. This isn't like the others." A shadow passed over her spine. Some called her an angel of mercy; she felt like the angel of death. "She's going to recover."

"I don't think she wants to. I think she's hiding something."

"What?"

Hands on his hips, he hung his head back, exasperated. "Come on, Nica. Something happened out there." He swung his arm inland. "Why won't she help us learn what?"

She could think of reasons. In fact, she understood Jade's reluctance better than he knew. Some things belonged to the shadows.

He cocked his jaw. "You don't really think she went off by herself and took a tumble."

"I don't know—"

"Anything about her."

"But—"

He raised his hand. "I don't want to fight. You called because you knew something wasn't right. Don't lose sight of that in your desire to help."

She did think something more was wrong than a hiking accident, especially with Okelani's warning. But that didn't mean she blamed Jade. She wanted Kai to help her, but his doubt was a quagmire sucking them both in. "Why are you so distrustful?" He hadn't always been, but she shouldn't have said it. "I'm sorry, Kai."

He brushed it off. "If she hasn't remembered by tomorrow, I'm going to the police. You could be harboring a—"

"Don't say it." She didn't want him planting thoughts that could shake her belief in Okelani, her trust in Jade. Cameron no longer believed or trusted, not without proof. And so many things in life happened without proof.

He looked toward the house where Jade had disappeared. "There's more to this than what we've heard."

"That doesn't mean Jade's keeping it from us."

He sighed and pulled her into a hug. "I just want you prepared for whatever happens."

As though that was ever possible. "Okelani would have told me if there was anything like that."

"Okelani has an uncanny connection to God's mind, but she doesn't know everything."

When he let her go, she felt the loss. There was no safer place than her brother's arms, head pressed to his chest. She could still sometimes hear his heartbeat, even after he'd flown back across the Pacific. More than anyone else, she trusted Kai, even when he pushed and questioned. That was why she'd called him.

If Okelani sensed a storm, Nica wanted the safe harbor of her big brother. Jade's injury might not be life-threatening, but that knowledge hadn't lifted the pall of impending death as she'd hoped. Kai must sense it too. In his less-spiritual but intuitive way, her brother saw what others missed. And this time, he didn't like what he saw.

⌣

He pulled with his arms, ignoring the suffocating pain of each jolt and drag. The swollen leg throbbed and burned as he inched nearer the echoing falls. Four days of inertia must have stabilized the bone somewhat, but the pain had increased incrementally, and he could no longer deny signs of infection.

The aching in the opposite ankle and knee had diminished, and he might manage to use it. If the ledge offered a way past the thunderous falls without having to swim beneath, he just might get through. But as he crept another four inches, he felt the ledge narrowing, dropping away. He reached forward and groped. No ledge. The wall fell sharply toward the falls and the rocks beneath that had chewed him up already. Groaning, he pushed back. The pain and effort had been for nothing.

No. He corrected his thoughts. He'd gotten information. Not the answer he wanted, but a fact nonetheless, a detail that contributed to a plan, if only by ruling out his first option. Gripping his leg with one hand, he eased back toward the wider surface.

He had remained still the first few days to stabilize the shattered bone. Now, even if he bled out inside his leg, he had to find a way out. He could no longer depend on rescue, and he was reaching the limits of his endurance.

It could have been worse, he reminded himself. He could have broken his back or neck. He murmured a prayer of thanks that he hadn't been paralyzed, then sank against the wall, exhausted. He'd used the dozen aspirin in the foil pouch the first two days when he thought help would come. It had barely touched the pain. Now it was too constant to register with the same ferocity.

He had refilled the water bladder that morning from the pool and treated it with the last of the purifying tablets. Four days with minimal food had left him weak, and even that was gone now. From his position nearer the mouth of the cave, he could see small dark shadows darting beneath the surface of the pool. If he could find a way before he was too weak to try . . .

SIX

Jade woke with a jolt, her body clammy, her heart thumping like a rubber mallet inside her ribs. The panic that had driven her down the mountains to the Hanalei Valley had returned in a dream that wasn't a dream. It was memory; fleeting, but real.

With a cry, she threw her legs over the side and pulled on the soft cotton robe Nica had lent her, tying the sash as she hurried out to the garden and up the stairs to the lanai. It was early and she might have to wake—

"Jade."

She shrieked.

Cameron Pierce, bronze-chested and dripping in hunter green swim trunks, had blended in with the plants on the lanai. Coffee steam swirled up from his mug on the railing, and she should have noticed the aroma at least. She couldn't afford to be careless.

"What's your hurry?"

She'd intended to tell Nica, but he would have to do. "I wasn't alone."

He straightened. "You remember?"

"Just a piece, a . . . glimpse. A path with water on one side and someone behind me."

He examined her with his hard blue stare. "Who?"

She struggled to drag it out, pressing her hands over her eyes. It

47

was there, agonizingly close. "I don't know. But someone was there. I need to go to the police."

"There's a thought."

She didn't have time for his sarcasm. "Look, someone's out there . . . somewhere. And it's been days." Hearing herself, she knew exactly what he thought; it wasn't enough. How could they mount a search without knowing who and where?

With his tanned, sinewy foot, he pushed one of the patio chairs away from the table. "Sit." He went inside with the gray-and-white cat following at his heels. A minute later he appeared with another mug that he put into her hands. "Kona. Plantation reserve."

Did he think she cared? But the first sip was amazingly smooth, and maybe it would clear her head. He took his place at the rail, and she tried not to notice his musculature, the crescent-shaped scar on his lowest left rib. She didn't want to notice anything about him. She wanted to find the person she'd recalled, someone who must be lost still.

He said, "Tell me what you remember."

She swallowed. "I came out of the mountains and—"

"How did you come?"

"Across the valley." She motioned out over the banister toward the mountains. "Before that, I came down a long way, and there was a stream. Higher up it was bigger, but it divided." Even to her ears it sounded vague.

He looked toward the mountains. "What were you doing up there?"

She frowned. "I had a hydration pack, energy foods, so I must have been hiking."

"You don't know?"

She wanted to say yes. It only made sense, but she really didn't remember anything for sure. "I had no overnight gear."

"You might have made camp and only taken what you needed for a day hike." He seemed to be taking her seriously, prepping her for the police?

"It's possible. But what matters is there's someone out there."

"One person or more?"

She frowned. "I saw one." Only she hadn't really seen, just glimpsed, a fragment of memory so brief, yet so real.

"Male or female?"

She shook her head. "I don't know."

"What's your guess?"

"Male." She didn't know why.

"Mine too."

She met his gaze. "I need to tell the police."

"You'll have to give it to them straight." He gripped his cup. "No holding back."

As though she had been. "I know."

"You're willing to risk it?"

She wanted to shake him. "I don't have anything to hide." She hadn't gone before because of vague, unsettling concerns. But if someone else was at risk, what did that matter? She stood up and turned toward the stairs.

"Hold on," he said. "I'll drive you."

⌣

At the police station, Cameron hooked fingers in a locals' handshake with Officer TJ Kanakanui, whose grip matched his size. "Howzit, brah; you busy?"

TJ shrugged. "Choke paperwork. Got someting bettah?"

"One, da kine, situation."

"What you got, Kai?" His glance slid over to where Jade waited by the door.

"Remember I asked about missing persons?"

"Someone lose one *ono wahine*?" TJ warmed to the subject. "You tinking finders keepers?"

"That *wahine* showed up at Nica's a few days ago. Doesn't know who she is."

TJ sobered. "You serious?"

"Dead serious. And now she thinks someone else might be lost. Maybe you better talk to her."

"Yeah, brah. Maybe bettah."

Cameron rejoined Jade. "He'll hear you out."

She looked past. "You know him. The officer?"

"Went to school together." He led her back to TJ's desk. "Tell him whatever you can." To TJ he said, "She's going by Jade," then perched on the corner of the desk beside a heap of papers TJ would get to when he felt like it.

Kanakanui slid out a chair for her and dropped the pidgin. "What can I do for you, Jade?" His chair protested when he sat, flexing his biceps to cross his arms. Behind his aloha smile the cop assessed her.

"I need you to find someone." Her voice thickened. "Someone who's lost."

TJ dug a clipboard from the chaos of his desk. "Okay, tell me what happened."

Jade described her trek out of the mountains and her realization that she'd lost her memory when Nica asked for her name. Though she didn't overdramatize it, as Cameron listened and watched TJ react, he guessed he could have gone a little easier on her himself.

TJ leaned forward. "Why didn't you come to the police then?"

She spread her hands. "I thought I'd remember."

Did he find that suspicious? Cameron kept his expression neutral to avoid coloring Kanakanui's impressions. TJ hadn't been the smartest kid in the class, but he could see when something didn't add up.

"And now you have?"

"I know someone was with me on the trail." Jade slipped her hair behind her ear.

"Who?"

She hesitated. "I don't know." She told him what the doctor had said about her injury blocking retrograde memory. "This is the first piece I've remembered of what happened."

"But you can't tell me what that was."

"It doesn't matter. I just need help for whoever's out there."

"Maybe this person attacked or assaulted you. Maybe that's why no one's reported your accident."

Her eyes as she took that in were an aqueous green that spoke of secret places and shadows. "It doesn't . . . feel that way."

Oh boy. Cameron turned to TJ. "She's spent three nights at Nica's. *If* someone's lost out there, time is critical."

TJ nodded. "We can circulate your picture. Someone who recognizes you might know who you were with. Then we'll know who to look for."

"But that'll take so long." She didn't object now to the public exposure. Either this concern outweighed it, or she'd only been buying time with that whole publicity thing.

TJ studied her face, looking, Cameron knew, for insincerity. "Once it's on the news—"

"All the islands?" Cameron said. "She probably hopped over. Not many choose the unplugged pace of Kauai—"

"I prefer it."

He turned on her.

"At least . . . it seems that way." She squeezed her hands. "If we were here to hike."

TJ had to be thinking what he was. *It feels, it seems, she thought, she guessed*—then a definitive statement that seemed to contradict her condition.

"What trail did you take?"

She shook her head. "I've studied the guidebooks at Nica's, but nothing sounds familiar."

TJ leaned back. "Not much to work with. I can put out the word to our helicopter tours and coast guard to keep an eye out. Fire department and park rangers can watch the trails. Until we learn who you are and if you were with—"

"You mean *who* I was with."

TJ nodded. "Yeah, who. But we don't have enough manpower to risk an all-out search over dangerous terrain." He stood, big and broad, bulky muscles straining the fabric of his uniform. "Is there anything else you want to tell me?"

Undaunted, Jade shook her head. Either she had no more, or she was disseminating only as much as she wanted to. It could all be a ruse, even with a confirmed head injury. Lots of people hit their heads without forgetting who they were. Maybe she'd attacked and killed her companion, faked her own injury. Anything was possible.

She stood up. "Thank you. I appreciate anything you can do."

When TJ fetched a digital camera and photographed her, Cameron tipped his head. Recognition teased. Should he know her face? But they were finished, and Nica would be worried. He led Jade out into the warm, lush morning. If she noticed its embrace, she made no sign. Even her stride was secretive.

She stopped at the truck door and touched his arm. It felt like a brush with an electric eel, though seemingly not on her end. She held his gaze and said, "Thank you. For believing me."

He frowned. The honest answer was he didn't. Yet. "We'll see."

"We'll see if you believe me, or we'll see what happens?"

"Both." No point misleading her.

"Oh." Disappointment washed her face, but she didn't try to convince him.

She got into the truck, and they drove back in silence. She exited without a word. He sat in the truck as she entered the room Nica had made into a shelter for wayward souls. Surprisingly unsettled, he tapped the wheel and wondered where the truth lay. Then he got out, climbed the stairs, and let himself in through the lanai.

Nica spun. "Kai. Where were you?"

"I took Jade to the police."

"What?"

"She remembered something. Oh yeah. Another person."

Nica clasped the counter. "Who?"

"Someone out there with her."

"Someone still out there?"

"Supposedly." He hadn't heard the door slide open behind him, but Nica's gaze moved past him. He turned.

Jade's expression was stony. She had changed into torn microfiber pants and carried her slim hydration pack. His inspection of its minimal storage pouches had revealed no illegal drugs or weapons.

"May I fill this with ice?"

Nica frowned. "What are you doing?"

"Retracing my steps. If I can get back to where I forgot, maybe I'll remember."

"What about the MRI?" Nica's brow furrowed. "It's in less than two hours."

"That can wait. This can't." Jade went past Nica into the kitchen.

Cameron eyed her. "You don't really think you can climb back in to wherever you were?"

She began loading cubes into the bladder. "Officer Kanakanui can't risk personnel in the wild. They'd have to cover too much ground anyway. If I can recognize the way I came . . ."

"You know the chances of that?" Even someone who knew the island would be hard-pressed.

"I was in or near the stream all the way."

"*A* stream. Going down. How do you expect to retrace that, heading *mauka*?" At her puzzled look he clarified, "Into the mountains."

She carried the pack to the sink and topped the bladder off with water. "If I can get close enough to remember, I could tell the searchers where to look." She sealed the bladder and tucked it back inside the nylon sheath.

"It's remarkable you made it out the first time. You're not in any shape to do it again."

"It's all I can think of."

She was turning his theories upside down, and he didn't like that. He threaded his fingers together atop his head, eyed her musculature. She wasn't soft like Nica. Maybe, as she'd claimed, she had come to

Kauai to experience the raw beauty, the treacherous terrain and un-spoiled wilderness. Maybe she did prefer it to the skin scene on Waikiki. But even so . . . "Can't you wait until your story hits—see what TJ comes up with?"

Wincing, she pulled the pack onto her shoulders. "It's been four days. I can't wait." She brushed past him.

"Hold on."

She turned and scowled. "I know all the arguments. You've made your opinion clear."

His lack of trust must have stung more than she'd shown. In spite of his doubt, he said, "I'll go with you."

"No, thanks. I seem to be losing companions."

"You won't make it up alone. It'll be dicey with two, but we might have half a chance."

She waited a full beat. "This isn't your problem. I won't bother Nica further."

"You're no bother, Jade. But I agree with Kai. You can't go alone."

Jade looked from Nica to him. "Kai? I thought your name was Cameron."

"Kai's my Hawaiian name." Though purely *haole*, Okelani had dubbed them both when they came under her care.

"It means ocean," Nica said. "Okelani named him that because he's as unpredictable as the sea."

He flicked her a glance. That was more information than Jade needed. On the mainland he was Cameron Pierce, but his island persona was different. Normally. Even there he wouldn't let a brain-damaged amnesiac trek *mauka* into native forest unassisted. "I've got a pack and boots in my room here, but we'll need supplies. Give me half an hour."

She still seemed reluctant. "If you're only coming to prove your point, I'd rather you didn't."

He appreciated her not pulling her punches. He wouldn't pull his either.

But Nica, the peacemaker, touched Jade's hand. "I'll come, too. The three of us—"

"No." No way was he putting his sister in danger. "I can't be responsible for both of you."

Jade raised her chin. "Responsible?"

Before she could get her back up, he said, "Technically speaking." She might be strong, but he was stronger. That made him the dominant partner in any physical situation, whether she wanted to admit it or not.

She assessed him coolly. "I only hope you won't slow me down."

Fighting words. They triggered an annoyed amusement, but he chose not to alienate her further. "Only where caution requires."

She leaned against the back of the couch and said, "Half an hour."

Nica fretted. Kai was right that Jade wasn't up to climbing back into the mountains. If she was recovered enough for that, she would have remembered more than one tiny fragment. After seeing the doctor yesterday Jade had slept most of the day. She should listen to her body, let herself heal. Another fall and she might never know who she was.

But that wasn't what scared her the most. *Malice.* She felt its presence. God had sent the warning through Okelani, and the essence of danger clung to Jade. Now Kai was caught up in it without protection, having all but dared God to interfere in his life again. Even a strong man was no match for malice. Not alone.

When he came back from collecting his supplies, she met him at the truck.

"Don't ask again, Nica. It'll be hard enough with Jade."

"I'm not asking to come. I want to bless you."

He straightened. "You don't need to worry."

"Kai."

He blew out a slow breath. "Can we do it without the whole armor and breastplate and legions of angels thing?"

She socked his arm. "Stand there and take it like a man."

He tucked his head back with a long-suffering expression.

She took his hands, closed her eyes, and brought him to Jesus who understood her concerns. "Please guide and protect Kai and Jade. Let all wickedness flee. Set angels beside them, before and behind them, above and below them." Her throat constricted with memories of her mother praying that over her head as she snuggled down to sleep. Why hadn't she remembered to pray it for her mother that stormy day so long ago? She squeezed Kai's hands. "Bring them back safely."

Kai didn't interrupt, but when she finished, he said, "Feel better?"

Her throat was tight.

He pulled her into a hug. "It's okay, Nica. We're just trekking *mauka*."

She nodded. Into the heart of the island, not out from its sheltering shores. He'd be okay. And he'd take care of Jade.

SEVEN

Just crossing the fertile valley had her breathing harder than she'd expected. Cameron had offered to drive as far inland as possible, but since she was working on intuition alone, she needed to walk it back, retracing the same line from Nica's.

As they tramped along, she studied the patchwork of flooded paddies they passed through. Since he'd crashed her party and she might as well make use of that, she asked Cameron what they were growing.

"Taro. A Hawaiian staple. The leaves are rich in vitamins, and from the tuber we get, oh joy, poi."

She laughed, then touched her temple, willing away the ache that was beginning there. Though he might not think so, she knew the danger of this undertaking. And dreaded it.

He didn't miss much, though. "Hurt?"

"I'm all right." Given the magnitude of their undertaking, a headache was the least of her concerns.

She jumped over a swampy area and glanced back to make sure she was still on track from Nica's, then startled as a feral rooster crowed. Draped in brilliant green, red, and gold plumage with an arched, iridescent black tail, he strutted out from the webbed roots of a tree. "Isn't it late in the day for crowing?"

"They crow day and night. No barnyard manners." Cameron lunged onto the higher ridge of ground where she stood. "Speaking of crowing, TJ is sending your story to the mainland. The chief ordered a full broadcast."

She stopped and stared. "How do you know?"

"I dropped into the station to tell him how to reach us if he learns something."

"You told him what I'm doing?"

"He said not to leave the island."

Don't leave town. Recollection flickered, then passed. She raised her chin. "No wonder he wouldn't help. If everyone wasn't so busy suspecting me, we might get somewhere." She'd hoped when she told the police what she knew, allowed herself to be photographed, her story to be broadcast, that help would be certain. Obviously it was still up to her. And Cameron couldn't be trusted. She moved on.

"It makes sense to include the mainland, where friends and family can identify you."

"Unless I live here."

"Then you'd know *mauka* and *makai*—toward the mountains, toward the coast. They're the primary directions on any of the islands."

"I might have forgotten."

"It's not something you forget. It's a circular sort of navigation absorbed by people who grow up on an island. It has little to do with north or south or even right or left, only toward the mountains or toward the shore."

She supposed that might be one of the intangibles that remained in lieu of memory, things more innate than filed occurrences, like the knowledge she'd retained without any recollection of learning the things she knew. Information must be stored separately from experience. "You grew up on this island? You and Nica?"

"Downline descendents of missionaries who came to do good and also did well, as the saying goes. Where we're different from others is that my grandparents, on passing, deeded the bulk of their land back to the Hawaiians who'd farmed it."

"Except for Nica's house?"

"Basically."

She stopped and studied the abruptly rising terrain. A stream tumbled down that looked and sounded like the waterway she'd followed into the valley. She turned and looked back, comparing the direction they'd come to the direction she'd gone the first time. A fairly direct line from Nica's, since she hadn't had the strength to wander. "This is it."

"You sure?"

"As sure as I can be."

He looked forward, then back, marking their position, perhaps, in his mind. "Anything coming back to you?"

"I remember coming out, just not what I was doing in there."

"Or what happened."

"Or what happened," she agreed. "Except . . ."

"What?" His gaze bored into her.

Shook her head. "Maybe I'm dizzy. For a moment I felt like I was falling."

"Try to feel it again."

She searched his face, then closed her eyes. The warm breeze encircled her as she tried, but the feeling was gone. "It must have been a spell." She'd had plenty of woozy moments, and the exertion didn't help.

"I wouldn't discount it."

"You think I'm remembering?"

"Could be." He hung his hands on his hips.

"Then it's at least possible I'm telling the truth."

"If there was no chance, I wouldn't be here."

"I can't tell you how glad I am." She brushed past. The terrain seemed familiar even though she'd been dazed the last time she passed that way. Her senses had been heightened then in a way that kicked in now—along with her aches and bruises.

The doctor had said rest. To let her energies realign. Right. She puffed up the first steep rise. As the incline increased, it put Cameron Pierce into position to break her fall. Might just be worth it.

Without a path, she worked her way up through red dirt, rocks, and ferns cloaking the stream's banks. A purple, jellyfish-shaped flower and other verdant plants perfumed the air. A dove cooed somewhere out of sight, but a brown-and-black myna shouted it down. The yellow triangular patch behind its eye matched its beak and bold yellow stockings. Under other conditions, she would have enjoyed exploring this island.

And then it hit her that she had. In that moment she sensed someone else's excitement too; the person who'd been with her. She focused on the feeling, trying to grasp the flesh-and-blood person she'd glimpsed. But as with the dream, when she tried it slipped away.

She squeezed between the slender trees along the shore to a place where the stream tumbled down a series of giant steps that looked familiar. As she mounted the boulders and pulled herself up, the aches and kinks faded. She inhaled through her nose, cleansed through her mouth, finding her rhythm.

When the incline steepened in the narrowing channel, she grabbed onto ropey roots and pulled herself up. A shower rolled down the mountains over them, swelling the stream and slickening the rocks, but on either side the jungle crowded in like linemen to contain her within the narrow passage. She gripped and pulled, digging in with her hikers, clawing for holds with her hands. Her muscles bunched and tensed.

Someone needed her. The need pumped in her temples, burned in her chest. Straining, she grabbed the wet, igneous rock, scrambled to catch her foot, slipped, then kicked again and pulled herself up against a stone face. The water beside her roared.

From below, Cameron gripped her shin, then pulled himself up behind her. "Take a rest," he breathed. "You don't have to prove anything."

She had almost shut him out, but now his presence encompassed and invaded her. She closed her eyes and breathed, only then realizing how fatigued she'd become.

"You sure you came this way before?"

She nodded. "I remember."

He pulled a thin nylon rope from his pack. "After I get past, attach this end. We'll leave it for the trek down."

Her stomach sank. She hadn't thought that far—not to going down again, only getting to the place where she could remember, finding the person she'd forgotten. But Cameron was right. They'd all have to get out again.

Her hands were caked with reddish mud, arms and legs smeared. Tendrils of hair clung to her cheeks and neck. Her left bicep twitched. None of it mattered—only getting there. As her heart rate slowed, she pondered her predicament.

She was in the Hanalei Mountains searching for someone she couldn't recall with someone she hardly knew. Two nights ago she wouldn't get into his truck. Now she was caught between him and . . . well, a rock. If she tried hard enough, she might explain that somehow.

"Stay put," he spoke into her ear.

As though she could move if she wanted to. He dug his boot in and pushed up past her, trailing the rope. Where the channel narrowed again, he straddled the water and spider-walked the walls. She knotted the rope around a sturdy root, eye level above the mud and stone, and waited until Cameron pulled it taut and tied his end.

Stopping had given her legs a tremor, but she ignored it. She had made it down, and down was worse. At least pulling against gravity gave the illusion of control. She took hold of the rope and worked her way up until she reached the top, where he waited shin deep in the water.

His wet T-shirt clung to him. "Might have been an easier way."

"Maybe. But I didn't want to lose sight of the water." She dipped her hands and arms into the flow and rubbed off the grime.

He surveyed the next stretch with a frown. The tree canopy had thinned and the undergrowth thickened. He motioned toward a break in the foliage. "Looks like a game trail."

"What game?"

"Wild pigs probably. Stop here to water."

She glanced around. "Are there predators?"

"Just us."

"I'm a threat to a wild pig?"

"Femme fatale," he deadpanned. "We might consider taking it."

She studied the animal path. "What if we can't get back to the water? Or if the creek branches out and we think we're back but we're not?"

He nodded. "Valid concerns."

Hands on her hips, she looked up at the next incline the water rushed down. Was it the same water that had carried her before? In the shallows where she stood, she closed her eyes and remembered it deeper, faster, more treacherous. It must have forked or the water would not be less here than higher up.

She opened her eyes. Even though the pressed-dirt path through ferns and palms as tall as she might prove easier, she couldn't chance losing her only point of reference. "I think we'd better stay with the water."

"What would your companion say?"

"He'd—" She expelled a breath. Her mind had responded automatically with the male pronoun. She was starting to flesh him out. "He'd want me to take the surest way. I've got to reach him." She couldn't come up with a name or even a face, but she'd caught an emotion. It was someone she cared about, someone she loved. She sloshed past, but Cameron caught her arm.

"You won't do him any good breaking your neck."

"We have to hurry." She tugged, but his grip tightened.

He made her face him. "You also have to consider we might not find him . . . alive."

EIGHT

Cameron had expected an outburst. Guilt or denial. Anger. Maybe he wanted her to snap—and snap out of it. But he got, instead, a deepest jungle stare. Her lips parted and drew his gaze against his will.

She said, "In the universe of possibilities, that is only one. And I refuse to breathe life into a worst-case scenario."

"In my world, it's better to be prepared."

"Doesn't leave much room for hope, does it."

He narrowed his eyes. "Hope rarely keeps its promise."

"Then you don't know God."

"I do. I just don't expect him to fix everything that's gone wrong in the world since he gave it a spin."

"Well, I'm not asking for world peace. Just trying to find someone. And if you don't want to help me, no one's forcing you."

"I never said that."

"It's bad enough having to drag your suspicions. I can't carry your doubts as well."

He hung his hands on his hips as her point sank in. On the off chance she was telling the truth in all this, his assumptions hadn't helped. Experience told him she was not being completely honest, but there was no need to push it now. If he waited and watched, she'd catch herself up. They almost always did. He motioned upstream. "Choose your path."

"We'll stay with the water."

They pushed on and up, fighting the mountain for every step. When neither the current nor the shore yielded, he took the lead, cutting with his hand machete only enough to make passage possible. Some survival instinct must have carried her down. What drove her now?

The most obvious explanation would be a true fear for the person she believed she'd left behind. But who was this mystery person? Jade wore no wedding band. A boyfriend or fiancé? Had they squabbled? She'd been obstinate enough to take off on her own this morning. She could have gone off, hit her head, forgotten the situation, and blown the whole thing out of proportion. Maybe the guy was camping somewhere, safe and free of a doomed relationship.

Probably this trek was a mistake. They should have waited to hear what TJ came back with. The big Hawaiian had given him the stink eye when he told him what she meant to do. Cameron glanced back and saw her struggling. He called a rest, but as they stood there, softly panting, she looked more vulnerable than he'd seen her yet.

Could the person she'd been with have attacked her, inflicted the head injury and left her for dead as TJ suspected?

"Jade."

She raised her eyes, and a protective urge caught him in the gut. "What?" She brushed a loose strand of hair behind her ear and braced herself for the next thing he might have to say.

He didn't want to bludgeon her with possibilities she couldn't or wouldn't face, but he needed to know what they were going into. Or if they should be going at all. One of his questions just might turn the key. "Is there a chance you'll be in danger if we find your companion?"

She stared at him long and hard. "Are you asking whether the person I came hiking with hurt me?"

"Might explain why he didn't report your accident."

She swallowed. "And now he's waiting out here to finish the job?" Hurt crept into her eyes.

"Or he's left the island."

She closed her eyes, tipped her face up to the soft rain shower that moved over them. Drops caught in her lashes like tears, but she didn't cry.

He shifted to ease a spasming hamstring. "Fear can block memory."

She lowered her chin, mouth set, brow creased. "I'm not afraid."

The tension in her body showed otherwise. Her strongest clues seemed to be sensations, and he guessed she felt something now. Why evade? "I'm not saying we should stop. Just trying to cover the possibilities."

Her shoulders dropped. She spread her hands. "Until now I wouldn't have thought I could lose my entire past. I guess anything's possible."

"You felt something."

She nodded. "But I can't identify it. And I can't let it stop me."

Again he got the unsought urge to keep her safe. Again he balked. He was here at Nica's request. *Aloha* required it. Jade was a guest on the island and he an ambassador. Though that sentiment was less prevalent now, it had been drilled into him from his earliest days. *"Aloha" means kindness, helpfulness, graciousness, and generosity. Whatever you have, you give. Whatever you can, you do.* No room for selfishness, for acting shamefully, greedily, or stingily. There was a saying for someone who did: *'A 'ohe paha he 'uhane*—perhaps he has no soul.

So he would help her, as far as he was able. But unlike Nica, he'd keep his eyes and mind open. "Let's go."

They moved on through the valley, finding the path of least resistance. He kept expecting her to say, "This is it," but she just kept plodding as shadows lengthened and the sun touched, then sank behind the mountaintops to their right.

At last Jade stopped in a semicircular patch of ground between the stream and a grove of kukui trees. She turned to him. "I spent the night here."

"What?"

"On this rock." She walked over to a boulder beside the stream.

"You were out here two days?"

"I don't know how long before this point, just that I woke up here and went on to Nica's."

He looked up at the steep, lacy falls behind her. "You came down that?"

Reading his doubt, she said, "I'm an experienced hiker."

Another definitive statement. "How do you know?"

"Because I—" Her face flushed. "I remember Chasm Lake. I can see it. The cirque with the lake reflecting the diamond face of Longs Peak."

Her excitement seemed genuine.

"Who were you with?"

Her lips parted, then closed. "I hiked it alone. I do that sometimes. It helps me clear my head."

He frowned. "Then how do you know you weren't alone this time?"

"Because I remember. There was someone." She shook her head. "I just can't see who."

"Jade, if you were with someone, why would you leave?"

She swayed. "Water." She pressed her fingers to her forehead. "I can feel it pulling."

"Think you got separated?"

"Maybe."

Then why wouldn't he have come after her? He'd had four days. Unless he couldn't. Cameron rubbed his beard. The evening was typically mild, cooler at this elevation than where they'd started in the valley, but well within the temperate range. As they said on the island, regarding the weather, "Sometimes same, sometimes little bit different."

That was a good thing since he hadn't realized how far Jade had come. He'd planned for an emergency overnight, just in case, but he hadn't known she'd been out there two days herself. She hadn't said, and he hadn't asked. She'd been all set to go alone, and he'd scrambled.

He assessed the setting sun, the climb up the falls, and his energy level. Streams were unpredictable. A hard rain would swell a cataract in minutes, turn even this stream into a force. Maybe she'd been caught in a flash flood, she and her companion.

This area was broad enough to handle a swell in the stream without washing them away, flat enough for the two mats he had coiled in the side buckles, and he could stretch a nylon tarp to keep the rain off. "We'll stop here." He unfastened his pack.

She pressed her hands to her waist, staring up at the falls. "I can keep going."

"We've lost the light." He pointed to the falls. "That's a major climb. And you don't know how much farther past that."

"Really, I—"

"Fatigue is when accidents happen." It was already too dark to attempt the climb safely. No point pushing past their strength.

She sat down on the boulder. "I didn't think it was this far."

Not what he wanted to hear. "Are you sure we've come the right way?"

"I'm sure I was here." She looked up at the shallow falls. "The rest is fuzzy."

"Another night's sleep might help."

"Another night." Her stare lingered. "And it's been four already."

At least. If she'd spent one night out, there could have been others. "We're doing all we can."

She nodded, then sighed. "I guess the story's run."

"Is that so bad?"

"I really don't know." She unfastened her pack and pulled it from her back.

"If TJ's learned something, there might be help coming."

"That's all I want." She rested her face in her hands.

He took out his cell phone, though as he'd guessed, there was no signal. "We'll have to wait and see." He removed his pack and set it on the ground.

Jade turned. "What do you want me to do?"

"Collect some driftwood and I'll make a fire."

She moved away from the stream for dry wood while he fitted together the collapsible poles and attached the tarp, then unrolled the two mats that would keep the worst of the rocks from digging in. Unless something unseasonable happened, there'd be no need for blankets or—

Jade shrieked.

He lurched out from under the tarp and shouted, "Stop!" just as she flung off a five-inch centipede.

He thrashed over and grabbed her arm. "Are you bitten?"

She panted. "I don't think so."

There was no think; she'd know. But he couldn't believe it. He searched her arm for punctures and found it unscathed—impossible with the length of contact and her frantic motion. The things wrapped around and struck with the fangs on the tips of their front legs. But though he could miss marks in the failing light, she couldn't miss the electrical socket experience of a centipede bite. The poison swelled, sickened, and disoriented bigger, stronger adults than she, and the pain was immediate.

He ran his hand over her forearm, still not believing. But she had somehow tangled with a centipede and emerged unharmed. He looked into her face. Her hair had come loose, and he knew how it would feel. Her eyes were weary and frightened, but that only enhanced their luminous depths.

Her body was fit and supple, and if she was a psychopathic murderer it could hardly be more dangerous than the effect she was already having. He let go. "Go sit under the tarp. I'll get the wood." He watched her creep beneath the sagging tent, his heart racing in a way it hadn't for a long time. *Get a grip, Kai.*

Jade shook all over. She hadn't felt squeamish about the tropical forest until now. But the feel of the creature's legs clinging to her wouldn't go away. She tried not to show it when Cameron ducked back under the tarp and rummaged in his pack. He hardly looked at her anyway; just said, "I should have warned you about that, with the night coming on."

"Are they going to be crawling all over us?" She'd keep moving in the pitch-dark if that was the case.

"We're in their habitat."

She eyed the flimsy cover that might keep off the rain but offered no barriers whatsoever to the creepy crawlies that until now wouldn't have concerned her. The loathsome feel of that centipede was one memory she wanted blocked, and the thought of lying down and sleeping . . . "I can't do this."

He pulled out the lighter. "They're out there, Jade. But you seem to be *ho'omalu ke Akua*."

"What does that mean?"

"Under God's protection."

"Ho'omalu ke Akua," she whispered.

"I've never seen someone wrestle a centipede and walk away untouched."

She shuddered. "I just . . . got it off me."

He cocked his jaw and eyed her in the deepening twilight, then ducked out and lit the fire he'd assembled near the streambed.

She joined him there. Wasn't fire the universal defense? The night was not cold, but she huddled as though a howling wind tore around them.

He tossed her a stick of teriyaki jerky for dinner. "Centipedes are predators. They mostly hunt at night. But they'll probably stay in the vegetation and look for bugs and lizards."

"Probably doesn't do it for me." She closed herself into her arms.

His mouth pulled sideways. "I don't blame you, but trust me, it could have been worse."

"I don't want to know. And I'm not staying here."

He took a flashlight from his pack and set it on the stony ground between them. "We have no choice. It's getting dark. Besides, you stayed here before."

"With enough brain damage to render me insouciant."

He tipped his head. "Big words. Maybe you're a teacher."

"Don't try to distract me."

"Now see, that's just the tone Miss Stafford used to take."

She wrapped her knees in her arms. "And it probably did no good."

He pressed a hand to his chest. "She struck terror in my third-grade heart."

"And you in hers, no doubt."

He grinned. "She loved Nica, though. And since we came as a pair—"

"You're twins?"

"We're eleven months apart, but she accelerated a grade."

Jade reassessed him. "I thought you were a lot older."

"She has a young quality."

"And he was hardboiled." Jade leaned her chin on her knees. "You're nothing at all alike."

"Oh, I wouldn't say that. We both have a weakness for squid luau."

She half smiled. The horror of the centipede had diminished a little. But her thoughts still churned as all around them insects sang. "What else is out there?"

"You've encountered the worst. The centipede is the only poisonous creature on the island. He took a ride over with the Polynesians. Lots of people have lived here since, sleeping out like this, whole families on little grass mats." He took out a bottle of repellent. "Use this for the mosquitoes."

"Malarial?"

"Only birds get malaria in Hawaii."

She shot him a skeptical look.

"Cross my heart. There's a few spiders whose bites can hurt, but nothing out here will kill you."

She applied a fresh coat of repellent, the caustic scent stinging her nostrils. "Maybe I'll just hang over that boulder again." She waved toward the stone near the bank where she'd huddled the first night unawares.

He shrugged. "Whatever suits you."

With a sigh, she turned back to the flames. "I won't sleep."

"Then you won't be much good tomorrow."

And she had to be.

He ducked under the tarp. "The light's on the ground there if you need it. Don't go far to relieve yourself."

She wished he hadn't brought it up, but better now than later. "Where's that big knife?"

He reached into his pack and held out the machete. "Just don't think I'm a wild boar if I start snoring."

It surprised her he could make her laugh. After everything. "Cameron?"

"Yeah."

"We're going to find him."

"That's why we're here."

It was why she'd sleep, in spite of centipedes, and push on tomorrow to whatever lay ahead. When she came back and lay down on the mat under the tarp, Cameron murmured, *"Ma ka malu o kona 'ēheu."*

She wished she could see his face as she settled her head into the crook of her arm. "What did you say?"

"Within the shelter of his wings."

NINE

Sweeping the drapes to the side to reveal the lights of Waikiki, Curtis Blanchard ignored Allegra's pout. Though unbecoming in a woman of her maturity, it was forgivable, definitely forgivable. In fact, it was encouraging. He'd take a pout over arguments, questions, and demands. His bird was no squawking crow; his was a nightingale. And the trick was to lure her from the bush into the cage, to capture her so completely, she thought of nothing else, no one else.

Without a hint of annoyance, he reached over and drew her to the window. "With all this, babe, who needs television?"

Allegra planted a hand on her slender hip. "I just wanted to see what's happening in the world."

"Happening? What could be happening?" He circled her waist and pulled her close, hoping she wouldn't sense his agitation. If she saw Gentry's story on the news, it would ruin everything, and he'd worked too hard for this time with her.

Seeing the report had shaken him worse than he'd expected. Allegra would insist on responding, or so he guessed, though this particular *femme* was complicated, a greater challenge and pleasure than he'd expected, but also hard to figure. Like a chameleon, she shifted, but what was going on inside? That was the question.

"Allegra, darling, we've escaped the world." He traced her lips with his fingertip, smoothing the pout and noting the fine lines gathered at the edges. Not even Botox was perfect. He didn't expect perfection, only attention, undivided. "I want to pretend it's permanent."

With a playful cast to her eyes, she took his gold chain in her teeth and tugged. "Presumptuous."

For a woman nearing fifty, she still had that *je ne sais quoi* that explained why her long-estranged husband would not let her go. "Perhaps. But I have great expectations." He kissed her mouth in anticipation of meeting each one.

After what he'd just seen on the TV he'd have to keep her distracted. But he could do that, especially when he considered how much she meant to him. How very much.

~

As darkness descended once again in the cave, despair closed in. None of the challenges he faced, lying there broken, exposed, and hungry, had the power that hopelessness wielded when each successive night fell. It was almost palpable, as though it oozed from the walls and ceiling and rose up like the mist from the pool.

He fought the thoughts that infiltrated his mind. Had he placed his hope in a straw God? Were his prayers no more than wishful pleading into thin, unhearing air? Faith a ruse?

He battled back with snatches from the Psalms. "'Answer me when I call to you, O my righteous God. Give me relief from my distress; be merciful to me and hear my prayer.'"

But his body couldn't take much more. It wasn't simply the injuries—there was something internal, systemic. How long he could hold on, he didn't know. What he did know was that even painful death would be preferable to this agonizing demise of his trust, his faith. He groaned. "Lord, forgive me."

And in the din and darkness he grabbed once again onto a lifeline of peace that invaded the pain, the doubt. Tears streamed from his eyes, and he raised his voice in praise that drove away the lying spirits and restored him more surely than the purest water, the richest food, the safest haven.

If this was to be his tomb, he would wait with the faith of Lazarus to be called forth either to his current life or to the next.

⌒⌒

People with hard faces pressed in on every side, pushing, grasping, shouting like carnival barkers. "Look here; over here; right this way." A macabre anticipation tainted the air. Vultures; they were vultures, there to pick her flesh. Cold metal banged her lip.

"Can you refute the allegation?"

"Are you going to fight it?"

"Is it true?"

True? How could they believe it? How could they not know? What kind of people were they?

"No. It's a lie." Her chest heaved; her heart raced. "It's a lie. It's a lie."

The cacophony grew. Loud raucous voices, drowning her out, drowning her. She couldn't breathe. A force strong and heavy pressed her down and swept her away. She thrashed and kicked, straining for air.

"Jade." Cameron's grip on her shoulder dragged her out. "Jade."

She gasped and opened her eyes. His face was grim in the morning light. Birds clambered. She was damp with sweat, or maybe it was mist and dew.

"What's the lie?"

"Lie?" She pressed up to her elbow on the mat.

He gave her shoulder another shake. "The lie, Jade. You said, 'It's a lie.'"

His forceful questioning mimicked something, but all she could remember was fighting for breath. "I think I was drowning. In my dream."

He hunkered back on his heels, scowling. Whatever she'd said had set him off again, but was she responsible for what happened in her sleep? She shook her head. "Drowning dreams are supposed to be symbolic, but I don't know what it meant."

"Why do you think it was symbolic?"

A wave of dizziness washed over her. He was right. It could be real. It could be memory. She looked over at the faithful stream that had led her out, then up to the white threads of water streaming over the black rock. Mist clung there like confusion. No sweeping torrent. But what lay beyond?

Her vision blurred, her thoughts stilled. The birdsong faded in her ears; the damp air clung to her skin until she melted in. A shout without words echoed in her head, and with it came a sensation of falling, so strong she swayed.

Cameron gripped her shoulder again. "What is it?"

Her lungs ached. Her head pounded. "It's right there, but I can't—" Frustration swept in. She wanted to scream. "You think I don't want to remember, but that isn't true." She scrambled to her feet. The sensations were too strong to be imagination, but until she broke through the wall, she was only groping.

Before he'd shaken her awake, he had struck camp and had the packs waiting, everything ready but the mat she'd been lying on. Even the tarp over her head had been stowed again. Good. The less time wasted the better.

She snatched her pack, slipped her arms through the straps, and started for the falls. A night's sleep had done nothing but frustrate her. Cameron's questions only bullied her mind. Halfway up the slippery rock face, she heard him beneath her. Maybe she'd be glad for his help when they found her companion, but right now his doubt and suspicions were an emotional drain she didn't need.

Reach and pull, cling, find a foothold. Her muscles strained, but it was a good strain. She clawed with her fingers, clinging like . . . like . . . Her head spun. Laughter . . . and a voice saying, *"Maybe the*

Hawaiians are right. I can see you coming back as a gecko." Her hand slipped.

Cameron caught her waist and braced her against the rock. "Now is not the time to lose it."

She grabbed hold and dragged herself up. Mist from the falls chilled her hot cheeks. Her knee banged something and pain emerged. Ignoring it, she heaved herself into a damp hollow to catch her breath. Since Cameron clung beneath her, she didn't wait long before pulling up to the next level.

Her legs shook. Two knuckles bled. Sweat ran down between her shoulder blades as she dug in and pulled up again. Water sprayed her in the face. She couldn't find a grip.

"To your left," Cameron called.

She reached and found the hold, dug in with her shoe and thrust herself over the top. She scrambled back from the edge to give him room and realized he was trailing a rope again. If she had let him go first, she'd have had it to hold on to. But she'd made it without. Gasping, she tipped her head back and found a piece of blue sky torn out of the clouds. She stared hard at it.

Cameron pulled up beside her. "Are you always this reckless?"

She shrugged.

"I bet you've got a guess."

Did she? Lying back on her elbows, drawing in the scent of mist and jungle and exertion, a certain exultation rose up from the danger and difficulty. Reckless? She didn't know. But the challenge had rejuvenated her. She caught the end of her water hose between her teeth and sipped the cold water.

Cameron balanced on one elbow. "So what did you remember, climbing up?"

"Someone saying I could come back as a gecko."

She thought it would surprise him, but he said, "Only the *kanaka maoli* come back as geckos."

"Kanaka . . ."

"Indigenous Hawaiians, or those descended from Pele, the volcano goddess, and all her numerous lovers."

"I see." She looked at him stretched out beside her on the rock, his hair wet with mist, the line of his beard fuzzy with new growth, a shadow of whiskers creeping down his neck. It made him look less arrogant than confident, less annoying than interesting. Or maybe it was that his anger had passed like the showers blowing down the valleys.

Removing his full-sized pack, he took out Ziploc bags of fresh shaved coconut, nuts, and dried papaya slices that he'd assembled. No chocolate. But she thanked him anyway.

Cameron dug into his baggie. "Who taught you to climb?"

She searched, but no answer came. "Part of the blank, I guess. Or maybe I taught myself."

"Which would you guess?"

"That someone took me along, pointed out the moss on the north side of trees, and told me which berries not to eat."

"And hauled you down from cliffs and asked you not to howl at the wolves?" He pulled a smile. "Bet you were one *lapa keiki*."

"I beg your pardon?"

He laughed. "Ho sistah. I ony call you one wild kid."

"And what kind of talk is that?"

"Da kine Hawaiian Creole. You want for talk story like a local, you learn da kine pidgin."

He was likable when he laughed, and his benediction the night before had kept all but the bad dreams away. She nibbled a soft, white coconut flake. "So teach me."

He chewed, then nodded. "Okay. Like the islands, pidgin's got roots in lots of languages and peoples. Most locals switch between it and standard English, depending on the situation."

"I see."

"In pidgin you change verb tense by using other words. *Wen* before the verb means past tense, *going* makes it future. No *is* or *was*. We say, 'da water cold.' Or, 'cold, da water.'"

Interesting.

"Don't make nouns plural."

"Even when there's more than one?"

"Nope. It's understood."

"What else?"

He thought a minute. "*Nevah* means not, except when it means never."

"Aha."

"We say *one* in place of *a*—dat buggah caught one beeg wave—and *for* in place of *to*—easy for say, hard for do."

She shook her head, puzzling that one.

He folded his baggie. "A few terms are indispensable—like *mo bettah* and *da kine*."

"Mo bettah?"

"You know; good, bettah, mo bettah." He slid her a smile.

"And *da kine*?"

"Mostly means 'the kind'—like da kine fruit, da kine flower—but it can stand in for anything you can't think of. You got any da kine?"

"Seems to be all I have." And the reminder was discouraging.

His eyes softened. "Yeah. Well. You can also throw it in anywhere the way people use *um* or *you know*."

"I see." She slipped her Ziploc into an outer pocket of her pack and stood up. "Thank you for the lesson. Are you ready?"

"If you are."

She turned and memory stirred, something dark and frightening. "I think the stream forks up ahead."

"We'll see when we get there."

His *modus operandi*. Wait until the evidence smacks you in the face, then accept it. An hour later, the channel they'd followed met back up with the larger river.

Cameron eyed the fork. "Could this be where you got separated?"

She stared out through the native forest along the other cataract, trying to remember. Had someone been with her in the water? She couldn't picture it, only her own struggle.

"I don't know. He could have gone that way."

Cameron planted his hands on his hips. "That way's west. If the river runs all the way down, it would end at the Na Pali coast, but passage might not be possible. That side of the island's not developed."

She swallowed. "What if he's out there?"

"Then it's out of our hands."

Into whose? Frustration choked her. She'd given Officer Kanakanui all she had, including her picture to broadcast, and he'd just crossed his beefy arms and said it wasn't much to go on. *Please.* Her spirit reached out. *Help me find him.*

"Jade."

She turned.

"There's nothing we can do if he's out there. You have to focus here."

He was right. She couldn't search the whole island. But she'd been compelled to retrace her steps, and she would.

The valley above the fork cut deeply. They'd have to inch along the slopes, or get into the water and progress against the current. She chose the river, but as she lowered herself into the cool, waist-deep water she had an overwhelming sensation of being carried away. "There aren't . . . piranhas on Kauai, are there?"

"No piranhas, no snakes." He slid into the water. "Unless you'd apply that term to me."

"Had noticed the fangs." Especially earlier.

"Only venomous snakes have fangs."

"If the skin fits."

"Ah, but it's the skin that's shed."

"Only when the thing's outgrown it."

He laughed. "Okay."

Moving against the current proved harder than she'd thought. Disorienting, too, when she watched the stony river bottom to avoid catching her foot or slipping. If she didn't look, the motion of the water pushing against her had an equally disturbing effect. She suddenly felt herself underwater, tumbling, churning. Panic gripped.

Somewhere ahead was a critical point, a place where she had no control. She faltered.

Cameron reached her. "What's the matter?"

"Nothing." The current strengthened as the grade rose, and with it, her feeling of helplessness. She fought it physically and mentally as fear took hold. Cameron had told her to pay attention to her feelings, but now she had to ignore them or she'd be swept away. She grabbed on to the roots dangling down the rocky walls. A little rest, then she'd press on, in spite of the dread swirling and tugging, threatening once again to wash her away.

Cameron came up tight beside Jade, feet planted, hip to the rock wall. He entwined one arm in the roots and caught her waist with the other. She might not like it, but he'd seen her flail, and it was easier to hold on to her than catch her if she got swept away. He scanned the precipitous banks, cloaked in green but inviting no trespass. "How much farther?"

She shook her head. "I don't know. It feels close."

She'd been right about the fork and seemed to be remembering sights along the way. She must have been processing information the first time she passed through and holding on to those memories. The doctor had said new ones were sometimes keener than usual.

She shuddered. "There's something bad ahead."

He studied her face, flushed with exertion; this woman who'd stumbled off the mountain into Nica's life and, therefore, his. "Bad how?"

"I don't know."

In spite of the fact that she'd awakened talking about lies, he believed her.

She swiped at the damp strands of her hair. "I think I was reacting at this point. Stunned, maybe. I don't think I had a plan."

Yet she'd found her way out, even with a head injury. Given the terrain and stormy conditions of the mountains, she could have panicked, given up, or miscalculated and died. Or else she was making it all up.

Turning to look ahead, she said, "What if the drowning dream wasn't symbolic? What if it's prophetic?"

He tightened his hold on her waist. "You won't drown on my watch." He pulled her in, breathing the damp fragrance of her hair, feeling the warmth from her skin. The desire to hold her had ignited the evening before. Now her mouth drew his like a hibiscus bloom luring a bee. He hadn't spent such intensive time with anyone in years, and she was brave and strong and desirable.

A tendril of wet hair clung to her neck. Her blond was darker, her eyes greener than Myra's stormy blue. But the similarities were strong enough to bring him back to reality. He wouldn't make that mistake again. *Aloha* was one thing; anything more would be masochism. He pulled away. "Let's go."

TEN

The nylon netting on the pack had proved harder to remove than he'd expected. Or else he was weaker than he wanted to admit. The malevolence breeding inside drained him even in his sleep, which was fitful and shallow. Hunger bored a hollow that rivaled the pain. If he didn't eat soon, what strength he had would be gone.

The idea to remove the mesh pockets and tie them together into a fishnet had come between dozes in the night, when the heat inside his body had cracked his lips and stuck his tongue to the roof of his mouth. He'd forced himself to think of one thing he might be able to do and come up with the net idea. He couldn't attempt it before daylight.

When it came, his hands were shaky, and he'd dropped the knife into the pool. Now he worked to tie together the pieces. The chances of a sizable fish running into the net were small, but he might be able to scoop up some minnows and eat them whole.

If he got down into the water he might find a school of something larger that he'd heard flipping around in the pool. He could find his knife, too, if the water wasn't too deep. He lay on his back with the net across his chest and wondered, if he went into the pool would he ever come out?

Nica walked down the red dirt path, dampened to russet clay. Her cheap rubber flip-flops sloshed as fresh rain drizzled down her bare arms. The afternoon sky was draped in gray gauze, and the mountains where Jade and Cameron had gone looked ghostly.

They'd been out all night, and concern ate away her confidence. But Cameron knew the island's moods, and though he'd been away, he could never lose his *aloha'āina*. The island would care for him and he for it. No matter their foreign *haole* blood, they were *kama'āina*, people of the land.

When their parents were drowned, their friend and neighbor Okelani had taken them as her own according to the ancient custom, *hānai*. There was no paperwork to document an adoption, only a person opening her home and her heart to two grieving *keikis*. They had felt a part of Okelani's *'ohana* before, but now she and her brother were truly Okelani's family. She'd been all that a natural *tūtū* could be and more.

She approached Okelani's small cottage and tapped on the door, but the old woman was already on her way. No matter how softly she stepped, Okelani heard her on the path.

"Like a rainbow in da mist your face at my door." Okelani smiled, her teeth gapped and crooked, yet the warmth sank in and remained. She pushed open the screen. "Come. Come." Her *mu'u mu'u* had a red hibiscus pattern on a sky-blue background and softly draped her still-shapely figure.

Nica slid her feet out of her rubber slippers and left them outside the door with Okelani's own pairs. In the shops, tourists were amused by plaques that read: *Mahalo for removing your shoes, but no take mo bettah ones when you leave.* None of the shoes outside Okelani's were worth stealing. Nothing inside either.

They went into the one sizable room in the cottage. It was empty and had a smooth koa wood floor, stained with the ash of kukui seeds and oiled by hand to preserve its beauty. The room was for teaching and learning and dancing the hula. Growing up, Okelani had learned the moves that only the *kanaka maoli* were taught; the dance dramas that told the ancient myths, preserving a culture of awe and gratitude to forces outside themselves.

But through her friendship with the Pierces, and their many discussions, Okelani had clarified the longing in her heart, and now directed her dance to the One who provided the great bounty and beauty of her world. The Almighty was the fire goddess of the volcano, the thunder god, the god of the sea and the shark. No longer the capricious, jealous, seductive characters of the ancient stories, these forces were manifestations of God's great power and love for his creation and his people.

This was the hula Okelani had taught Nica and which they now taught to the young girls who came every week to train their minds and bodies in the demanding steps and motions, but most of all to train their spirits. When Okelani danced, there was such reverence, such truth, Nica could hardly bear it.

When she walked out of Okelani's three hours later, the sky had cleared, and TJ was waiting. She ignored him as she started up the path, but he turned and walked behind her, the bulk of his shoulders filling the space between the trees. The day was mild and clear. The path had dried. But she could hear him huffing with the steepness.

He didn't complain or ask her to wait, just kept plodding after her until they reached the top, where she turned toward her yard. Again he followed without speaking. A smile touched her lips in spite of herself. The gardenias, pikake, and plumeria in her garden sent a potent welcome as she entered. TJ stopped at the edge.

She turned and glanced over her shoulder. "Well?"

He shoved his hands into his pockets. "Your friend, Jade? Her name's Gentry."

Nica turned, unsure she'd heard him right. "Gentry?"

"Gentry Fox."

"The actor?"

"Only got maybe one tousand calls. Da first hour. Now we got one recording say we know already."

She turned and stared *mauka*. Cameron was up there somewhere with Gentry Fox, whose debut in *Steel* had earned her a Golden Globe Award. Hers was the supporting role, but she'd come out of nowhere and stolen the show. How could they not have recognized the timbre of her voice that sent her words right down inside? Not known the face that had portrayed such powerful emotion. "She seemed so . . . normal."

TJ shrugged. "She nevah know who she is."

When she remembered, would it all change? Or was she really the way she'd seemed here, when she wasn't in front of the cameras? Cameras. "Wasn't there . . . something else . . ."

"Da kine scandal?"

Nica nodded. "Wasn't she in court or—"

"No court. Jus all over da news for maybe six weeks. *Oprah*. Dat kine stuff."

Nica looked into his face. He must be humiliated. He'd broadcasted an unknown person report on her. He'd never live it down. "Did you find out who she came here with?"

"Going screen messages for da kine personal stuff. Chief going handle it now."

She touched his hand. "TJ, you're not *lōlō*. No one else in the department recognized her. And I've had her here three days without knowing."

"Whatevers."

She slid her fingers into his big palm. "Come inside."

His face softened. "Yeah?"

She gave a little tug. "Come have a cup of tea. Okelani brought fresh jasmine pearls." They climbed up past the room where Gentry Fox had slept, as helpless and needy as any of the others. Just a person. And maybe that was what she'd needed.

Watching Cameron's back as he forced a path across the steep incline, Jade tried to shake off what she'd seen in his face. She didn't want to think of him as a man, didn't want him seeing something in her he couldn't have. They had climbed out of the water when it turned into a frothy rapid, but she still felt it swirling and pulling. In the same way, the tug of that momentary connection would not wear off.

Cameron's cynicism and distrust had been annoying, but kept her from any interest that could prove unfortunate. Out here, working together, they were forging something in spite of his doubt. Friendship, she told herself, because the person they were going to find might already have her heart.

A noise penetrated her thoughts, something that had been there for a while but now rose above the bird and insect calls, the wind, and their own breathing. A roar and pounding that echoed inside her like doom. Perched at an angle on the steep incline, Cameron pulled himself around a promontory and stopped. She ran into his back. Without turning, he steadied her.

She pressed around and stared at the force before her with waves of recollection as Cameron closed his arm around her waist. "This is it," she gasped, as memory almost took her legs. "I went over those falls."

He assessed the white column in silence, the black rock that formed its backdrop, the sheer walls of the basin enclosing it. "These falls are not accessible to tourists. There's no trail."

"Up above." She clutched his arm. "We—"

"Jade. You're tearing the tendons from my bone."

She let go of his arm and stared. Weren't they in this together? He had pushed and pushed. They'd expended serious energy. Now that she remembered, he just stood there frowning? "This is it; I know it."

He said nothing.

"You don't believe me." She pushed away, scrambled down the stony slope and splashed into the pool.

"Jade!"

She ignored him. Her companion was here somewhere. "Hey!

Hello! Where are you!" Why didn't she have a name to call? She'd thought everything would come back. Most of all the person she was there to find. Why couldn't she remember?

Cameron removed his pack and wedged it onto the basin wall, furious. She could have broken something, crashing into the pool that way. Lava basins were treacherous. He lowered himself behind her. "Jade."

She didn't answer, just moved farther into the churning pool, searching the narrow shore at the foot of the basin where someone might conceivably have lain injured—or dead. *If* she'd gone over these falls, she was lucky to be alive. *If* she had a companion, he might not be. He didn't want her to find a corpse, bloated and fetid after this many days in the elements. But she wouldn't stop or listen.

"Jade." He caught hold of her.

She scathed him with a look that made him let go, then turned and hollered, "Hello!" Her voice rasped, thick with need, but only the echo mocked a response.

She hadn't called out a name. Either she didn't remember as completely as she wanted him to believe, or the whole thing was one impossible ploy. But what would she gain? Why pretend someone else was involved?

He pushed through the troubled water. The day had alternated clear and stormy, but now thick gray clouds closed in. The wind sent spray into his face from the falls, and a fresh rain began. He swam after her, calling, "Jade, wait."

She turned on him. "Why are you even here?"

Great question. "Get up on the bank. Let's talk."

"No." She moved closer to the falls, her gaze scouring the igneous bowl.

He'd seen death, and this one could be bad. She'd have no idea. He caught up and hooked her waist with his arm. She fought, but he hauled her up the narrow bank and sat her down. "Just hold on a minute, okay?"

She gulped back her anger and surprise.

"Look around you." He circled the basin with his arm. "Do you see any way someone could last in here five days?"

Her breath came hard and sharp. She frowned at the steep, unyielding walls, the churning water, the bare, thin strip of ground around the pool. In spite of his skepticism, he'd wanted to find something to justify her hope. But while she seemed to have some kind of supernatural protection, there was no evidence her companion did. Unless he'd been carried out like her through the rapids, he'd most likely been dashed to his death beneath the pounding water.

The only other possibility was that he'd been the reason Jade went over the falls. Cameron looked up the unforgiving column of water to the edge of land. "Jade, think. Did you see anyone in here with you?"

She searched the basin, falls, and pool with pain in her eyes. "I wasn't looking. I must have hit my head when I fell. I did. I know it now."

"Stop."

"What?"

"Making your case. I believe you."

Her lips parted. "You do?"

He'd said it without thinking, some instinct speaking for him. "Yes. But you have to face the facts." He swallowed. "If he's here, he hasn't made it."

Her chest rose and fell with abbreviated breaths. Tears filled her eyes. What had he expected? Another lesson on the universe of possibilities? He didn't want to be the one to tear her illusions apart, but now was the time for reality. "I want you to sit here while I go back to my pack."

"Why?"

"To get my flashlight. It's waterproof."

Her gaze jerked to the pool. "You think he's in there."

"I don't know."

She started to cry.

"Stay here and let me do this."

She dropped her face into her hands. It was the best he'd get, so he left her there and made his way back to his pack. He took out the light they'd used the night before, checked that it worked. The thought of a corpse in the pool made diving in unpleasant, but how else would they know?

With a glance to make sure she'd stayed put, he got a good breath and went under. The light illuminated the foggy surface that cleared and darkened as the water stilled deeper down. He shined it over branches and rocks and even a cow skull that must have been carried over the falls. But no body. Yet. He surged to the surface for air, treaded, and went back down, moving around the perimeter, then the deeper center, using what he knew from years of skin diving to clear his ears and gauge his breath.

She stood in the water up to her knees when he surfaced next. "Anything?"

He held out a handful of netting that he'd grabbed because it looked like the pockets on her hydration pack. If the guy's pack had been torn apart . . .

With a cry she splashed over and took it. She pressed the scrap to her chest, obviously realizing what he had. Fighting tears, she fingered it, then gasped, working it around in her hands. "Wait. It's tied together. Like a net." Hope sprang fresh in her face. "He's here."

"Jade . . ."

"Look. The pieces are tied."

Cameron looked from the net to the steep walls of the enclosure, the pool and the falls. Lava basins frequently had caves and air pockets. He'd been looking for a body, but now . . . He rubbed the water from his beard. "I'll try again. I haven't searched the falls."

"Is that possible?" She clutched the net to her chest.

"I'll have to go deep, get under if I can. Will it do any good to tell you to wait?"

She swallowed hard and nodded. "They're too strong for me." As he started to dive, she caught his arm. "Be careful. And hurry."

"I can hold my breath a long time, so don't panic."

She nodded.

Gripping the light, he dove down near enough to feel the push of the falls. The rocks beneath were bad. No one driven down would surface unscathed. Was that where she'd hit her head hard enough to cause amnesia, yet still walked away? Her light weight might have been a factor. That or what portion of the falls carried her over; anything. But he pictured her throwing off the centipede and wondered again what kind of protection she had.

Pressure built in his ears. The percussion of the falls pounded his chest. He ran the light over the floor, the walls, the—

Cave. No way to tell if it extended above water. Not without going in. Could he make it through the falls without getting crushed? He went deeper, his lungs urging him up for air. With his chest almost brushing the rocky bottom, he caught sight of a lava tube under one side of the cave wall. If it was open at the far end, he might get inside without fighting the falls. But not without air.

He pulled to the surface, emptying his lungs as he went. He broke the surface, sucked air.

Jade grabbed his arm, barely holding her own in the turbulence. "What did you find?"

Not *was there something*, but what? Her expectancy shook him. How could she know he'd seen anything?

"I'm not sure. I'm going to look again." He hollered, "Stay here." Then down he plunged with purpose, heading straight for the lava tube. Just wide enough to pull through, it blocked the pounding force of the falls, though the water still surged and tugged. But then he was through and kicking for the surface. If the cave didn't clear the surface of the pool, he'd have to retrace it all in the same breath. His lungs burned already. Thrusting with his arms and legs, he propelled himself up, shining the light to keep from smacking his head on the roof.

His face broke the surface under the low dome of the cave. Breathing hard, light raised, he turned a slow circle, saw the ledge along one wall, and the man lying there.

ELEVEN

Waiting for Cameron to surface, Jade tried with everything in her to remember what had happened. Had someone else gone over the falls? Why would she leave, why let the water carry her out if she'd known? She looked up and imagined her plunge over the powerful falls. She didn't really remember, but it explained the feeling of falling.

If she'd hit her head, concussed, lost sight of who she was and whom she was with . . . Even now she fought the pull toward the rapids where the pool drained. The swift water had swept her along until she'd pulled herself ashore. By then how disoriented had she been? She had trekked to Nica's without knowing she'd left someone behind. But if they were too late, how would she ever forgive herself?

She took a breath and dove under the water, whipped white with the action of the falls. She remembered its nightmare strength. Here was her assailant. No person, as the cop had assumed, but the raw power of nature and her own human error.

She pulled deeper, but there was no sign of Cameron or his light. Where had he gone? What if he'd been trapped, crushed, knocked unconscious? Lungs burning, she surfaced. He'd said not to panic, but this was too long. He couldn't hold his breath so long. She dove under again, saw his light shining up from the bottom and met him halfway. They pulled to the surface together.

He grabbed hold and gasped, "I found him. He's alive."

Exhilaration seized her. "Where? How?"

"There's a cave."

"A cave! Show me. Take me to him."

"I don't know if you can make it." He started swimming toward the side.

What? "Cameron. Wait." She had to see, had to reach her companion, but Cameron climbed out onto the shore.

"Cameron!" She splashed up with him. "You can't—"

He raised a hand. "Hold on a minute." He bent tight at the waist, wrapping his arms around the backs of his thighs, then down to grab his ankles. He'd either strained something or was cramping. The moments it took for him to get his breath nearly drove her wild.

At last he straightened. "The only way in is through a lava tube almost under the falls. It's tight and deep."

"But you got through and he's there. Is he all right? Is he injured?"

"He's unconscious. Feverish. His legs are beat up. Pulse is thready." He rubbed his hand over his mouth and beard. "I don't know how much time we have."

Her heart pounded. "Can we get him out?"

"Not without air tanks and stretcher." His gaze circled the basin. "I need to climb up to get a signal."

"We can't leave him."

He chewed his lip, causing the narrow line of beard to jut out beneath. "How long can you hold your breath?"

"Long enough."

"It's more than twenty feet deep, at least twelve along the lava tube, then up. No room for error."

She straightened. "I'll do it."

"If you get caught under the falls, there's not much I can do."

Caught under the falls. Tumbling, flailing. She turned back to the treacherous white column and felt its brutality. She shrank inside, but this wasn't the time to quit. "I beat it before."

He forked his fingers into his hair. "Okay. We'll dive down together to the tube. If you think you can go on, take the light and get through as fast as you can. If you have to turn back, do it."

She nodded. But she wouldn't. She was going to get through to the person she'd left behind. Whatever it took.

If he was paying attention to his gut, he'd have convinced her to wait until he called for emergency rescue operations. But if the guy in the cave died before help came, it would be worse for Jade than finding him dead already. He had to give her this time. He only hoped she could handle it.

Holding the light between them, they dove. Down, down to the long, jagged gap in the lava rock. No time to question, to doubt. At the opening, she took the light and entered the tube, kicking and pulling herself inside. He waited in case she had to back out, then went through himself, surfacing right behind her. She sputtered and choked, then turned toward the ledge where her companion lay.

With a cry, she swam to him, pulled up on her elbows, and caught hold of his hand. Cameron joined her, grabbing on to the ledge as she started to cry. The gray-haired man made no response, just drew thin, reedy breaths. Jade's reaction was hard to decipher.

He had to get out and make the call, but he wanted answers first. "Who is he?"

She clutched his hand and shook her head. "I don't know."

Anger surged. How could she not know? The man was lying right there. Cameron let go of the ledge. "I'm going for help. Don't come out without me."

She nodded, already pulling the hose from her slim hydration pack toward the injured man's mouth. Cameron swam out, climbed to his pack and pulled out his cell phone. He started for higher ground. Only after his muscles burned and his chest heaved and sweat ran down his sides from climbing, did he let himself ponder the fact that the man had to be twice Jade's age.

The man beside her murmured in his delirium, but even the sound of his voice brought no name, no relationship, to her mind.

His grave condition tore at her, but her lack of recognition hurt more. What kind of person was she to forget him? She had sensed the relationship in her waking memory, but hanging on to the ledge beside him now, she could not remember ever having seen him before.

The doctor had said days or hours. But it had been days. What if her past never came back? As bad as that would be for her, it would be torture for those who'd known her. For this man who must have been counting on her all this time. His grip tensed as he muttered.

She leaned close. "Hang on. Help is coming." The words seemed to soothe him. "I'm sorry it's been so long. If I'd known—" Her voice broke. She didn't want to say she'd forgotten and still didn't recognize him. Looking around the cave, she tried to imagine what the days had been like in there. With no direct sunlight it was chilly, and her head throbbed with the pounding of the falls.

Had Cameron gotten through? She had to believe he had. A search-and-rescue team would know how to get in to them, and how to get her companion out. She looked into his haggard face. Cameron was right that they'd need a breathing apparatus and stretcher. It would be complicated and it would take time.

Lord. Please, don't let it be too late. What if they'd gotten there even a day earlier? If she hadn't resisted going to the police—but she'd acted as soon as she remembered him, or rather, someone. This someone she couldn't recognize no matter how she studied his pinched brow, his sunken eyes, his cracked lips. His hair was silver around his face and in the stubble of his beard. His physique might have been healthy, though now he looked wasted.

Was he cold? If there was room on the ledge she would lie beside him for warmth. What was her relationship with him? A man so much older? The thought triggered nothing. Could he be a relative, a friend? She clenched her jaw, wanting to jam the memory back into her mind. She brought his hand to her forehead. *Who are you?*

Rescue teams would be hard-pressed to get them out before nightfall. Could he last through another night? He'd been unable to suck the water from her pack, so she'd removed the mouthpiece and drizzled it over his lips and did so again.

It grew dark in the cave, but so quickly it must be a storm, like so many others that had passed over on this rainy side of the island. She'd seen how fast the clouds closed in. Could a helicopter come if visibility was poor? Would they risk it? She groaned. *Please, God. Please.* She didn't think this man had another day in him.

⌐⌐

Nica rubbed the shame and embarrassment from TJ's shoulders through the stiff fabric of his uniform. He had joined the force when he could think of nothing else to do, but he'd become a conscientious officer. That he hadn't recognized a rising star from the tabloids and talk shows was hardly surprising, since he spent most of his free time bamboo fishing. As far as TJ was concerned the ragged shoreline of Kauai could be the edge of the world.

After attending community college in Lihue, he'd done his law-enforcement training on the mainland and come back with hardly an impression of anything outside of that instruction. Only Kauai could impress itself on him.

She squeezed the big shoulder and sat down. "Are you hungry?"

Silly question. She took the cup with the unfurled jasmine pearls in the bottom to the sink. Time, attention, and food would lure TJ back to cheerfulness. She took from the refrigerator an aku filet and vegetables and set a pot of rice to boil. He didn't move from his seat as she worked, as much to not disturb her as to ponder the situation.

She knew what troubled him. If he had recognized Gentry Fox, he could have gotten help for her companion before she took it on herself to go *mauka*. Cameron's accompaniment was his best hope that nothing further would happen to Gentry, but they'd been out there a long time.

Nica set the plate of tuna before TJ. His phone rang, and he took the call, jerking up straight with the first words. "What? Yeah. Kay den." He lifted the cat off his lap, pushed up out of his chair, and looked at her with relief flooding his broad face. "Dey found him."

Nica raised her brows. "Jade—Gentry's companion?"

TJ shoved the phone into his belt. He'd come over from work without changing his uniform, and now he seemed to fill it with purpose. "Dey sending in one chopper. Den a ambulance to da hospital."

"Let's take your truck."

He didn't argue her going along. But she opened her door and stopped short. Where had all the people come from?

～⌒

Curt shook. The situation was deteriorating. He pressed in to hear the news report over the soft tones of Enya and the swishing of Allegra's bath. Gentry had been identified, naturally, the fools on Kauai eating it on that one. He wished he could have seen the face of the officer who'd put out the plea for identification of Gentry Fox. He snickered, then rubbed his face, acid rising in his stomach.

He'd never wanted to be a soft-stomach guy, the kind who couldn't take it when things came down wrong. He had abs of steel, but inside? He'd have an ulcer before he hit forty.

He wove his fingers behind his head and watched the tenuous rescue. The weather wasn't helping. Bad visibility. No telling whether the helicopter would get in, what they'd find if they did . . .

A news babe came on to say that the storm and nightfall could force the helicopter crew to abandon the rescue until morning. Duh. Gentry Fox was believed safe, but there was no word yet on Robert Fox. No news was good news.

He raised his head when the CD ended, but another, equally bland, began. He returned his attention to the live action. At some point Allegra might need to know, but until then— He clenched his fists and willed things to happen as he wanted. What better chance would there be?

They showed an aerial view of the section of island being searched for Gentry's companion. In the corner of the screen, a picture of Gentry, recognizable from all her recent publicity. Everyone in the world watched the star's personal drama unfold, everyone except Allegra. He could still hear the music, but what about the water? Better not take any chances. The rescue could take hours, days. He had to make sure she heard nothing. Nothing that would interfere.

She was too precious to lose. He turned off the TV and crept to the bathroom door. Soft swishes of the water. It got him going. She'd insisted on a suite and allowed nothing but kisses. Now was the time to change that. With one hand on the knob, he loosened the tie of his robe and let himself in.

~

The thumping of the helicopter blades sent a surge of relief as it came into sight through the clouds. For a while Cameron had thought the storm would keep them out. For a while it had. He'd climbed back into the basin after making the call and now sent up a small emergency flare.

The copter approached and hovered. The wind from the blades beat the water and stung his eyes with tears as they lowered the stretcher with small air tanks strapped on. He tried to gauge whether it would fit through the lava tube. If not, what would they do? But these were the guys who'd figure that part out. Watching the helicopter hover low in the narrow space, he appreciated the skill and courage of the pilot. Conditions weren't exactly ideal.

By the time the team had been lowered into the basin, another storm forced the helicopter up away from land. If weather permitted, the pilot would be back. If not, the paramedic and the rest of the SAR team would have to get Jade's companion through the stormy night before they could bring him out.

Weather was already a factor. If they lost the helicopter, the team could not hand-carry him, given the lack of anything like a real trail.

He and Jade on foot had fought a way through, but carrying a stretcher over the steep terrain? Not likely.

He didn't know the team leader, Lieutenant Jeffrey Maxwell, or the other SAR team member who'd come down, but he knew the paramedic, Jason Becker. He'd grown up in Waimea on the hot, dry side of the island. They tapped fists.

"So here's the thing." Cameron filled them in on the man's location. "You can scope it out for yourselves, but I've searched the pool and cave area. I think the only safe access is through the lava tube."

Maxwell nodded. "Given the time and weather constraints, we'll take your word for that. Jason and Mitch will go in; I'll stay in communication with the helicopter. Can you guide the guys down?"

They spent some minutes assessing equipment and preparing to go in.

"Watch yourselves getting into the lava tube," Cameron told Mitch, who would be right behind him, towing the stretcher. "The falls are brutal, and there's an undertow action inside the tunnel." Since Jade had managed, he figured they could too. "Ready?"

At their nods, Cameron led the way.

⌒

At first he'd thought Gentry's voice a dream. So many others had come and gone. What was real? He'd had a hard time discerning that; he didn't know for how long. But her soothing words had sunk in, giving comfort without rousing. The voice of an angel, murmuring prayers on his behalf, from her lips to God's ear.

He thought she held his hand, thought she wept for him. If it wasn't Gentry, he'd have quite a story to tell. How many guys had been ministered to by an angel? When other voices joined hers, he wondered. And when someone took hold of his leg, swollen and festering, he leaped from wonderment to wakening—with a shout.

Someone was speaking as an oxygen mask was placed over his

face. He wanted to respond, but it was hard to hear over the constant barrage of the falls, and anyway, no words would come. A needle punctured the muscle of his upper arm. Unbelievable. His tomb had been transformed into an echoing emergency room.

He blinked in the near darkness. Maybe he had imagined Gentry, because he saw only two men working over him. The ledge was narrow, and they worked shoulder to shoulder alongside him. As they immobilized his leg, pain and nausea struck, no longer subdued by his stupor. He cried out, shock waves coursing through him until, mercifully, the pain drove him back into the place where shadows dwelled.

Hanging on to the far end of the ledge, Jade cringed as they moved her injured companion onto the stretcher and fitted him with an oxygen supply for the underwater journey out. From the moment they'd entered the cave, their focused intensity had confirmed her fears. She'd stayed out of the way and quiet. Cameron, too, was silent as he treaded water beside her.

She'd been in the pool so long she had shriveled and her body chilled. Her head ached, and she battled fatigue and muscle cramps, but that was nothing compared to what her delirious companion suffered. He must have hit the rocks beneath the falls—rocks that she'd miraculously missed. What strange quirk of fate had sent her one way and him the other?

But she knew it wasn't fate, and she guessed this person did too. She sensed rather than knew that somehow he was part of her believing. *Oh, Lord, why can't I remember?* It wasn't right. He deserved recognition.

She wanted to encourage him, to give him something to hold on to as they prepared to take him out, but she couldn't even say his name. *You know him, Lord.* She prayed automatically, no idea how or when she'd come to believe, only that she did. Cameron didn't expect God to fix things—but she did. Otherwise the helplessness would smother her.

They slid the stretcher into the water. Cameron stayed back with her as the others swam to the far side in preparation for their plunge into the lava tube. The bearers were also equipped with air, so they could go as slowly and carefully as needed. She hoped her companion didn't panic when they submerged. How much had he understood?

They had described their intentions, saying, "We'll be underwater some time," but had her delirious companion grasped it? Would he panic underwater? She remembered fighting for the surface, for breath and freedom. How helpless he must feel.

After a moment's consultation, the rescuers dove with the stretcher between them into the dark water of the cave. The pool swallowed them whole. She was alone with Cameron, who'd been a silent shadow since emerging again with the others behind him. Now she noticed his grim and accusatory expression.

She swallowed the painful lump in her throat. "What's bothering you?"

He hooked his elbow on the ledge. "A lot."

"Like?"

"What you're really up to."

She expelled her breath. "Up to?"

"You don't know the guy; he's old enough to be your father; and he's wearing a wedding ring."

Her mouth dropped open. She hadn't even noticed. But Cameron's implication was clear. "You think I'm involved with a married man? Maybe he *is* my father."

"Then why don't you remember?"

"I don't know." Jaw clenched, she fought a fresh spate of tears. "Do you think I haven't asked myself that a thousand times? That I haven't tried?" Whatever friendship they'd found evaporated, filaments of trust and respect swept aside like spider thread in a flood.

She pushed off the side, gulped air, and dove under the water, down to the opening of the lava tunnel. The men with the stretcher were just rising from the far end. The water tugged as she crawled and kicked through, forcing her lungs to hold on to the angry breath she'd taken. Past the pummeling falls, she pulled to the surface and broke free, gasping.

The rescue team had reached the side with the stretcher. She swam over and climbed out to them. One of the men spoke over a handheld radio. Minutes later she heard the thumping of helicopter blades before it emerged through the clouds. Their motion beat the water around her as the copter hovered overhead and lowered a line.

One of the rescuers turned to her. "We've only got a short window here. There's more weather moving in." As he spoke, the other two affixed the stretcher to the line.

Fear and hope mingled as the injured man was drawn into the sky. That was what she'd come for. "Just take him and go." She'd done what she had to, and she would stay another night out if it came to that.

Cameron climbed, dripping, out of the water as the stretcher approached the belly of the helicopter. A voice came over the rescuer's radio. "Roger," he communicated back as they hauled the stretcher into the hovering body. After a while, the cable was lowered again with a harness this time. The paramedic Jason went next, then the other EMT. They would continue medical assistance on the flight.

Another spate came over the radio. The ground man responded and turned to her. "There's time for one more." He explained how she'd be strapped into the harness as the cable was lowered once again. Then he turned to Cameron. "They've marked the location. Once the injured party's transferred to the ambulance, the pilot will attempt a return. Weather's chancy."

Cameron nodded. "I'm prepared to stay the night."

A thin guilt accompanied her relief that he wouldn't share the helicopter. She wouldn't mind if they went back for him, though. Jade followed directions as the man strapped her into the apparatus and gave the hand signal to the team member above. Just as she felt the tug lifting her from the ground he said, "There you go, Ms. Fox. Hold on."

Swung into the air, her thoughts latched on to one thing. *Ms. Fox?*

TWELVE

Cameron watched until she was inside the helicopter and it had sunk back into the clouds. Flying the islands, pilots encountered clouds and rain and the prevalent winds, but it gave him a twinge to see her swallowed up after being responsible for her safety. They'd penetrated substantially inland, and helicopters had crashed into the high, steep mountains for lack of visibility.

"So." Maxwell turned with a smile. "What's she like?"

Cameron raised his brows. "Jade?"

"Gentry Fox."

He stared for a full beat before looking back up to where she'd disappeared. "Come on."

"Guess you didn't hear."

He shook his head. "No way."

"Since Kanakanui put out her story, the island's been flooded with press."

The scene she'd described flashed in his mind. Cameras, reporters, microphones. He'd called it gross exaggeration, but he realized now she'd been right on. And she was flying into that scene unawares. "Can you radio up and tell them not to let her ride with the ambulance?"

"Why not?"

"She hasn't remembered who she is. They'll eat her up."

Maxwell caught his point and radioed the helicopter. "Uh, any indication our gal doesn't know who she is?"

The response was audible to them both. "Yeah, we're getting that impression. Name didn't seem to strike a chord. Not like you'd expect."

Then she really didn't know. A twinge of guilt passed through him. "I need to climb up and make a call. Where is the ambulance waiting?"

"Princeville."

The man didn't try to stop him. It would be a while before the chopper could return—if it could. Cameron climbed the wet and stormy mountainside but remained within earshot of the falls. As soon as he could get a signal, he called Nica.

"Cameron, where are you?"

"Stuck on a mountain. But listen. Jade's on the rescue copter, and they're putting down at the Princeville heliport. I need you to meet her there."

"I'm with TJ at the hospital. It's a madhouse. Cameron, Jade is—"

"I know. Gentry Fox."

"She remembered?"

"She's been told. But she doesn't know what that means. She's completely blocked."

He could hear Nica's dismay, a short side conversation, then TJ came on. "Got one mess here, brah."

"TJ, Gentry's coming in blind. She's been told her name, but it doesn't mean anything to her."

TJ made a sound of comprehension.

"I need you to intercept her at the Princeville heliport and get her back to Nica's."

"No can. Press all over dere."

At Nica's? They must have learned where Gentry was staying. He thought hard. "Okelani's, then. Get her to Okelani's and keep her there until I get back." He waited while TJ processed the idea. *Come on.*

"Kay den."

Cameron expelled his relief.

"Dis some kine mess."

"You know it, brah." And they'd all contributed, one way or another. He, worst of all.

⌒

Gentry Fox, she thought. *Gentry.* Seated up front beside the pilot, she couldn't see past the back of the EMT as they worked to stabilize the accident victim. Robert Fox. Same last name. They must be related. But even learning his name triggered nothing.

What was it going to take? Why wouldn't her mind work? She pressed her fingertips between her brows. *Gentry, Gentry, Gentry. Remember something!* But as the helicopter lowered to the ground, she was no closer than she'd been.

The EMT turned. "Don't worry about your uncle. We'll be taking the best care of him that we can."

Her uncle.

She hadn't assumed the SAR team knew. But she wouldn't have revealed his ignorance. Not after Cameron's reaction. Why was she so afraid of what people thought; what they might say?

They removed the stretcher, one man holding the IV drip they'd started to stabilize him. Her uncle, Robert Fox. As he disappeared through the side door, it seemed that his color was better, and maybe he was resting. Probably pain control. The thought of him lying there all that time on the ledge in that thunderous cave, waiting, hoping for someone who couldn't even remember his name . . .

Waves of sorrow swamped her. She had to stop blaming herself. She couldn't help amnesia. Nor could she cure it, apparently. But it hurt to think how badly she'd let him down. With a SAR member's hand upstretched to help her, she climbed out of the helicopter and was half blinded by a camera's flash in the twilight.

The rescue would have made the news, but the flash seemed to open a door into her mind that quickly filled with fear and aversion. Before she could react, Officer TJ Kanakanui pushed between her and the journalist. The crowd wasn't large. Only a few voices shouted, "Gentry, is it true you've lost your memory?" "Is it a permanent injury?"

And one nasty voice, "How convenient, Ms. Fox."

Convenient? She stared into a hateful pair of pale blue eyes in a weasel-sharp face. A flicker of recall teased before another flash blinded her.

TJ pushed her through to a battered white pickup and pulled open the door. She was relieved when Nica slid in beside and closed the door. TJ cranked the engine and screeched out of the lot with the cherry top on his roof flashing circles across the trees along the road.

She clutched the seat as his momentum thrust her against Nica. "Are we going to the hospital?"

"Not yet." Nica gripped the armrest. "The crowd is worse there. Much."

Jade's knuckles whitened as she held on around a curve and tried to make sense of it. Cameron had thought her scenario overblown, but obviously he'd been wrong. She pictured the ambulance team whisking Robert Fox inside. Why did she matter? Wouldn't the press get the rescue information from the emergency personnel? "Is it such a big story? My uncle's rescue?"

TJ increased his speed, whizzed past a string of cars that had pulled over when his light flashed them.

"You're the story," Nica said.

"Me?" The reporters hadn't been asking about the man on the stretcher. Only about her memory, her injury. And there'd been the snide comment about its convenience. A bad feeling rose up like déjà vu, only she couldn't recall the source.

TJ swung the wheel and she landed up against him. Why was he driving like a maniac? Jostled from side to side, she held on until, at last, he veered into a dirt track and slammed the brakes. Before she could ask what had happened, Nica grabbed her arm and pulled her out the door. TJ peeled out in reverse, throwing dirt and pebbles that stung her hands and face. The moment his tires hit pavement, he screeched off.

Jade stared. He was one crazy cop.

"Come on." Nica pulled her arm. "Before they see you."

Before they—Had the whole world gone crazy? They came to a ramshackle cottage patched together to look homey. A delicious aroma engulfed her as they reached the door. Nica slipped off her sandals, so Jade did the same with her soaked and muddy hikers. The door opened, and a woman stood there like someone from a storybook.

Her black-streaked gray hair hung loose past her waist to the back of her thighs. Her blue dress draped her softly, ending at her brown calves. Her teeth required repair, yet there was something in her smile that cancelled out that thought. And it was her eyes that ended all other inspection. Ghostly white, they could not possibly see. Yet the woman swung wide the door and said, "Bring her inside." She must have been told to expect them.

As they stepped inside, Nica said, "Gentry, this is Okelani."

Nica had mentioned her before, this woman who led them into a shabby kitchen the size of a closet. Something bubbling on the miniature range gave off the delicious aroma and caught hold of her stomach with a growl. But before she could think of food, she had to understand what was happening.

Nica had called her Gentry not Jade. Someone must have identified her, and TJ could have told Nica. But how did everyone else know? This must be a big story for the island of Kauai. Or else . . . what?

Swallowing back tears of exhaustion, worry and confusion, she turned to Nica. "Will you please tell me what's going on?"

Okelani slid a folding chair out from the card table on the cracked linoleum floor. "Sit, *mea aloha.*"

Jade collapsed into the chair, feeling all her muscles. Her trek had been long and grueling, her time in the water exhausting. She hadn't realized how much so until this moment. Yet something told her it wasn't over. She groaned softly.

Nica took the chair across the table, her gray eyes settling like flower petals on a still pond. "Cameron said you haven't remembered anything."

And she could imagine the tone in which he'd said it. Resting her elbows on the table, Jade clutched the sides of her face. "Just feelings, and not enough of those obviously."

Nica smiled. "He guessed what you'd be coming into and asked TJ to spirit you away."

"He guessed?" She raised her face.

"Once he learned who you are."

"How . . ." But that wasn't what she wanted to know. "What do you mean who I am?"

Okelani set bowls of stew before her and Nica. The fragrant steam triggered her saliva glands, and once more her stomach reacted audibly. The old woman set a hand on each of their heads, tipped her face up and closed her eyes. *"Mahalo e ke Akua."* She patted their heads. "Eat first, then talk story."

Nica raised her spoon and dipped it into her dish. Jade couldn't fight it. She took a spoonful of her own and sighed. "This is wonderful." A creamy coconut fish chowder with flavors she wasn't sure she'd ever experienced.

"Muhe'e." Okelani smiled.

Jade glanced at Nica, who smiled, as well, but didn't translate. No matter. Within minutes, she had emptied her bowl with the greatest satisfaction her stomach had known for days. Then she thought about Cameron, still out on the mountain. Did he have any food left?

He'd said he was prepared to stay the night, but how would he sleep in the steep-walled basin in the rain? At least one search-and-rescue member had remained with him. And they had communication. They'd figure something out.

She thanked Okelani, and the woman took away her empty dish.

Nica dabbed her mouth with her napkin, folded it across her empty bowl, and said, "I'm sorry I didn't recognize you."

Jade widened her eyes. "Then you know me? I'm local?"

"No. In fact, if it hadn't been Kauai, people would probably have known you right off. Cameron almost did. Remember him asking if we should recognize you?"

Jade clenched her fists. "I'm a criminal?" Was this TJ Kanakanui's idea of house arrest? Cameron had issued the orders.

Nica's smile settled deep in her eyes. "Not unless stealing the show is a crime."

"Stealing . . ."

"Okelani, they're not arresting people for Golden Globes, are they?"

What was she talking about?

Okelani pulled a stool to the table and sat. "You plenny good kine actor. But your hair a different color."

Nica nodded. "It was darker on the screen."

Jade ran her hair through her fingers. "I'm an actor?"

Nica nodded. "Do you remember playing Rachel Bach in *Steel*?"

This was crazy. How could she remember someone she'd pretended to be, when she couldn't even remember who she was? Maybe that was why. If she'd played enough parts, her mind could be hopelessly confused. "You're telling me I've been in a movie?" No wonder people were making a big deal—

Her head spun. A crowd squeezing her in, hollering, badgering. The woman's weasely face. Accusations. Lies. Hungry faces all around waiting for one slip. She gripped the table edge. That was no fan club.

⌒⌒

Cameron shook hands with the last of the rescue team, tossed his pack into TJ's truck bed, and got into the cab. "Hit it."

TJ started the engine. "Nevah tink you get out tonight."

"Almost didn't. That pilot's good." As TJ pulled out of the heliport, Cameron fastened his seat belt. "He picked us off like ants on an anteater's tongue."

TJ grinned. "Ant taste bettah."

"No doubt. You got Gentry?"

TJ slid him a glance. "How you hang wit one movie star?"

He frowned. Jade hadn't seemed like a movie star. But she wasn't Jade. She was Gentry Fox. The only screen performance he'd seen her in had been extraordinary. But she'd been a brunette, and she'd spent much of the movie with bruises and dirt on her face. Maybe if he'd seen her the first night she stumbled out of the wild, he'd have known her right off.

"Does she know?"

"Nica wen tell her."

His stomach tightened. Another person might get hurt if Gentry snubbed her; Nica would feel as though she'd released a stunned bird back into the forest. She wouldn't expect Gentry Fox to remain on the same plane. "Guess she can pay the medical bills."

TJ snorted. "You tink?"

"Who's the guy?"

"Her uncle. Robert Fox."

Her uncle. Cameron settled into his seat, taking that in. Uncle. He supposed famous people had uncles, just hadn't considered such a benign relationship. He'd accused her of worse. Well, not accused. Insinuated. Her reaction should have told him.

They rode in silence until TJ turned into the dirt track that led to Okelani's cottage. He pulled to a stop, and Cameron braced himself to go inside. He was thinking crow was on the menu.

Jade looked up as Cameron and Officer TJ Kanakanui came through the door. Cameron's expression held something she didn't recognize on him. Humility?

TJ went straight to the pot and raised the lid. "Mmm, Auntie. Squid luau?"

Okelani rose to serve him the squid in coconut milk. Cameron leaned against the refrigerator, arms crossed.

A hard defensiveness seized her when their gazes collided. "Why am I here?"

"You wanted to avoid publicity. The hospital's a madhouse."

TJ nodded over the bowl he clasped in both hands. "Plenny TV crew and journalist."

Jade sank back in her chair, touching the aversion. How would she face a crowd of reporters when she couldn't fathom what they'd told her? A movie actor? A Golden Globe? How could she not know? The thought of facing a crowd worse than the one at the heliport—the crowd in her dream—made her legs weaker than if she were on a slippery cliff without ropes. But she said, "That's not really the point anymore. I need to be with my *uncle*."

Cameron didn't miss her emphasis. He couldn't begin to know how his suspicions had stung, but he had the decency to look away. He asked TJ, "Has other family come in?"

Other family. Her family. People she knew and loved—and might not remember.

TJ turned to her. "Your mother's finding a flight as soon as—"

"No. She can't leave Dad. He—" Gentry jerked up as memory rushed in. "He just had bypass surgery." Taking sharp, quick breaths, she thrust out her hand, images filling her mind like a film on fast forward. "Let me use your phone."

Cameron came off the refrigerator, his gaze rapier sharp, as though he shared whatever frequency her mind had seized to download her life. "Use mine." He slipped it into her hand. "Keep TJ's for official communication."

She touched in a number without hesitation. She knew the voice that answered. "Mom?" Tears stung.

"Oh, Gentry, I knew you'd remember. Your dad—"

"Please don't let him worry." But as she said it she realized how unlikely that was. Her parents paid lifetime tuition to the school of positive thinking.

"And Rob—he's all right?"

"I'm not sure." She didn't want to pop their balloon, but Uncle Rob had looked far from all right.

"But they found him, and . . ."

"Yes." She relived in a flash the moment Cameron had said, *"I found him. He's alive."* "They've taken him to the hospital, and I'm sure they'll do everything they can. Mom, please don't leave Dad. He'll root out every bag of chips in the house."

"You're right."

Her mother's laugh sparked more tears, but she blinked them back. "I'll stay with Uncle Rob. He'll be fine. You know how tough he is." And with another rush of memories, she did too. *Uncle Rob!*

From the time she could keep up, they'd escaped to the wilderness, rugged mountaineering in remote locations where it seemed that only the two of them had ever stood. Had he considered Kauai such a spot? And there she found the gap. She didn't remember coming to the island, or taking the trail or anything that happened before she went over the falls. She stopped the sinking feeling in its tracks. She would remember.

"All right, then, if you're sure you can handle it. Well, of course you can. Dad said you would."

Right. Sure. She could do anything. "I love you both."

She signed off and handed Cameron back his phone, relief and fear running neck and neck inside her. Ecstatic to have a past again, she nonetheless focused on the present. "I need to get to the hospital."

Cameron set down his bowl of squid and pocketed his phone. "You want to face it?"

"I want to be with my uncle."

He looked at TJ. "They know your truck?"

TJ shrugged. "Probly. Though I wen drive like one NASCAR racer."

"Lucky you nevah get one ticket."

"Why I'm one cop."

Cameron set his dish in the sink and turned to his sister. "Still got press hanging around the house?"

"I don't know."

Press at Nica's? Gentry slumped. "If they've staked it out, they're still there." And now she found another hole. Her experience with the press. So how did she know what she'd said was true? From a bad feeling with no specifics? Her memory was Swiss cheese, as intact as if it had never been gone, except for the holes as blank as air bubbles.

Cameron raised Nica to her feet. "You and TJ drive around and engage them. I'll sneak up the path and get my truck."

He would take her, with all his doubts and suspicions? Or did he deign to believe her? It didn't matter. Anything that got her to her uncle.

He bent and kissed Okelani's cheek. "Thanks for dinner."

The Hawaiian woman patted his bearded jaw. "Special for your return, Kai."

"My return wasn't certain. That squid could have been wasted on TJ." He jabbed his thumb at the big Hawaiian.

She tapped her heart, her face warm with affection. "I wen know you be here."

He kissed her again. "Keep Gentry till I get back."

Strange, hearing her real name from him, from the others. As the screen banged shut behind them, she was left alone with Okelani, who seemed too competent, too aware, to be blind. "Nica told me you helped her that first night I came. Thank you."

"Sure." Okelani sat down across from her. "You like da kine squid?"

From the moment it had been mentioned, she'd tried not to think what she'd just eaten, but in truth it had been tasty. She nodded. "What was the chopped green?"

"Taro leaf. Healthy. Keep you *nani kōkī*."

"Nani . . ."

"Supremely beautiful." Okelani smiled.

She couldn't be talking about her personally, because she couldn't see one way or the other. Or could she?

"Da beauty come from inside. One *mā'ona 'ōpū*, filled-up stomach, bring a peaceful spirit. Da woman's *hina* power, like one sun leaning down, da sunset."

Gentry smiled at the imagery. A fat, filled-up sun leaning toward the horizon. "And the sunrise?"

"*Ku.* Man stay da morning and hot noon."

Yes, she could see that, a different sort of energy.

"*Ke Akua,* he make 'em for complement, strong and beautiful." Okelani exemplified her lesson, her supple beauty potent in spite of gray hair and poor teeth. In spite of eyes clouded white.

She reached over, and Gentry felt heat from her fingertips before they touched her forehead. But the tips were cool when they rested just above and between her eyebrows. They sat in that strange position a long time, yet it didn't feel awkward.

"Your *hina* strong. Fruitful. *Ke Akua* bless you." Okelani removed her fingers and shook her head. "My Kai, all close up, all cloud cover da sun."

"You mean Cameron?"

Okelani sighed. "His wife squeeze da heart till it wen shrivel like one lousy guava, all seed and no juice."

His wife? Gentry straightened. And she'd been out alone with him for two days, overnight. Just perfect. She knew without knowing it was the kind of thing the press would jump on. Why? What would anyone care? But a dark shadow rose up inside, nothing more—once again—than a feeling, yet there must be something behind such a negative impression.

She turned at the sound of a truck outside the front screen door. She had the unreasonable desire to run out the back, but she stood up, thanked Okelani again, and headed for the truck. Her legs had no more running in them.

THIRTEEN

Cameron let Gentry into the truck, noting her exhaustion. He guessed she knew what she could handle—or at least believed she could handle whatever she had to. If she had to walk the gauntlet to get to her uncle, she'd do it. At least now she knew what she was in for—which was more than he could say.

He could have let the emergency personnel convey her at once, or had TJ provide a police escort. Instead he'd assumed responsibility. She hadn't asked for his help before and didn't ask now. The urge was his, like a toothache he couldn't ignore.

It had sent him into the mountains when she would have gone after her uncle alone. She might even have found him. Then what? She'd have had no phone, no way to get him out of the cave or off the mountain. Had she thought of that?

No. As in the pool beneath the falls, she just jumped in. And there he was jumping in behind her. Was it some subliminal manipulation? Was he chronically exploitable? Or was it his own need to get at the heart of the matter, to make sense of things that had no sense—was it him trying once more to order a universe spun out of control?

He reversed down the track from Okelani's cottage to the road, spun, and started for the hospital in Lihue. Traffic after dark on the Kuhio Highway would be minimal. Except for the handful he'd outmaneuvered at Nica's, the press were probably at the hospital, knowing that sooner or later she would show up.

Her uncle's rescue would have been news, but Gentry made it big news. The numbers of reporters would be greater and the boundaries lower for the mob awaiting them. Celebs were fair game and couldn't expect the privacy of a tourist or local. She must know that. But he couldn't shake the look on her face or the tone in her voice when she'd described the scene they were going into. And that was why she was in his truck and no one else's.

He glanced over. "You okay?"

She nodded and turned back toward the window.

On the mountain they'd experienced cooperation, companionship. More than that if he was honest. They'd formed a bond of hardship and endeavor. Then he'd offended her. He swallowed. "Gentry." The name felt wrong. He wanted to backtrack to Jade, to the forest, the cave. He wanted to take back what he'd said. "I made an assumption."

"It doesn't matter."

True enough, but he couldn't leave it at that. "I shouldn't have said it. Even if— It wasn't my business."

She turned. "Are you apologizing?"

"Pretty poorly."

"I forgive you."

"Wow."

"What?"

"Dat one, da kine, chilly pardon."

She leaned her shoulder to the door and eyed him. "I thought you'd stopped."

"Stopped what?"

"Suspecting me."

Had his assumption been rooted in doubt and distrust? "Well, suspecting . . . it's what I do." Their gazes locked long enough for her to transmit disappointment, and for a moment he shared it. He had his reasons, but that wasn't something he intended to discuss.

Turning in at the hospital, he viewed her nightmare. Cars and vans choked the lot, reporters standing ready, cameras on shoulders, lights and microphones, the press en masse with eager fans intermixed. A handicapped spot was all he could find.

Gentry brought her hand up to the side of her face and said, "You can go."

"Not likely."

"I appreciate what you've done, Cameron, but I've got a bad feeling about this, and it's not going to help that I spent the night in the jungle with a married man."

He jerked. "Married?"

"Okelani told me." She frowned. "It wouldn't be any big deal; nothing happened. But things get twisted."

His throat felt like paste. Okelani had no business bringing that up. It had no bearing on this or any other situation. "You can cross that off your list of concerns. I'm not married." With a bitter taste in his mouth, he got out of his truck. She'd given him the chance to walk away. Why hadn't he taken it? Because she had gotten under his skin, and he wasn't finished, even if he wanted to be.

He could blame it on Nica's phone call, dragging him into the mix. But everything since then had been his choice. Or had it? Maybe they were all molecules on a crash course, bouncing against each other with no pattern and no control, every choice a random act of futility.

He would get her inside, then make his escape. Someone else could pick up the slack. He didn't have to be the one. Who was she anyway?

He rounded the hood as Gentry Fox emerged. Transformed from the woman in Nica's kitchen to a magnetic presence that drew every eye, she stepped out. She had not even run a comb through her hair, yet the strength and courage she'd pored into her performance as Rachel Bach, the vulnerable but indomitable spirit, could not be mistaken. Every stupid thought he'd just had coalesced into a fist that caught him low and hard.

People started squealing. The reporters pushed in close, shooting questions from all sides. "Look here, Gentry. Over here." A flash and more flashes.

"How did you lose your memory? Do you know who you are? What happened? Tell us what happened."

"I don't remember." She moved toward the entrance.

"Is it a closed-head injury? Is it permanent?"

"The doctor says I'll recover." She could barely move. "I'm sorry but I need to get in to my uncle."

"Why did you leave him out there?" From a woman on her right.

Gentry turned. "I didn't remember."

Someone else jumped on. "How long have you known? Why didn't you get help?"

"I tried, but . . ." None of them had seen how hard she'd tried once she knew.

He'd intended to stay out of it, but now clamped his arm around her shoulders and moved her through the microphones and flashing cameras. People shouted questions, but she followed his lead and kept walking.

A short man with a rash of moles darted in front of them and flashed his camera. "New lover, Gentry? One past puberty this time?"

She stopped. "What?"

Cameron shouldered the man aside as his own recall kicked in. Accusations of Gentry's affair with a minor. All the tabloids had carried a version, complete with photos and the young man's claims. No wonder she'd avoided publicity.

"What did he—"

"Keep walking." Cameron pushed her along. If she didn't remember, the parking lot was not the place to explain. He thought the claims had been discredited, but obviously the scandal lingered.

Questions shouted at them blurred. The reporters merged into a human jungle, a force to engage and defeat. He had vowed to avoid personal involvement, but he ignored that to aid Gentry once more. He didn't ask himself why.

She was shaking by the time they got through the police stationed at the doors into the relative quiet of the lobby. He sensed her confusion. That last question had thrown her. But why?

An attractive Asian woman followed by a chunky security guard approached and offered to escort her. Again Cameron ignored the chance to escape. Gentry might not even know he was there, so tight was her focus. She had closed up like a Japanese puzzle box after the jerk accosted them, and he wasn't sure how to unlock that rigid control. But she needed an ally, and he was in position.

He'd seen her determination. He'd also seen her shaking from the centipede, sobbing at her uncle's side, stinging from his assumptions. He'd seen her unguarded—or had he?

She was Gentry Fox. Professional pretender. His doubts kicked in big time. Who was he fooling? She didn't need him. And yet . . .

They entered a tiny room where her escort indicated they could wait. "We'll try to keep them away, Ms. Fox. No guarantees. The doctor will come see you when your uncle is moved to recovery."

Gentry's face paled. "He's in surgery already?"

"He gave consent in the ambulance and was prepped on arrival."

"Then, he was conscious."

The woman shook her head. "I don't have any details. Sorry."

Gentry sank into a chair. "Thank you."

"Coffee and soda machines down the hall." The woman pointed in their direction. "Mr. Pierce can go out for it. Adam will watch the door." The guard nodded, and they both walked out.

Gentry turned. "You know her?"

Cameron shrugged. "I don't think so."

"When did you tell her your name?"

He caught the implication. "The SAR team and police knew I was with you. Word spreads." Far and wide around Gentry.

She removed her ponytail holder and combed her fingers through her hair, pushing it back and away from her face, then looked up, eyes weary. "I should have been here."

"They'd have taken him right in."

"He was conscious. I could have said something."

"You hadn't remembered."

She sighed. "I know, but . . ."

"You'd have been swarmed without warning." Having her intercepted hadn't been his call, but he'd made it. And if she hadn't been in Okelani's kitchen when TJ delivered the news about her mother, she might not remember yet. He imagined the confused Jade stepping out into the crowd instead of the poised Gentry Fox.

Her brow pinched. "You know what he meant, don't you. That reporter."

He lowered himself into a chair, feeling the release of muscle and sinew and a general post-exertion letdown. "Don't you?"

She shook her head. "I thought it had all come back. But I'm finding holes." She turned. "What—"

"You've got enough to worry about."

She looped her ponytail holder around and around her finger. "That look on his face. His lip curled up like . . ." She spread her hands, then dropped them in her lap. "Past puberty?"

He rubbed his beard. He hadn't paid enough attention to the story to explain it to the person involved, especially when she looked so vulnerable. He should have ducked out when he had the chance. "Let's just focus on now."

"That bad?"

He weighed what he knew against what she might imagine and said, "There were allegations that you had an affair with a minor."

"How minor?"

"Sixteen, I think."

"Sixteen?" She sank back as if he'd walloped the air out of her. "Who?"

"I don't know the name." He rarely tuned in to celebrity scandal, but the pain that gripped Gentry's face had substance. "You don't remember any of it?"

She pressed her palms to her temples. "No wonder they're out there." Her voice squeezed.

"Comes with fame. You must have expected it."

"Not really." She let her hands drop. "I've done some TV parts and stage productions, but my focus the last few years has been a troupe called Act Out. An improv ensemble I started with my friend Helen Bastente for at-risk teens."

He remembered that now. Oprah had emphasized its purpose, providing a creative avenue for troubled kids to express their tangled emotions. He'd been on the rowing machine when Gentry's interview aired. Mostly he remembered his annoyance that someone had switched from ESPN.

"I wasn't seeking a script." She caught her hair back with her fingers. "Helen was reading for the part in *Steel*; I went along to support her. But for some reason, the casting director had me read too."

Some reason? Gentry could have been typecast for the gutsy Rachel Bach.

"It was a small, independent production, so I didn't think it would take much time from the theater. Then it got legs and attracted some serious interest. Big shots took over, renegotiated contracts—the works. I almost bailed, but I'd fallen in love with the character."

That had come through on the screen, Gentry playing the wife of a striking steelworker who took his place as a scab to pay for their child's operation. Even he'd seen how she peeled the character off the page and breathed life into the part. "And you thought afterwards you'd slip back into obscurity?"

"I'm not that naïve." Her gaze returned bruised. "I knew things had changed. I just wasn't prepared for the rest."

"You remember now?"

"Not a memory as much as . . . I can feel the hatred."

Once again she'd accessed the emotion, but not the facts. "Hate's as potent as love; maybe more."

She shook her head. "I won't believe that."

Her universe of possibilities must be rose tinted.

She got up and circled the room, the only sounds the ticking clock and the low buzz of the lights. She bit off the broken nail of her index finger, and once again he had a hard time visualizing her as a

Hollywood personality. Was it something she turned on and off, as she had when she stepped from the truck? Or had that been a subconscious shift in response to the crowd? How would anyone know what was real with Gentry Fox?

She looked at the clock and rubbed her neck. "How long do you think they'll have him in there?"

"No way to tell."

She gripped and released her hands. "You don't have to stay."

"I'll stay." Nervous energy had built up in her, but now it seemed to seep away and leave her empty. "Want something to drink?"

The time it took her to answer revealed her exhaustion. "Diet Coke if they have it."

"If they don't?"

"Anything diet."

He went out past the guard and strolled down to the vending machines, waited while a slight woman clinked in her quarters, and the machine clunked out a soda. This late at night, those were the only sounds except for the distant *ding* of an elevator.

A flowery perfume wafted from the woman, who stepped aside from the machine, but it didn't quite cover an underlying sweat. She looked up with eyes like pale sea glass in a face as sharp as a prow. "Cameron Pierce, right? Kapa'a High. Ninety-three."

He brought up his guard. "You local?"

"Waimea. I won't tell you what class." Her teeth formed a narrow arch to fit the sculpting of her face.

He could usually tell a local even if they'd left the islands, but not always. Just to check, he said, "Any class in your age range, you must have graduated with one of the Barretos." The twelve Portuguese-Hawaiians had actually attended his own Kapa'a schools. He'd graduated with Miguel.

She nodded. "Telling which one gives it away." And she'd just proved herself a liar, though why she felt the need puzzled him. She could have simply said what paper or station she was with.

He scanned the soda selection, slipped in quarters, and procured a Diet Coke.

She said, "Running back, first team, but you prefer the long board when the surf's up. Won the '97 Haleiwa Surfing Championship."

"You know this because?"

"I talk story."

"That's how, not why."

She popped her tab. "Aren't you going to drink your Coke?"

He started down the hall, then thought better of giving away his destination. The guard would keep her out, and in fact, she probably already knew, but it still felt like leading the wolf to the door.

"Did she tell you the boy overdosed?" Her voice grated.

He didn't have to ask who she meant. The media had played up the youth's attempted suicide. He'd smelled a rat, medical fraud being his specialty. But it wasn't his business. He headed for the room.

"His mother's filing a civil suit for pain and suffering. Now Gentry's lost her memory." The woman kept at his heels like a terrier. "I'd call that convenient."

He turned. "Look, Ms. . . ."

"Walden. Bette Walden."

"You need to fish another stream, Bette."

"She's reeled you in?"

Whatever answer he gave to that could be spun. Even saying she was Nica's friend would shift the scent a direction he wouldn't want it to go. "What's your part in all this?"

"What's yours?" She slid her purse strap up her narrow shoulder.

"Wouldn't you rather make that up? Isn't that what you people do?"

"I'm not a rag reporter."

"What, then?"

"An investigator. Like you, only impartial."

He stopped walking. "Let's see."

She took out her identification.

He frowned. "Who's paying the bill?"

She smiled without teeth.

"Then tell me this. Why are you investigating a hiking accident?"

"Accident? Funny how people get hurt around Gentry Fox."

Not what he wanted to hear. Had he lost his impartiality? But if she'd injured her uncle, why go back for him? The amnesia seemed real, though a good actor could pull it off. He'd watched her transform in the time it took to round the hood of his truck.

He expelled a breath. The clock had tipped toward morning, and he was nearing exhaustion. Not a good time for judgment calls.

Bette slid her card from her wallet. "Maybe we can help each other."

"We'll see." He took the card and left her standing in the hall, then let himself into the room. Gentry sat with her face in her hands. The expression she raised to him was so bleak, it tugged the doubt right out of his head. He walked over and set her Coke on the table, then laid the card beside it. "Anyone you know?"

FOURTEEN

Gentry stared at the name on the card, but nothing came to her. "Should I?"

Before Cameron could answer, the door opened. A doctor came in, sandy hair receding from a slack-cheeked face. His chin all but disappeared into his neck, but his eyes were sharp and aggressive. She jumped up and faced him.

His nostrils collapsed as he drew in his breath and spoke in a thin, nasal voice. "Ms. Fox, I'm Dr. Long. Your uncle has come through surgery but has not yet stabilized. I repaired injuries to the knee and ankle of his right leg, but the extensive damage and septic condition of the lower-left extremity could require amputation."

She startled. *Amputation?*

"That is a solution we hope to avoid, but the infection is severe and his condition critical." His robotic delivery set her teeth on edge.

"Is he conscious? Can I see him?"

"He'll remain unconscious until he's stabilized. From recovery, he'll be taken to ICU. Someone will let you know, but . . ." He tipped his head back and sighted her down the narrow barrel of his nose. "I won't have a circus in there." Understandable, considering the circus outside, but his expression suggested that, on top of everything else, this was her fault. Guilt hit her so hard she staggered.

The doctor's icy manner started her meltdown as he left the room.

Cameron's hand on her shoulder undid her. She turned, and he pulled her into his chest. Uncle Rob critical and unstable? She had thought as soon as he reached the hospital everything would—*Amputation?*

She refused to think of Uncle Rob without both strong legs. Uncle Rob unable to conquer a boulder field, to leap rock to rock across a stream, to set a pace only the hearty could match to reach a summit at peak light. If infection caused the loss, then it would be her fault for not remembering, for not finding him sooner.

Cameron's *"I found him; he's alive"* had been a clarion call to hope and expectation. A feast of relief. *Fait accompli.* Even her uncle's dire condition hadn't quenched hope as this surgeon's words did now. She clenched her jaw and refused to surrender the field. "They won't take his leg."

Cameron's face was grim. "There might be no choice."

It hit her like a cold splash from the falls. She pulled away, remembering he scorned hope. "I'd ask you to pray, but you don't expect anything." She shook him off like an irritating fly and circled the room, issuing her own orders to God. Specific and vehement, she still couldn't help feeling that Cameron was canceling her out.

Why was he even there? He didn't know her, didn't know Uncle Rob. He was an investigator like the woman on the card, Bette Walden, PI. She stopped short. A face flashed, the sharp, pale-eyed face of the woman, sneering, *"How convenient, Ms. Fox."*

She spun. "What did you tell that woman, that PI? That if I'd gone to the police, my uncle would be fine?"

"You don't know that."

"I'd have been identified. They would have known that first day he was out there."

Cameron crossed over to her. "That doesn't mean they'd have found him. You did that. And you couldn't have done it sooner. You needed to heal."

She pressed her hands to her face. "If it's too late. If I've ruined his life . . ."

"You saved his life."

She jerked her face up. "You don't know him. He can't stand to stay cooped up, to be constrained. What I've done to him is a crime."

He took hold of her shoulders. "Don't say—"

"Anything that can be used against me?" He had come to the island to investigate her. He'd admitted it. Just like that PI and the reporters—waiting, hoping for a scandal. "Anything damning enough—"

He gave her shoulders a shake. "Are you through?"

Her chest heaved. They were both ragged and sweaty, their scents mingling with fear and tension. "You've thought from the start—"

"Forget what I thought." His mouth took control, kissing the words and thoughts away, then softening, giving back what he'd taken. That first sight of him had stirred something in her. She had fought even the thought of connection when she didn't know who she'd lost, but now she couldn't help responding so deeply it took her strength away.

He propped her against the wall and leaned on his elbow, looking frayed. "I didn't plan that."

"You want to forget it?"

"Unfortunately my mind's a trap."

"Must be nice."

He cupped her shoulder. "It's coming back, Gentry. You're going to remember."

"I'm not sure I want to." Had she blocked things she couldn't face? Mistakes she'd made and regretted. She looked away, beyond tired and incapable of reason.

"Look at me." His voice was low and steady. "Whatever happens isn't your fault. You're Gentry Fox, not God."

A short laugh escaped her. "That's perspective."

He needed it too—a step back, a fresh view of the whole situation. Things had gone a far sight from what he'd intended. He slid his fingers into her hair and tipped her face up. "You're going to be okay."

"And Uncle Rob?"

"If he's anything like you, he'll handle whatever comes."

She released a jagged breath. "I'm sorry I dragged you into this."

"You didn't drag." He'd taken every step. "But it's gotten crazy, and I don't want Nica involved." He rested his thumb in the soft depression above her collarbone. "No offense, but you can't go back there."

Her lashes dropped and lifted wearily. "We must have had a hotel or something."

"You don't know?"

"I don't remember coming to Kauai or anything until after I went over the falls."

None of the trauma. This or the one months ago. She was blocking things that hurt. He'd suspected that. "Who might know your itinerary?"

"Uncle Rob. He'd have made the plans; he always does. Maybe Aunt Allegra, though that's another story. His housekeeper . . ."

"Who would you have told?"

"Probably no one."

At his skeptical look, she said, "We started hiking together when I was a kid. He always made the arrangements and surprised me. As far as I know that hasn't changed."

"All right." He looked at his watch. "In a few hours you can make some calls."

She leaned her head against the wall. "In the meantime?"

His body liquefied. "Don't look at me like that and ask."

Her languid eyes reflected shade and mists and mossy alcoves. Her lips pulled into a slow smile. She was every inch Gentry Fox, but she was also the woman he'd fought beside on the mountain. What was he doing?

He brought her back to a chair, but she'd only been seated a few minutes when a hospital staff member came for her. Cameron escorted her but stayed outside the ICU. While he waited, he made some calls.

Not long after she'd gone in, Gentry came back. "They suggested I get some sleep. I think that translates into 'give us room to do our jobs.'" She had to be dragging, but she didn't show it to the press line who took her picture and murmured encouragement as they made their way to the elevator.

Badges and microphones identified the major news networks. Only local and reputable press had been allowed into the hospital in the middle of the night. He knew they were dying to press for details, and he couldn't help thinking it was Gentry's amazing comportment that kept them at a respectful distance.

Once the elevator doors closed them in, his own ordeal began. He did not repeat mistakes, and he didn't break vows, even those made only to himself. No longer in the spotlight, Gentry leaned against the wall and handrail, eyes closed. She was comfortable with him, enough to let her guard down.

His throat tightened. Twenty minutes alone had cleared his head. He meant to keep it that way. His cell phone rang; hopefully TJ with answers. "Talk to me."

"One Jeep Wrangler for two weeks. Her uncle wen give Hale Kahili for da address."

Cameron silently cheered. He had hoped that information had been phoned in from the rental company when the police asked for information regarding Gentry and her uncle. It didn't matter who had the itinerary if Robert Fox had left a paper trail.

"Hale Kahili." He sent a peripheral glance over his shoulder. "What's that place going for these days?" None of his business, but Ginger House was one of the sweeter rentals on the island.

"Don't know, brah. Seven, eight hundred maybe."

A night. Only the best for this girl. The elevator dinged, but he held the Close button. "Can you get someone from the management company to open it up and meet us there?"

"Now?"

"Yeah now. And, TJ, you available?"

"For one bodyguard? Tink you want dat one."

"Yeah, well . . . I've got cases waiting." Cameron rubbed his face, sheer exhaustion weighting his limbs. "We'll talk about it later. Just meet us out there, okay?"

"Okay, Kai."

Cameron shoved the phone back into his pocket and turned. "Ready?"

Gentry nodded. He let go of the Close button and the doors opened. It was two-thirty in the morning, but there were still hangers-on. And these were less polite. He was getting the hang of moving through the strobe effect of the flashes, the hollered questions, the incendiary comments. If they were hoping to provoke an outburst in Gentry, they didn't realize how spent she was. He got her into his truck, assuming they'd be followed. But it didn't matter. On an island this size, she could no longer hide.

The drive to Hale Kahili took less than half an hour, paying no attention to the speed limit. Not huge; two bedrooms, kitchen, dining, living, lanai, the house commanded top dollar for its ocean and mountain views, sumptuous appointments inside and out, private pool, and flowering ginger gardens with lily ponds. A narrow path led to the private beach, but most of the cost was due to its seclusion. Robert Fox had been keeping Gentry from the limelight, but that was no longer possible.

They met the property manager at the front door. As the woman let them in, he watched Gentry for any spark of recollection, but saw none. Having ascertained that all was in order for Gentry Fox, the manager left them. Maybe she'd go back to bed; maybe she'd talk to the press who'd followed.

He rubbed the back of his neck. "Anything?"

Gentry shook her head. She crossed to the table where a cream-colored leather purse slouched. She opened and looked inside it, drew out a wallet and found her ID and credit cards.

Cameron slacked a hip. "Insurance?"

She flicked him a glance. "Of course."

She wouldn't have needed her purse on a hike into the heart of Kauai. Made more sense to leave it locked in the house than in the

Jeep, especially if they'd intended to hike some distance from where they'd parked. Her uncle had probably driven. With the recent rains, the Jeep might not be immediately retrievable from its remote location—wherever that was—but he imagined things would be squared away soon enough.

Gentry yawned, all but dead on her feet.

"You need sleep." He drew his keys from his pocket. "I do too." Where was TJ?

Trancelike, she crossed the ceramic tile floor to the polished wood staircase. At the base she paused. "Thank you. For everything."

"I won't leave before TJ comes."

Her face fell.

"He doubles as a bodyguard." His size was usually enough to make someone think twice. If not, he put his muscle to use with seemingly little effort. Like on the football field where, just by flexing, he'd opened holes for Cameron to run through.

She relaxed. "I'll be fine."

"I'll stay down here until he comes." And try not to think about her up there, changing out of the soiled hiking clothes into something soft. "Go to sleep." He almost closed the distance between them and took her back into his arms. But he didn't repeat his mistakes.

He watched her climb, heard a door close upstairs to the left. He scratched his ragged growth of beard and took a seat on the soft suede sofa. After a minute, he removed his boots and brought his feet up. What was keeping TJ? He curled onto his side and closed his eyes.

⌒

Though she didn't remember the house they'd supposedly rented for their stay, its contrast to Nica's home and Okelani's cottage drove home her reality. She didn't belong in their world. She was Gentry Fox, star and pariah.

He'd said it gently, but Cameron's implication had been clear. Stay away from Nica or anyone else whose life she might contaminate. She entered the bedroom where someone had made the bed and left a fresh spray of flowers on the pillow. A maid, no doubt. She crossed to where her clothes hung in the closet—clothes that must have come with her since she recognized them, not part of the black hole that was her arrival on Kauai.

Quality clothing. Designer labels. She ran her fingers over skirts and shells, tanks and shorts, sundresses and sheaths. Her spring to fame had been a story worthy of its own screenplay. An unknown actor finding acclaim and fortune—and more enemies than she could have imagined.

The wave of hatred swept over her, condemning faces, malicious comments. Had she been involved with a sixteen-year-old? Wouldn't she be in jail? She staggered. Maybe she'd run to Kauai to hide. Was that why she hadn't gone to the police? She gripped the closet door. Had Cameron been right all along?

It felt so wrong. Wouldn't this sense of self, even outside of recall, be real? She shook her head. How valid were feelings anyway? What she needed were answers. Who had accused her of such an affair? One of the youths in Act Out?

She'd been too shocked to push the issue with Cameron. His hazy grasp on it had been comforting, but now she wondered if he'd been trying to trap her into saying something incriminating. Maybe he'd known all along who she was. And Nica too? Was that why she'd called her brother, the investigator?

He was downstairs waiting for Officer Kanakanui to take charge of her. Bodyguard. Guard. Somewhere out there, was someone writing up a warrant for her arrest? While Uncle Rob— A sob caught in her throat.

She tried to focus her questions into memories, but exhaustion had muddied even the part of her mind that worked. Too tired to more than drop her clothes from her body and sink into the generous jet tub, she pushed all thoughts away beyond the warm wrap of the water and the scent of mountain-rain kukui nut soap.

FIFTEEN

Cameron woke to the vibration of his phone in his hip pocket and managed a groggy, "Pierce." The voice on the other end carried on for a full minute before he turned the phone off and set it on the teakwood table. In fairness, Barry didn't know he was on Kauai or he'd have considered the time difference.

He peeled his eyes open enough to ogle his watch. Five-thirty. On cue, the island birds burst into song. He groaned, buried his head back into the soft suede, then realized TJ hadn't shown up. Either that or his knocking hadn't penetrated the sleep Barry had just interrupted. More likely something had come up that ranked higher for Kanakanui than a side job protecting Gentry Fox.

Gentry. The thought of her upstairs obliterated the last vestiges of sleep. He sat up, rubbed his furry tongue along the roof of his mouth, and felt every minute that had passed since he'd washed. He hadn't meant to stay the night. But now TJ had left him in the awkward position of slinking out, greeting Gentry in his grungy condition, or going upstairs to make use of her uncle's shower and toiletries.

Since slinking out would leave her without transportation or protection and he couldn't stand his condition one more minute, he climbed the stairs to the next level. A door on the left was closed. He turned into the one across the hall. In the bathroom, he eyed her uncle's Dopp kit that held shaving cream, razor, and mouthwash. Pretty invasive.

On a hunch, he opened the cabinet under the sink. Bingo. For seven hundred dollars a night, he found those items plus a packaged toothbrush and paste. "Now we're talkin'," he said under his breath. The shower sent prickles of pleasure down his back, heat and pressure purging the sweat and grime and all evidence of their mountain adventure. If he could just find a brainwash as effective as Gentry's to wash away last night's mistakes. He stepped out and toweled off, noting the need for a haircut; but a comb through the hair, shave around the beard, and thorough toothbrushing made him human again.

Not wanting to get into the grimy clothes he'd worn for days, he made use of the white Hale Kahili monogrammed robe. It would do until Nica could bring him something clean. He tidied up the steamy bathroom and went out, but he'd neglected to close the bedroom door.

Gentry stood framed in the jamb in a robe matching the one he was wearing, her luminous eyes perplexed. "I thought you were leaving last night."

His heart quickened over the triangle of green silk revealed at the neckline of her robe. "TJ never showed."

She slid her fingers into her hair. A yawn arched her neck and deepened the circular hollow at its base where he'd rested his thumb. After thirty-one years, he forgot how to breathe.

She lowered her hand, and the rumple in her hair was more alluring than French perfume. "Am I under arrest?"

"What?" His heart rate increased.

"Are you holding me until Officer Kanakanui gets a warrant?"

That question had an effect he vigorously resisted. "A warrant for what?"

"You tell me." Her voice had sleepy overtones that gave it a throaty resonance.

He swallowed. "As far as I know, you haven't done anything wrong."

A ripple formed between her fine peaked eyebrows. "Then . . . the allegations . . ."

Comprehension dawned. He should have been thorough in his explanation last night. "The investigation discredited the kid's story. Your appearance on *Oprah* quashed it."

She released a breath, relief shimmering under her gutsy exterior like a secret she couldn't keep. Its impact was powerful.

He turned and opened the closet. "Can I borrow some clothes from your uncle?" *And will you please walk away.*

"Of course." She came up beside him. "You're about the same—"

"I'll find something." His voice graveled. She smelled like kukui nuts, the same body rinse he'd used compliments of Ginger House.

She reached in. "He's got . . ."

"Gentry."

She turned. This woman had laid bare the hearts of movie watchers everywhere, yet unless she was putting in another impeccable performance, she didn't realize how much he wanted—

"I can find something myself."

Understanding flickered, then blazed. "Oh. Okay." She moved out of his way, and something stoic entered her spine. She walked out of the room, crossed the hall, and closed her door behind her.

Great move, Kai. Had he learned nothing the last four years?

He dressed in a pair of lightweight khakis and a Lacoste polo. Her uncle and he were nearly the same shoe size, so he slipped into a pair of Hugo Boss leather loafers that hardly looked worn. He'd deliver Gentry to the hospital, then get out of there. Barry had called to say Golden Years Insurance wanted his findings yesterday. He had to get back to the mainland and complete his report.

He dug his phone from the soiled pants he'd worn into the mountains with Gentry. That excursion had all the relational elements team builders looked for; challenge, cooperation, goal. His behavior last night, while unfortunate, was understandable. Its continuation would not be.

He called TJ. "Where are you?"

"Da hospital. My tūtū wen fall last night. Broke er hip."

"Eh, brah, sorry. What happened?"

"She need one drink and wen fall over da beagle."

"She in a lot of pain?"

"Dey got her comfortable now. I kep tinking I get away, but it wen get so late. Nevah want to wake you."

"That's okay."

"Lucky I got tree days off, but, brah—"

"I know. I'll handle things here." Right.

He hung up and called Nica. "Still got press over there?"

"Good morning, Kai. Let me look." He listened to the sounds of motion as she must be checking through the front window. "I don't see any. Where are you?"

"Hale Kahili."

"You stayed with Gentry?" Her tone was cautious, probing.

If his own sister wondered . . . "TJ was supposed to come. His *tūtū* broke her hip."

"Not Auntie Hanah."

He'd forgotten how well Nica knew TJ's grandmother. "She fell over the beagle." Neither of them laughed. Nica would be taking the blow, feeling the old woman's pain and fear, imagining the arthritic dog licking her apologetically. "TJ said she's doing all right."

Nica released her breath. "And Gentry's uncle?"

"Don't know yet. The surgeon wasn't too encouraging."

Another sigh.

"Stuff happens, Nica. You have to stop taking it personally." And so did he. Gentry Fox wasn't his problem. She could take care of herself. She'd shown that already.

Nica asked if he was going to the hospital.

"I'll take Gentry over. But I've got cases that need attention."

"I know, Kai."

"Are you working today?" Her position at the nursing home paid for her half of the property taxes, food, and gas. He provided her benefits and funded her IRA, a situation that had irked Myra. A sour taste filled his mouth. She'd resented his relationship with Nica and didn't try to understand her limitations. *"You can't keep her in a cocoon forever."*

Maybe not. And maybe it was true that if she moved to the mainland her cost of living would be lower. But Nica had found her equilibrium right where she was, and it pleased him to safeguard her future. She'd been his to protect and sustain long before Myra. From the start of their existence.

"Yes," Nica said. "But I'll see TJ and Hanah first."

"If the hospital's anything like last night, I'm not sure you should go." She wouldn't listen to him, though, not when someone had been hurt.

"How's Gentry?"

Gentry was no longer her concern. "She's fine. You did all you needed to."

"It's not just about need, Kai. It's what I want to do."

"I know. But Gentry's a hot item right now, and it's not pretty."

"Then she needs a friend even more."

He should have kept his mouth shut. "I can't be worrying about you."

"Then don't." Her voice softened. *"Aloha,* Kai."

He hung up, went downstairs and waited. A short while later Gentry came down clothed in beige shorts that showed off all six miles of her legs and a soft top the color of her eyes.

She slipped her purse over her shoulder and glanced up. "Ready?" There was something brittle in her calm.

Responsibility for that settled in his chest. "Gentry . . ."

"You don't have to explain."

"I—"

"It's simple. You don't see me anymore; you see Gentry Fox."

A strand of hair slipped forward, and she slipped it behind her ear, mesmerizing him. She wasn't right, but he liked her version better. His was something he didn't want to deal with right now. She tucked her chin and went to the front door.

The press had deserted Nica's and bivouacked at Hale Kahili. He followed her out to the small enclosed parking circle in front of the house. When did these people sleep? The questions came immediately.

"How are you feeling, Gentry?"

"Is your memory back?"

"Can you tell us what happened?"

Gentry looked that last woman in the eye, sensing a fair voice, maybe. "I'm sorry, I can't."

"You still have amnesia?"

The crowd had silenced, listening now that Gentry was giving information, taking it down word for word—to be parsed and spun later, no doubt.

"I don't remember the accident."

"Then it was an accident?" That from a reporter for the local news.

Gentry turned. "What else could it be in the middle of the native forest in the mountains of Kauai?"

When she put it that way, it seemed obvious, and yet . . . Cameron searched the crowd for Bette Walden, didn't find her. Nor did he see the guy who'd insulted her.

"What is your uncle's condition?"

"It was critical last night." Strain crept into her voice. "I hope he's better now."

"Why didn't you go to the police right away?" *Ouch.* The newspaper reporter named Hammel liked to stir things up.

Cameron moved up between her and Hammel, but Gentry answered him.

"The doctor said I'd remember. I didn't know anyone else was involved."

Before Hammel could follow that line, another voice hollered, "What's the relationship between you two?"

Not even a breath of pause. "Mr. Pierce helped me find my uncle. He's an investigator."

"What did he investigate last night?" A snide voice off to the side.

Gentry turned. "He provided security last night. If you'll excuse me, I need to see my uncle."

"Gentry, how long are you staying?"

"As long as it takes." She pressed her way toward the truck.

Cameron followed but didn't touch her. Any contact would be magnified, by them—and him. He let her in, pressed the lock, and closed the door. He was on the island often enough to justify keeping the truck at Nica's—had to have something to carry his board when nothing but catching the waves would do. But he'd have to find out what happened to the Jeep her uncle had rented or get Gentry some other transportation.

As they left Hanalei and Princeville behind, he thought about food. The place that came to mind wasn't open yet, but someone would be harvesting fruit from their fields, receiving more from local farmers and setting up for the day. He pulled into the small gray-gravel parking lot in front of the grass-roofed gazebo and quaint yellow building of Banana Joe's.

He told Gentry, "I'll be just a minute," then followed the path around the side, petted the tabby cat lying there and found someone to let him in. Chatting as briefly as possible, he purchased a bag of lychee, freshly picked, and a small bunch of apple bananas with a sweet custardy flavor Gentry might enjoy, then went back out.

"Hungry?"

She accepted the fruit when he climbed in. "Thank you."

"That's *mahalo*."

"What?"

"Thank you is *mahalo*." He put the truck in reverse.

"*Mahalo*, then. What are these?" She held up the nubby red fruit the size of a large grape.

"Lychee. Peel the skin off, eat the flesh, but watch out for the seed."

As he pulled back onto the road, she peeled one and held it out to him. He took the slippery, grayish white fruit and popped it into his mouth, then chewed around the dark brown seed at its center. That, of course, presented him with the need to spit it out and hand it over or toss it out the window. His *aloha'āina* would not allow the second, even if it was biodegradable, so he dropped the seed into his palm and pondered his next step. She held out the bag.

He dropped it in. *"Mahalo."*

A smile flickered on her lips. She couldn't think he was hung up on her being Gentry Fox if he was spitting seeds into the bag she held. Just as he hadn't been when they were waist deep in turbulent water, or clinging to a steep, slippery slope. Her fame was not the attraction.

Courage, loyalty, determination. Yeah, beauty. Those were the things that had grabbed him inside, caused the kiss in the waiting room and the repetitions he'd considered thereafter. He no longer claimed he wouldn't repeat the mistake. He'd repeat it all right. Unless he got out of there. If Gentry was aware of or shared his struggle, she was a better actor than he'd ever be. Maybe she was so used to men dissolving in her presence, she thought nothing of it.

Kauai had its share of famous visitors. He'd lost count of the shows and movies filmed there, but none of the stars had been so recently in the news in such an attention-getting way. Now that her cover was blown, she would have no peace. He walked her, once again, through the press.

"How did you find your uncle?"

"Was the cave visible?"

"What part did Mr. Pierce play?"

Gentry paused. "He found the cave."

The cameras turned on him. Whether she was giving credit or deflecting he couldn't say, but he hadn't intended to be spotlighted. As the questions came at him, he got a little picture of what she went through. The smarmier characters seemed to be absent, though, so he did his best to answer until it turned personal.

"How long have you known Ms. Fox?"

"What's your relationship?"

"Why didn't *you* go to the police, Mr. Pierce? Were you protecting her?"

He found the speaker—Bette Walden. "No crime had been committed. The medical opinion Ms. Fox received indicated her memory would return. She was not avoiding anything but this kind of publicity and got help the moment she knew another person was involved."

He pushed Gentry toward the door.

"Funny it's always the other people who get hurt." That got the attention Bette wanted, as the press turned to her.

He didn't know whether he'd done more harm than good, but at least it was over.

As they entered the lobby, a tall redhead swooped in. Cameron started to ward her off, but Gentry moved past him.

"What is it, Darla?"

She shoved a tabloid into her hands. Cameron caught only the headline. *Fox's Mind Lost to Aliens.* How inappropriate would it be to laugh?

By the woman's face, very. "Three weeks without a headline was more than you could stand?"

Gentry half turned. "Darla, this is Cameron Pierce; my publicist, Darla Graves."

Darla gave him a skewering glance, then turned back to Gentry. "We need to powwow. What have you said?"

Before Gentry could answer, a young man closed in with an armful of publications. Gentry murmured, "Hi, Jett," as Darla hustled them toward the elevator, flipping through the papers. The woman stopped and glared back. "You'd better come too."

Wasn't a publicist supposed to be on Gentry's side?

As they got into the elevator, Darla slipped a different publication from the stack and shoved it at him. *Fox and Lover Leave Uncle for Dead.* The picture was taken in the parking lot when they'd first arrived last evening at the hospital. How had they jumped on it so fast? But the press had known who she was long before he did. They had no doubt jumped on it as soon as TJ's bulletin went out. No trouble for the snide creep in the parking lot to sell his photo to a tabloid rabidly awaiting a break.

The photo showed him and Gentry locked in a clutch, her face turned toward his chest. He knew it for the protective pose it was, but it left room for interpretation. People would take it and run.

"Congratulations." Darla gave Gentry a thin sneer. "You've bumped their front pages—again."

"I didn't—"

"The important thing is what we're going to do with it. I have—"

The doors opened. Publicist and assistant blazed into the hall, Darla yammering. Cameron reached over and held Gentry back. Darla turned, her glare a masterpiece of disdain.

He walked Gentry out of the elevator. "Excuse me, but Gentry has a sick uncle we're here to see. This other crap can wait." He slapped the paper back into her assistant's torso.

As the woman stood, gape-mouthed, he walked Gentry to ICU. She was shaking under his arm. This was not some jaded movie queen. She was a person with feelings and fears like anyone else. Darla hadn't even asked about her uncle's, or Gentry's, condition. She saw only a situation. Sensing Gentry's need to see her uncle privately, he didn't go into the unit, but he told her, "I'll be right here."

Her eyes teared. "I know you need to go. Handle your cases."

"That can wait." It was only income and security. He'd been called to the island for a reason, and while he didn't look for God's hand in everything, he paid attention when it slapped him in the face.

She touched his chest with her fingertips. "*Mahalo*, Kai." Then she went inside, and he was left wondering, once again, how to get the air into his lungs.

Darla came up beside him with a barely disguised smirk. "You're not the first. You won't be the last. She can walk down the sidewalk and men imagine they're part of her world. She's got what's known in the industry as 'it.' She also has the worst luck of anyone I've represented. And she's made a lot of enemies."

"How?"

"She didn't pay her dues."

"She can't be blamed for that."

"Oh, but she can." Darla looked him over. "What do you do?"

"Investigate fraud."

She drew her gaze over him like a cold shower. "Did you sleep together last night?"

His heart thumped. "You're asking this because . . ."

"It's my job to airbrush her mistakes."

"Sleeping with me would be a mistake?"

"Under the circumstances."

Under his circumstances too. "No."

"So your power play in the elevator was anticipatory."

He rarely had violent thoughts toward women. This one had potential. "Gentry's faced enough antagonists. She could use a little support."

Darla showed a scant softening. "She doesn't realize how serious this is. She's only just ridden the last wave. And believe me, we've not seen the end of it." She thumped the papers in the young man's arms. "Next week's issues will be worse, tying this new love affair—"

"There's no affair."

"To the other. Which supposedly didn't happen either. Do you think that matters?"

He frowned. "It should."

"It doesn't. Because that scandal had the legs of one of your centipedes. And they grow back."

He looked at the door through which Gentry had gone to sit with her uncle. That should be all she had to worry about. Would it be better if he disappeared? Maybe. But he'd told her he'd be there. "So what now?"

"Now we discuss keeping your mouth shut. What will it cost?"

She'd just topped his list of repulsive people. "Cost?"

"You've spent two nights with a star. The rags will pay handsomely for details. True or not."

He studied her fire red lips, burnt orange hair, and hard hazel eyes. "Did you offer a deal to the kid the last time?"

"That's none of your business. Just tell me what it'll take to make you go away."

She matched Bette Walden's ire. Had he missed something in the days he'd spent with Gentry? Something that turned these women into sharks? One supposedly for, and one stridently against; both trolling murky waters, ready to bite.

He squared his shoulders. "It won't cost Gentry anything. I'm going as soon as I've finished here."

"When will that be?"

"When I decide I'm through."

At the direction of a hospital staff member, they moved into the small waiting area that served the ICU. No press hassled them there. The hospital must have made it clear harassment would not be allowed on the premises. Or else Darla had brought in the National Guard.

She would obviously like him keelhauled. He might have assigned her attitude to the star rather than the mouthpiece, but he relished the challenge. Bring it on. Anything to take his mind off Gentry's husky voice calling him Kai.

SIXTEEN

After a room-service breakfast of soft-boiled eggs, lox, and cottage cheese, Allegra stretched and ran her fingers through her tastefully highlighted hair. What she wanted was a dip in the pool, but Curt was on the phone. So much for getting away from the world. His business wouldn't wait.

But he'd been right about the TV. Who cared, really, what problems the pundits were pummeling to death. If there was a terror attack on Oahu, she'd be of no consequence. And complying with Curt's wish was a small price for joy, something so sorely lacking in her life that sometimes she wished a terror attack would simply take her away.

Maybe she should stop denying the depression that had seeped like fog into her mind and heart until nothing bright or beautiful penetrated deeply enough to make a difference. She pulled on her swimsuit, fully aware that she was not the supple beauty she'd been when— before. Envied by women her age for good genes and a good surgeon, she was nonetheless sliding into decline.

Did that bother Curt? Did she care? She pushed the doubt away. Not care? He'd been wonderful. He adored her. Would she rather go back to her lonely patio home? To shop and play Bunko and host dinner parties for her single friends whose husbands had the good sense to divorce them? A familiar ache resonated through her, reaching its tentacles around until it slithered into her heart with stabbing pains she wished were real.

Now, that was a cheery thought to take into the pool with her. Next she'd be picturing herself on the bottom, lying still and breathless. Drowning was said to be so peaceful. Why resist?

She tied a sheer wrap around her waist and motioned to Curt that she'd be swimming. He gave her a salacious appraisal that shot warmth through her like an infusion, then went back to his conversation. She closed the door and strode down the hall toward the elevator. A thin man and his emaciated wife, both reeking of suntan lotion, had already pressed the button, but the thing took forever.

She glanced away from them and noticed the newspaper on the table by the wall. Not a paper reader, she looked back at the down arrow above the elevator, lit but seemingly ineffective. Annoyed, she took a step and glanced over the front page of the *Honolulu Advertiser*, confused, then stunned to find Gentry staring back.

⌒

He knew the minute she stepped in that the gig was up. She tossed the paper on the table beside him, and he told the person on the phone, "I'll call you back. Something's come up." He turned off the phone and stood. "Babe, what is it?"

"Gentry and Rob have had a terrible accident."

He looked down at the paper, picked it up and read. Gentry, of course, was all right. He'd seen that much on TV. He read on. *The star's partial amnesia has kept her from telling authorities how the accident occurred. Dr. Yamaguchi, who examined Gentry, says that is not unusual. An injury to the central part of the brain can result in the exact sort of memory loss Ms. Fox has experienced. He added that the partial block could be permanent.*

Curt shook his head and expelled a disbelieving breath, then flipped pages to the continuation. *After a hazardous rescue, Gentry Fox's uncle, Robert Fox, is in critical condition.* It then gave a brief synopsis of Rob's successful career and segued into Gentry's movie credits and one sentence regarding her appearance on *Oprah* following the sex scandal that was settled out of court.

He set the paper down and managed a soft exclamation of dismay.

Allegra, pale, obviously shaken, sank into a chair. She raised one delicate hand, then dropped it. "I . . . I don't know what to do."

"What do you want to do?" It was risky. He still didn't have the certainty he'd expected by now. Even after last night. He'd hoped for more time.

She lowered her face and pressed her fingertips to her forehead. Her hand was shaking. "I feel like I should be there."

He went over and dropped to his knees beside her, taking her hand between his. "It's your call, babe."

Her face pinched. "But . . . it's so wrong after . . ."

Good thing he'd followed his instinct. "You could go to the hospital, patch things up. Pray with him. If he's a Christian, he'll forgive this indiscretion." Out on a major limb there. Indiscretion was not how he wanted her to view it. But he knew how she felt about the man's conversion. A little salt in the wound might work in his favor.

Her eyes filled with tears when she turned them to him. What happened next would be pivotal. Her lips moved, and at last words emerged. "His condition's critical. I can't lay something like this on him."

Good. That was good. He dropped his chin. "Of course, you're right. I'm not thinking straight. I just . . ." He looked back into her face. "I want what's best for you."

Tears streamed down her face. "Curt, that's . . . I don't deserve you."

Oh, but she did. And more than that, he deserved her. He brought her hand to his lips and kissed her fingers. "You're the best thing I have." By a long shot.

He rose up and held her tightly. Nothing sensual, just sweet, unselfish comfort. That was what she needed. Guilt would keep her from Rob and Gentry. He knew that road. He'd walked it before. An angel of understanding beside the penitent in sackcloth and ashes.

⌒

Uncle Rob looked like a shell of himself. Not even a hard, durable shell but a crushable, papery casing that hardly resembled the man she knew. A sickening sweet odor hovered around him, and Gentry stifled a moan when she felt his fiery hand, cooking with fever.

She ran her gaze down the two ridges under the sheet, both legs wrapped and bandaged; damaged, but not beyond repair. How could the surgeon even consider amputation? This wasn't the Civil War.

She sat down beside the unresponsive version of her uncle, fighting doubt and fear with the words Uncle Rob would say: All things are possible with God. From the moment he'd taken his leap of faith, he'd scaled its mysteries and procured its power. If their places were reversed, he'd be calling her on with unflagging confidence, but she felt unequal to the task.

Cameron's revelation of a scandal she couldn't even recall had triggered nightmare vignettes of all the kinds of things she could have done and forgotten. Darla's intensity, the fresh assault by the press, and Uncle Rob's condition dragged her down into a dark, uncertain place she resisted only feebly.

She needed to call home to update Mom and Dad on Uncle Rob's condition, but couldn't bear to burden them with the truth. She'd tried to reach Aunt Allegra and wasn't sure how to interpret the lack of response. But it was coming clear that the decisions were up to her.

She sighed. The most important thing was being there for her uncle. She pressed his feverish hand between hers. "Uncle Rob," she whispered, "can you hear me?" No response, but she felt his attention somehow. Or imagined it. "I need you to know—"

The strains of "Für Elise" rose out of her purse. Identifying that particular ring, she dragged the phone out. "Hi, Dave."

"Are you sitting down?"

She'd better be, because one more blow . . . "Yes."

"Up for costarring with Alec Warner?"

"I've been offered the part?" Where was the exultation?

"Pretty nice package, though they might've thrown a little more Alec's way."

"Oh yeah, you think?" Alec Warner, the heartthrob who could carry off a part without nudity and heavy petting because he could actually act, who delivered his lines as though each character he played was the real man.

"Of course, we'll talk." Her agent was licking his lips at the opportunity.

"They're not concerned about *Oprah* and . . ." She still didn't have a grasp on the scandal.

Dave laughed. "Honey, all that business gave you more recognition than we could have paid for."

"People who think I'm deviant want to see my next movie?"

"No one thinks you're deviant. The guy was nuts. Trust me, Gentry. And this amnesia thing's a great angle. Everyone loves a comeback kid. They'll want to see if you've still got it."

"You haven't seen the morning papers."

"I'm in the Caymans trying not to."

She told him about the tabloids and Darla's concerns.

"What's the spin?"

"I haven't read them yet. But do you think they'll play nice?" Throat tightening, she told him about Uncle Rob. Her voice only broke once. "Right now, he's all I care about." Great thing to tell her agent in the midst of hot negotiations. But Dave wasn't just her agent. That pot-bellied, salt-and-pepper-haired bulldog was one of a narrowing field of her friends, and she knew this offer meant as much to him as it might to her.

A scene jumped to her mind. She and Uncle Rob discussing their escape, an adventure equal to the crud she'd been dragged through. They'd laughed about Antarctica but must have settled on Kauai. She'd believed no one would consider her for another part, least of all the one that had been dangled before everything went crazy.

"Look, kid." Dave's voice, wrecked by thick, smelly cigars, could still rock her like a baby. "You focus there, and I'll handle things here."

Tears stung. She had to get control of that. "Thanks, Dave."

"Don't let them get to you."

She sniffed. It was his kindness, and Cameron's, that was getting to her.

"Hang in there, darlin'. We'll talk."

"Okay." She dropped the phone back into her purse as Dr. Long came in. She stood up, ready to do battle if he even suggested taking off her uncle's leg. She stopped the thought before it started and replaced it with one more deserving. *No eye has seen, no ear has heard, no mind has conceived what God has prepared for those who love him."* And who loved him more than Uncle Rob?

The surgeon's pessimism would not dismay her. Hope would keep its promise. He looked at the chart without addressing her, looked at her uncle, then pulled the sheet aside and began to unwrap his leg. An odor seeped out. No denying the seriousness. But there were drugs to fight infection, to heal and restore.

The doctor spoke without looking at her. "What happens today will determine the protocol. I've consulted with two colleagues on his condition."

"And?"

"It's grave."

Grave certainly. But Uncle Rob was in God's hands. She would not believe, could not believe, God would want anything but the best for his servant, his son. She knew it with all her soul.

The nurses joined them, and she had to go out while they changed the dressings. Things might be dire, but she would not flag in expectation. *Lord. Show your power. Do not allow anything but your perfect will.*

She went out and found Cameron still there with Darla and her assistant, Jett. By their expressions they'd read every applicable word in the tabloids. Though Uncle Rob's condition outweighed everything, she tried to care. In fairness to the other people involved, she'd have to face it, and fighting a battle on another front might dilute her combative feelings toward the doctor. "Which one's the worst?"

"Worst written or worst implications?" Jett arranged the papers into a fan on the low table.

She appreciated his humor. "Implications."

"Ah." He slid out the one where she and her lover had left her uncle to die.

Anger snapped at her heels. Uncle Rob was not going to die.

Cameron shook his head. "How do they come up with this junk?"

Darla glared at him. "You gave them opportunity; they took it. You didn't know." She redirected her glare. "But Gentry ought to."

Cameron frowned. "How about we all get on the same side here."

He hardly knew her, yet he'd nailed it. Darla was all gushing enthusiasm talking *about* her, but lately she'd hinted of battery acid whenever they interfaced in person. Might be time for a different publicist. But that would make one more enemy.

Cameron moved one seat over to make room. Gentry took the place he'd vacated, felt his warmth. Funny that he should be supporting her now, when he'd been so cynical. But then, he'd fallen for the mystique. She couldn't hold it against him.

She picked up the paper, read about her steamy ordeal in the jungle with the new love interest, a mystery man who had made her desert the one who'd been a second father to her. It hit her hard in the stomach. Where had they gotten that? Who outside her family knew how close she was to Uncle Rob?

Pain welled up. Why did people feel justified betraying her? She faced Darla. "This is the worst they had to throw?"

"So far."

One by one Jett handed her the papers. When she'd digested the current trash fest, she said, "Now I need whatever's out there from before."

"You mean the situation with Troy?" Darla's eyebrow arched.

"Troy?" Gentry took the blow unprepared. "It was Troy?"

Darla looked at Jett and back. "You don't remember?"

Gentry pressed a hand to her eyes. Troy Glasier. She'd had him in the troupe from the start. They'd worked so hard together. How could he . . .

She drew herself up. "Show me."

Darla took her Pocket PC from her purse and accessed her files. Gentry read article after article, each one dragging her deeper. Though she filled her mind with information, it didn't trigger actual memories, and that was the one grace in it all. The last thing she accessed was the transcript of her interview on *Oprah*.

Tears stung as she read. She ached to be back there with the troupe, feeding them lines, drawing out their laughter and their tears, leeching away the anger like venom from their blood—and creating some wonderful vignettes in the process. But Helen had the program now.

Fine. She'd have to make her own way. She blinked away the tears and told Darla, "They've offered me Eva Thorne."

For the second time that morning, Darla gaped. A smaller gape this time; not disbelief, but wary amazement. "Alec pulled out?"

Of course. Only if everyone who mattered removed themselves from the project could she still be considered. "Not according to Dave."

Darla clicked the table with her fingernails. "Well." She looked as though a sugar cube had just melted on her tongue. "That's great." She exhaled sharply. "We can use that."

"It could all blow up if this does."

Darla's cheeks bloomed roses. "I'm in control here. This is not blowing up like the last time."

That would take the grace of God, not Darla, and she wasn't as sure of God now as she should be. Gentry turned to Cameron.

"Think we could find some coffee?" She allowed a flicker of desperation to show.

He stood up. "I'm sure."

Darla and Jett rose as well.

Gentry gave them her best smile. "Where are you staying?" Darla gave her their lodging information. Gentry didn't give hers; everyone already knew it. "Okay, then. We'll be in touch."

"In touch? Gentry, we need a plan. I don't want you talking—"

"Right. Got it." She started out of the room.

"You've got a chance here," Darla hissed. "Don't blow it."

Gentry stayed calm until the elevator doors closed, then slammed her palm to the wall and held it there, breathing hard. Cameron stayed back, sensing her need to find her own control. Or maybe after a glimpse of reality, he regretted his brush with her world. Couldn't blame him.

But his voice sounded warm. "Would you put her in the friend or foe category?"

She glanced over her shoulder, a smile creeping to her lips. "To be honest, I think there's no divider."

"Must feel that way."

"I didn't intend for you to get snarled up in it."

"Doesn't take much, does it?"

She shook her head. "Not even the truth."

The doors dinged open, and they exited. Cameron directed her outside. No fans hung around that early, and the press had seemingly had their fill. Only a few were left to cover any new developments.

"Gentry, how's your uncle?"

"He's going to be fine." She telegraphed hope, no matter what that doctor said.

"Turn this way, please." A flash.

"Now over here, Gentry."

She turned the other way. Cameron would be in these pictures, too, unless they digitally removed him, but he was keeping his distance. The gossip rags would look for more provocative shots, and she and Cameron provided none as they reached the truck. He had learned from last night, but she still felt the need to warn him again.

"The press isn't done with you."

"Okay."

"They'll follow you, talk to everyone you know, look for anything scandalous." Her brow pinched. "They'll twist everything."

"Nothing to twist." Cameron entered the highway, traveling the opposite direction from Hanalei. She didn't push it, though if he knew how little it took, he might not be so sure. She sat back as the tropical countryside passed and tried to release the morning's strain. Closing her eyes, she bargained with God: help Uncle Rob and she'd deal with her own problems.

Yet she knew it wasn't so simple. Her situation was serious. Darla might be obnoxious, but she was working hard to clean up the mess. Things could get out of hand for Cameron and Nica. She wished her mind was devious enough to guess what next week's rags might hold. They'd be digging everywhere. If Cameron or his sister had secrets . . . She sighed.

Cameron slid her a glance but said nothing. Amazing how they could be together without having to fill the silence. It had started out as ignoring each other. Now it was something rare and sweet. She couldn't recall the last time she'd met someone who didn't pump her for details about her life. Who did she know; what was it like; how did she get so lucky? As though they could rub her like a charm for good fortune to come their way.

She stared out the window. To her right, tufts of gray clouds crawled down the more distant mountains. Sunshine warmed the grass and trees along the road. They passed through the quaint town of Kalaheo. The land flattened and the trees thinned. Fields of something like a cross between corn and palms stretched out, then more fields with rows of small, bushlike trees.

Amidst these, Cameron pulled into a parking lot, and she read the sign on the building that looked like an old house. The sign said Kauai Coffee Plantation.

"You wanted coffee."

So he'd taken her to the plantation?

At her surprised look, he added, "Best-quality beans are only available at the source. It was either this or hop to the Big Island for Kona, my personal favorite." He looked as though he'd have done it.

"I didn't expect this." She shook her head. "I just had to get out of there."

He draped his wrist on the steering wheel. "You don't want coffee?"

"I do."

"Then let's go." He climbed out of the truck.

He'd been accused of sordid conduct and malicious negligence by a tabloid read and believed by too many people. He thought he could handle it, but he didn't know how personal they could get—or how cruel. Most of the poison had been spent on her, but that was because they hadn't had time to dig up his dirt. Unless something bigger drew their attention, that would come next.

The morning was warm, tempered by the ever-present breeze, and as they walked up the boardwalk, she breathed the aroma of coffee so fresh it had come from the fields around her. They entered the gift shop and passed through to a covered patio area where a video was describing the process of growing, harvesting, and roasting the beans. With the surprisingly few people there, she lowered her guard. She and Cameron could be two tourists, or even locals, or a local showing a friend the island; each scenario better than the reality.

They ordered and she paid. Her own credit card with her name. The woman inside didn't even read it. Her heart soared until someone seated near the window approached. "Excuse me, aren't you Gentry Fox?"

Cameron reached between them for the cups and smiled at the curious gal. "She gets that all the time." He nudged her toward the outer courtyard, and they sat down with their backs to the shop.

Had the woman read the tabloids, she'd have recognized Cameron as well. Gentry shot him a glance. "That was so smooth, I'd think you were used to this."

"It's true, isn't it?" He sipped. "You probably have people approach you like that everywhere."

"It's just that you slipped into diversion so seamlessly. I could use you in the improv troupe."

"I read and react to situations all the time. Amazing what scammers'll spill when they think you're in." He dabbed a drop of coffee from his freshly trimmed mustache with his thumb.

She studied him. "Can I ask you something?"

"Shoot."

"Why the beard?"

He stroked the line he had reestablished that morning. "You don't like it?"

"I like it. I just wondered what . . ."

"Intimidation."

Her brows raised. "You're kidding."

"I'm not built like TJ. It gives me an edge."

"I thought I was imagining the effect."

His eyes crinkled. "That's why you wouldn't get into my truck?"

"The intimidation came through loud and clear."

He leaned back and cradled his cup. "Still intimidated?"

"I wouldn't want you after me."

"After you?"

She flushed. "I mean professionally."

He narrowed his eyes. "Is that blush real?"

She pressed a hand to her face.

"Come on . . . You've been in front of a camera for an audience of thousands, and you can still blush?"

"A camera doesn't look at me like that."

"Take your hand down." His voice was soft and thick.

She slid her fingers off her eyes.

"All the way. Let me see you."

No starstruck gaze. He appraised her as he had on their trek;

curious, skeptical, amused. "Sort of miss the mud and soggy leaves."

She laughed, then clutched her cup. "Cameron, I don't want you hurt if this gets ugly."

"Let me worry about me."

She fought back tears. "You don't know how bad it can get."

"Yeah, Gentry, I do." The way he said it sank in. "You're not the only one who's been dragged through stuff unjustly."

She wanted him to say more, but he looked away and drank his coffee in silence.

SEVENTEEN

In the hospital room, Nica rested her palm on Hanah's head. "How are you, Auntie Hanah?"

The old woman gave her a slow blink and the flicker of a smile.

TJ said, "They wen give her mo pain stuff."

Nica turned to TJ's mother wedged into a chair beside the bed. "Have you had any sleep, Auntie Malia?"

She shook her head. "Doze some, nevah sleep. Dis chair da kine tight."

"Why don't you let TJ take you home? I'll sit with Auntie."

"You so nice." Malia looked from her to her son. "Why you nevah speak up? You nevah see da kine good girl?"

TJ's complexion deepened.

She hefted herself up. "I go home now. You bettah make some kine use of dis time."

TJ bent to give her a hand. "Drive careful. Go slow."

"Go slow? You da kine slow." She waved her hands at him, then turned back to her. "He tink you break." She looked her up and down. "Maybe he right." She waddled from the room.

TJ stood by the wall trying to disappear inside himself like a sea turtle. He mumbled, "Sorry," then pulled the chair his mother had vacated over to her. "Sit?"

Nica looked into his face without sitting. "What did she mean

157

break?" Or need she ask. People thought she'd been on the verge of a nervous breakdown her whole life. Yes, she gave sensitive new meaning. Why God had made her feel others' pain so acutely, she didn't know. But she wasn't going to break. "TJ?"

He spread his hands, then dropped them at his sides. He rubbed his palm across his forehead.

"How am I going to break, TJ?"

He extended his hand. "You so small." His face had reddened to a fierce mahogany. "Mama want grandkids. I tink no room for da kine baby. . . ." He swallowed. "My kine baby." A drop of sweat rose at his hairline and slid down his temple.

Her jaw fell slack. "You and your mother talked about me having your babies?"

He tried to shrink into the wall.

"You've been following me around thirteen years without saying how you feel, but you talked to Auntie Malia about having babies with me?"

His forehead streamed.

She moved the chair back to the corner by the bed and sat down. Hanah had fallen asleep. With her gaze fixed on the old woman's face, she said, "I'm no smaller than my mother, who bore two babies eleven months apart with no problem."

TJ pulled a wad of tissues from the box on the shelf and swabbed his face, then stuffed it into his pocket and puffed out his chest. "I wen weigh twelve pound. You tink you could manage dat?"

She looked up. "Not much chance, since you've never so much as kissed my hand."

Having spent half the night in the hospital in his uniform, he was rumpled and soggy, but he stepped over and took her hand. Instead of bending to kiss it, he pulled her up from the chair, circled her back with his muscular arm, and kissed her with the softest mouth she could have imagined.

Cameron cleared his throat. The last thing he'd expected to find back at the hospital was TJ finally making a move on his sister. The big guy let go so fast, she tumbled back into the chair. Her face pinked, but TJ's was downright scary.

"What're you doing, brah? Can't you see this is private?"

What he saw was that TJ was more than a little worked up. If he decided to put his muscle where his mouth was, Cameron would feel it for weeks. But then it was Nica he'd dropped. "You better work on your technique, bruddah."

Nica crossed her knees, and they shared a smile. "Where's Gentry?"

"With her uncle. Thought I'd scoot in and see how Auntie Hanah's doing." He glanced at TJ's grandmother. "Some chaperone."

The storm brewed in TJ's face. Had to be the most emotion he'd seen there in years. Hospitals did that. So did love. He'd pretty much decided that neither of them would cross the barrier they'd maintained since he and TJ had turned seventeen, the year TJ decided Nica was the prettiest thing he'd ever laid eyes on. Cameron wasn't sure he'd actually laid eyes on her again for the next decade. Instead he'd had some sort of homing device that pulled him around to wherever Nica was but rendered him dumb and mute.

She said, "I looked for you when I first got here. A woman said you and Gentry had left."

"Gentry needed coffee."

"You flew her to Kona Le'a?"

He smiled. "The local plantation was the best I could do on short notice." He turned to TJ. "How's Auntie Hanah?"

"It's only a hairline. The dog is so fat, he cushioned her fall."

The same could be said for Hanah. "How's the dog?"

"Indestructible. It's the poi."

TJ without the pidgin wasn't entirely new. He dropped it when dealing with tourists, especially when giving out tickets. But a whole conversation in front of Nica? He must be chest-puffing proud of himself. A pang worked its way through Cameron. He hoped—no, prayed—they wouldn't get burned.

TJ moved toward the door. "I gotta make a call."

When he'd gone out, Cameron turned to his sister. "So . . ."

"So?"

"Let's see." He counted on his fingers. "Only thirteen years. Dat's da kine quick for TJ Kanakanui."

She pushed his arm.

"Guess he'll be over for dinner tonight."

"Maybe."

Like it wasn't a foregone conclusion. Once TJ got moving, his inertia was an unstoppable force. "What are you making?"

"Spam musubi."

"Ah, break da mout!"

Nica laughed. "He wants to smuggle some to Hanah."

Fried Spam on sticky rice wrapped in nori seaweed was an island tradition, but somehow the hospital hadn't put it on the menu. A serious oversight.

She slipped a tendril of hair behind her ear. "You're welcome to join us."

"And risk TJ's wrath?"

Nica tipped her head. "Have you ever seen him angry?"

"Once. When I blew up his lunchbox." That hadn't been pretty. "And a minute ago when I interrupted."

"He wasn't angry. Just . . . surprised."

Cameron sobered. "I'm glad he'll be there tonight. I had wanted him to keep an eye on Gentry, but I'd rather he watched over you. The tabloids are making a big deal out of this."

"Why would they care about me?"

"Because you had Gentry in your home." He rested his hands on his hips. "And you haven't had the most normal life the last few years. If they connect you with some of those people . . ."

"Those people needed compassion and care. You know I couldn't turn them away."

"These hounds are not concerned with the facts, only the sensational impact."

She shook her head. "Poor Gentry. I can't imagine."

"I hope you never have to."

It hurt to see Uncle Rob looking so vulnerable. Part of her wished she'd let Mom come. Or that she could reach Aunt Allegra. Or that she knew which of her friends she could still trust, that she didn't have to watch every word, every glance. And she wished other people's lives weren't damaged by contact with hers. She left her uncle and found Cameron, TJ, and Nica all together in the waiting room.

Nica stood up and hugged her. "How are you?"

"All right. Uncle Rob hasn't stirred, but that's probably good." She turned to TJ where he sat, hands planted on his brawny thighs. "How's your grandmother?"

"She's okay." He rubbed his thighs. "You remember what happened yet? I need to make a report."

She shook her head. "Things are coming back, but nothing to do with the accident."

Cameron must be right that she'd blocked the worst parts. Sitting with her uncle, she had thought about Troy. He'd joined the troupe at thirteen, a precocious, angry foster kid. He'd been the most consistent of them all, never missing a rehearsal, gaining skills and confidence, and shedding his belligerence. By fifteen he'd gained a special position, more apprentice than student. All *that* she remembered, but she couldn't remember what had gone wrong.

Cameron met her gaze. "It's all in there. Just needs a way out."

That was what frightened her. Would she remember something she'd done? A mistake on the trail with Uncle Rob, in the troupe with Troy? Words or actions that had devastating results?

Reading the articles had shocked and depressed her. The reporters had embellished his smallest suggestion, twisted and pumped it up. Then there had been an investigation. Legal authorities had taken it seriously. And she recalled none of it. She shook her head. "The whole world knows more than I do."

Nica sat down beside her. "The pressure must be awful. Everyone watching, speculating. No wonder celebrities cut themselves off."

Gentry shrugged. "It's a reverse process, really. Friends betray you; peers want to know why you and not them. Everyone else just wants a piece of the action. I'm a commodity." She smiled into Nica's soft gray eyes. "For a few days, I got to feel what it was like before. Thank you."

Nica squeezed her hand. "I'm glad you came."

Cameron moved to the chair on her other side. "The two gaps could be related. If you deal with the first, the rest might come."

She turned. "You think this accident has something to do with Troy?"

"Think of what you know and go from there."

She shook her head. "I only know what I read this morning."

"Try."

"I am." Or was she fighting it with all she had?

Nica stood up and put a hand on Cameron's shoulder. She said, "I have to go back to work," but the current that passed between them was a plea for gentleness. Gentry read it as clearly as if Nica had said it aloud. When had she become party to their inner communication?

TJ got to his feet and walked Nica out with reverence. Another revelation.

She was more attuned to their realities than her own. Why couldn't she remember?

Cameron leaned back in his chair. "Tell me about Troy."

She looked away. "I don't want to."

"Was he upset that you left the troupe for *Steel*?"

She felt the gears shift and lock into place. "Yes," she whispered as the details rushed in.

"Did you know how he felt about you?"

"I knew he was crushing. But he was fifteen! He'd been part of the program for two years and rightly believed he held a special position. I thought he understood what kind."

"Who else knew how he felt?"

"It's a small troupe. New kids come in when their needs are matched with the program, but we had a semipermanent core who'd gotten pretty close. I'd say we all were aware of his fixation, but no one took it seriously. No one thought anything physical happened."

"What about the pictures?"

She scowled. "The shots in the tabloids were taken during rehearsals, a stage kiss. It only looks real."

"Who took the pictures?"

She was quiet a full beat. "Helen." She swallowed. "She took candid shots all the time for publicity posters and the Web site."

"Those shots were on the Web site?"

She looked away. "No."

"So the rags got them from her?"

Gentry stared into her hands. "I don't know."

"Then what?"

"Then it all got crazy. The investigation, the press. I was forbidden contact with Troy, so I couldn't even ask him what happened. I was so worried." The ache gripped her stomach afresh.

"About what?"

"The pressure was eating me alive. I couldn't imagine how bad it must be for him."

"You're not thinking in context. An attention-hungry adolescent at the center of all that publicity, claiming an affair with an actor who'd suddenly become a star. Someone he'd idolized, dreamed of."

Her throat ached. "His walls were covered with pictures. I don't know where he got them all."

Cameron digested that. "Then what?"

"The investigator found holes in his story. I think it got bigger than he could handle. He . . . took some pills."

"Kids do that."

She shot her gaze up. "Kids—"

"He was manipulating the situation. Trust me, Gentry, I deal with this stuff all the time."

It stunned her to think Troy could have done that for effect, but Cameron looked so sure.

She sat back. "They never pressed charges, but the publicity had gotten so out of control my agent arranged an interview with Oprah to tell my side."

"I saw you."

"You did?"

He nodded. "Then what?"

She frowned. "Then . . . Uncle Rob and I planned an escape."

"To Kauai?"

She shrugged. "I remembered that piece earlier this morning. We joked about needing something big, like Antarctica."

"You didn't tell me."

She crossed her arms. "No, I . . ."

"I need to know when you remember something."

She raised her chin, confused and piqued. "For your investigation?"

He frowned. "I can't help you if—"

"I don't need your help, Cameron. My uncle's found. That's all that matters."

His gaze ran over her like sandpaper. "What happened matters."

She sank back and closed her eyes. "I don't remember."

His sigh was audible. Silence spread, but it wasn't warm and comfortable. Finally he said, "So what's next. The new script?"

She remained reclined but opened her eyes. "It looks that way."

He rested his palms on his knees. "If you don't like publicity, why take the part? That'll just bring it on."

"I need to work. Helen and I decided it would hurt the troupe right now if I'm involved." Helen's words had sliced her to the core. *These are at-risk kids. They need people they can trust.*

Cameron frowned. "The allegations were proven false."

"The allegations were not proven; insufficient evidence to charge me with a crime."

"Innocent until proven guilty."

"In court, not public opinion." Pain found her voice. "My actions, my interaction must have led Troy to believe, or at least desire, a relationship beyond his maturity." She looked into Cameron's eyes. "Until I know what I could have done differently . . ."

"You're not responsible for other people's choices."

"I was responsible for every kid in that program." And the loss of their respect left a hollow she wasn't sure she'd ever fill.

He didn't tell her she'd never control the effect she had on others. Part of him wanted to shake her and say if she set herself up as a target, she'd get shot. Part of him wanted to shoot. But the scariest part wanted to take her home and keep her safe.

He'd seen the innocence, moments before she recognized his attraction in front of her uncle's closet. He believed she hadn't realized the extent of Troy's infatuation. He also believed Darla's assertion that when Gentry Fox walked down the street, every man fantasized. The industry would devour her. He swallowed the knot in his throat.

"I'm going to check some things out. Will you be okay here?"

Gentry nodded. "Darla's arranging a press conference."

Just the mention of that woman heated his blood. "Don't leave the hospital."

The look she gave him was pure Jade. She'd do what she needed to, and he could try to keep up. He went out to his truck at the far end of the lot. Tucked into his windshield was a business card with *Big bucks for the inside scoop* penciled on the back. Two others had been tossed to the ground, probably by each successive hound. He wanted to grind them into the parking lot, but he picked them up and slipped them into his pocket to burn later.

He drove to the rental company at the Lihue airport and traced down dead ends until hunger sent him to Bubba's for burgers and fries, and then he went back to the hospital. He'd spent two hours without Gentry and it felt like days. As he laid the food out, she eyed his offering with alarm. Burgers with raw onions, fries in a paper boat.

"It's a staple." He held a paper-wrapped burger to her. "Bubba's grease in your pores makes you buoyant." He unwrapped his. "Be thankful I didn't get you the signature shorts."

She raised her brows.

"'Bubba's. We relish your buns.'"

Her glare pinned him to the wall. Good. He could handle antagonism.

"How's your uncle?" He took a chunk out of his burger.

"I think he looks better."

He chewed on both the burger and her answer. She'd been consistently positive, but he wasn't getting that vibe from the staff. "I've been working on the Jeep he rented. Can you remember anything about it?"

"Like . . ."

"Where it might be." He took another bite. The onions bit back.

She dragged a fry through the ketchup. "My best guess is we drove as far as the vehicle could go and hiked from there. Normal M.O. for Uncle Rob." She sectioned the fry into her mouth.

"So it's parked somewhere *mauka*, but you don't know where?"

"That's my guess. I can't say for sure."

"Close your eyes." That served two purposes; giving his heart a rest from their impact and shutting out her distractions. "Try to picture flying in to the island."

"I—"

"Just imagine it. A little improv." Maybe keying into her creative side would cause answers to surface. "You land in Lihue, rent the Jeep."

Concentration furrowed her brows.

"What color is it?"

"Red."

His pulse quickened. The paperwork had listed red. "Where did you go from there?"

"North."

Interesting. "What next?"

"We found a locals' hangout."

"Why?"

"Because Uncle Rob never takes a beaten path. He always wants the most obscure adventure, so he finds the people who know those kinds of places."

"Who did he talk to?"

She stayed silent so long he must have stumped her imagination. She opened her eyes.

He couldn't read the expression. "Nothing?"

"A dragon."

"Dragon."

"I pictured a long black-and-red dragon."

He narrowed his eyes and studied her. "Medieval or Oriental?"

She licked a drop of ketchup from her lower lip. "I don't know."

"Like on a temple?"

She frowned. "Maybe."

"Come on, Gentry. Don't quit now. Did you talk to someone at a Hindu temple or—"

She shook her head. "I don't know."

He settled back. "Okay. Eat your burger."

"Do I have to?"

"You could wait for the Spam musubi Nica's smuggling in to TJ's grandma."

"Spam?"

"Da kine ham in da can? Slap it on da sticky rice, wrap da buggah wit seaweed. Broke da mout." He leaned back with a grin.

"That's amazing."

"What?"

"How you go in and out of it."

"Offering me a job in show biz?"

She laughed. "Right now, I wouldn't do that for my worst enemy."

"And I don't qualify?"

She tipped her head. "Worst . . . no."

Oh man, he had it bad. He grabbed his burger and stood. "Anything else you need?"

"You're leaving?"

"Got a dragon to slay."

She folded her fingers together. "Hadn't pegged you for a knight."

"Not even with the beard?"

She melted his flesh with her gaze—like Nimue to Merlin, who foresaw his own death and went for it anyway.

No wonder her debut had packed a punch. It wasn't even a romantic role, yet something had come through. Something he needed to extract himself from immediately. "Eat."

She took a bite of her Bubba burger and looked less than impressed.

"They're better right off the grill, before they congeal. Fries are good for a day or two, though."

"Nice to know." She smiled.

He could get used to that smile. He and every man on the planet.

EIGHTEEN

A brown hen and four speckled chicks skittered out of his way as Cameron crossed the parking lot and climbed into the truck. As he keyed the ignition, his cell rang. "Pierce."

"Gentry Fox? Four years without a date and now Gentry Fox?"

He felt as though his teeth had just bitten down on chalk. "It's not—"

"You? Under the headline 'Fox and Lover'?"

He'd expected harassment, but not from the woman whose voice he hadn't heard in four years. He activated the window and let in some air. "What do you want, Myra?"

"Is it true?"

He flipped through all the possible reasons she might want to know. His chest tightened. His fingers itched to disconnect. His heart, thankfully, had been ground to a dust of disillusionment. "I can't imagine why that's any of your business."

"You don't have to get angry."

The British accent he'd once found so alluring now sounded stilted. But she was right; anger was a choice. He closed his eyes and breathed slowly. Because he'd once loved this woman, and some pitiless part of him always would, he didn't hang up.

"Do you want to hear what I have to say?" Her voice broke just enough to trigger guilt.

"I'm listening."

"I think it's good that you've . . . found someone."

"Gentry's a friend. I helped find her uncle."

"A friend."

He should have said client, considering how loosely Myra defined friend. But technically he'd been neither retained nor paid. And for some warped reason he felt compelled to be honest. "That's right."

"The article—"

"Is there a point to this?"

She huffed. "Same old Cameron."

"You said I'd never change."

"Yes, but I . . ."

Sweat dampened the base of his neck. He needed to get moving, let the wind blow, find some way to breathe that didn't feel toxic. How could the sound of her voice thousands of miles away still have a physical effect on him?

"Cameron . . . do you miss me?"

Anger and confusion hit him in the stomach. Miss her? The last thing she'd said to him was, "That's it, then," at the divorce table. As far as he knew that had been it for her. He'd walked around eviscerated, unable to think, to feel anything but the suppurating wound until shock and numbness had scarred him over. Now, when he'd spent one week with someone else, Myra wanted to know if he missed her.

He pried his sweaty fingers from the steering wheel. What he might have missed, what he'd thought he had with her, were the things she'd thrown in his face. *What does that mean, two becoming one? Explain the physiology of that. You know what I think? You're a dependent freak, and in case you haven't noticed, I'm not your bloody sister.*

"Cam—"

"No," he said. "I don't."

She disconnected. He held the phone to his ear another half a minute. Myra hadn't been mean at the start, but she'd been dangerous—potently. He'd never taken speed, but she'd been close.

He dropped his head to the wheel. What had made her call now? His gut clenched like a giant fist inside him. *Focus.*

With his mind fixed on the present, he methodically went into every local's hangout in Lihue, reconnecting with guys he hadn't seen in a while, showing Robert Fox's picture, asking if anyone had seen him, spoken with him, given him directions to that waterfall that had proved so dangerous? Was there a temple around, a restaurant or bar with a decorative dragon, something he might have missed since moving to the mainland. Even on Kauai things changed.

He also asked if anyone had come across a red Jeep parked somewhere *mauka.* Using a topographic hiker's map, he'd marked the approximate location of the falls. Though the island's economy depended on tourism, that far *mauka* could be another story.

Had Robert and Gentry trespassed onto *kapu* territory? Or taken a four-wheel track that led to crops people didn't advertise, like *pakalolo?* If Gentry and her uncle had happened onto one such operation, an accident could have been arranged to silence them.

Probably he was way off base, and someone had simply fulfilled Robert's hopes for a different sort of adventure. He had to stop assuming criminal elements in every situation that went bad. He heard Myra's voice in his ear, *"You're so suspicious."*

Except where it had mattered most.

He rubbed a hand through his hair. The rental company would pay him if he recovered the Jeep before Robert Fox regained consciousness. But he didn't care. He had other work to do, cases that wouldn't solve themselves. One Ponzi scheme could escalate exponentially while he spun his wheels on Kauai. And the insurance fraud he was working on for Barry needed attention. A rash of supposed victims, all being seen by the same clinic, filing huge damage claims for pain and suffering. He collected evidence by surveilling the bogus victims, but it was the doctors perpetrating the scam whom they'd nail.

He had to get home. There was nothing he could do for Robert Fox or his niece that others couldn't do better. He went back to the hospital. He would tell Gentry he'd come up blank and had to go.

But outside the ICU, her publicist was playing pugilist again. He walked into the psychological fray, took Gentry by the arm, and hustled her out.

He regretted it the minute the door closed behind them. He was supposed to be leaving. Gentry could take care of herself. Then why didn't she? "I'm not sure that woman's good for you."

"She's doing her job." But Gentry sounded battered.

He didn't care for people who turned on the charm in public and dispensed with it in private. At least he was equally rude in both. He let her into the truck and drove north by way of the east shore.

"Where are we going?"

"I want to take you a few places and see if anything triggers your memory the way the waterfall did." Where had that come from? He should be heading to the airport, getting back to work, going home.

"What do you want me to remember?"

"How about everything?"

She rubbed her temple. "I'm not sure it matters. Insurance will pay for the Jeep." She flicked him a glance. "Guess you hate to hear that."

"There are legitimate claims. What I do helps companies take care of those who need it, by stopping the ones who don't. How's your uncle?"

"They're keeping him comatose while they fight the infection." She sounded weary and frightened and, for the first time, honest. "He looks awful. Worse than when we found him." Tears glistened in her eyes.

This vulnerable Gentry was not making his departure easy. Where was her optimism?

"Every time I have to leave his side, I think he'll be better when I go back. But then it's the same thing all over again."

In her place, he'd think next time he returned the man might be dead. He followed the highway all the way to Kapa'a and pulled into a surfers' hangout. At Gentry's odd expression, his anticipation rose. "You remember this place?"

She frowned. "I don't think so."

"Then what's wrong?"

"I'm not exactly . . . incognito."

He looked around the crumbly parking lot. "I don't see any press."

"The ones you see aren't the problem. And it's not just press. I might have kept a low profile before this new wave of publicity. But now . . ."

He tapped his lips with his thumb. "Locals play it cool. I doubt you'll be mobbed."

"I know, but . . ."

"Just say it."

She turned her vibrant teal gaze on him. "You can't touch me."

His heart thumped his chest.

"They'll be looking for fresh shots, and this is the sort of place that invites speculation. Darla didn't want me near you. That's what she was hollering about."

He stroked his beard. "I might be able to restrain myself."

Gentry shoved his arm. "That's not what I meant. It's just that protective bodyguard thing. A camera doesn't read your intent." She raised her face. "That look is all it would take."

"They could catch that look on every guy on the island."

"I didn't mean yours." Her lashes dipped and rose.

Ah. What would Myra say to that? He stared out the front windshield.

"You look like you just sucked a lemon."

He shot her a glance. "Got one sour face?"

"Yeah, brah." She sounded just like TJ when she said it, only an octave higher.

"If I didn't know better, I'd say you were an actor."

"If I didn't know better, I'd say you were a friend."

He forked his fingers into his hair. "I guess I can handle that." But Myra's voice still mocked. Jaw clenched, he opened his door. Gentry let herself out. He touched the lock on his remote, and kept distance between them. No bodyguard contact.

As soon as Gentry's feet hit the pavement, a handful of teen girls hurried across the lot, squealing for her autograph. No harm in that. Gentry obliged. He watched to see if it was a trap to hold her up so the vultures could move in, but it seemed the girls were on their own.

The heavyset one in long, dark braids thanked her. "You're the greatest. I loved you in *Steel*. I'd have done the same thing if it was my kid. Your husband was mean not to do it for you."

"You were so brave. You, like, made me cry." The second girl looked as though she might do it again, just standing next to Gentry. What was it about her?

A car pulled into the lot, and he scanned it automatically; a woman he knew from high school and the hotel manager from Oahu that she'd married. Margot waved, and he thought for a minute she'd join them, but the husband marshaled her inside. It violated *aloha* to swarm famous visitors. Too much money would be lost if they stopped coming.

Gentry finished with the girls, who walked off calling thank-yous over their shoulders.

Another car pulled in and parked. His chest tightened as Bette Walden got out.

Gentry shrank into Cameron's side before she realized what she'd done. His hand went to the small of her back, responding to her. But she gathered herself and stepped away as Bette approached with the sharp look of a hawk fixed on her prey.

Only it was Cameron in her sights. "What a surprise I haven't heard from you."

"Were you expecting to?"

She shrugged. "Some information suggested I might."

"You checked me out?"

"One investigator to another."

Gentry clenched her jaw, remembering Bette throwing bones to the press. Why? What did this woman know, or think she knew?

Bette held an envelope out. "These were e-mailed to me a couple hours ago. I made the prints from the file and copied the note that accompanied it."

Cameron took the envelope but didn't open it.

Bette held out another business card. "In case you lost the last one."

Gentry wanted to slap the card out of her hand. Cameron slipped it into his pocket. Bette's expression shifted to smug as she turned and walked back to her car.

Gentry's legs were wooden. Instead of continuing into the bar, Cameron let her back into the truck. With a concerned mien, he handed over the envelope. Chest tight, she opened the unsealed flap and gasped. She didn't have to see any more of the photo to know how wrong it was.

Blood pulsed in her throat, her ears. She closed her eyes, breathed deeply. "This . . . is not me. Someone put my face . . ." And Troy in the background looking on. *God help me.*

"Read the note."

He didn't ask to see. That small courtesy meant so much. She slipped the paper out from behind the two photographs. A short note: *These are the pictures I didn't show. Leave that guy or I will.*

Oh, Troy. She had enjoyed his quick wit, his patience with the younger kids, his natural stage presence. How could an innocent crush—But then nothing about the improv kids was innocent.

She swallowed the ache. She didn't want him hurt anymore, but she had to preempt this before the rags got it. They couldn't print the photos without blurs, but blurs were no big deal to them. And if people thought she'd posed like that for the kid . . . She turned. "You have to go."

"What do you mean?"

"I can't be seen with you, or he'll show these pictures." She slapped the envelope against her knee.

Cameron stared hard. "And what about the next demand? Are you going to let someone threaten you into a cave?"

"People believe what they see. Truth is . . . meaningless."

He leaned his forearm on the wheel. "Truth is never meaningless."

"Well, sometimes it doesn't stand a chance."

How could he have turned on her like this? A young man with such promise and those big dreams. Tears stung. She fought, but couldn't stop them. Cameron pulled her to his shoulder, wrapped his arm around her neck. She could almost hear the cameras clicking. Darla would be livid. Not for the first time, she hated it all.

"Gentry." His beard against her forehead was softer than she'd expected for a man who wore it to intimidate. "You can't give up. Think what it took to find your uncle. That's who you are."

She drew back. "Who I was. Before I knew."

He raised her chin. "Don't buy into that." He held out his hand for the envelope. "Let me have it."

She shook her head.

"There are ways to tell when a photo's been doctored."

"Not without seeing it." She clenched her fist. "I was so careful in my contract; no nudity, nothing flagrant. Once those images are in people's minds they don't go away." She groaned.

"Give me the pictures, Gentry."

She pinched the bridge of her nose, sent a sideways glance, then turned the envelope upside down and thrust it into his lap. "Do not look."

The corners of his mouth twitched. "What would I need with pictures when I've got the real Gentry Fox in my truck?"

She sniffed. "Red-nosed and bleary-eyed." Her voice broke.

He tapped the envelope on his thigh. "I'll deal with these on the mainland, okay?"

She stared out the windshield and nodded, then realized what he'd said and turned. "You're leaving?"

"I have to. The Jeep'll turn up, or your uncle can tell them where it is." That was the most hopeful thing he'd said about Uncle Rob. "If you remember anything . . ." He pierced her with his gaze. "Call me."

She nodded, but she wouldn't. Things were complicated enough. "Can you take me to Hale Kahili? I can rent a car from there."

"I'll make sure TJ knows."

"I'll be fine."

He drove her along the highway through broad, umbrella-shaped trees that parted now and then to reveal rolling green pastures streaked with sunset hues and fragments of rainbows. Sorrel horses grazed among pink-and-white flowering lily ponds. At Hale Kahili, Cameron walked her through the few press vans still hanging around, to the door of the cottage. He waited while she unlocked it and looked inside.

She turned back. "All clear." If only that were true.

"Anything, whether it seems important or not." He took out a business card and wrote his cell number on the back.

She palmed the card. "Thanks seems inadequate."

He stroked her with his gaze. "Try *mahalo*."

She smiled. "*Mahalo*, Kai."

He leaned in and kissed her cheek. "*Aloha*."

NINETEEN

Gentry slept fitfully. A weight had settled on her chest like sand-bags pinning her down. She thrashed and kicked. When her eyes flew open she was alone in the Hale Kahili rental Uncle Rob had chosen. It was dark and silent, but the burden remained.

The photos were a nightmare waiting to happen, but that wasn't it. Something worse, something wrenching drove her to her knees on the floor beside the bed. She poured out her heart for Uncle Rob. Didn't the Lord desire to heal? He'd done so with the crowds that swarmed him on earth. It had to be what he wanted. *Oh, God, I beg you.*

Leaving the hospital with Cameron last evening, she'd let her confidence waver. He made it difficult to be less than totally honest, but now she regretted her lapse. Did doubt have power to interfere? In the dark, alone, she felt its power.

No. Even if her faith wasn't staunch enough, Uncle Rob was a rock. His love for the Lord could be a force field around him. But then . . . he'd had troubles of his own. They both had. Aunt Allegra, Troy, now this. How exactly had giving their hearts to Christ almost three years ago made their lives better?

Anger licked. Was optimism foolish? Cameron's outlook, to believe in God but not expect him "to fix everything," seemed like wisdom. She felt naïve. Had she made God Santa Claus? If she asked nicely and promised to be good, she'd get everything she wanted.

But hadn't he already given her the ultimate? When she had gotten on her knees and surrendered her life with Uncle Rob, she'd anticipated a new kind of adventure, a spiritual journey to challenge and enlighten them. But hadn't she agreed to live for Christ no matter what? Pain coursed through as she realized the Lord could be preparing her.

She couldn't bear to lose Uncle Rob. She wouldn't even think it. And if he lost his leg, the self-condemnation would smother her. She didn't have the strength, the knowledge, the experience to handle it. She'd be swept away. *Please, please let it pass—* The Lord's own prayer stopped her thought. Could she complete it? *Not my will but yours be done?*

She had prayed for the Lord's perfect will. Making a rash assumption that God must be in agreement, she'd prayed it. But what if his will wasn't hers? She buried her face, unable to give God Uncle Rob, his leg . . . or her guilt.

The room seemed to close in like the cave where Uncle Rob had waited. She imagined him there, hoping, praying, day after day as infection took hold. She could hate herself for what she'd done, what she hadn't. *Uncle Rob!*

Dad was supportive and encouraging, but when his health deteriorated, his younger brother had stepped in like a magical godfather and whisked her off on adventures too rigorous for Dad's heart. Out in nature, they'd talked about goals and dreams, boyfriends and plays and hopes for the future.

Now . . . what would his future be? *Whatever God has determined.* The thought lanced her festering doubt. God knew the plans he had for them, plans to prosper, not to harm. She had said that to the kids in her program, a positive-thinking mantra she'd believed wholeheartedly.

She dropped her face to her hands. What did it mean not to harm, when all around her believers and nonbelievers suffered? There must be a spiritual element Uncle Rob probably grasped, but she didn't. She groaned. It hurt too much to give in.

Should she pray for what she wanted, or pray to want what God wanted? Did she trust him? On the mountain she'd have said yes. And later, when the waters of baptism had poured over her, she'd been carried to a place of exquisite surrender. But ever since, it had been one long freefall, the accusations, the gossip magazines, her plunge over the falls, and now Uncle Rob.

Again her spirit groaned. The burden grew. She didn't know what else to do, so she prayed for Uncle Rob's leg to heal, that in the morning when she went in, the smell would be gone, the flesh would have lost the fiery streaks. She prayed the fever would come down and his former strength return. She prayed for the doctor's astonishment. Then she prayed for strength to bear it if none of that came true.

Nica woke with a sorrow so fresh she expected to find someone at her door, strung out or near death. But when she looked, no one was there, needing her. No source to the sorrow. What then? Kai?

The thought took the legs from her. She rushed to his room. He'd told her last night he'd be ducking out early to get home, and only the kitty slept now on his neatly made bed. She hated that he flew so far so frequently, but it didn't usually hit her like this. She went to the kitchen and brewed some jasmine tea, hands shaking.

Growing up, she'd felt his moods, his intensity; he'd absorbed her hurts, cushioned her sensitivity to cruelty and sorrow.

He'd been the one to bring her back to reality that day when she was five. *We can live at Okelani's, but I'll take care of you,* he'd promised, his childish certainty undaunted by forces that could sweep away lives in a moment.

When their parents' spirits slipped from the world, she had inadvertently followed. That was the first time she'd seen Jesus, warm and sorrowful, climbed into his arms and felt the warmth of his breath. If it had been her time, nothing could have brought her back. She would never have left that embrace. Sometimes she wished she hadn't.

But Kai would not let go. He'd said he would take care of her, but it was his need that brought her back. In that choice, she'd received her calling. She didn't like straddling the realms, but she'd seen that death was only a small step away, and she could comfort those whose time had come to pass over.

But not without a toll. She'd been exhausted when Gentry came, her spirit drained. Now she realized Gentry had not been a burden but a gift. Part of something bigger, maybe, that had yet to be revealed.

Nica sipped her tea and dared to believe Jesus did not intend to take her brother from her. But there was something still. She closed her eyes and found Jesus waiting. Drawing close, she pressed her head against his chest, felt his arms around her. "I'm ready," she said. "Tell me."

⌒

Gentry knew when she approached the hospital administrator, the surgeon Dr. Long, and two doctors she hadn't seen before that what they had to say would break her. For the first time, she appreciated the surgeon's cold brevity. "The leg is septic. It can't be saved."

Grief smothered her. She had called her dad, Uncle Rob's only brother, before the sun was up on Kauai. She'd spoken with her mom as well. True to form, they'd voiced the optimism she had clung to until last night. No mystery where she'd gotten that particular trait.

She had tried to reach her Aunt Allegra, as she'd been for days, getting the answering machine each time. They had no sons or daughters to call. No one else. The weight of the decision had weighed so heavily on her, but now she saw, in reality, she had no control at all.

"You've tried everything? There isn't anything else that might work?"

"My colleagues agree."

He'd brought them in because of her, she thought, her public platform, her notoriety. But none of it would help Uncle Rob. She glanced at the others, hoping for one dissenting voice.

Dr. Long repeated, "We are all in agreement."

Including God. She'd known it last night.

"Your uncle gave permission for treatment."

In the helicopter before he'd lost consciousness. "Not for amputation."

"For all life-saving measures."

"And he'll die without this surgery?"

"I've held off as long as I possibly could." For the first time the doctor's voice held something human.

Her heart labored like a lump of wax. She nodded. "Save his life."

From the copilot's position beside his friend Denny Bridges, Cameron had watched the morning sun gild the water as the string of islands slid away behind them. A bank of clouds scuttled across the left horizon, but the sky ahead was clear cerulean. Even so, the charter jet that was earning Denny a nice, fat income jumped and wobbled in the trade winds until they'd settled out over the ocean for six hours of contemplation.

Denny would converse when they grabbed food at the airport diner, but he liked it silent while he flew. He'd been awestruck the first time he took the controls and experienced the rush of keeping a plane aloft over the Pacific. They'd trained with the same instructor, so Cameron had been waiting when Denny came back from his first solo, looking as though he'd been on the mountain with Moses. It had been a God thing ever since. But *everything* was for Denny—as he'd said this morning when they hooked up at the Lihue airport.

He had flown a group in the day before and was right there to provide this flight back. Coincidence? "God's got his hand all over it." Denny's smile was radiant.

Cameron hadn't pointed out that he made the trip two or three times a week, and odds were good that they'd hook up the morning he needed a ride. He'd simply finagled the seat Denny usually held open for the Lord and was thankful for it.

As they cruised over the deep blue expanse, Cameron let his thoughts run over everything. The pictures were in his shirt pocket, but he hadn't looked at them; partly at Gentry's request, partly because of the missionary blood coursing through his veins, but mostly because the thought of seeing Gentry's face on some porn model's body disgusted him. It would ruin the images of her that he'd tucked up into his heart, whether he wanted them there or not.

He would take the pictures to the authorities if he had to, but even as he and Gentry had sat in his truck on the island, he'd contemplated another way. He hoped to minimize the chance that those pictures would get out, but even more he wanted to quash the real purpose behind them. She hadn't feigned embarrassment in his truck. Her reaction had proved her a mark for blackmail.

After the six long hours, Denny soared in for a nice, tight landing. He offloaded the foursome who'd ridden in comfort behind them, as well as their luggage, then led the way to the diner for a late lunch according to their bodies' timing, though it was dinnertime in California. The diner's scent of fat, fried and seared, marked the place as a staunch holdout against sprouts and low-carb wraps. He'd work it off later.

They'd barely put seats to the booth when Denny came out with it. "Gentry Fox."

May as well start explaining with someone who tended to believe him. Even so, the less said, the better. "She showed up lost and injured, and Nica asked me to look into it."

Denny's face danced with amusement. "Great for your press conference, buddy. Now give me the real story."

"That's it. Nica called me to investigate when Gentry couldn't remember who she was. Then she remembered, and all hell broke loose."

"Hell tends to break loose a lot on that woman." Denny sobered. "Is she lost?"

Denny didn't mean in the forest. "Hardly. Reminds me of you."

"Ah." Denny gripped his hands together. "When I watched her in *Steel* I thought: a light shining in the darkness."

Only Denny. His own reaction had been far less elevated, cynical absorption. Darla could hardly hide her envy, the press their rabid curiosity; Nica, of course, responded with tender mercy. Maybe Gentry brought out people's most basic natures. One thing was sure; there was no lukewarm response to Gentry Fox.

Shaking his head, Denny said, "When all that persecution started, my spirit ached."

"Did you think her innocent?"

Denny V-pointed to his own eyeballs. "Windows to the soul. I saw it in her eyes."

Cameron didn't doubt it. His reaction had been more physiological than spiritual, though. Until a few days ago, he'd been sealed tighter than a time capsule—a condition he preferred to whatever it was Gentry had released. Now he couldn't stop thinking about her situation. "I didn't know you followed that kind of thing."

"It was everywhere. Shuttling my clientele, I hear too much."

People in the motion picture industry formed a large customer base for charter flights to the islands. Denny's business depended on them and the corporate bigwigs all along the coast.

"So you'd have recognized her?"

Denny shrugged. "It's hard when you see someone out of context."

Their shapely, black-haired waitress approached the table with a tall strawberry shake and the metal blender cup it was mixed in. She set it in front of Denny and received his thanks with deepening dimples, then turned. "Something for you?"

Cameron ordered iced tea, and she sashayed off to get it.

Denny sucked the shake through his straw with hollowed cheeks, then licked his lips. "Still working for her?"

"Unofficially."

"No retainer, no expenses?"

"It's a favor to Nica."

The pert waitress brought his tea and said, "I know what he wants. How about you?"

"Whatever he's having."

She nodded. "Right-o."

With his flaxen stubble and sky-blue eyes, Denny's piercing gaze gave him the look of an archangel on truth detail. "A favor for Nica."

Cameron sipped the cold, tannic tea. "It's not like that." Now that he'd put distance between them, the days he'd spent up close with Gentry seemed surreal. "She's a rising star, and I'm not ..." He pressed back from the table. "I'm not looking."

Denny stirred the shake with his straw. "To everything its time; to hate, to love; to kill, to heal."

Cameron stared into his glass. Some things didn't heal. And some people learned from that. He chose not to hate, not to kill. He could avoid the rest as well.

Denny drew the straw out of the shake and licked it. "Myra called me."

Her name jolted him like a cattle prod. "What did she want?"

"To know where you were."

"Before or after the stories hit?"

"That day."

Yesterday, the same day she'd called him, spurred by the thought of him and Gentry? Or him and anyone at all. Maybe it was Denny who'd told her he hadn't dated.

"Since I'd flown you over, I couldn't say I didn't know." Denny's brow furrowed.

"It doesn't matter. She can reach me anytime she wants. My numbers haven't changed."

"Did you talk to her?"

Cameron nodded but offered no details. That conversation still left a sour taste. Miss her? Like an addict missed the hit that would kill him.

Denny emptied the remainder of the shake from the metal cup into his glass. "It sounded like she'd been crying."

"I'll bet." She'd have turned on whatever it took to get what she wanted, in this case Denny's sympathy and cooperation. But why bother?

Denny replanted the straw in the shake. "A time to forgive?"

Cameron sighed. "She doesn't want forgiveness, doesn't need it. She has no regrets."

"No chance of reconciliation?"

Besides Nica, only Denny knew it all. The night she'd unloaded her sordid details, he'd staggered to Denny's and bled. *"How could I not know? Not even suspect?"*

Then he'd called Nica because even two thousand miles away she would be feeling it. She'd answered in tears. *"Tell me I'm wrong."* They had sobbed together because he didn't know yet how to stop the pain.

Because Nica had borne it, too, he answered, "No. No chance."

The waitress brought two burgers, thin as cardboard, with ragged edges on buns the size of saucers, two sides of shoestring fries, and dollops of chunky applesauce brown with cinnamon. She clunked ketchup and mustard bottles on the table, Tabasco in front of Denny. Either she was clairvoyant or she'd memorized his personal preferences.

Denny watched her all the way back to the kitchen, then refocused. "So the gossip is the typical tripe?"

"Well, aliens did steal Gentry's brain, but I didn't sleep with her."

Denny nodded. "That's what I thought."

⌒

Driving home from the airport, Cameron dug his vibrating phone from his pocket. He checked the ID and answered, "What's up, Nica?"

"Kai." The pause was so long, his adrenaline kicked in. "Kai, they removed Rob's leg."

"What?"

"They couldn't stop the infection, so they took him back to surgery."

He had doubted Gentry's optimistic reports but hadn't really thought it would come to amputation. She must be completely unprepared. Her universe of possibilities didn't include unanswered prayers. How would she handle the fact that this time God hadn't come through?

"How is she?"

"Brave. Strong. Devastated."

She'd been so determined to keep it from happening. "Are you there with her?"

"Yes."

"Anyone else?"

"Okelani's on her way."

Good. Okelani was a *kahuna lā'au lapa'au*, healer and plant specialist, and didn't trust Western medicine. But even she knew nothing could heal a septic limb spreading poison. Some wounds were beyond herbs and prayer alone. At any rate, Okelani would make sure Nica didn't overinvest. "Any press?"

"Not yet. But as soon as they hear . . ."

"It's what she's chosen, Nica."

"Chosen?"

"It's what her life looks like. Don't let it take any more out of you."

"Kai?" The tone of her voice told him he'd spoken more harshly than he'd intended. "What's the matter?"

"Nothing. There's nothing wrong."

"It's me, Kai."

He was silent a full beat. "Myra called." Her name tasted like dead fish, a salt pool cut off and drying out in the sun, stagnant and brackish.

"What did she want?"

"To remind me never to make that mistake again."

"Oh, Kai."

"Listen, I've got to go. Tell Gentry I'm sorry, okay?" There was nothing he could do two thousand miles away. It irritated him that he wished there were.

TWENTY

Nica ached. Once again Cameron bore the brunt of Myra's pathological selfishness, shoring himself up against past hurts and future possibilities. Her sting spread like poison through his mind and body. He still believed he could resist. He didn't realize that only by opening to the suffering could he pass through.

She closed her eyes, knowing pain would come unlooked for in the night or the bright of day. Sorrow struck in rainbow-drenched fields, in shaded valleys, in crystal coves. There was no resisting, no avoiding, only discovering what could be learned and given in its midst.

Gentry had touched something in Cameron. Okelani's kitchen had been charged with their electricity. But he was backing away so fast, he would stumble over the possibility—and be grateful for the fall that saved him taking a chance.

Now Gentry had her own heartache. When the doctors had come out to say her uncle had made it through surgery, she had looked grim and sublime, in the midst of her dismay, radiating courage. She didn't pretend the strength she'd shown on film; she embodied it. She'd been tested, but not broken. Unlike Kai.

But her strength didn't make her impervious. Maybe, as Cameron said, she'd chosen her high profile. But she was still human, still hurting. Nica rejoined her. "How are you doing?"

Gentry paused her pacing. "I wish I could reach my aunt. She should know what's happened."

"Rob's wife, or sister?" Nica took one of the beige chairs.

"Wife, but they're separated." Gentry sank into the other chair.

"She's ignoring your calls?"

Gentry shrugged. "It's possible things got worse between them, but I don't remember."

With Cameron's ache fresh in her throat, Nica shook her head. "Was it hostile?"

"Decorously. Aunt Allegra would never fight. But she's been on slow simmer since Uncle Rob realized he needed God in his life."

"She objected to his faith?"

Gentry released a slow breath. "She didn't know what to expect. She said things like, 'Are you going to sell all we have and give it to the poor?'"

"And?" Nica glanced sideways.

"And Uncle Rob said if the Lord asked him to."

Nica raised her brows. "I can see where that might elevate her blood pressure. Did she have much to lose if the Lord suggested an estate sale?"

Gentry managed a smile. "Uncle Rob's invented some important things in the tech and communication fields—and invested well. It would be a big sale."

"How sad that what turned her away was what she needed more than everything else he'd provided."

"She doesn't understand." Gentry crossed her arms. "We'd had this mountaintop experience—just the two of us at eighteen thousand feet on Mount St. Elias. For a year we'd been pondering what mattered in life. And then up there, with the spectacular display all around, it just happened. Uncle Rob said, 'I need this inside me.'" She turned with tears in her eyes. "We wanted the abundant life Jesus promised. And that's what he gave us. Now . . ." She sat down, chin trembling. "How will I tell him?"

Nica rested her hand on Gentry's knee. She didn't try to say his life could still be abundant, only, "You'll have the words when you need them." Because Jesus wouldn't leave her alone in this. When they hurt, he was closest of all.

Gentry sniffed. "Does Cameron know we were too late?"

"Gentry, you saved your uncle's life."

"But not his leg." She gulped back her tears, then gave in.

Nica hugged her, wishing Kai had stayed, then startled when a photographer leaned into the room and snapped a photo.

Gentry pulled back as though singed while two hospital personnel escorted him out. She sniffed. "I'm sorry."

"For what?"

"Cameron didn't want you involved." Gentry buried her face. "Everything I do hurts someone."

"Oh, Gentry. I'm sure it feels that way, but—"

"I thought the troupe would change lives, but look what it did to Troy." She rubbed her knuckles under her nose. "Being offered the part in *Steel* felt like a gift from God, his plan for me to make a difference. I was so excited, so afire with the challenge and opportunity."

"And you walked into the realm of darkness with the Shekina glory still fresh."

"Shekina glory?"

"The touch of God visible in you, like the light Moses covered with a veil. If viewers could see it, I assure you forces of darkness were even more aware."

"But I didn't tell anyone, didn't pray out loud or preach at my fellow cast members." She had fit in as well as she could, better than some whose egos or addictions caused conflict. She hadn't trumpeted her belief that God had given her the part, the platform.

"It showed in your work. You were brilliant."

And that meant she'd attracted evil forces, brought on persecution by revealing her faith in ways she didn't realize?

"I don't mean to diminish your talent."

Gentry waved her off. Lots of people had talent; few soared to recognition overnight. But if God had directed it, why had he allowed such wreckage to follow? If God had led them to Uncle Rob, why take his leg like some bait-and-switch used-car salesman? You think you're getting all this, but you end up with that. And even that'll cost you.

"Every gift has its own trials." Nica's face took on an otherworldly glow. "Believe me."

"How do I stop it?"

"You can't. Not without squandering your talent. You've been given the chance to touch millions. Do you really think the ruler of this fallen world will let that happen without a fight?"

She had believed she was meant to make a difference. She just hadn't thought it would make her enemies, or that they'd be so vicious. Being raised in a home where everything had a bright side had not prepared her to recognize evil.

She looked up when Okelani came in, bearing the subtle sweet scent of the buttery yellow lei she wore. In her own home, she'd carried herself with such ease Gentry had wondered if she could see after all, but here her blindness showed as she approached on the arm of the Asian man beside her.

Okelani removed the lei from her neck. Gentry breathed its scent as the blossoms settled over her own chest. The brush of Okelani's lips was like butterfuly wings on her cheek.

"Da Lord say you *mea aloha*. Beloved. He want you know dat here."

The warmth of Okelani's palm against her heart brought tears again. "I prayed so hard."

"*Ke Akua* wen pour out da lava and make dis world. He going take care dis too."

She sniffed. "How?" When Uncle Rob would never be the same again?

"Big, his love. Bigger dan all dis."

And there it was, the reason she would face the trials and not squander the gift. Even in her despair last night, she'd felt the over-whelming presence of the one to whom she'd surrendered upon the Alaskan mountaintop. Love bigger and deeper than any accusations or mistakes.

Nica handed her a tissue, and Gentry pressed it to her nose and cheeks. Though it sometimes felt as though the whole world was against her, the Lord had provided these two women, new friends in place of those who misunderstood her faith, resented her success, and deserted her in the scandal.

She embraced them both, drawing in their warmth and caring, and giving back her own. Then Darla walked in and reminded her she was Gentry Fox, star and pariah. Her dubious celebrity could bring misery to Nica and Okelani.

"There you are, Gentry. I was hoping to find you alone." Darla came to a stop before her. "The press wants a statement. We need to plan our take on it."

"Our take?" She stared.

"I'm sorry; that was poorly stated."

Darla, the master of the perfect phrase, couldn't manage the simple compassion Nica and even Okelani had expressed. Anger stung with a realization of her power. Two words could drop Darla to her knees. *You're fired.* This was her chance to strike back.

Darla fanned her fingers through her short, coppery coif. "We're all under a lot of pressure—"

"Darla." Her voice was low and controlled. She had to keep it that way or she'd scream so loudly they'd hear her in Hollywood. "My uncle has lost his leg, and I'm devastated. You can phrase that any way you want. Now please . . . go." Before she acted on all too human desire for revenge.

Nica and Okelani flanked her.

"I know this is hard." Darla tried to look compassionate. "But they'll want to see you. You have to give them something."

A little more Shekina glory? She'd given them her best, and they'd dragged it through the muck. What would she lose by not making an appearance? Nothing near what the man she loved as much as her own father had lost. If the press, her fans, and the whole world rejected her, it couldn't hurt worse than what Uncle Rob would feel once he knew how she'd failed him.

⌒

Alone on the balcony in the ruby glow of the setting sun, Allegra placed the call. The surprise in Gentry's voice disturbed her.

"Aunt Allegra, I've tried to reach you for days."

"Well, I'm . . . out of town." She'd had to call once the stations stopped carrying updates. After a surfeit of Gentry's travails, they'd moved on. But for those living it, life didn't jump from one point of attraction to the next. It dragged through every single hour, every minute, piling up like grains of quicksand sucking her under, and the more she resisted the faster it swallowed her alive.

While she swam and sunbathed and shopped, Rob lay in a hospital with Gentry beside him, watching and praying, united in that life-changing religion they'd found. Even so, did Gentry really think she didn't care? Estrangement wasn't enough, not nearly enough to destroy—but stupidity was.

Shame and sorrow dragged her deeper. "How is he?"

Gentry's silence lasted too long. "I don't know what you've heard."

Her pulse raced. "That Rob was injured in an accident and airlifted to the hospital." Gentry's hesitance tortured her. "What's happened?"

"They had to amputate his leg just above the knee."

"What?" She sank to the chaise on the lanai overlooking Waikiki.

"His leg got infected, and they couldn't stop it from spreading."

The ache hit her like a punch in the stomach. She gasped.

"Aunt Allegra, I'm so sorry."

"Is he . . . Does he know?"

"He's still unconscious. He won't know until he wakes up."

She closed her eyes, pain triggering tears she'd sworn she'd finished with.

Gentry's voice broke. "Do you think you could come?" An understandable request, for his wife to be there for him when he awakened, to share his desolation. But Rob had lost his leg, and she was having an affair.

Curt came out on the lanai with chilled flutes of champagne, his hair combed back and showing only hints of gray. His shirt fell open to the sternum to reveal a smooth, suntanned chest. With a crooked smile, he held out a flute. And another piece of her died.

Allegra's eyes had reddened, Curt noted as she told the person on the phone, "I'll have to let you know," and disconnected.

He handed her one of the champagne flutes and pondered her expression. Dazed, maybe. "Everything all right?"

"They've amputated Rob's leg."

He stared a full beat, processing what she'd said and what it could mean. "Allegra, that's terrible."

She stared at the champagne in her flute. "The infection was killing him."

"I'd rather die." He spoke without thinking but meant it. The thought of a stump horrified him. He hoped it horrified Allegra as well. But there was always the sympathy factor.

"To someone as active and athletic as Rob, it may as well be death."

The first fuzzy edge of a buzz tickled his head from the champagne he'd downed in the room to congratulate himself . . . prematurely?

She closed her eyes. "He might not make it. That serious an infection . . ."

Not good. If she started to internalize the situation, she might pull away.

"This has nothing to do with you, babe. It would have happened wherever you were, whatever we—Whatever our relationship looked like. He's had two and a half years to change things, and instead he's been off climbing mountains with his niece." He probed the wound without mercy. She needed to get angry. And Gentry was already a sore spot.

Allegra's throat worked as she pulled out the words, "He'll never make another ascent."

"He'll find something else. Puzzles, or chess."

She raised her gaze to him with more than a hint of disgust.

"I'm sorry. That was callous." He'd gotten cocky, and that didn't work with Allegra. "I just want you to see all the more that it was right to make a break. He wouldn't want you to see him as less than a man."

Her brows pressed in together. "Less. . . ?"

"Trust me, babe. The best thing you can do is let him start over with dignity."

A tear slid down her cheek. "Do you really . . ."

She sniffed and stared off into that place he hated, where he couldn't guess her thoughts. She stayed there so long he almost lost it. But then she looked up with aching eyes. "That's what he said he'd found. A new beginning."

"Well, then." Curt raised his flute. "To beginnings."

TWENTY-ONE

Cameron jolted awake and scrambled out of bed. He caught the LED display on the clock radio as he dragged on a pair of athletic shorts. 4:00 A.M. Someone better have died. He stumbled down the stairs, groped through the dark foyer, and opened the door.

A fatality would have been preferable.

"Can I come in?"

"No."

"Please, Cameron, I need to talk to you."

Glass shards filled his throat. He pressed a hand to his eyes and motioned her inside. He considered leaving the door open for witnesses, then closed it with a sigh. He swiped the switch and blinked back the stab of light in his sleep-deprived eyes.

Myra walked halfway into the room and turned. Her collarbones jutted above the scoop-neck shirt that fitted softly over her breasts and down her ribs—each of which protruded. She'd always been tall and slender with legs that wouldn't quit; now she was dangerously thin. She ran her fingers into the hair at her nape, silky hair that now seemed brittle. She hadn't weathered the last four years well. Neither had he.

"Aren't you going to offer me a drink?"

He cleared the shards. "What would you like?"

"Tea? I can make it."

"I don't have any." And she didn't drink coffee. "The best I can do is hot lemonade." He used to make that for her when she'd gotten sick; a quarter inch of lemon juice in the bottom of the mug, that much thick golden honey, and hot water.

"That would be nice." Her voice broke as though she'd stumbled over the memory as well.

He went into the kitchen, turned on the light, and blinked again at the brighter infusion. A lingering aroma of lasagna remained from the frozen dinner he'd microwaved and wolfed at the computer around midnight. Four hours later, he did not want to be in the kitchen. Or the living room. Or anywhere near Myra.

He went through the steps on the lemonade; bottled lemon juice, honey a little grainy, water from the hot faucet on his sink that kept it near the boiling point. He stuck in a spoon and set the mug on the table. She could stir it herself.

Myra took a seat, drew the mug to her, and stirred. "I want to tell you something without making you mad."

He rubbed his face. "I'm too tired for much of an outburst, so go ahead."

She raised her eyes. "I think I made a mistake."

Why she chose to confess that now in his kitchen was beyond him. Unless it was . . . "Something illegal?"

She raised the cup and sipped. "I should have known you'd think that. Are you imagining me embezzling, maybe, or faking my death?"

He scratched his beard. "I'm just going with this four-in-the-morning thing."

She startled. "Is that what time it is?"

He sighed.

"I thought . . . I haven't been sleeping."

Or eating, by the looks of her. He felt no pang of compassion. For the first year after she'd filed for divorce, he'd wondered how bad it would be to run into her unexpectedly—like a stab in the gut, he'd guessed. The second year, he'd stopped looking for her everywhere. The third and fourth had brought a sort of numbness. Now . . .

"What mistake did you make, Myra?"

She drank from the mug as though it was a ritual cup, cradled in both hands like a chalice. "I remember when you first made this for me. That time I had strep throat?"

He was not willing to unpack their baggage. "What's your mistake?"

She hit the mug a little too hard on the table. "You still won't listen, will you?"

"What obligation do I have? You're not my wife, not even my ex-wife. You're my non-wife, remember? The psychiatrist said for you the marriage never happened."

"Yes, but now—"

"Now?"

"I made a mistake." Her eyes pooled. "I see that now."

That was her mistake? That was what she'd come to discuss? It was too rich. No, it was derelict. He didn't trust himself to speak.

She pushed the mug away. "Don't look at me like that."

He didn't know how to look. Away, he supposed. He leaned against the counter and stared at the wall. "And you want me to say what?"

She stood up. "That you'll think about it." She walked over to him, the tears interred in her eyes without falling. She could always cry with the least amount of hazard to her face. "Just that you'll think about it."

His mind would churn it endlessly, but he wouldn't tell her that, couldn't. Or she'd think there was an opening.

She rested her fingers on his arm. "Consider it in light of every-thing we had." And now a tear slipped down her cheek, choreographed.

He'd wanted to see her face every day for the rest of his life. And he probably would—in his nightmares and times of despair and hope-lessness. That was where her stormy eyes lurked, her smooth, creamy skin. Her perfume encircled him, intoxicating and toxic. He shook his head and whispered, "No."

She closed her eyes and rested her forehead on his shoulder. "Because I hurt you?"

Hurt, betrayed, ripped out his heart and shared it with her dogs.

"Or because of Gentry Fox?"

He moved his shoulder away. "I told you Gentry's a friend."

"I saw the pictures."

"I was helping her through the press."

"I saw your face."

He expelled a breath. "What do you want me to say? That after a week I'm in love with her?"

She stared into his face. "It's there, though, isn't it? The potential."

"Myra." He took her shoulders and moved her away. "It's no longer your business to know."

"But I do. I know everything about you." Her voice held bitter truth.

He steeled himself. "Not anymore."

A look of hurt disbelief passed over her face. She wanted to speak, but he willed her to silence. She'd already sunk her poison. Another word could make the dose lethal. "I'm going to bed. You can see yourself out."

She turned and walked out of the kitchen. He heard the front door open and close and felt the draft of her passing. Her perfume and the stale lasagna formed a malodorous partnership that drove him from the kitchen, up the stairs, and into his bed. There, alone, he lay on his back in the dark and remembered loving her.

⌒

"'Where can I go from your Spirit? Where can I flee from your presence? If I go up to the heavens, you are there; if I make my bed in the depths you are there. If I rise on the wings of the dawn, if I settle on the far side of the sea—'"

In a whisper Rob joined in with Gentry. "'Even there your hand will guide me, your right hand will hold me fast.'"

Her eyes jerked open. "Uncle Rob."

He smiled, taking her, and the light, and the blessed quiet into his soul. No more pounding roar. No damp shelf. Dark thoughts and doubts had fled. He was in the land of the living. Barely, though, judging by his struggle to draw breath enough to speak.

"Guess you found me." He'd meant it thankfully, but her eyes brimmed with tears.

"I'm so sorry."

He didn't know what for, but he was too tired to ask. He managed a faint thank-you, then drifted back to sleep.

The next time he awakened, Gentry was there again, her smile brighter than the light blazing in the window, yet there was something forced about it, in a way she never was, even on stage. She straightened in the chair beside the bed. "Like your new room?"

Anything would be heaven after the cave. "Like it fine." His voice rasped, but it was a little easier to talk than the last time.

"I special-ordered the view." Again the smile that took her face by force.

He looked at her with deep affection. "The view's great." He raised his fingers, and she took his hand like the daughter he imagined her. And then, because he knew her so well, he asked, "Gentry, what's wrong?"

The smile slipped away. Her fingers tightened on his. Maybe his battle had been closer than he realized, but they were both there, alive, even if his body felt like lead. He tried to raise his head, but that wasn't a good choice.

He gathered his strength and said, "Are you all right?"

She swallowed. "Mostly. I hit my head under the falls and still can't remember some things." Tears filled her eyes. "Uncle Rob, I didn't know you were there. I didn't even know who I was. But if I'd gone to the police at once . . ."

He was getting the picture. All those days in the cave.

"I can't tell you how awful I feel."

"Honey, don't." He squeezed her fingers. "Don't blame yourself." He knew what was going through her head. If only she'd known, thought, acted differently. She'd had enough of that.

"Uncle Rob." She drew a jagged breath. "You were out there so long, your leg got infected."

He must be doped not to feel it. He tried to look down his body. Her grip tightened. "They had to take it off above the knee."

He couldn't have heard her right. But the look on her face said he did. When he struggled again, she raised the bed up a little so he could see past his chest. One leg was under the sheet; the other, tightly wrapped, was only a stump.

Stunned, he stared at the stump as though someone had left a package there for him to unwrap. It didn't look like a part of him, nothing he recognized like the shape of the other leg under the sheet. *Was it . . . ? How . . . ?*

He'd resigned himself to death, but not this, not— He should be grateful, but he only felt confused—and angry. He'd recognized the gravity of the injury, but how dare they take his leg without his knowledge, without his consent?

Gentry broke down, sobs shaking her. "I'm so sorry."

He dragged his stare from the stump to her face and squeezed her hand until it hurt. "Stop it."

She blinked.

"You're not in control." He swallowed hard. This wasn't Gentry's fault, whatever part she'd played. But where to lay the blame?

A nurse came in with a thin, sallow man. Rob pulled up inside himself like a child expecting a blow, his mind pinging on the truth and retreating, his body in full-surge denial. He even found the pain, pain he'd known in the cave, the deep, throbbing ache down his shin. How could it be there if the leg was not?

"I'm Dr. Long, the surgeon in charge of your care."

The heaviness in his chest and a smothering weakness muted any response.

"As Ms. Fox may have told you, your leg was infected and had to be removed." The doctor shifted from foot to foot, a motion so automatic the man could not realize the effect it was having. Foot . . . to foot. "As you can probably tell, we're still fighting the systemic infection. Although this is a shock, you need to be careful to not overexert."

Overexert? Over— What did the doctor think he could do? Hike the world, ascend its peaks? The man grew blurry, the lines of his face melting with his words. Rob wanted to sleep. Sleep and forget this nightmare. He wanted them all to disappear, leave him alone—as in the cave? Yes, even that. In there he had hope. Not this warped reality. He wanted to forget, wanted to . . . sleep. Sleep and forget. Forget.

~~

Walking through the tropical landscaping outside the hospital, Gentry pressed her face into her hands. Soul-quaking sorrow burrowed deep inside her, sorrow beyond tears. Now that Uncle Rob knew what she had done to him, nothing would be the same. *Why?*

Why hadn't God healed him? He could do anything. As Okelani said, he'd poured out the world; why could he not stop the infection in her uncle's leg? Bathed in sunshine, she could not purge the gloom from her mind. Bright, glorious blossoms glowed along the paths, yet she could only see the horror on her uncle's face. If she had not been so selfish, if she'd not been a coward, hadn't resisted when Cameron and Nica said go to the police—

Her phone played "The Entertainer," a ring she hadn't heard for a while and one she wasn't sure she should answer. But she took it from her purse and said, "Hello?"

"Gentry, I just heard. I'm so sorry."

She didn't ask how Helen had heard. Since she had humored Darla with a personal appearance for the press between Uncle Rob's first waking and the next, everyone had now heard that the uncle she'd forgotten had lost his leg. She had hoped that telling the awful truth herself might soften their fangs, and the mood had been subdued, conciliatory. Why now, when she so didn't deserve it?

"He's not doing too well. His fever's still high." Her throat clenched. "I'm so afraid he won't fight." She hadn't intended to say that, to Helen of all people. Once, maybe. But now . . .

"Oh, Gentry. I know how you're feeling. But you can't blame yourself."

Can't? A gush of memories filled her gloom, Helen's blame and disappointment. She had believed—*Don't. Don't add on.* Helen had been her best friend, and she was calling as a friend now. Of course she knew how she felt. Who better? "Thanks, Helen." Silence pulled between them. Gentry said, "How's the troupe?"

"Not as fun without you."

That surprised her. She'd expected Helen to say how well she was managing it, how great the kids were, what a good decision they'd made to separate.

"Are you doing okay?" Helen asked.

Gentry slid her fingers into her hair. "I guess. Still have a hole in my memory." The hole that had cost Uncle Rob his leg.

"But your head is okay?"

Gentry laughed. "As okay as before."

Helen laughed too. Oh, if she could cut-print the moment. A simple laugh with an old friend. How good it felt.

"Rumor has it you've been offered another part. With Alec Warner."

Gentry let the breeze take her hair and cool her face. Darla had been adamant she drop enough hints to titillate the reporters. A diversion from the present fiasco to future success. "It's on the table. Dave's handling it."

"It's really happening for you, isn't it." She couldn't hide the hurt in her voice.

Gentry cleared the hurt from her own. "It looks that way. All the publicity—Helen, it's insane."

"You can handle it."

"I don't know. I truly don't. I mean, if it's this bad after one part . . ."

"You were fantastic." Now her sincerity came through.

"Thank you." She swallowed. "You would have been too."

Helen sniffed. "I didn't have what they were looking for."

She was too pretty for the part in *Steel*. Helen needed a lead in a romantic comedy, not a gutsy girl taking a stand.

"Pete took one look at you and . . ." Helen's voice trailed off.

"Strange since you're totally the pretty one."

They laughed, but they'd watched it play out party after party. Helen drew guys over, but they'd end up engrossed in Gentry Fox. The memory had a bittersweet tang. "Go figure, " Gentry mused. And then a thought crept in. "You know, Helen, there might be a part for you."

The other side went silent.

"Um . . . earth to Helen."

"You mean you'd get me a reading? Put it in your contract? *I can only accept if my friend Helen—*" The nasal tone of her voice made them both laugh.

"I mean it. There's no reason you shouldn't read for a part."

"There's the troupe."

"We can skip a season."

"Season?" Helen snorted.

"You know what I mean. Think about it. I promise not to do anything scandalous." Wrong thing to say, obviously.

Helen cleared her throat. "Well, I just wanted to say how sorry I am about Uncle Rob."

Grief smothered Gentry again. "Thanks."

They hung up and she released a long sigh. For a while there, things had felt right. She crossed her arms and rocked. But how could they? *All things are possible with God.* How easy to think it. A great Pollyanna platitude that paled beside Cameron's assertion. Hope didn't keep its promise.

TWENTY-TWO

Cameron had used his resources and called in a few favors to get the information that brought him to the duplex in the less-than-affluent L.A. suburb. The cool summer evening did little to cheer the dried-out strip of yard and rubbish stacked along the cracked driveway. The place had an unwholesome quality enhanced by what he'd learned of its residents.

He went to the door and rang, guessing he'd timed it right to see the kid alone. Happy hour raised his odds. The young man who opened it was taller and heavier than the pictures in the papers, but he was half a year older and hopefully wiser. Recognition hit him too.

"Hey, Troy. Cameron Pierce." He extended his hand.

"What do you want?" The kid didn't join the handshake.

"Thought we might chat."

"About what?"

Cameron hooked his thumbs into the belt loops of his khaki slacks. "A mutual friend."

Troy looked past him as though Gentry might be there in his truck. "I don't know what you're talking about."

"I think you do." Cameron slipped the Baggie that held the note and photos from his shirt pocket. He'd taped paper over the pictures and labeled them Exhibits 1 and 2. "Do you know perpetrating a fraud is a crime punishable by law?"

"I don't—"

"Doctored photos, come on." He hadn't brought them to a lab, but Troy didn't know that. "They're not even good fakes."

"I didn't take those."

"And that note. You're saying you didn't write it?"

He started to turn away.

"You don't care if Gentry and I continue our affair?"

Fire flashed in his eyes. "She denied it. I read it in the paper."

"Yeah, well, she denied yours too."

His hands clenched.

"But that's not really the point. The fact is, you've given me everything I need to prove you were lying—both times." He flapped the photos. "These are so clearly manufactured, no one will believe anything you said before. Pretty much kills your mom's lawsuit."

Troy's jaw muscles rippled.

"Add that to the lies you told before, all the man-hours the police spent investigating and Gentry's expense refuting it, not to mention damage to her reputation. Gonna be a lot of flack flying your way."

"I didn't make the stupid pictures."

"You mean take?"

The kid rocked back on his heels.

Cameron pressed. "Which is it—take or make? Hard to keep the story straight, isn't it. That's what tripped you up before, why the police failed to believe your so-called evidence. They'll tear you up on the witness stand when this goes to court."

He flicked the tawny hair from his darting eyes.

"I know you didn't take the pictures. You're standing in one of them. But, hey, there's a lot you can do with Photoshop. You good with computers?"

"It wasn't my idea."

He digested that. "Not your idea, but you went with it?"

Troy didn't answer.

"She suggested you use the photos to break us up, didn't she."

"Who . . . what are you . . ." The boy clenched his teeth. "I don't have to talk to you."

"It's me or the police."

Troy's brows pinched. "I didn't do anything."

"You know what I think? This was a test. If Gentry was scared enough to cut things off with me, then next time she might pay to keep it quiet."

"I don't care about her money. I care—"

"About her? Funny way to show it."

His face flamed, but he didn't break. "You don't know anything about it."

He wished that were true. "I know what it's like to get caught up in your feelings, to want something so much you'll risk more and more, maybe listen to someone who ought to know better. Someone you want to trust."

Troy sagged against the doorjamb, looking away to keep back the tears.

"Your mom's done time for embezzlement. It's not that big a step to blackmail."

"She doesn't even know Gentry."

"But she knows you, your feelings for Gentry. If the tabloids get hold of fresh evidence, the story's hot news again. Guess she forgot how hard it was for you when things got out of control."

His eyes hardened. "What else is new?"

"You stopped her the first time, didn't you. By going to the tabloids. When she saw your infatuation, all the pictures on your walls, she threatened to sue Gentry for causing pain and suffering to a minor. She knew it would settle out of court. She'd get lots of money. She's done it before. But you resented being used. You didn't want Gentry hurt; you wanted her to care. So you went public, let the whole world know how you felt about Gentry Fox. You'd save her and win her all at the same time. Not your fault it didn't work out that way."

Troy dropped his chin.

"Now here we are again. Your mom's found a new angle. This time you were mad enough about me to go along."

Troy's jaw cocked.

"We can trace the e-mail back from Bette Walden to the source."

"Who's Bette Walden?"

"Come on, Troy."

The kid looked him hard in the face. "I don't know who Bette Walden is." Hope flickered in his eyes that maybe he'd been scammed.

"Then who'd you send the file to?"

"Why should I tell you?" His lip snarled. "Gentry's lover."

Cameron expelled a slow breath and studied the youth. "Because maybe you do care about her. And you shouldn't believe what you read. People will say anything."

Their gazes locked. Troy wet his lips. "I sent it to the person who helped me the first time."

Cameron waited.

"To Helen. She was supposed to send them to Gentry. I don't know that Bette person."

"I need that file."

"Are you going to the cops?"

"Let's just say it's insurance. Against any future harassment."

Troy nodded and led him inside. He accessed his mother's computer and copied the file of the photos that had been combined to create the prints.

Relieved, Cameron tucked the CD into his pocket with the prints Bette had made. "You know, Troy, I think you've got a future."

"Gentry used to say God knows the plans he has for me, plans for good, not harm." He frowned. "I'm not sure that's true anymore."

Cameron landed squarely in his own doubts about God's plans. "Well, it's a coordinated effort. You can only do your part."

The side of Troy's mouth pulled. "Guess this is a start."

Cameron nodded. "Quite a start."

⌢

Anger surged, fever feeding fear. Rob wanted to split open his body and get out, just get out. He had lingered long in the corridors of confusion, but now knowledge burned into his mind, pumped his sluggish heart in a chest of mud. If he opened his eyes they would see a stump, a useless half leg.

Eyes closed, he remembered running track—that moment of release when he launched himself over the hurdle, then landed with fleet feet, bursting on to the next barrier and surmounting it. His strength resisting even the gravity that might hold him down. That was his life, his essence. Soaring over the roadblocks, the pitfalls. Finding the way and . . . and now . . .

He clenched his hands. Days of praise in that pit of darkness turned to ash. God had not played fair. Rob shuddered. What had he done, or not done, to deserve this? He'd changed his life, given everything to the Savior he trusted. And this was his reward?

No wonder so few made the effort. He grappled with the disillusionment, and fresh anger stirred. How had he failed—what detail had he overlooked? If you do not do thus and so, you will never walk on two legs again. Why? Why. . . .

He opened his eyes to the half-light of a hospital night, turned his head on the thin pillow. Gentry slept in the chair beside him, her face drawn, even in slumber. He knew her pain and regret, but it was swallowed by his encompassing anger. Why hadn't she gone at once for help? Even if she hadn't known—

Again anger shielded the hurt. He had sung and glorified the Lord, trusting . . . trusting. And God had betrayed and abandoned him. The ache of separation seized him, even as he recognized that he was the one pulling away. He groaned, not wanting to see this for what it was. A setback. A hurdle. An opportunity.

My son, my beloved . . .

No! He didn't want to be called on. He'd done enough. His experience of Christ had been so real, so personal. He'd given everything, lost . . . so much. Tears stung his eyes. Again he groaned. What had believing brought but pain and loss. Aching loss.

Gentry stirred. He willed her back to sleep, but she opened her eyes.

"Uncle Rob?" her whisper thick with worry. "Are you in pain?"

Couldn't she see the flames? "Yes." Numb it. Kill it. Silence it. She pressed the button for the nurse.

Silence Him.

Rob sank back in the bed. Silence. Dark, empty silence.

⌒

Cameron opened the paper to Gentry's face. A side column, but front-page nonetheless. Unlike the previous drivel, the article had a sympathetic tone: *Beleaguered Film Star Faces New Shock As Uncle Loses Leg.* Her sorrow and self-condemnation must be extreme, but she'd cope. If there was any quit in her, he hadn't seen it.

And his news would help. With the disk in his possession, any further attempts at blackmail would land Troy's mother back in jail. One down, half a million to go. It was too much to expect that people would stop taking shots at Gentry. She'd chosen the high profile, but he'd shielded her this time. He could rest easy in that.

He tossed the paper aside and booted the computer. He had plenty of things to nail down for other cases, plenty to keep his thoughts far from the woman who'd touched something he'd buried deep inside him. Mercifully, there'd been no time for it to develop.

He forked both hands into his hair and leaned back in his ergonomic chair, chosen to minimize the lower-back pain from a surfing injury. Not bad enough to keep him off his board, but bad enough to need to sit right when he worked.

Things had gotten so crazy with Gentry, he'd only surfed once on Kauai, the morning he'd startled her on the lanai. Why was every moment as crisp as Kodak? He closed his eyes and pictured her, then jerked them open and shook his head. He typed his password and brought up the Ponzi scheme he'd be reporting on for the FBI. He'd have to testify when it went to trial and made sure now that everything was documented and in order. Then he processed his bill.

Opening the file for the whiplash insurance fraud, he thought of the Jeep on Kauai. They'd recover it as soon as Robert Fox could tell them where. He pictured the battered man they'd taken from the cave, fevered, delirious, with a mangled leg. He sat back and steepled his fingers against his mustache. If he had forced Gentry to talk to TJ after seeing the doctor, would that one day have made a difference?

He ran his fingers down the line of his beard. Hindsight was lethal. It could kill confidence. But what had happened? There had to be more to it than Gentry remembered.

Maybe he should have focused there and let the pictures wait. Even though it had seemed like a cold trail, he might have found something. People didn't realize how much they left behind for someone like him to follow. But he hadn't been hired or even asked. If a crime had been committed the police would pursue it. He'd done what Nica asked and more.

So why did it nag him still? He sat back in his chair and sighed.

Gentry sat with her face in her hands, glad that Uncle Rob slept. With the fever broken, he could begin to heal. The leg had been killing him, but now she could see strength returning. Even so, every time she looked at the stump where his strong leg used to be, guilt crushed her. Her pride, her self-preservation, and stubbornness had caused his loss. And it hurt.

She looked up when Darla came in. This was not the time for another battle, but for once Darla didn't stalk in like a commando. She held out a stack of publications and smiled. "You did it."

Gentry looked down at the papers, mystified.

"You won them over. Next time they'll be eating out of your hand."

"I sincerely hope there's no next time."

Darla arched a brow. "There will be. And soon you'll hope *for* it." She leaned against the window seat. "You're a real person now, not just some actor on the screen. They want to know about you, connect with you—Gentry Fox, not just the part you play."

The thought was surprisingly intoxicating. After all the negative press, the idea that people wanted to know the truth about her soothed the wound. She returned Darla's smile. "Thanks."

Darla shrugged. "It's what you pay me for."

"Sorry I wasn't cooperative."

Darla cocked her head. "Next time you'll know better."

Next time. Darla was right. If she stayed in the industry, this would always be a factor. Her movie with Alec, if it happened, would be a giant step up—pass Go, collect $200. Was she ready for that kind of attention, when just the thought of publicity had kept her from getting help?

"Jett and I are flying back today. I trust you'll avoid further catastrophe?"

Gentry shrugged. She'd learned not to make promises she couldn't keep.

Darla rolled her eyes. "Touch in when you get back. I want to keep ahead of this thing with Alec."

"Okay."

When Darla went out, Gentry turned back to her uncle. Something in his position suggested wakefulness, though his eyes stayed closed. Avoiding her? She understood. As much as she wanted to talk to him, she didn't know what to say. She stood and paced the room.

While her night of struggle had prepared her to accept whatever happened, it hadn't told her how to handle it. Uncle Rob was alive, and she was deeply grateful for that, but the burden of his injury took a toll.

As Nica said, gifts came with trials. She folded her hands under her chin and closed her eyes. Instead of telling God what she needed, she asked for the strength and wisdom to deal with this and to know how to support Uncle Rob. "Your grace is sufficient, Lord. Be his strength and courage. Surround him with your love."

Persistent and irrepressible. Rob recognized the traits he'd fostered. How often he'd imagined Gentry his own daughter, loved her as his own—and she'd forgotten him. He'd jumped in to save her, and she'd left him alone, battered. And now maimed.

He couldn't blame her, but he did. He shouldn't blame God, but he did. He blamed himself for blindly believing. If he hadn't trusted so completely, he wouldn't be so completely disappointed. Where was the grace in that?

The only good thing he could find was that Allegra wasn't there to see. It had ripped him apart when she left, but now it was a blessing, one of the crumbs that led to false expectation. Treacherous tidbits of hope.

Gentry bent and kissed his cheek. She murmured, "I'll be back in the morning."

Yes. Go. Leave me alone.

The halls grew still; the lights went down. As night came on, other thoughts loomed, thoughts he'd carried with him from the cave, an infection of the spirit. While Gentry had sat beside him he'd kept his eyes closed, feigning sleep. He hadn't wanted conversation. But she'd employed something far more devastating—prayer. Didn't she see how it stoked the fires?

She was gone now, her prayers wafting away, filtered through the air ducts into particles of nothing. He was alone. Alone.

"If I make my bed in the depths, you are there."

No.

"Your right hand will hold me fast."

He groaned, wishing he had not impressed the words on his mind.

"You hem me in—behind and before; you have laid your hand upon me."

"Lord," he groaned, and tears slipped from his eyes.

"All the days ordained for me were written in your book before one of them came to be."

And what happened in each of those days was for the Lord to decide; his to determine whether Robert Fox walked on one leg or two. He had snatched him from the cave and breathed life back into his body. Now God desired to resuscitate his soul.

Wherever he went, however great his resistance, the Lord would pursue him. Humility and unworthiness settled on him like the mist. Who was he to question what the Lord chose for him? Did he know more than God? Did he think, like Job, he could interrogate the Creator of all things, demand an accounting? He was nothing, and yet the Lord had plucked him from the pit. Gratitude rushed in, and praise tumbled from his lips.

TWENTY-THREE

The stain would not come off. She stood in white, yards and yards of satin and toile, but the stain would not come off the bodice. The more she rubbed, the more it spread. She needed to get it off before anyone saw, but when she took a step, she found the floor thick with garbage.

She grabbed up her skirts, pulling in the train, foul with slime and rancid food. Her hands grew slick and putrid, but still she pulled and gathered the fabric into her arms. The miasmic odor cloyed. She gripped and pulled, armful after armful of rotting lace until her own vomit coursed down the front of her.

Allegra opened her eyes, surprised her spasming stomach had not actually spilled its contents. The white hotel sheets gathering like pursed lips into the depression made by the man who should not be there. Bronze and golden, Curt lay like a burnished treasure half buried in sand.

With the vigor and glow of a lesser decade, he slept unknowing, while she slipped from the sheets. His rum-fed slumber cradled him through her hasty dressing, stealthy packing, and silent departure. The message of her dream was clear. She'd tried so hard, rubbed and scrubbed until the outside looked, sounded, and seemed like class, but deep inside she was trash.

She'd taken the girl from the trailer, but she'd never get the trailer out of the girl. It had only been a matter of time before it showed. As she waited for the elevator, her hands rubbed each other with Macbethian persistence.

⌒

Rob awakened without protest when the nurse came in the next morning. In place of the thorough but taciturn woman of the previous days was a husky guy with a blond ponytail and freckles so thick he looked tan. His name tag read Paul.

"You're my nurse?"

"And drill sergeant, otherwise known as physical therapist. You been lying around long enough, and Hawaii or not, vacation's over." The man had the build of a linebacker, the hands of a meat-packer. He cracked jokes while removing the catheter. Had to be sent from God.

He assembled a plastic thing with a hose and said, "I need you to breathe hard into this to clear the gunk from your lungs, cuz they're awful swampy in there, and that ain't good."

No, swampy lungs were not good. He'd always had superb cardiovascular health, and he could feel the difference, like breathing through sludge.

He did his best with the machine, but the nurse looked at his results and shook his head. "That's it?"

Rob scowled.

"Every thirty minutes give it another suck 'til you can get it up to here."

"Okay." Rob eyed the hosed contraption, wondering if it was rigged like a carnival hammer that never reached the bell until someone released the lever.

"Now, here's the deal. The sooner you're up on that leg, the better it heals." He called it a leg, not a stump. "We gotta shrink it down; that's why it's wrapped in that elastic." He spread his palm over the wrapping with no hint of repugnance. "They'll probably transfer you to be fitted with a permanent prosthesis, but soon as you're ready, we'll get you started with some standing and balancing exercises. Nothing on the tightrope right away, though."

If Paul had come in the midst of the black funk, it would have seemed cruel. Now his humor took the edge off. Rob had released the rage, but he was still raw with fear and uncertainty. What would life look like? How would he do it?

By the time Paul had bathed him and assisted his toothbrushing and shave, fear had become a shadow in the corner, waiting for weariness or discouragement to lure it back out. He'd do his best to keep it there.

Paul made him suck the float up the tube again, then shook his head. "Maybe I better get you the kiddie unit."

"Maybe you'd better—" Rob tugged the sheet over just as Gentry arrived. The hesitance in her step cut him to the heart. Was she repelled by shame, or him? Would this form a wedge between them, the elephant in the room their relationship would skirt until it gave up finding a way around?

As Paul gathered rubbish from the small table, he caught sight of her and stopped moving. He'd pushed and bullied as though he ran the world, but as Gentry approached, he went stock-still. She reached the bed and smiled. Rob had never enjoyed a meltdown so much.

She held out her hand. "I'm Gentry."

Paul detached his hand from the rail and took hers. "You're better looking than the papers make you."

"They try for my worst moments."

"You look pretty good on the page, but rounded out ..." He waved the hand that held the trash, realized he still had hold of her, and let go.

She smiled. "Taking care of my uncle?"

Paul looked down at him. "Yeah. Uh, trying."

Trying? After the diatribe he'd had to endure about not trying hard enough? Oh, did he have ammunition now. And for a moment he stepped out of the dread. The little vignette had cheered him, the previous darkness exalting the lightness of the moment.

Paul obviously wanted to linger, but said, "I'll leave you two," and neither of them stopped him.

Gentry's eyes welled up. "Uncle Rob—"

"Gentry." He took her hand. The tears glistening in her eyes did not belong there, nor the weight of guilt on her soul. He had this chance, this moment to protect and define their future. To determine the tone, the target, the goal. He drew the strongest breath he had. "It's just another mountain."

On the lanai at Hale Kahili, joy welled up again. Overnight the man she knew and loved had surfaced. The balm of his forgiveness soothed her afresh.

"You can only do the best you can with what you have to work with."

He'd always told her that, expecting her best, but always within her ability. The first time they'd attempted Longs Peak in Colorado, she couldn't handle the ledges. The vertical drop had raced her heart and spun her head. Uncle Rob had tried to talk her through it, but when it came clear that she couldn't break through the fear, he'd commended her effort and begun the descent. The next time, she faced the ledges and the narrows and reached the summit.

Though she couldn't tell him what caused their accident, she had sat beside his bed and explained everything that had happened while he huddled in the cave, how she'd followed the stream to Nica and realized she'd lost her identity. She described her trek back in with Cameron and how they'd found the falls, the piece of netting that had told her he was there.

"So my little net caught something after all."

"Cameron searched the pool until he found the cave."

"That was God." He'd closed his eyes. "Not done with me yet."

"Not even close." She had squeezed his hand as he fell asleep.

Now, on the lanai, relief filled the places hollowed by worry. Uncle Rob had barely begun the fight ahead, but their relationship was intact.

"It's just another mountain." His words were a promise. He would take the challenge, face what came. And so would she.

The photos were a time bomb. She had awakened with sharp memories of the whole ordeal with Troy. How ironic that the improv skills she'd taught had been her undoing. Troy had a great talent for getting into character. He truly became the role he played. Maybe that explained his ability to create such a thorough delusion.

She'd stood up for him on *Oprah* even though he'd hurt her badly. As it turned out, his claims had given her the mystique of a woman enshrined in one troubled teen's mind. She'd run the gamut of public opinion from predator to goddess. The last thing she wanted was to churn up the speculation again.

Darla would be livid if the fake photos came out and she hadn't been told. Stomach clenching, Gentry stood up and looked over the rail to the flowering ginger garden. She drew in the fragrance, but no sweetness could mask the stench of those photos.

If he wanted, Cameron Pierce could sell the pictures to the highest bidder, saying truthfully that he'd received them from her. Why should she think he wouldn't? Longtime friends had done worse. Or one, at least.

She rubbed her forehead. She had no proof of that. The tabloids could have gotten the pictures . . . somewhere else. She hadn't asked, sparing Helen the pain of suspicion and herself of knowing for sure. If Helen had realized the boost of recognition the whole incident would cause, she'd never have done it. Or maybe she would—because she knew what Gentry really wanted; to use her talents to impact lives.

Impossible. Daniel, her almost fiancé, had rejected the possibility that anything but evil could come from an industry steeped in sin. He'd said before she changed anything, she'd be changed. Wherever he was now, he probably thanked the Lord they'd broken off before she dragged him down too.

But then there was Nica claiming she could reach millions, shining light into the kingdom of darkness. Shekina glory. Gentry cringed. If those pictures came out, her witness to anything higher, anything pure, would be destroyed.

She didn't pretend to be perfect. She had legitimate faults people could criticize and exploit. It was the lies that left her feeling helpless. How could she climb a mountain that didn't exist? That was what had left her exhausted, emotionally and spiritually, and why Uncle Rob had chosen Kauai and this particular rental.

Serenity and seclusion. He had known how badly she needed both, but he couldn't have known how good it had felt to forget altogether, to live as though no one knew her name or her face. To be Nica's friend Jade, to not wonder if Cameron saw her or some fantasy. She could kiss Officer Kanakanui for not having had a clue—but the tabloids would be all over that one, wouldn't they.

With a sigh, she yearned for a simple conversation, the kind friends had when they didn't have to worry they'd be overheard. Or betrayed. Longing squeezed her throat for just one person to share Uncle Rob's progress with. On impulse, she took her cell phone from her pocket and placed a call. Monica answered on the second ring. "Nica, this is Gentry."

"How are you? How's your uncle?"

She filled her in, and it felt so good to share the news that she went one step further. "Would you like to come over this evening?" Why did she feel so vulnerable? It was a simple invitation.

"I'm so sorry, but I'm meeting TJ at Choy's."

"Oh." So she hadn't imagined that dynamic, but it had become evident.

"You could join us there."

Gentry leaned on the banister. "A third wheel?"

"We'd love it. TJ was just asking about you."

"He needs his report."

Nica laughed. "He would like to know what happened."

"Uncle Rob told the police where to find the Jeep and traced our route as well as he could from a hospital bed." He had gotten directions from a local, as she'd guessed, but he didn't know what caused the accident. He'd only seen her fall. "Anyway, I don't want to intrude on your date."

Nica laughed. "TJ Kanakanui's had fourteen years to light a fire. What's one evening more or less? Besides, I want to tell you something."

She wavered between a companionable night with Nica and TJ's possible interrogation.

"TJ's finishing some paperwork. The way he procrastinates, it could take a while."

She bit her lip. "Okay. If you're sure."

"Gentry, I'm sure."

She hung up in a surprisingly buoyant mood. What were the chances it would last?

⌇

Nica turned down the high crooning of IZ's *In Dis Life* as Gentry slid into her car, looking less harried than she'd been. It still seemed impossible to think of her in Hollywood terms. She was Jade in the ways that mattered. "I'm glad you're coming."

Gentry settled into the seat. "I'm sure Officer Kanakanui will be less so."

Nica laughed. "If he's upset, it'll take a year or two for him to realize it."

Gentry clipped the seat belt. "I didn't know you were together."

"We weren't, aren't . . . Actually, with TJ it's like interpreting the clouds."

Gentry raised her brows. "Interpreting . . ."

"An ancient Hawaiian skill. Is it simply *ao*, which means cloud, or *aokū*, dark with rain, or *ao pōpolohua*, purplish cloud. TJ expects me to see with Okelani's eyes and know what he thinks but won't say, what he feels but won't admit."

As they reached the end of the private drive, Gentry turned abruptly from the window.

"Is something wrong?" Then she saw the white compact near the hedge with a single driver, camera raised.

"Just your friendly neighborhood paparazzi." Gentry expelled a breath. "He'll follow us."

That rudeness violated *aloha*. "I'm not sure I can elude him between here and Choy's."

"Just don't give him a clear shot of your face, or Cameron'll kill me."

Nica pulled onto the highway. "Kai's protective, not homicidal."

"That could change if you're plastered on next week's tabloids."

The thought sank in, and Nica shuddered. "It's not right."

"Would you rather take me back?"

She shook her head. "I meant for you, for anyone."

"As Cameron said, I chose the limelight. But you didn't." She put a hand to her cheek as the compact angled for position around a turn.

"Kai doesn't—"

"He was explicit. He doesn't want you bothered." Gentry faced her. "You should take me back."

"No. He's not going to spoil our evening."

"Cameron or the photographer?"

Nica laughed. "Kai means well."

"I know. That's why I don't want anything to happen."

Nica turned into the small lot outside Choy's and parked. "If this photographer continues his rudeness, Pele will show up and singe him."

As far as she could tell, Pele didn't make an appearance, so Gentry positioned herself between the photographer and Nica, who shrank naturally from the attention. She was just going to a restaurant with a friend, but Cameron had been adamant. At the door, she allowed the guy a face shot while Nica slipped inside, then stepped in herself.

Despite the balmy trade winds wafting through the open side windows, the piquant aromas of Choy's savory fare filled the room they entered. The space was cluttered with black enamel tables and red vinyl chairs. White silk banners hanging from the ceiling flapped airily, and Oriental music twanged over a grainy sound system.

She didn't miss the stares and comments, but no one asked for an autograph as they found a table.

Nica scooted her chair in under the table. "Do you think he'll wait? That cameraman?"

Gentry took her own place. "He's probably perched outside with his telephoto, hoping to catch me with sweet-and-sour sauce dribbling down my chin. 'Gentry Fox drinks latest victim's blood.'"

Nica's eyes widened.

"Open to interpretation, of course. I might have a bleeding disorder with only days to live." At Nica's troubled sigh, Gentry smiled. "It's okay. Really." She glanced around the simple square room. "You picked a good place. Not too many hiding spots."

"TJ picked it. I wish he'd get here."

Gentry tried to share her enthusiasm. The waitress brought them water, and they told her they'd wait to order when their other member arrived.

Nica sipped. "I had an interesting thing happen at the nursing home today. One of the residents saw your picture in the paper and said, 'Isn't it nice she has such a strong angel watching over her?'"

Gentry puzzled that a moment. "Meaning Cameron?"

"No." Nica reached into her purse and took out the photo from the local paper, taken during the interview Darla had arranged. She laid it flat on the table and pointed to a blur in the corner. "Right here."

Gentry frowned. "That's . . . an angel?"

"According to Gayle Falstaff." Nica looked up. "She was adamant."

"Is she . . ." How to say it kindly?

"Senile?" Nica shook her head. "She's one of the sharper ones."

Gentry stared at the picture again, not sure what to make of it.

Nica leaned back. "Kai thinks you have divine protection."

Gentry shook her head. "The centipede?"

"And the falls."

She looked at the photo. Intellectually she believed in angels. But this . . . "Why me and not Uncle Rob?"

Nica searched her face. "Not your uncle? Gentry, he hit the rocks and lived. And what were the chances Cameron would find that lava tube?"

Gentry released a slow breath. How easily she limited God, focused on what he hadn't done, instead of all he had. "I can't see an angel there, but . . ."

Nica fixed her with a deep gray gaze. "When you came, I thought you'd bring me grief. Most of those who find me—"

"Find you?"

Nica nodded. "I don't ask how or where they get my name. Most are past any help except love and understanding for their last days." She dropped her gaze. "Someone I'd cared for had just died, and . . . I was raw."

Gentry's heart sank. "I'm so sorry. If I'd known . . ."

"I wished you hadn't come. But I knew if Jesus brought you to my door, there had to be a reason."

Gentry didn't know what to say.

"I'd started having nightmares, seeing all the people who had died. I felt like the angel of death and thought you were one more face to haunt my dreams."

"But you took me in."

"And I haven't dreamed of the dead since."

This had to be the strangest conversation she'd ever had.

"I'd been pulling away from people I loved because I couldn't take any more. The night you came, I had prayed for the Lord to take me instead."

Her breath suspended. "Does Cameron know?"

Nica shook her head. "Please don't tell him. Besides, everything's changed."

"How?"

Nica tucked a strand of hair behind her ear. "I think because I was willing, even when I had nothing left to give, Jesus brought me a gift instead of a burden."

"Nica—"

She laughed. "I know it sounds crazy. But I don't know how else to explain the joy I've found."

"I haven't done anything. It's been you and Cameron helping me."

"Well, maybe that's how it works." Her eyes moistened. "Thank you for landing in my yard."

The door opened, and they checked for TJ, but it was a Hawaiian bigger than TJ who headed for a stool at the bar. Gentry started to turn away, but as he took a seat and rested his fists on the bar, her glance caught on his hammy arm and the red-and-black dragon running down it.

Dizziness seized her. She clutched the edge of the table, felt herself falling, falling . . .

"Gentry?"

"I need to use the rest room."

Nica's quizzical gaze followed as she wove through the tables. At the curtained entrance to the rest rooms, she raised her phone and took a picture. The guy half turned, and she ducked behind the curtain, breathing hard. Was she out of her mind? She moved down the narrow hall into the bathroom and phoned Cameron.

"Pierce," he almost barked.

"Cameron? It's Gentry."

"Hold on a minute." She heard a motor gear down, then he came back on. "Gentry, what's up?"

She drew a shaky breath. "I found the dragon."

He waited a beat. "Talk to me."

"I took a picture. I'll send it." She put him on hold and accessed the function that sent the photo to Cameron's phone, then brought him back.

"A tattoo? You're sure that's the dragon you saw?"

"I'm not sure of anything. I just had a feeling when I saw it." A debilitating, head-spinning feeling. "I'm at Choy's with Nica. The guy came in, and I saw it, and . . . something feels wrong."

"Can he see you now?"

"I'm in the ladies' room."

"I'd tell you to wait until I got there, but I'm two thousand miles away."

"I know. I'm sorry. But you said to call." Taking the picture and calling had been knee-jerk reactions. What could he possibly do?

He released a slow breath. "Let's assume he knows who you are."

"Likely assumption." Even if he had nothing to do with anything else.

"Does he know you recognize him?"

"I don't. If it weren't for the tattoo, I wouldn't have looked twice."

"Okay, listen." His voice took authority. "If he saw you take out your phone, let him think you were only making this call."

"Okay."

"I want you to keep talking and go back out. Don't even glance his way. And act like you're enjoying the conversation."

"Sounds like stage direction."

"Play it."

Laughing softly, she opened the bathroom door, stepped out and gasped. He was coming toward her, all but filling the hallway. She had less than a second to slip into character. "No, really. So close I could touch it. You know how dangerous that would be."

"He's there?"

"Would I lie?" She pressed into the wall so they could pass each other, but the guy didn't do the same, just stood with his stare fixed on her face.

Play the part. "Listen, honey, I better get back to the table. Nica's waiting."

"Don't hang up."

"Love you too. Bye." She closed her phone and slid it into her pocket. "Excuse me." For a moment she thought he would pin her into the wall.

"Gentry?" TJ Kanakanui came up behind the dragon man in his Kauai PD uniform, with side arm and cuffs.

"Oh good, you're here. I'm starved." Nica might have sent him after her, but his expression didn't show whether he'd expected trouble or just wanted to eat. The man turned to let her pass. Her heart pounded so hard as she squeezed by that she was sure the tattooed Hawaiian would hear it. He went into the door marked *Kane*. She had hardly cleared the curtain when her phone rang.

Cameron's pulse raced. The second she answered, he snapped, "Do you understand *don't*?"

"It's all right; TJ is here."

He expelled a breath. "Let me talk to him."

When TJ came on, Cameron said, "TJ, that moke in the hallway?"

"Yeah?"

"Take him in for questioning."

"For what?"

Good question. "Gentry recognized his tattoo. I think he's involved with whatever happened to them."

"I nevah can take him in cuz you tink something."

"He might be the local who sent them out there. Get him."

"What charge? Bad directions?"

A lowly patrolman, TJ Kanakanui was most often on traffic detail. He was no detective, and there was no evidence of a crime. Cameron clenched his jaw. If he were there they could hammer out a strategy. He could question the guy without the formalities that bound an officer of the law. But he wasn't there. He tried again. "What if it wasn't an accident? Okelani sensed malice."

"Sorry, brah. Not enough."

Cameron scowled. "What was he doing in the hall?"

"Going to the john."

He expelled a breath. "Just find out who he is, okay?"

"I know who he is. Glenn Malakua's cousin."

Cameron gripped his hair. "Then talk to him!"

"No can."

"Why not?"

"I wen put Malakua in jail when he wale on his wife."

"Great." He dropped his hand. "Help me out here, TJ."

"I keep one eye on Gentry. Das all. Now gotta go." TJ hung up.

Cameron stared at the picture Gentry had sent. The guy was big and gnarly. Picturing him with Gentry in the little hallway at Choy's made his skin crawl. Had she been scared? He wished he hadn't told her to pretend. She was too good an actor. His throat squeezed. *"Love you too?"* He dragged his hand over his beard and frowned.

What was going on in his head? Potential? He could strangle Myra for planting the thought, except she'd only reported what she saw. Even though his only intention had been to protect Nica from another heartache, something had crackled between him and Gentry like sheet lightning.

He wanted no part of her life, and had no room for anyone in his. But that didn't stop potential from working on him like acid eating away the rust and corruption of the last time.

TWENTY-FOUR

As she strolled Hale Kahili's private beach the next morning, Gentry pondered her encounter with the dragon man. She had told TJ that she recognized the tattoo, but had not mentioned the feelings it churned. He'd been unimpressed by her hunch the last time, and it was possible she'd overreacted in the hallway. With the sand shifting under her feet and the rhythmic *whoosh* of the waves in her ears, she tried to shake off her unease and relax.

A lot had happened, and she needed to find her balance. Alone on the little beach, she turned her thoughts to Nica's angel theory. She'd shared it with her uncle and now recalled the warmth of that moment. How he'd beamed. *"I knew there was something about you."*

The wind ruffled her hair with caressing fingers, and she took in the beauty of the golden sand licked by the frothy surf, fringed by lush, blooming foliage. A few lanky palms stretched up under the noon sun, ruffled by the breeze. Though it was a different beach from where she'd met Mai-Tai Sam, she recalled that evening—how frightened and confused she'd been, seeking recognition, wanting to be known, and yet afraid of what she'd find.

Without memory, what had remained were the pillars of her personality; hope and perseverance. She'd been foolish, stubborn, and self-protecting. But Nica had convinced her she was part of something bigger and more real. Something eternal. She stopped walking and watched the waves. They no longer looked lost or forgetful. They simply followed the eternal pattern designed for them.

She drew in the salt scent and wondered at the pattern of her life. From the time she could talk, she'd parroted lines beyond her understanding, sensing a drama to life that had to be presented. Her sisters, ten and six years older, had paraded her around like a performing doll, and she could still remember the smiles and hands clapping. Nothing except her adventures with Uncle Rob had ever come close to her calling in the dramatic arts.

She had played in a number of stage and TV productions, but when nothing seemed to come of it, she'd thrown her energies into the troupe. Having Act Out recognized as a valuable resource in the community, working with the kids, was incredibly rewarding. But the joy of acting, of leaving herself and becoming someone new, speaking not as Gentry Fox but as Cosette or Dulcinea or Ilsa remained. And when the part in *Steel* came without her trying, she had known it was God.

She reached the line of wet sand, slipped off her sandals and stepped closer to the foamy surf that wrapped itself around her feet and ankles, a cool rush that pulled the sand out from under her heels. Rainbows rose up from a shimmering tide pool at the black stony edge of the shore. She smiled and raised her face to the sun's rays. The warmth sank into her cheeks as if they were butter. Was it foolish to believe the storm had passed?

Cameron hadn't told her whether he'd taken care of things as he'd promised. There hadn't been a chance to discuss it. But the concern in his voice had stayed with her. It triggered memories of their time in the mountains—his fingers brushing her arm in disbelief, his yielding to her choice of path, his strong arm in the rushing water.

Because of Uncle Rob, she measured men by the way they handled a mountain. It didn't have to be a geological slope, though. One guy had needed to crest every intellectual peak. While she'd been attracted to his widespread knowledge, his egotistical delivery grew thin fast. Someone who had to constantly air his vocabulary wasn't much fun to talk to.

There'd been those determined to surmount her resistance and conquer her virtue. And then there was Daniel—her spiritual superior—more rigid and experienced in faith, styled perhaps for his namesake, the prophet. He'd answered her questions with the patience of a parent, giving her only what he believed she could handle. Daniel had subtly revealed his maturity and wisdom. She had only to trust in him. No wonder she'd fashioned a Santa Claus God.

A rooster strutted across the sand, raised his head and crowed. Smiling, she remembered Cameron saying they had no barnyard manners. Unlike this feathered popinjay, he hadn't tried to impress her. No boasting. No list of achievements. She knew almost nothing about him. Yet in the Hanalei Mountains, she and Cameron had found a natural partnership. Pushing the limits of their strength and experience, they'd become a team. He hadn't held her back until they reached the pool where he thought they might find her uncle's dead body.

But that was before she'd become Gentry Fox, and the mountains a piece out of time.

The phone rang in her pocket, Nica calling to say they were on their way. Gentry had laughed when Nica invited her to TJ's sister's baby luau. Since Uncle Rob's therapy took most of the afternoon, a baby luau had sounded like something she shouldn't miss. And TJ didn't seem to mind her tagging along.

She started up the ginger- and orchid-bordered path to the house. No cameras jutted from the foliage; no one hounded her with questions. Cameron's exit had thwarted the love affair thread, and her uncle's recovery wasn't juicy enough since he hadn't disowned or threatened to sue her. She rinsed the gritty sand from her feet in the cool water from the outside faucet and went in.

In the bedroom, she plugged her phone in to charge until they came, then went to the closet. She had asked Nica the appropriate dress for a baby luau. *Mu'u mu'us*, T-shirts, and rubber slippers, Nica had told her.

"*So no Vera Wang?*" She loved wearing nice things, and it mattered in L.A. But the locals on Kauai wore whatever had been in their closets long enough to fade and grow soft.

"*Wear anything you want, Gentry. Janie will be thrilled you're coming.*"

The thought still surprised her that people she'd never met before would get excited about meeting her now. She fluffed her fingers through her hair, letting it fall carelessly to her shoulders. Minimal makeup. She'd chosen a sage green sundress with spaghetti straps and a pair of beaded sandals she'd picked up at a local boutique. Close enough, she hoped, that she'd fit in with the other guests.

Behind the wheel of Nica's Saab, TJ greeted her with a jut of the chin; Nica and Okelani with hugs. On the drive, Okelani gave her a little family history so that by the time they arrived she knew Janie was TJ's half sister, had three kids, and ran a fruit-and-vegetable stand on the weekends. TJ had a brother on Oahu and two who were grounds keepers for local hotels, a father who'd disappeared twenty-seven years ago, and a stepfather who'd died of cancer while TJ was in the police academy on the mainland. His mother and grandmother were eager to meet her.

All TJ said was, "You remember what happen yet?"

She didn't, but that no longer mattered. She wanted to move on and accept it all as part of a divine plan. Hope had reestablished itself, and she celebrated its return. Once Uncle Rob was strong enough, they'd leave Kauai and whatever had happened behind.

From the highway, TJ turned into a grid of small yards, houses with carports strung with laundry lines; a workingman's neighborhood where people made ends meet. She realized at once the birthday of a one-year-old must be serious business. The party expanded past the boundaries of yards and streets.

Though pregnant clouds had come and gone over Hale Kahili on the north shore, the day stayed sunny for the south-shore luau. Trade winds puffed around a few cotton balls but carried no smell of rain. No one swarmed her when she climbed out of the Saab; no one screamed for her autograph, though the aloha warmth of the gathering enveloped her.

While TJ gave an arm to Okelani, Nica wound her through to a woman whose deep hourglass figure perfectly adapted to supporting the chunky baby. "Gentry, this is TJ's sister, Janie."

With her free hand, Janie slipped a potent, yellow plumeria lei around Gentry's neck and kissed her cheek. "*Aloha*. And welcome to Davy's baby luau."

"Thank you for inviting me. He's adorable." She stroked the hand of the smiling baby whose dimples resembled his Uncle TJ's. Maybe the rolls on his arms and legs and neck would someday translate to muscle, but for now, his eyes were almost swallowed by his cheeks.

Okelani put a hand on Davy's head. "Strong, da baby."

Janie beamed. Her house was tiny and past due on paint and repairs, but she received Okelani's words as a greater gift than a diamond choker. The way she cuddled her son gave Gentry a pang. Not that long ago, she'd contemplated marriage and children.

Daniel would make someone very happy—the sort of Christian woman who wasn't called to shine her light into the world, but only for him. He'd accepted the troupe as a mission ground, but the first whisper of Hollywood had stunned him. *"You can't really mean it."*

To a degree, he'd been right. The men she'd met since had thought faith in a spiritual power all right as long as it didn't interfere with ambition and immediate gratification. She'd found herself in a no-man's-land, caught between extremes and out of step with either side. Somewhere in the middle, she hoped, was someone who would matter.

In the backyard she placed her gift among the others on the table. TJ seated Okelani and introduced "Auntie" Hanah, his grandmother, who spread across a good portion of the picnic bench with an old beagle in her lap. The dog could have been a member of the family. Gentry greeted her and asked how her hip was healing. A string of little girls in grass skirts and flowered headbands ran over and touched her, one by one, then wove away like a multicolored ribbon in the wind. As her gaze followed them across the yard, she caught Cameron walking in.

Unprepared, her heart reacted with a quickened staccato. Myriad details her mind had hoarded surfaced now; first impressions that had triggered childhood memories, clashes that had forced instinctive bursts of recall, the way he'd defended her, and the trust she'd felt in turning over the photos. Shared experience spiced with opposition and seasoned with respect.

Dressed casually in a white T-shirt and frayed shorts, he set a package on the gift table and moved through the crowd. His bold Shakespearean beard contrasted with his loose gait, a rolling stride that might come from riding the waves. His leaving had simplified things, but his return caused a visceral anticipation when his gaze locked on and held all the way across the yard.

He stopped in front of her, the corners of his mouth deepening inside the parentheses of his mustache. His eyes still held unfathomed depths, but no longer threatened survival. "Hi."

"I didn't know you were coming."

"Miss Davy's baby luau?"

She smiled. "Quite an event, it seems."

"A celebration of life. The baby's completed his first year, and everybody parties. Traditionally no gifts are given until then. Used to be the baby wasn't named until the first baby luau."

"Not named for a whole year?"

"Infant mortality."

She shook her head. "Wow."

"So you see, dis baby luau ting one, da kine, big deal."

She laughed. "Is that really why you're here?"

"Not entirely." He sobered. "Let's go somewhere."

She'd like nothing better than to hike off into the woods with him and experience the island as they had before. But sneaking off to be alone was not a smart move.

"I need to stay visible, Cameron." She didn't want to spell it out in terms of celebrity or bad press. If he'd forgotten that element, so much the better. "And I'm not missing that kalua pork."

He surveyed the party. "Okay. Eat first, den talk story." He rested his hand on the small of her back.

She glanced over her shoulder. "I don't think anyone here's a threat."

"You haven't met TJ's brothers."

Seth and Jacob Kanakanui dwarfed Cameron, in heft if not height, and spoke just like TJ; locally and sparingly. "Dunno whassamattah; you hang wit dis guy," Seth told her with a grip on Cameron's shoulder that shook him like a rag doll.

Jacob said, "Must be spooky kine weather make people funny kine."

The weather looked anything but spooky. Clear and hot with a sapphire sky. Cameron took the ribbing and moved her on to someone else he had grown up with, and then someone he knew from surfing, and someone with whom he'd gone deep-sea diving. It seemed as though everyone at the party was related somehow, but there were too many aunties, honorary aunties, cousins, and removed cousins to make sense of it.

With everyone, the gracious *aloha* drew her in. She'd expected to spend time with Nica, but got her brother instead. By the glances and nods, there seemed a gleeful conspiracy to make more of that than there was. Cameron appeared oblivious, but then, it wasn't easy to tell his thoughts. He'd be a complicated leading man to play beside.

With the tantalizing aromas demanding attention, they approached the tables. Cameron identified the foods as they passed platter after platter; char siu, kim chee, lomilomi salmon, laulau, chicken adobo, chicken katsu, huli-huli chicken, and of course the smoky roasted pig that had shredded and fallen from the bones. Who could possibly eat it all?

Her plate dangerously heaped, she sat down on a bench under a papaya tree where she could swear she smelled the fruit ripening. To her right grew an avocado tree that held thick-skinned orbs in various hues of green to black, a pepper bush, and poled tomatoes. To her left, guavas. Such natural abundance. Heart swelling, she offered a blessing for the food, the day, and the company. No elaboration.

Cameron added, "*Amama.*"

"Amen?"

He cocked his head. "Literally that the prayer is free, or flown. We send it out, then it's up to God to catch it or not."

That explanation fit his lack of expectation, but she got the image of prayers trapped inside until she gave them wing. Prayers being freed, flying far and wide; grace aloft. *Amama.*

She bit into the slow-roasted kalua pork and sighed.

"Yeah." He smiled. "Break da mout."

She laughed. "What *does* that mean?"

"It's good." He shrugged. "Breaks the mouth." He dipped her fork into the dab of purplish gray goo on her plate and held it up. "Poi."

If he hadn't globbed some onto her plate, it wouldn't be there. But since he held the fork to her mouth, she tasted it. The slightly tangy paste did not inspire praise.

But as he handed back her fork, he explained, "Alternating poi between the strong flavors lets you go from mahimahi to kim chee to smoky pork to squid luau. It's like bread to the French. A pause for the palate."

"Ah." Something bland between strong, varied flavors. Now she got it.

He dipped a finger into his own. "Usually eaten like this." He sucked it off. "But you have to be careful." He pointed. "See the dog in Auntie Hanah's lap? Poi."

"That's its name?"

"Its diet."

Gentry looked from the obese dog to her plate. "You fed me dog food?"

He laughed. "Just warning you it's hard on the figure."

They'd managed to ignore, for the moment, the business hanging between them. But mentioning her figure brought the photos front and center. She flushed. Had he handled it as he'd promised?

Before she could ask, the band in the yard began to play. The drummer struck the rhythm with the guitar hitting the strong counter-beat she recognized from other island music. Then the ukulele came in with two tenors whose high, sweet voices didn't match the thickness of their necks. She sat back against the bench.

Little girls gathered and danced impromptu hula, their hands and arms already graceful. She nibbled the red spare ribs, salt butterfish, and cold diced salmon with tomatoes and onion. People wandered by and chatted, maybe to say they'd spoken to Gentry Fox, maybe just being friendly. Through it all, she sensed Cameron's impatience—felt her own.

He dumped their finished plates into the big plastic can at the end of the table, and huddled with TJ. From the look on Cameron's face they weren't reminiscing.

Nica caught her by the arm. "You won't want to miss this."

A hush came over the gathering, as Janie positioned Okelani in front of the band. The drum and one of the singers accompanied her with more of a chant than a song. Though Gentry didn't understand the words, when Okelani raised her arms and danced, tears stung.

Nica murmured, "Every movement has meaning, significance in each expression, each position of her hands. She's dancing an ancient creation story now. When she imitates the water or a shark or a palm or a stone, she becomes that thing."

Gentry nodded. Getting into character was something she understood, but she'd never tried to become a stone.

"Hula is also a prayer. It opens the spirit. Okelani is a great *kumu*. She teaches not only the motions, but also the discipline to direct this prayer to the Father." Respect rang in Nica's voice.

"Did she teach you?"

"Yes. And now I assist her with the *keikis*—the little ones. It's very strict. But by showing the way through dance to the Father's heart, Okelani changes lives."

The rapt expressions of the students showed how deeply she had done so.

"Like you, Okelani shines light into the darkness. She dances now to bless the baby. Then we'll have cake." Nica smiled as though it were completely natural to transition from something deeply spiritual to something delicious. And maybe it was.

Janie and three others cut the mango, coconut, and banana cake and gave the baby the first bite. Then slices were passed around and more cakes brought out. It tasted as good as it looked, but Cameron's warning had struck home. She couldn't afford the calories, not if she intended to play alongside Alec Warner. TJ accepted the remainder of her slice and downed it in three bites.

Cameron caught her elbow. "Let's go talk." He hadn't interrupted Okelani's dance, but his mood had shifted. The intensity he'd carried into the party had earlier drained off him like rain, but in the way of the islands, the clouds had returned. He took out his keys.

She glanced over her shoulder, unsure if she'd satisfied *aloha*. "The party isn't over."

"It'll go all night, maybe tomorrow too. We'll take a drive and come back if you want." He led her around the house and down the street to his truck.

The last time, she'd sat there gripping dread in an envelope, but now she imagined grace aloft. Hadn't God turned the hearts and minds of the reporters? There'd been no more talk of aliens or lovers, in spite of Darla's doomsday attitude. Without a juicier scandal, Gentry Fox might not warrant a second week's attention. But she believed her prayers had not flown off to an inattentive God. "So what did you—"

"Hold on a minute." Cameron checked his side mirror and pulled out. "Been up the canyon?"

"Um, no, but . . ."

"We'll do that, then."

"Cameron, did you—"

"Wait." He lifted his fingers from the wheel. "Just a minute."

She stayed silent while he took a roundabout way from the neighborhood through the small town of Waimea, and stopped at the intersection of highways 50 and 550. He glanced in the rearview mirror. "We've got a tail."

"Oh." The photographer who'd followed her to Choy's? At least he hadn't hassled her at the party, though a telephoto could have captured plenty. "Hope he enjoys the drive."

"It's not a he. It's Bette Walden."

She sucked a breath and almost turned around. "Are you sure?"

He slid her a glance.

"What is *with* that woman?"

"She's obviously been hired to follow you."

Gentry frowned. "Why? And by whom?" Bette was a bloodsucking gnat. Through everything with Troy, she'd been there, insinuating, trying to force a confession, watching, waiting to catch her in the act. Only there wasn't an act to catch. She must not have heard.

"I don't know." Cameron started up the canyon. Whatever he did know would obviously wait.

Gentry stared out at the semi-arid landscape—pale grasses and scrubby bushes on scrabbled, red-and-gray slopes broken by crumbly shelves of rock. Why was Bette Walden after her? Did she think the new pictures proved Troy's old lies? If she'd bought into it, the whole thing could blow up again. Her stomach churned.

Cameron glanced over. "What do you want to do?"

"About Bette?"

He nodded.

"What are the choices?" They couldn't exactly outrun her on the single highway creeping up Waimea Canyon.

"Let her follow us to the top and see what she wants, or take one of the trail roads off the highway. My truck'll handle it. Her compact, maybe not."

She hadn't seen anything but scenic turnouts, but he would know. As they climbed, the landscape had changed from hardscrabble hills to scraggly forest. Did she want to confront or avoid Bette? She clenched her jaw, resenting the intrusion. "I'd rather choose my time, my place. I'm tired of her ambushing me."

"Okay." He sped up. "Hold on."

Gentry gripped the armrest and reconsidered her answer. Avoiding Bette on the tortuous road wouldn't matter if they rolled off the side. Thrust against the door, she wished she'd chosen Plan A.

The trees grew taller, denser, and greener as they climbed, closing them in. The temperature dropped noticeably. With a screech, Cameron swerved to the left and dove down a dirt road that had opened with almost no warning. She stifled a cry as they rumbled down, then jerked to the right onto nothing more than ruts between the trees. Jostled and bumped, she clung to the seat until he came to a stop at a small turnout on the edge of a plummeting precipice. The colorful canyon gaped below.

She clutched her stomach and expelled her breath. "Do you have a death wish?"

"Nah." He put the truck in gear and set the brake. "Dat would be, da kine, murky water at high surf."

She dropped her head back.

Cameron opened the windows and turned off the engine. The scent of eucalyptus wafted in from the trees overshadowing them. Cool, shady air filled the cab. He turned and rested one arm on the steering wheel and the other on the seat back, pulling his T-shirt tight across his chest. He drew his knee up and sat like the surfer dude he'd sounded; murky water at high surf.

Her heart was only starting to still. "Does Bette—"

"We'll talk about that after. First tell me about the dragon man."

She frowned. "What about him?"

"What happened at Choy's?"

She sent her thoughts back to that night. "Nothing. After I called you, he left."

"I thought he'd just come in."

"He had. I took his picture right when he sat down. Then he cornered me in the hall—"

"Cornered you?" The intensity in his voice warned her off careless phrasing.

"He was so big, maybe he just took up the space."

His eyes narrowed. "Tell me the truth."

She released a slow breath. "He didn't move when I tried to get by. He looked . . . determined."

"Threatening?"

She pictured his face. *Oh yeah.* "If I wasn't used to it, I'd wonder why some stranger took my picture."

"Stop evading, Gentry. Did you feel endangered by this guy?"

No use finding a positive spin. "Until TJ came. Then, like I said, the man left."

"Well, at the luau TJ filled me in on his record. Grover Malakua isn't someone to mess with. Like the cousin TJ arrested for beating up his wife, he's got a history of violence."

She swallowed.

"I want you to think. Before Choy's, had you seen him?"

She'd recognized his tattoo, but . . .

"Close your eyes."

She shook her head. "I don't know him. I thought about it all night. I can't remember seeing him anywhere else."

He clutched her shoulder. "Close your eyes."

A deep reluctance seized her. Her mouth went dry. What on earth?

"Gentry." His grip softened. "Try."

TWENTY-FIVE

What TJ had told him was that Grover Malakua had a record of assault and battery, drug trafficking, and vehicular manslaughter. There'd been suspicion of intent in the accident, but it couldn't be proved. TJ had emphasized that nothing remotely connected him to Gentry. But she'd recognized the dragon. They had to have interacted at some point, and inside she knew it. He'd heard it in her voice. It was that phone call, not Davy's baby luau, that had brought him back to the island.

As she closed her eyes, her shoulder tightened with tension. She hadn't reacted that way the last time he led her through this exercise; she'd gone with it, picking out fragments of thought that had proved accurate. That's what he wanted again, but he'd hit a wall. Fear?

"You knew the dragon when you saw it. You remembered it before. It's in there, Gentry."

Her throat worked.

"Where else did you see it? When?"

Her arms jerked. Her eyes flew open, and she drew hard, clipped breaths. "Falling. I felt like I was falling."

"Long and slow or hard and sudden?"

"The second. There was a jolt, and I tried to catch myself."

"A jolt? You were pushed?"

She turned, confused. "Was I?"

"I don't know." The first time he'd seen her, she'd been too wary to accept his ride even when he'd shown his relationship to Nica. She'd scrutinized him as though trying to recognize a threat. "Was someone else with you and your uncle?"

"No." She frowned. "But . . ." She shook her head.

"Say it."

"It's so minute."

"Gentry, a minute recollection saved your uncle's life. Tell me."

Her brow scrunched. "Branches. And a face. A face in the branches."

"Malakua?"

"It doesn't make sense."

"Don't try to make sense. Was his the face you saw?"

"I don't know." She sighed. "Maybe."

But she was right. It didn't make sense. What motive would Grover Malakua have to hurt or kill Gentry Fox? "You said your uncle found someone to recommend a trail. Was he the one?"

"Uncle Rob talked to lots of people."

"Did you ask him about the tattoo?"

She shook her head. "He has so much to deal with already. I don't want him worrying about me."

"Okay." He slid his hand behind her neck and rubbed the tension out.

She lowered her chin. "I thought you were going to tell me what happened with the pictures."

"It's taken care of."

Her mouth fell open. "How?"

"Since you guessed Troy sent the note, I dug up what I could find on him."

She groaned.

He'd slogged through every article, transcript, and blog to get the public version of the whole previous mess, then extracted from the police report a clearer picture. "Gentry."

She turned.

"I know you." What he'd meant was that all his digging had pointed to her innocence, and his meeting with Troy had confirmed it. He tried to rephrase that, but her eyes pooled, and maybe he'd said exactly what he meant.

"I found a more likely suspect in his mom."

Gentry shook her head. "His mom? I've never even met her."

"If you were someone else, that might matter. But you're Gentry Fox." How could she still not get it? "Darlene Glasier did time for embezzlement on a plea that dropped two counts of fraud. She's filed seven lawsuits ending in nuisance settlements. She knows a mark when she sees one."

"I don't—"

"She sent the photos to blackmail you."

Gentry expelled her breath. "But they're not real."

"Real or not, think how you reacted. Your first response was to kick me out." The corner of his mouth pulled.

"Well . . ."

"I understand. You'd been sucker-punched. But based on that reaction, you'd soon be paying to keep her quiet."

Gentry bit her lip. "She hired Bette Walden?"

Bette had delivered the pictures, but he doubted Troy's mother could afford a PI. "That's the piece I haven't figured out. Might've been worth talking to Bette."

"She's just so vindictive."

"I'll catch up with her later. You don't have to be part of it." He lowered his knee from the seat. "The important thing is, I got the file. Ms. Glasier would be supremely stupid to pursue it when I've got evidence of her fraudulent behavior."

She turned and stared out the side window. "Then you saw—"

"Only enough to make sure of the file." Her discomfort touched a chord in him. He hadn't expected modesty in a Hollywood actor. Maybe he'd bought a little of the hype. Maybe his own attraction— and that of countless others—predisposed assumptions. "Look at me."

It took a long moment before she turned, but he wanted to be clear. "I didn't see. I didn't want to." Potential had already slid in its talons. If he threw it one tidbit . . .

She drew a jagged breath. "So it's over?"

"Your part. Troy's got some issues."

Her brow creased. "Is he okay?"

Amazing. She still cared about the kid. But that didn't surprise him. Her search for her uncle had revealed a tenacious outward focus. If she cared about someone, she meant it. And apparently there wasn't much that person could do to destroy it. More than her courage, strength, or beauty, that loyalty threatened to undo him.

"His mom's giving him grief."

Gentry dropped back in her seat.

He leaned over and caressed her shoulder. "He'll be all right. He's getting it."

"Getting . . ."

"That you can't manipulate people. He was hurt when you left the troupe to shoot *Steel*. In some warped way he thought he could get you back."

She shook her head.

"When he got me the file, he said you were the only person he trusted. You'd gotten down and dirty—not the way it had come out—but role-playing his anger, his hurt, until he could laugh in its face."

"He said that?" Hope filled her smile.

"Said he'd gotten caught up in the hype, made more of it than there was. He said he'd tell it straight if you wanted him to."

Tears sparkled in her eyes. "I wouldn't put him through that."

"I didn't think so." He drew her close and kissed her mouth, hating what she made him feel, and wanting it. No one but Myra had ever grabbed so deep inside him, and he knew what it cost. He knew.

They hadn't kissed since he'd stifled her ranting in the hospital, but this kiss held the pull of strained muscles, hope and fear, confusion, suspicion . . . triumph. They'd saved Uncle Rob's life, and her own would be marked forever by the sight of Cameron drenched and gasping, *"I found him. He's alive."*

Maybe it was reckless, but she knew herself better for having lost her identity. And Cameron was part of that. He'd been unwilling to leave her lost any more than she could leave Uncle Rob. Because of that and so much more, she welcomed his kiss. But he pulled back abruptly.

She searched his face. "What?"

"I shouldn't have done that. It was presumptuous."

A moist breeze came in the window, cooling the air between them. "That depends on why."

He frowned, unable or unwilling to hold her gaze. "Because you're . . ."

"Gentry Fox?" She had thought he knew her, but in fact he was kissing the myth. And it hurt. "I'm not a character on a screen."

"I know you're not."

"It's just easy to pretend?"

"Gentry . . ."

She looked away. "I thought you didn't want the fantasy."

"This started before, when you were Jade. That first evening you wouldn't get into my truck. The night of the centipede. In the water under the falls . . ."

"Then what's wrong?"

"All of it. Your reality is way outside mine, your 'universe of possibilities' infinite." He clutched the steering wheel. "I know you won't let this go anywhere."

It almost sounded like a plea. *Stay up on your pedestal. Don't be real.* "Then you're right. It's presumptuous."

"It won't happen again."

Good. She'd rather stage-kiss Alec Warner with a camera in her face than Cameron Pierce in his truck in the woods. "Have we shaken Bette?"

"She's probably realized she lost us, but she'll go to the top to be sure."

"Then let's get back."

He hesitated as though he wanted to say more, but she kept her gaze out the window. He started the engine and backed up with a little too much force. If he was angry, he need look no farther than himself. But it wasn't anger that came off him in waves; it was something bleaker by far.

They took the jarring track back to the road and the road down the canyon in silence. Leaving the green forest and gray skies behind, they returned to the arid sunshine as they emerged from the canyon. Nature had captured it. Two different worlds; two different lives. Time to find closure. "I don't want to go back to the party. Can you take me to the hospital?"

His response was void of inflection. "Okay."

Then the silence solidified as he drove through Hanapepe and Koloa, to Lihue and Uncle Rob. When he pulled into the hospital lot, she turned. "Do you mind parking? My uncle wants to meet you."

After messing up that bad, he'd expected to be dismissed, not invited in. But this was a chance for answers he might not get again. He parked and locked the truck behind them, scanning the lot. He saw no sign of Bette, or paparazzi. Gentry's life might not always be the circus it had seemed, but he kept his distance anyway.

She was right that he'd kissed her in part because nothing could come of it. Potential required opportunity to become reality. He didn't deny the desire to touch and hold her, and kissing her was like shooting the curl of a cruncher, toes on the nose. He knew better, but something crawled inside his head and told him to catch it in spite of the damage it would do. He hadn't meant for that damage to spill out on her, though.

She chewed her lip as they made their way to her uncle's room, and he couldn't help visualizing a trapped animal chewing off the offended part. The time to speak had passed, and he didn't know how to make it right anyway. What he needed was to put the whole business behind him.

Robert Fox sat in a wheelchair by the window when they entered, the remaining half of his leg wrapped but uncovered. How would he handle a stranger seeing that? How would anyone?

"Uncle Rob," Gentry said. "This is Cameron Pierce, the one who helped me find you."

Her uncle held up his hand, his grip vigorous, considering what he'd been through. And he wasn't as old as he'd seemed in the cave. Fifties not sixties, with the build of an athlete. With modern prostheses, amputees could live an active life, but still, what a blow it must be.

"Mr. Fox."

"It's Rob." The man gave his hand a squeeze to match the warmth in his eyes. "Gentry's told me what you did. Thank you."

"The way things looked in the cave, I wasn't sure I'd have this opportunity."

"Me neither." Rob's mouth made a grim line.

"Without the lava tube, we couldn't have gotten through."

"Wish I'd known that way was there." He sighed. "At least the Lord showed you."

Cameron didn't argue the point. "I'm sorry about your leg." By the lack of a drape, he assumed forthrightness. In Rob's place, he'd want the same.

Rob's throat worked. "All things for a reason."

Could he say the same if their roles were reversed? He doubted it. "So what now?"

"Now I work to keep what's left."

Gentry effused. "Paul says you're doing great."

Rob glared. "That man's an insult encyclopedia. Do not give him your autograph."

"That man thinks you're awesome. It's your autograph he'll want." Gentry settled cross-legged at the foot of the bed, a position evocative of cozy conversations. Forced levity for her uncle's sake, or her own?

Cameron took the remaining chair and faced Rob. "I know you've spoken with the police, but can you also tell me what happened out there? Why you went over the falls?"

"I jumped in to catch Gentry."

"You saw her fall?"

"I heard her scream, saw her hit the water."

"But not how or why she fell."

"No. And she can't remember. But Gentry's no novice. And it wasn't a place that concerned me, or I'd have kept a better eye out."

"You were behind her?"

He nodded. "About six yards."

Yet he'd seen nothing. "Was anyone else with you?"

Rob shook his head. "Just the two of us."

She had said the same and looked annoyed that he'd checked her answer, but part of investigation was cross-questioning, and her memory was still faulty. "Who else knew you'd be there?"

Rob pressed his palms to the arms of his chair. "You think someone caused her fall?"

Cameron got up, thinking in motion. "Gentry's got sensations of being pushed."

"I'm not—"

He silenced her with a glance, then continued. "She may have glimpsed a face in the forest, and recalls a dragon tattoo that matches a gnarly dude named Grover Malakua."

"Dragon." Rob ran his hand over his shoulder and arm. "Here?"

Gentry stiffened. "Yes."

"Remember in that tavern we were planning our hikes. That guy came over with something mo bettah."

She turned. "Then that's where I saw him, Cameron. Not in the woods."

Maybe. "Did he know you'd taken his suggestion?"

Rob frowned. "Knew we planned to. He sat down and helped us lay out a route for the best view of the falls. Though why he sent us to the top . . ."

Gentry stood up and stalked to the window. "He couldn't know how fast we'd hike, what time we'd get to any particular point."

"He could have been waiting." Rob's voice was gentle.

She turned. "Then why didn't you see him?"

"I was filming. Out across the water, toward the crest of the falls."

Cameron knew the answer but asked anyway. "Do you have the camera?"

Rob shook his head. "Dropped it when I jumped." Something passed over his face. Pain? Post-traumatic stress? He masked it before Gentry looked back at him.

"Why would someone push me?"

Cameron hung his hands on his hips. "You've got enemies, Gentry. Haven't you listened to Darla?" As much as he couldn't stand the woman, she'd grasped the situation.

"You think he meant for me to go over the falls? I could have died." She clenched her fists. "This is real life, not some script."

And movies couldn't touch real life. "Maybe I've got Darlene Glasier's motive wrong. Maybe she thinks you used her son."

She shook her head.

Rob said, "Gentry, who knows what whacko you've picked up with all the publicity."

She turned on him. "I will not believe someone wants to kill me because I lucked into a movie part. Or because someone else told lies. Listen to yourselves." Hurt and anger played over her face like clouds above the waves. "Then . . . I live and Uncle Rob—" Her voice broke.

"You think I'd want it the other way around?" Rob reached up and took her hand.

Cameron dug for his phone. "We need to call the police."

"No." Gentry fired the word. "The press will be all over it."

He'd watched them eat her up, and she might not have it in her to face it again. Balancing that with any possible threat, he had to admit what they had against Malakua was pretty slim.

Rob turned. "Can you protect her? I'll pay for it."

She expelled a breath. "Cameron lives and works on the mainland. He can't hang around."

He did have cases pending, though none with imminent danger

to his client—or himself. For more reasons than one, he was ill-prepared to accept.

"Can you do it?" Rob's voice crackled with effort or exhaustion.

Looking from one to the other, Cameron nodded. "I'll keep track of her overnight."

"I don't need a baby-sitter."

Her petulance actually betrayed the fear she was trying to hide. "We'll look at it fresh in the morning."

Gentry could deny it, but his gut told him something had happened out there. He kicked himself now for going after blackmail instead of attempted murder.

TWENTY-SIX

The moment they left, Rob curled up in pain. It had intensified as they spoke, and by the time Gentry and Cameron had helped him into bed, he'd nearly screamed. It had started with the flashback of jumping into the water. The cold, the rush, the plunge, and—*Oh, God*—the pain. *Lord.*

He was on Demerol, but this was different, this pain in the part of his limb that no longer existed. No drug would take it away. What had Paul said? Flex and relax. Stretch the muscles. Rob focused. They'd made clear the seriousness of contracture, but he didn't think this was physiological.

Phantom pain. A disorientation of his brain, thinking him whole. He closed his eyes and felt the rocks like teeth mangling his flesh, shattering his bone. *It's not there anymore.* He gripped the stump with his hands, squeezed and rocked. His breath wheezed as panic rose. He could not live with this pain.

Lord. The effort it took to keep from Gentry the horror of his condition was more than he could stand. He had to get away from her. She believed what he showed her, but he couldn't keep hiding it. Cameron had seen and almost asked, but he'd warned him off with a glare.

This was his battle. She would only hurt.

"*The Lord is my strength and my shield. My heart trusts—*" Pain screamed through his leg. *But this is too much!* He rolled and writhed. How had he failed? Why could he not grasp the grace he knew was there for him?

His chest felt heavy. If only he had died . . .

But God had never given him the easy way out. His life had so many if onlys. But every time, he'd fought through the harder way. He'd do it again. He clenched his jaw and confronted the pain. He sank right to the center of it. And there he found grace. In the pain. In the suffering.

He drew shallow breaths and absorbed God's presence. *"My heart trusts in him, and I am helped. My heart leaps for joy. . . ."*

He was not alone. Broken and maimed, he was not abandoned. *"Your right hand will hold me fast."* The hands of Christ covered his, squeezing the tortured leg, sharing the pain. Rob rested in that grasp until sleep carried him away.

⌒

Thrown back into turbulent waters, Gentry had fought just like the last time, but once again the current proved too strong. She had not intended to have Cameron for a watchdog. She had wanted closure. But worrying about her wouldn't help Uncle Rob. By the end of their visit, he'd looked drained and ashen. She would not add to his burden.

She walked to the door at Hale Kahili, picturing Cameron helping him into bed with one hand under the maimed and bandaged leg. Neither had shrunk from the infirmity or obsessed on it. She was the one overwhelmed every time she saw the result of her mistake.

Uncle Rob had called after her, "Gentry, be careful."

But what did that mean? It was bad enough when people wanted to kill her career, her reputation. Now they believed someone wanted her dead.

"Wait here." Cameron walked inside and searched the immediate level. Coming back to where she stood in the entry, he said, "So what does your uncle do?"

The question took her by surprise. Was he distracting her with a thin sort of normalcy? Helping her forget she'd been a target, after working hard to convince her of it? "He's an inventor."

"Really." He checked the entry closet. "What kind?"

"His first patent had to do with cell phone technology back when it was all piecemeal and none of it worked very well. His contribution was revolutionary. Now he's working on some kind of chip for a satellite."

Uncle Rob wasn't a Mensa-type genius—just amazingly able to make things work, not quitting until they did. He never quit. Not even now, with a kind of challenge he'd never faced, an extreme physical limitation. Like Dad's. But while Dad skirted his heart condition and pretended everything was bliss, Uncle Rob would meet his injury head on.

"Widowed?"

She turned. "What?"

Cameron moved from the closet to check the front window locks. "He's got a wedding band, but I haven't seen—"

"Aunt Allegra moved out two years ago. I tried to get her to come here, but I guess it's asking too much."

"They're divorced?"

She shook her head. "Uncle Rob provides everything she needs, and I guess that's good enough for her. As far as he's concerned, she's his wife, no matter what."

Her words stiffened Cameron like starch. Okelani had said his wife squeezed his heart until he'd shriveled up, and now she saw it. He started up the stairs, and she followed, weary, angry, and scared. Cameron ducked into her uncle's room on one side of the hall, and though he would doubtless complain, she moved past him to hers and shrieked.

"What! No." She clenched the jamb.

"Don't move." Cameron pressed past her, stalking through the disaster with purpose. Closet. Bathroom. Under the bed. Back to her. He moved her out of the doorway into the hall, took out his phone.

Her head reeled. She felt herself falling, but this time there was no bottom. She just fell and fell and fell. Cameron talked to the police, but she just wanted to curl up someplace no one knew her name. The thought of making news again sickened her, but worse still was admitting she could have caused what happened to Uncle Rob. Didn't this prove it? Someone wanted to hurt her, and he—

Cameron touched her arm. "They're going to want to know if anything's missing. Can you take a look without touching?"

Anger burned. "Shouldn't be hard. It's all laid out for me." Everything she'd brought was thrown around the room. He'd said no touching, but she lifted a Versace silk tank torn down the front and brought it to her throat.

"Jewelry?" Cameron had come up beside her.

She went to the room safe in the closet, worked the combination. She wasn't huge into jewelry, but what things she'd brought were there. "Couldn't crack the combination, I guess."

Cameron turned and scanned the room. "What would someone be after?"

Then it hit her. She turned to the nightstand where a thin, black cord dangled. "My phone." She'd forgotten it when TJ and Nica picked her up for the luau. Was it just hours ago?

She rushed over and searched behind the stand, dropped to her knees and looked under the bed. She sat back on her heels and covered her face. "All my contacts."

"And pictures."

She dropped her hands and turned. "Grover Malakua?"

"He's first on my list." Cameron raised her to her feet. "You're sure it's not in a pocket or something?"

She shook her head. "I was charging it after Nica called, but I forgot to take it with me."

Cameron moved from one window to the other, looking out.

The implication clenched her stomach. "He was watching?"

He fingered the louvers. "Were these open when you left?"

"I haven't changed them. With the foliage so thick over there . . ." She gripped her hair. Stupid. She knew better. She knew. Her throat swelled. It was only clothes and a phone, but she felt violated. "It's like I'm some carnival target. Knock me down, I'll flip back up."

"I'm sorry, Gentry."

"It's not your problem. You shouldn't even be here." She swiped at the angry tears, stooped and picked up a skirt and blouse and—

He caught her hand. "Leave it. The police need to see."

"You know what? I'm tired of people seeing. People thinking they have rights to me. Thinking they know me." It wasn't fair to dump it on him, but he was part of it, kissing the fantasy who couldn't hurt him as his wife had. "Would you mind leaving me alone?"

He let go of her hand. "Come downstairs; I'll wait outside."

A tear streaked down her cheek. She wished she was made of steel. Or that she really was the character she'd played. That was who people thought she was. Undaunted. Unbreakable. She went past him, out the door, down the stairs, into the living room, and closed herself into her arms.

Cameron passed behind her and went outside. A frisson of panic tightened her spine. Where could she go and not be seen? What could she do if someone wanted her dead? In Uncle Rob's words, *"Who knows what whacko you've picked up with all the publicity?"*

And now there'd be more, a cycle of publicity and repercussions repeating itself until she was afraid to show herself and, like Nica, just wanted it over with. She rubbed her arms and told herself it was only a break-in. An inexperienced thief who couldn't crack the safe and didn't realize her wardrobe was worth more than the cell phone he stole—without taking the charger. She covered her face. *Don't be stupid.*

The dragon man had it, because she'd taken his picture. He'd torn and tossed her clothes as a warning, or a threat. He didn't know her, had no reason to hate her. But he did. And Bette Walden did. And the people who'd sent nasty letters. And the callers who believed she'd had an affair with a minor. And the nasty reporter who said she and her lover had left her uncle to die.

She sucked hard breaths through her nose. No one wondered, no one cared what it did to her. She went to the kitchen and grabbed a water bottle from the refrigerator. She wrung the plastic cap off and yanked the stopper top with her teeth. She sucked the cold water down a throat swollen with fury.

A knock came at the door, and she admitted the police officers—one young and ruddy, the other older than her uncle, with sharp, gray hair that stood out from his neck beneath his cap like a hedgehog. He lumbered in and introduced himself, but she missed the name. His partner stood silently. Cameron lingered outside, unsure, she guessed, where she wanted him. She left the door open and led the officers up the stairs.

He understood her feelings better than she could imagine, the sense of trespass and desecration. He understood how it felt to be used, and chastised himself as he climbed the stairs behind the cops. He'd been more than presumptuous. Cavalier. Thoughtless.

Gentry motioned them into her room. She had control of herself, but it was a hard control. She stood in the doorway, arms crossed, while the officers surveyed the mess. A minor burglary didn't warrant a major investigation, even with the malicious nature of the mess. Only connected with other events could this seem portentous.

The officers surveyed her private space, her garments and under-garments with thinly veiled curiosity, breathed the cloying essence of her spilled perfumes. Gentry took a drink from the water bottle in one hand and tapped the fingers of the other against her ribs. He wanted to hold her, and not because she was safe, but because she was hurting. And because she was brave. And he was falling in love with her.

He and Nica had been so close growing up that he'd left the island so she could find herself without him. Months later, he'd met and married Myra, and maybe he'd been the one who couldn't find himself. He'd wanted too much. Or else he'd chosen poorly, a woman unable to think outside herself.

Nica had found her balance, even if things still rocked her. He hadn't. The loneliness of the last few years was a monster gnawing inside, eating away his confidence, his faith. He took personally the lies, the deceptions, the plots he uncovered, found satisfaction in the convictions, but that was a vindictive sort of caring.

He rubbed a hand over the beard he wore as a front. Confident, intimidating, bold. People seldom looked past it to the hurt inside. He knew how it was to play a role and have people believe it was real.

The younger officer named Severt, whom Cameron knew slightly, had a hard time keeping his mind on business. Cameron wanted to shield Gentry from the fantasies in the man's mind. But he'd been just as invasive—worse, because she'd trusted him.

After a thorough inspection of the room, the older cop, Bender, asked the standard paperwork questions. Cameron prompted Gentry to tell them everything, including her encounter with Malakua at Choy's, the picture she'd taken with the now-stolen camera phone, her reasons for doing so. She answered robotically, then said, "I don't know why I took it. It was stupid."

"You were afraid," Cameron said.

She looked up, but neither acknowledged nor denied his assessment.

"Do you feel threatened, Ms. Fox?"

Her arms closed tighter. "I don't feel anything at all."

Not knowing where else to take it, Bender closed his notebook. "When you clean up, let us know if you find anything that's not yours."

She nodded. Fatigue hollowed her eyes, but she looked her best in extreme situations. That was why they'd cast her for a movie like *Steel*, why she'd shone in the forest, sweaty and flushed. Why Severt had responded to her aura.

Cameron walked the officers to the door and underscored the situation with Malakua. "I can't say he's responsible for what happened to Gentry and her uncle, but there's some connection. Who else would take her phone and nothing else?"

"We'll ask around, look for anyone who might have seen someone around the place," Officer Bender assured him. "And we'll question Grover Malakua."

No cop liked coincidence, and this had the feel of cause and effect. The trouble was it pivoted on Gentry's spotty memory, and she would not say that Malakua had threatened or harmed her. He understood her refusal to blame someone without certainty after her own agony of false accusation. Understood, but didn't like it. If she'd thrown her weight, even a little, they'd have notched up the investigation.

"The thing is . . ." Severt hesitated at the door. "There's no sign of forced entry."

That hit between the eyes. He'd checked the place out when they came in, and the cops were right. No broken windows; no jimmied doors. They weren't close enough to this thing to be drawing the same conclusions.

Bender tucked his notebook under his arm. "Now, I'm not saying she likes the attention—"

"What?" Cameron planted his hands on his hips.

"You've got to wonder when someone keeps ending up in the news."

"In radical ways," Severt added.

Cameron expelled his breath. "Gentry did not—"

"I'm not saying she did. But it wouldn't be the first celebrity high jinks we've seen."

Cameron spread his hands. "She's desperate to keep out of the spotlight, didn't even want you called."

They both nodded. Neither believed him.

"We will check it out." Officer Bender scratched up under his hat. "Just . . . looks more like a tantrum in there than a burglary."

Severt barely squelched a grin. "And she's not awfully clear on the rest. To be honest, it felt . . . evasive."

Evasive? Was he the only one giving Gentry a break? But it had felt evasive. And how could he explain no forced entry? Maybe he had lost his objectivity.

As he closed and locked up behind them, his gaze caught on the alarm box beside it. Gentry had touched in the code when they arrived, as she had each time since they'd met the manager at the door. But how had . . . ? Heart hammering, he took the stairs two at a time. Gentry stood shipwrecked in silky designer labels.

"Gentry."

As though he'd touched her in freeze tag, she tossed the water bottle into the trash and snatched up a pair of shorts. "You can use Uncle Rob's room tonight. I need to check—"

"Did you lock up when you went out today?"

"Of course."

"Set the alarm?"

She drew a jagged breath. "I . . . probably."

"Talk to me about the code."

"The manager gave us a card. I memorized it; Uncle Rob put the card in his wallet."

"Your uncle had a key?"

She dropped her arms. "Yes."

"Does he have it now?"

She shook her head. "He left it in the Jeep. The glove compartment."

"How do you know?"

"He told me. He had the Jeep keys in his pocket but lost them in the water. He was worried about his . . . wallet."

Cameron picked up the business card Bender had left on the dresser for Gentry. He called the number and identified himself, then asked, "Has the Jeep Robert Fox rented been recovered?"

Officer Bender seemed reluctant to share that information.

"It pertains to your concerns here." He would not name their doubts with Gentry standing there.

Bender said, "The Jeep was recovered this afternoon."

"And the wallet in the glove compartment?"

The two officers conferred briefly, then he said, "The glove compartment was broken open and emptied."

Hearing the answer for herself, Gentry held his stare as he hung up the phone. "You think he has the key?"

"And the code, if that card was in Rob's wallet." They could change the code on the alarm, call in a locksmith. But the place was too isolated and unfamiliar. "We need to go."

He expected a fight, but she drew her mouth into a hard line and dragged a suitcase onto the bed. "Give me a minute to pack."

He went into the other room and packed her uncle's things, then found Gentry in her bathroom. Her cosmetics had been tossed and stepped on, lipsticks crushed and creams smeared. He wanted to hurt Malakua. More than that he wanted to know who'd put him up to it. The man didn't fit the "whacko" mold, and he didn't seem to have any personal connection to Gentry. But he'd been the hired heavy more than once.

She picked up a lotion bottle and tossed it in the trash. "I don't want the maids to have to deal with this."

He went down to the kitchen for paper towels and helped her swab the floor. When they'd done the best they could, he hefted her luggage into the hall, then went into her uncle's room and fetched the others. He loaded the bags into the bed of his truck and let her into the cab. Before getting in himself, he called Monica.

"Nice surprise today, Kai. I didn't know you were coming."

"I can't talk, Nica. I'm bringing Gentry over, and you need to go to Okelani's."

Silence.

He blew out his breath. "I'd stay here at Hale Kahili if I planned to ravage her."

"I didn't—"

"And don't think I missed all the Cheshire grins at the luau. This isn't personal. Someone broke in and trashed Gentry's place."

Nica gasped. "Oh no."

"I need somewhere to keep her safe." He should have told her uncle he had no idea how to do that. The plots he uncovered for a living were seldom life-threatening.

"Kai . . ."

"I'll be fine." He rounded the back of the truck. "But can you stay with Okelani a few days?"

"Yes, but—"

"Thanks." He hung up and drove to Hanalei through a drizzle that felt just about right.

TJ Kanakanui stood inside the carport at Monica's when they pulled up. Gentry started for the lower room she'd used before, but he didn't want her on ground level. "Upstairs, Gentry. Use the big room in the back."

His parents' room, that neither he nor Nica had taken over after their deaths. They'd lived with Okelani and rented out the cottage for income until Nica turned eighteen and moved back in. He went off to college but came back often enough to call it home until he relocated on the mainland. There'd never been a question of selling it. A modest enough home, it was still their heritage.

He waited until Gentry was inside, then said, "Why you nevah stick it to Grover Malakua?" He didn't usually talk stink, but if TJ had confronted the man on the spot, there'd at least have been a record of the incident.

TJ crossed his brawny arms and gave him back the stink eye.

"Okay, look." He planted his hands on his hips. "I need a gun."

"What for?"

"To protect Gentry while Kauai PD sticks its head in da surf."

"You can't get one gun, brah."

"I'm licensed."

TJ shook his head. "Not here."

Cameron rubbed his face. That was true. Applying for a gun license in Hawaii was only slightly less offensive than infesting the islands with snakes. And his weapon was at home in Pismo Beach. Airports frowned on his carrying it along.

TJ rolled back on his heels. "Dey broke up her place?"

"Not they. He. Malakua stole her cell. The one with his picture in it. You should have grabbed him."

TJ looked pained. He was in over his head and had the sense to know it. They both were.

Cameron stuck his keys in his pocket. "Did Nica get to Okelani's?"

"I got her dere."

"You were here when I called?"

TJ nodded.

"I interrupt something?"

"Nevah your business."

Cameron forked his fingers into his hair, then groaned.

TWENTY-SEVEN

Troubled, Nica stood beside Okelani as the last of the day's light gave way to the shy moon. A soft brush against her ankles heralded a new arrival, as Okelani laid the pie pan of milk on the porch. Seven scrawny kitties pressed in and lapped.

Geckos *kekek*ed in the bushes, and one clung to the screen, watching the act of benevolence toward the feral cats. Okelani straightened and pressed her palms to her lower back. "Too old fo dance."

"Never." Nica scooped up a striped kitty that stepped away from the bowl and shook its head.

Okelani grunted. "Tell my bones dat."

The cat pressed its nose up under her chin. "You were beautiful, Tūtū. You honored Janie." She studied the woman she loved as fiercely as Kai. "And pleased everyone."

Okelani smiled. "Cute, da baby, ay?"

"TJ says he looks like him."

"What uncle nevah tink dat?"

They laughed, but the shadow stayed over Nica's heart. Cameron's call had shaken her. Okelani had sensed a storm with malice in its heart, and now it seemed that storm was brewing.

"*Mea aloha.*" Okelani grasped her forearm. "Gentry *ma ka malu o kona ēheu.*"

In the shelter of his wings. Like the bony cats that leaped onto

Okelani's porch, wayward creatures finding blessing. On the island, they had no enemy but the carelessness and cruelty of humankind.

"I'm worried about her. And Kai."

Okelani pulled open the screen door. "Strong, da attraction."

She hadn't meant that. Only that Gentry's trouble put Cameron in danger too. But maybe the other was worse. Kai's heart was shattered glass—and it could cut.

Curt held the disposable cell phone to his ear with utter disdain. What did he care about someone else's problems? Especially when the fault landed smack in the middle of the idiot's own chest. "No, I don't think so. See, 'upon completion' were the key words. You don't complete the project, you don't get the money."

"I gotta have it now. Gotta get outta here."

"Uh-huh."

The guy's voice notched up a level, desperation creeping in. "You nevah help, someone might hear tings. Someone you don't want hear tings."

"That's how you do business?" But he'd known that. Scum. "You know what? Go ahead and spew. You can't touch me."

"I'm talking cops."

"Oh, that's what you meant?"

The thug growled.

"See, here's the thing. You're working with some wrong information. First, you think I care. Second, you don't even know my name." He hung up and turned off the phone, then turned it back on, just in case.

He couldn't believe there'd been no word. No note, no call. He could not believe she'd left. Left!

He rolled one shoulder, then the other. *Loosen up. Don't get edgy.* Things hadn't gone so good for her. He shouldn't have kept Rob and

Gentry's situation from her. Made him seem untrustworthy. No wonder she didn't turn to him when she got confused.

He went and stood in front of the mirror. Okay, so forty wasn't twenty. But his thirty-nine was plenty good for Allegra's forty-nine—a forty-nine she clung to by her fingernails, the big 5-O coming up. She'd cosmetically regressed at least ten years. Still fine, but not sure of it. That's what made things work.

He shrugged his shoulders and let them drop, turned sideways and cocked his chin, eyes narrow and sexy. Staring at himself, he wrung the anger out, drop by drop. She'd been confused, upset. Who wouldn't be? It did signal a stronger tie than he'd expected with two and a half years of separation. But, okay. Just another hurdle. Things hadn't gone right, but he could fix that. There were new possibilities. And he wouldn't rely on anyone else. Only himself. That was the best way. Always the best way.

Gentry hadn't opened her suitcases. The thought of sleeping in something that the dragon man had handled sickened her. The phone had been lying in clear sight. Malakua could have simply taken it. Instead he'd fouled her nest.

It wasn't that the phone was that valuable—it was that personal. Uncle Rob had fitted it with a GPS chip that would communicate with his new satellite system, but she didn't know how close to completion that project was, and he had none of his equipment available. So all her messages, her rings, the phone numbers of her friends and colleagues, and as Cameron said, her photos were in his hands, and she couldn't retrieve it.

She sat down on the bed under a painting of a Hawaiian woman who could have been Okelani many years younger. She wished Cameron had brought *her* to Okelani's instead of Nica—or with her. She needed wise counsel, and though she'd only encountered the old woman a handful of times, she sensed a spirit steeped in grace. She understood why Cameron had sent his sister out, but it made her feel like a toxic element.

Nica's cat jumped onto the bed and made its strange and tortured meow. She cupped its bony head and rubbed its neck as it rose up on its haunches with another ratchety meow. Had it sensed her need for a friend? A knock came at the door.

It didn't surprise her, but it took all her energy to respond. He'd want reassurance that she was all right. She wasn't, but hey, she was an actor. *I'm fine, thanks. No, I don't need anything.* She opened the door.

He held out a toothbrush, paste and comb, a roll-on deodorant and shampoo. He hadn't asked, just gathered up the things Nica had given her before. She took them. "Thanks."

"Can we talk?" His face held more than the surface inquiry she'd expected. But then, he always forced the issue, had from the very start.

"I'm tired, Cameron." Tired of being pursued, imagined, threatened. . . . She was without boundaries. A cell with no wall, no protective membrane. That, she realized, was what allowed her to connect on such an immediate level with viewers, with the kids in the troupe, cast members, friends, strangers. It was that accessibility Cameron had kissed. But right now she wished . . .

"Okay." He turned to go. "Get some sleep."

Those simple words sank her heart. Sleep? How? Her mind would turn everything over and over. She sighed. "Want a cup of tea?"

His brows rose just enough to show relief and surprise. "If there's one thing Nica has, it's tea." He led the way to the kitchen, filled the kettle with hot water and put it on to boil. "Jasmine?"

"Sure."

He took two mugs from the cabinet. The tension between them stretched. She didn't want to be alone with him and didn't want to be without him. Thin tendrils of fear snaked up like smoke, and being alone would fan it. She tried not to let it show.

He found the jar of jasmine pearls and dropped three into each mug. Her few days as Jade had given her a chance to relate to him on a different level, and she wished they could have kept it that way. It was almost as though Gentry Fox was an alter ego that collected troublemakers and worshipers but very few true friends.

A memory came back to her, not current but applicable. Maybe it would help him understand. "When I was twelve or thirteen, we took a family vacation to London. Dad especially wanted to see the changing of the guard." She leaned against the counter. "It was pageantry at its best, of course, perfect choreography."

"So I've heard." He set the mugs next to the stove.

"What really stayed with me happened afterwards, though. Once the guards had taken their places, they stood there, motionless. This woman came up to one while her husband readied the camera. Then she stretched up and kissed the guard's cheek as though he were a bit of statuary placed there for her Creative Memories book."

He sighed. "I'm sorry, Gentry. There's no excuse for before. But it wasn't because of who you are, or rather it was."

"Don't make me parse your words, Cameron. I don't have the energy."

He spread his hands. "Then here it is. I wish you weren't Gentry Fox."

Well, that made two of them, but she was.

"You're tough, loyal, beautiful. . . . It messes with me so bad I don't think straight. I want to know you. I want . . ."

She waited for the other slipper to fall with a rubber slap.

"I said you wouldn't let it go anywhere." The kettle started a low hum. The first wisp of steam spiraled up. "But the truth is *I* won't."

The hum rose to a scream as he reached for a potholder. He took the kettle from the burner and poured the steaming water over the jasmine, releasing the green, exotic aroma. He placed a mug in her hands. "Want to sit on the lanai?"

She nodded. "Okay."

They sat down among the damp plants with the half-moon climbing naked out of the ragged cloud. The rain had stopped, but the smell of it remained and a mist tingled her skin. In all the time they'd spent, this was the first glimpse inside he'd given her. She didn't expect it to last. He'd been shaken by the intrusion, knocked off his guard. But she said, "Are you going to tell me why?"

The mist closed in around them, though the sky still looked clear.

He sat back, cupping his mug. "I don't handle loss well."

"Does anyone?"

He sipped. "When Nica and I were five and six, our parents drowned. They'd gone marlin fishing and got caught in a storm. I kept saying they'd be back, but Nica sat in a ball on the floor with a look on her face I can never forget."

He stared into his mug. "I believe she would have died too. But I wouldn't let her go. I held on so tight Okelani had to pry my arms off her."

Gentry lowered her mug and stared. She'd hoped for a glimpse, hadn't expected a fissure.

He swirled the buds in his tea that would have opened like hers and stretched into leaves and stems in the bottom of the cup. "I don't remember who was watching us that day; Okelani took us in. She raised us like her own, but there was always the fear I'd lose Nica too. So I learned to hold on tight." He looked up. "Okelani told me I love too hard."

Gentry shook her head. "It must have been devastating for you both."

"In different ways. Nica's never gone into the water since, but I can't stay out."

"Why?"

"I have to keep beating it."

"How?"

"One wave at a time."

"Surfing?"

He nodded. "That's why Okelani called me Kai."

What kind of man stuck it to the ocean, wave after wave, year after year? The kind who didn't let go.

"Can I watch you sometime?"

He shrugged. "North shore surf's best in the winter, but we can go south and catch what's over there."

"Notice I said 'watch.'"

He smiled. "Wear your suit."

Hurt and anger welled up. "I don't want to put on anything he's touched."

Cameron set down his mug and stood. "Come on."

In her bedroom, he opened both suitcases and scooped up armfuls of her clothes. She followed with the trailings that fell behind. He stuffed them into the washing machine, poured in the soap, and started it running. Then he turned. She looked into his face and smiled, even though almost everything she owned was dry-clean only.

Cameron went into his room and got a clean T-shirt and a pair of soft drawstring shorts. He carried them into the hall and handed them over. "You can sleep in these."

She brought them to her chest. "Thanks."

"I guess I could have gotten you something of Nica's." He spoke as the thought occurred.

"This is fine."

"Are you tired?"

"Beat. But I won't sleep. I'll keep thinking."

That made both of them. He hadn't planned to reveal his underbelly. But then he hadn't planned any of it.

She put a hand on his arm. "Can we sit a little longer?"

He drew a slow breath. "Sure. But I can't be held responsible."

She searched his face. "Am I a bit of statuary?"

His throat filled with gravel. "Hardly." The uptilt of her chin sent a subliminal code he instantly deciphered. "You're making me break my word."

"I said it depended on why."

He closed her into his arms. Her lips tasted like jasmine.

She dropped the clothes he'd handed her and circled his waist as sobs threatened. "Someone wants to kill me."

"They'll have to get through me."

Her eyes brimmed.

"Don't cry. The world's full of screwed-up people. You can't let them break you."

His phone vibrated in his pocket. He had no intention of answering, but she felt it too.

"Your phone."

"I don't care."

"It might be the police."

He dug it out and looked, then jammed it back in, stomach clenching in a knot.

Gentry read his face. "Someone you know?"

"Someone I never knew."

Her hands rested on his chest. "You want to talk about it?"

"Not tonight." He ran his fingers down her cheek. He had heard reality sinking in for her and dragging fear behind. Angry that someone had shaken her resilience, he took her hand and led her to the couch.

Rain splashed against the windows with renewed vigor. The under-cabinet lights in the kitchen shed the only glow. He stretched onto his side on the couch, motioned for her to join him, and considered it a measure of trust that she did.

"Tell me more about you and Nica."

He talked about them, about TJ, about Okelani, and about the island. He felt her breath deepen and slow, let his own match her rhythm and woke, hours later, with her back against him on the couch, her neck cradled on his arm. The dress she'd worn to the luau hadn't weathered the night as well as his T-shirt and shorts. Her hair smelled faintly of kukui nut oil. He rubbed his face in it.

She stirred, opened her eyes, and rolled over in the crook of his arm. "Did I fall asleep?"

He twisted his wrist to show her the time.

"It's morning?"

"Almost."

She caught her fingers in her hair. "I can't believe I slept with you. Again."

His other arm encircled her waist. "That's all it was, Gentry. Sleep."

"I was scared to be alone."

"I know."

"But it doesn't look good."

"I promise nothing happened." His thumb ran the line of her rib. "Except I'm falling in love with you."

Her lips parted. Her eyes were the green room inside the tunnel of a wave, and this time the sea was going to win.

"There are a thousand reasons that shouldn't happen."

"I know them all." He splayed his hand over her flat belly and kissed her lips, a warm kiss that held no hint of jasmine.

"Cameron."

"I like it better when you call me Kai."

"I can't make a mistake, Kai."

Five years of his life had been a mistake. The next four a train crash.

"Not with everyone watching." She searched his face. "You saw how it is."

"That's not real." He didn't intend to perform in that circus. She shouldn't have to either.

"Tell that to Darla and Dave and Alec Warner." Her eyes misted. "Tell it to the person who wants me dead."

He rose up to his elbow. "Then don't do it anymore. Don't take the new part."

She closed her eyes. "That sounds so easy." Her lashes swept up like a curtain on her stage. "But I want to. Something in me comes alive on stage, behind a camera, with lights and scripts and cast."

He'd seen it. He knew. He'd watched *Steel* seven times after going home. She was amazing, but not because of lights and cameras. "It's alive in you right now. It was alive on the mountain before you remembered. You made *Steel* real, not the other way around."

She drew breath to answer, but his phone vibrated. She rolled and picked it up from the floor. He didn't want to let go, but she got up and headed for the bathroom.

He answered with a gruff, "Pierce."

"You're there, aren't you. You're with her."

Four years she hadn't cared. An argument could be made for nine. He almost said yes and had it out right there, but that would affect Gentry's reputation, or at least attract the gossip hounds again. He rubbed his face. "What do you want, Myra? What can you possibly want?"

"A chance." It came through more desperate than he'd ever heard her. Bad connection. Had to be.

"Five years wasn't chance enough?"

"I didn't know what I wanted, Cameron."

Wrong. She'd gotten exactly what she wanted, from everyone. And he was the last to know. He'd denied it until she gave him names and dates, shoving his stupid face in it so he would let her go. She knew exactly what she wanted. Always.

"Are you making love to her?"

He sank back. "You were the one playing the sex-outside-marriage card."

"It wasn't a real marriage."

Now he understood the psychiatrist's point. She'd been able to cheat with impunity because she'd never entered the covenant. It took two people to make a contract. Each had to bring something to the table. He couldn't make it by himself. "I guess you're right." It felt strangely free, like a crack in the door of his crypt.

Eager now that he'd come to her side, she said, "Do you remember the first day we met?"

He hunched forward and rested his head on his splayed hand. As though he'd ever forget seeing her on the beach the year he'd won the competition. "Myra—"

Gentry went from the bathroom to the laundry closet. He heard her in there dealing with her clothes. There was no dryer, only the clotheslines in the carport. He'd have to move Nica's Saab out.

"I have to go."

"No, wait." A long breath seeped like a vapor into his ear. "I'm sorry."

He sat back like a punch-stunned contender. Sorry? Myra?

"I never say I'm sorry."

Her brash smile had intoxicated him. *"Never?"*

"I'd die first."

"What if you were sorry?"

"I'm not. Ever. I am completely without regret."

Her brazen comment had intrigued, ensnared him. He hadn't thought how it would be to live with someone incapable of remorse. A stone grew in his throat. The other night she'd admitted a mistake but offered no apology. Never once had she offered an apology, in all the years he'd known her. And what was he supposed to say? It's all right; don't worry about it?

Gentry came out of the laundry closet with the basket full of clothes. He wanted to get off the phone, but a tentacle had snaked out and coiled his neck.

"Regret is death. If I'm ever sorry, I'll die." And her laugh had faded, replaced by the stormy turbulence of someone who couldn't look back.

His voice rusted. "Okay."

"Can we talk?"

"Um, yeah."

Her relief was audible. "When?"

He glanced up at Gentry, feeling gutshot. "When I'm back." He hung up and stood. "Let me move Nica's car. We'll hang those in the carport."

TWENTY-EIGHT

The silks had lost sheen and shape, the cottons color; everything grayed like the dawn, hung over from the night's rain; the dragon man's taint washed away, but damage done. How did one rewind past the part where someone tried to kill you? Grover Malakua had reprogrammed her brain to fear.

Holding her against him, Cameron had leeched it from her until she slept. Now, once again, threads of relationship entangled them. She wanted to thank him, but the phone call had put him in a funk, and he needed to work his way out of it. She hadn't asked who called, but the impact was palpable; his efforts to brush it off ineffective. Maybe it was related to her situation, but his bleak expression had suggested a more personal hit.

As they neared the bottom of the laundry basket, he found her bronze Esteban Cortezar bikini and straightened. "This isn't too damp."

"For what?"

"Hitting the surf."

He'd taken her seriously? "You mean now?"

"Definitely."

"Shouldn't we—"

"No. There's nothing we should do instead." He wore an expression that brooked no dissention. "Would you rather borrow Nica's?"

"Why would Nica have a swimsuit if she won't go in the water?"

"She sits on the shore and watches. If the surf's off the Richter, she prays."

"Oh." Gentry looked down at her rumpled dress. "I can pray in this."

He held out her bikini.

She planted her hands on her hips. "How do you know *I'm* not afraid of water?"

"I've seen you, remember?"

"Okay, but . . ."

"Come on. Trust me."

She couldn't fight rivers and cling to cliffs with a man and not trust him—as she'd learned last night, settling into the curve of his body and not admitting even to herself that she didn't want to leave it. Fear was a terrible decision maker.

"I'm not sure I want another encounter with powerful water."

"When fear is strongest, you strike back."

"You sound like Uncle Rob."

"You've got balance and strength. You'll do fine." He stuck two boards in the bed of his truck. "This shorter one got me the junior championship. Should fit you close enough." He'd said last night he had to keep beating the sea. Now he was doing his best to ask, but she had the feeling argument was futile. He needed to take control of something.

Deciding she wouldn't mind a measure of it herself, she put on the damp swimsuit, T-shirt, and shorts.

"When fear is strongest, you strike back." She could be hiding, dreading what might happen next, fixating on the fact that someone had tried to kill her. Instead they were heading to the shore.

Cameron focused when the surf report came on the radio. It meant nothing to her, but he must not like what he heard.

"Why the frown?"

He glanced over. "We're not going to get much. Acid Drops at Lawai can be a good, strong right with steep, hollow barrels. But today's conditions ... Maybe we'll try Pakalas." He nodded. "Yeah, that should work. It's a mellow left that peels forever."

"Is that English?"

"Some da kine surfin' slang." He touched his temple. "Got one choke vocabulary."

She shook her head.

When they reached the beach, he took out the boards. "I'll teach you a few points on the sand first." He stopped near the line where the waves foamed in and set the boards aside. "Lie down on your stomach."

The brittle, lightweight sand gritted and clung as she and Cameron stretched out like two seals who'd scooched onto the beach to sun.

"This won't be the first thing we'll do, but it's easier to learn how to stand up on solid ground. Watch."

He did a push-up and, in one swift motion, pulled his knees to his stomach, hopped to his feet—right in front of left—and stood back bent, arms outstretched. The sharp, lean muscles of his calves were eye level as she watched, the tendons of his feet revealing years of clinging.

He dropped down again. "You'll be holding the rails, the sides of the board." He positioned his hands as though a board lay beneath him. "About halfway between the nose and your chest."

"Shouldn't I practice on the board?"

"It would damage the fins. Just get the feel of it for now."

Imagining his junior championship board beneath her, she pushed up, dragged her knees up under her, and stood.

"Your position's good, but do it faster."

She did.

"Hanah hou."

"What?"

"Again. Do it over and over until it's in your subconscious."

She repeated the process, gaining speed and balance.

"That foot feel good forward?"

She shrugged. "I guess."

"I showed you regular, but you can do it goofy if you want."

"Why would I want goofy?"

He shrugged. "Some dudes like the left foot up. Some, da kine, like me switch it by the wave."

"I'm thinking basic English, Mr. Choke Vocabulary. And basic surfing, if you don't mind."

Climbing another step out of his funk, he took hold of her sand-crusted T-shirt and pulled her closer. "Lose the shorts, but keep this on for now to prevent a rub rash."

In spite of the fact that her body had been rated and discussed by tabloids during the scandal, she felt self-conscious removing the shorts. But Cameron pulled his shirt over his head and reached for his board, already focused on the water and the waves he would beat.

Though the sun was barely up, a few other surfers were out already. Noting her glance, Cameron said, "We're not going that deep yet."

She nodded. "Good."

He stood his board at the edge of the surf. "The board's got a center of gravity; you want to distribute your weight so that it floats on the water just as it would without you."

Floating sounded okay.

"We'll start in the mushy surf. I'll show you how to paddle out, but first I want to tell you about duck-diving."

"Cameron."

"That's what it's called. Now listen up."

After taking a while to find her balance, paddling, duck-diving under the oncoming waves, trying not to cork or dig the nose or rails, and lifting her chest in the chop, she made it out among the sloping swells that were not yet, as Cameron put it, "standing up straight."

From his position a short distance away, he said, "Watch me sit." He straddled his board as easily as though it weren't bucking and rocking. "Keep just below the center point so you can swing the nose left or right, but not so far back it tips you off."

She planted herself as he directed, wobbling on the board but managing not to topple.

"Kay den. First you need to know when *not* to catch a wave."

"Great."

He held up his fingers. "Three mistakes'll give you a jarring experience called—you'll appreciate the terminology—going over the falls."

She groaned.

"Catching a wave too late, when it's already pitching over, is the first mistake. Do that and it'll just be you and tons of water arching down to the seabed. While you're rolling around in fetal position on the bottom, the whole wave dog piles on."

Her stomach turned with a sensation that struck too close to home.

"Mistake number two, falling in front of an arching wave, will get you a ride up with time to anticipate the over-the-falls crash and roll experience previously described."

She pushed the wet hair from her face. "And we're out here, why?"

He smiled. "The third thing to know is that big waves tend to stand up and crash over in about the same spot. Loitering where the curtain drops is one *lolo* idea."

"This whole thing is *lolo*. Did I tell you I've just recovered from a head injury?"

"We won't have any of that here unless conditions change. Surf's so mushy, it's a baby cradle."

"Uh-huh."

"So now you know what not to do. Let's have some fun." His smile had a dangerous edge. "When the wave you want comes, lie down. When you feel the lift, paddle hard. Lean forward and raise your chest. On these mushy waves, wait until you're in the flat water, but as soon as the momentum flows faster than you can paddle, stand up; just like we did onshore."

Sure. Just like solid ground.

"Remember, keep your eyes forward, not down at your feet. Ready?"

He sounded so eager something inside her awakened, and she laughed. "Okay." She was probably out of her mind, but she pushed against the fear, and it felt good.

The contest had hardly been fair, conditions almost a forfeit, but being out there had still worked its magic. By the time they splashed ashore, Cameron had pressed his conversation with Myra into the hard place that held the previous nine years. Guarding Gentry was enough to think about.

She'd done great in the water—as he'd expected, given her natural athleticism. If they got a high surf before she left, he'd show her how good it could be. Now, in her soaked T-shirt and bikini, she signed autographs and allowed a few photos while he searched the faces of fans for murderous intentions.

A guy he knew by the broad nose he'd gotten from too many face-plants on his board nodded toward her. "Geev 'um, brah."

Cameron smiled, but "going for it" with Gentry Fox made as much sense as surfing the boneyard. If it came to choices, she'd take the cameras and the lights. She'd said so.

He toweled off, his thinking cleared by the sea. Kai. His name-sake. Sometimes brutal, sometimes deadly; beautiful, seductive, ever present. Since his parents' deaths he couldn't remember a dream without the ocean in it. It was more alive than their memories. He'd dived its depths, forced out its secrets, ridden its crests, swum its currents. He breathed its scent even miles from the shore. He tasted its salt in his sleep.

Gentry said she could still feel the waves as they drove back to Nica's, but he carried their loft and thrust inside always. Anytime he started to stray, he had only to ground himself in the sea.

While Gentry showered, he called Bette Walden, got through on the third ring and said, "I think we should talk."

"I might agree if I knew who you were."

Cameron leaned against the wall. "Your bag of tricks doesn't include voice recognition?"

"Fancy maneuvering yesterday."

"That was nothing."

She sniffed. "What do you want?"

"To meet, come together on this thing."

"We both have a job to do." Her avoidance grated. "I skidded into a rock yesterday."

"Sorry to hear that."

"My client can't afford those kinds of expenses."

Possibly informative. "Send me the bill."

"So Gentry can pay? That's almost worth it."

He looked at his watch. "Where are you?"

"Lihue."

Exactly where he'd be taking Gentry. The hospital should be safe enough for the span of time he'd spend with Bette. "I can be there in an hour." Forty minutes for the drive and time for Gentry to clean up and dress. It wouldn't be long before the police had questioned Malakua.

The island wasn't that big. After the vehicular homicide, he'd skulked at his cousin's house, but that cousin was in jail, and Malakua was easily recognized and unpopular. Not many would stick out their necks for him.

Bette said, "Good, you can buy me lunch."

"Paradise Grill. South of town." He'd try to have an appetite.

⌒

Gentry sat down beside her napping uncle and lifted the booklet from the side of the bed where it had fallen, one of his favorites, *Living the Psalms*, written by his pastor. It fell open from use on the page titled: *Being a Man After God's Own Heart*. Was he finding solace in words that had shaped and defined him the last few years?

As her gaze slid to his sleeping face, his eyes shot open; he hollered and jolted up.

"Uncle Rob? What is it?"

He stared at her with reddened eyes. "What are you doing here?"

"I'm—"

"I can't keep you safe. Don't you see?" He gripped the bed rails. "I can't do anything for you! I can't do anything . . ." He dropped back down.

She clutched his hand, feeling his anxiety and agitation. "It's okay. Everything's okay." But her heart raced. Was this the post-traumatic stress Paul had warned them about?

Her uncle's face pulled into a tight grimace as he sank into the pillows. He'd been so confident last night, meeting Cameron, charging him with her protection. Loving, strong, real.

He groaned.

"What is it, Uncle Rob? Were you dreaming?"

He rolled his head her way. "I've lost her, Gentry."

She frowned. "Aunt Allegra?"

"You know how she is. Botox, tucks, liposuction, implants."

More than she wanted to discuss, but no way would she stop him.

"She thought I wanted her that way." He turned. "Maybe I did. I never stopped her, never told her she didn't have to be thin, voluptuous, and wrinkle free. Not until I realized what mattered. Then telling her invalidated everything she'd done."

"She didn't understand."

"Neither did I."

"She wouldn't listen."

"Neither would I." He groaned. "Now look at me. Look."

She took in the maimed limb that would surely horrify Aunt Allegra, whose quest for perfection never ceased. The ache in his face showed how much he still loved her, how he needed her. She felt his fear and desolation.

She almost sank back into the mires of guilt, but the rhythm of the waves still rocked her. God had a plan, even in this. Life wasn't random. They had only to do the best they could with what they had. "Hang on, Uncle Rob. Hold on to what you know is true."

His breath made a slow escape. "Tell me what's true."

She lifted the booklet. *"Because your love is better than life, my lips will glorify you. I will praise you as long as I live, and in your name I will lift up my hands. My soul will be satisfied as with the richest of foods; with singing lips my mouth will praise you.'"*

⌒

The last thing Allegra wanted was a manicure. But she'd kept her standing appointment, because Gloria expected her. Allegra met people's expectations. She knew how to qualify, modify, nullify. Like the real nails ground off to make room for the fake, a smoother, stronger self poured into the holes.

She'd been scheduled to return from Hawaii the day before so, of course, Gloria wanted to hear all about it. Allegra described the beach, the hotel, the sunset view with the correct excitement. She had told her only that she was going with a friend, so needn't discuss Curt, but when Gloria took her hand, Allegra shrank back, wanting to shout, "Unclean, unclean!"

Gloria chattered over her nails, blind to the pestilence, deaf to the silent screams. Guilt remained an invisible specter, and in fact Gloria would think nothing of it if she laid out the whole sordid affair. "Happens all the time," she'd say. "Do you really think you're the worst? Honey, the stories I hear . . ."

She wished she could put it behind her, out of her mind away from her thoughts. Instead, as Gloria worked, she imagined pulling each ground, shaped, and painted nail out. How people would stare at her bloody stumps. Bloody stump. Her gorge rose, and she pressed it down.

She couldn't think of Rob that way. He'd always been so . . . whole. No pieces missing, nothing that didn't fit. He knew so many things, did so many things. He was the fixer and the doer. He was the standard by which she measured—and always, always fell short. That was the downfall to marrying the perfect man—even before he found Divinity.

Waves of agony scoured her. Gentry had asked her to come. Instead she'd flown home. Gloria saw nothing. But Rob ... Rob would look into her soul and recoil. The horror she felt for his mutilation wouldn't touch what he'd feel for hers. Her amputated spirit writhed. *Unclean.*

TWENTY-NINE

Cameron ordered broiled-fish tacos; Bette Walden the fish and chips. With all her angles and points, she must shed fat like sloughed skin. Or else she burned it away with white-hot spite.

When the waitress left, he said, "Who sent you the photos?"

Sweet'N Low dissolved in the whirlpool inside her tea glass. "You know I won't say."

"Whoever did is accessory to fraud and possibly attempted murder."

She paused the spoon in her tea. "What are you talking about?"

"Gentry's face; someone else's lewd poses. I have a copy of the file used to create them."

Bette brutalized the lemon that had hung innocently at the rim. "And you got this file . . ."

"From the source. Troy's mother."

Bette wrung the last drop from the fruit and drowned it. "She gave it to you?"

"Troy did."

She looked up. "Troy, who's on suicide watch?"

He frowned. "Since when?"

"Two months ago. Admitted to a juvenile facility for emotional distress resulting from sexual and emotional abuse. Gentry might have the biggest platform for denial, but—"

"You'd better check your source."

"What do you mean?"

Cameron studied her face. "Troy Glasier, son of felon Darlene Glasier, sandy hair, small scar on the bridge of his nose?" He touched the side of his own to mark the spot. "He's not in any facility, nor has he been, except for the brief examination after his supposed overdose. I spoke with him personally just days ago."

She looked baffled.

"If your informant is your source for the pictures—"

She leaned forward. "What did you mean, attempted murder?"

"Gentry was pushed. Over the falls."

"Of course." Bette rolled her eyes. "I'm sure she played *that* well."

"Actually she denied it. She couldn't believe someone wanted her dead, until she found her place trashed. You wouldn't know anything about that, would you?"

She jerked back. "You don't think I had anything to do with it?"

He shrugged. "You're harassing, stalking, and making false accusations. Collaborating in a fraud."

"Those pictures were sent to me—"

"Who's to say you haven't taken it a step further?"

"That's—"

"You've made this your personal vendetta. Why?"

She snapped her teeth together. "I'm doing my job."

"Your job requires you get the facts. Fact one: Troy Glasier never had an affair with Gentry Fox. A true, if misguided, adoration, maybe. He's offered to set the record straight. What he got from Gentry was someone who believed in him, who gave him an opportunity to deal with the junk in his life. Other people took it and twisted it."

Bette still looked skeptical.

"He gave me the file because he's tired of being manipulated by his mother, who planned to blackmail Gentry. Is she your client? Your source? You delivered the threat."

Bette shook her head. "I saw his interview. I believe him."

"He lied. What kid wouldn't lie to cover his backside? He'd already boasted. Now he was getting national attention, not to mention the potential legal pitfalls of a false investigation. Who knows what Mom threatened. She's a professional irritant."

Bette grabbed her tea and drank.

"Not only is Troy not suicidal, not contained in a juvenile facility, he's taking steps in the right direction, facing up to his mistakes."

She worked her jaw side to side. "You don't—"

He took out his phone. "Call him yourself, if you don't believe me. He's under G."

She stared at the phone but didn't take it. They'd gotten a table on the covered porch enclosed by a half wall. The heat of the day was building. "My client has not been anywhere near this island. She couldn't possibly be involved in Gentry's accident."

She. "You and I both know things can be orchestrated from a distance. Look how well she played you."

Bette tapped her nails on the table. "I think you're wrong."

"Based on what? Your animosity toward Gentry?"

"I have nothing—"

"Your own baggage?" He pushed his napkin-clad place setting aside. "Admit it. You can't wait to nail her. You're so eager you didn't even get the facts."

"Fine." She drew herself up. "I can't stand people who damage kids. They ought to pay."

"Big time. But Gentry hasn't damaged anyone. Her program gave at-risk kids a place to deal with their damage."

She moistened her lips. "So *she* says. I heard otherwise. Ego, disloyalty—"

"Disloyalty?"

Bette picked up her purse and planted it in her lap, a prim and protective position. "You have your opinion—"

"I have firsthand experience."

"I'll bet."

He seethed. "You think this is about sex?"

She looked away. "Women like Gentry—"

"You don't know the first thing about Gentry. But you and the press have all but destroyed the positive things she did with her troupe. You've let your own issues temper the truth, and it stops now." He stood up, thankful he hadn't had to eat. "I'll get the check. If you harass Gentry further, you'd better have concrete proof, or I'll come down with everything I've got."

She stood. "I don't harass. I investigate."

"Investigation 101; let the evidence tell the story."

She jutted her chin, protruding her hawkish mouth. "If I've been mistaken . . ."

He walked away before she could finish.

In the lot, he phoned TJ in his patrol car. "What's the word?"

"Bender and Severt tried for question Malakua. He wen bolt."

"He ran?" If he'd played it cool, the officers might have taken him at his word. *"No, brah, never seen dat woman."* Their heads nodding. Celebrity tantrum.

"He one *lōlō* buggah. He do what he get told, but he nevah tink right on his own."

"That doesn't make him less dangerous."

TJ sighed. "Got one APB on him. We going get da buggah."

Unless he went *mauka* and lived off wild fruit, they'd run him down sooner than later on an island as minimally populated as Kauai. With that mug and the dragon sprawling his arm he couldn't exactly blend in to a crowd.

"Okay. Keep me posted."

"You got Gentry?"

He fired the engine, wishing he hadn't left her at the hospital. "She's with her uncle. I'm on my way there."

"Bettah watch her, brah."

It wasn't the PD's job to keep her safe, though she could have hired an officer for extra duty. It was their job to determine if a crime against her had been committed. They'd assume Malakua guilty of something, since he'd run, but that might make him take risks. Cameron put his foot to the gas.

⌒

Gentry had not told her uncle about Grover Malakua breaking in and stealing her phone. His mental state had deteriorated—a predictable stage in the psychological elements of the rehabilitation, Paul had said—and she could not lay anything else on him. But she'd been out of communication since the luau yesterday, and people would worry if they couldn't reach her. So when Uncle Rob went for therapy, she used his cell.

Starting with her parents, she let them know her phone had been stolen. She said it as matter-of-factly as she could, but still it amazed her how easily they took it at face value. "At least you weren't mugged," Mom offered.

"Of course she wasn't mugged." Dad's tone suggested the very thought absurd.

They spent the next five minutes discussing Uncle Rob. Gentry told them he was being transferred to a treatment center in Palo Alto in the morning. It made no sense for anyone to come now. She didn't tell them someone had tried to kill her and maimed her uncle in the process, but the irrational desire took hold to curl up between them as she used to in their lofted bedroom.

They would point out all the positives in the situation. Someone pushed you in? Good thing you had all those years of swim lessons. Remember how you threw kisses from the side of the pool?

"I need to call Dave now. If he's tried and couldn't reach me, he'll be frantic."

Someone wanted her dead, but as long as it didn't interfere with future contracts he'd be all right. No, that wasn't fair. If she couldn't get her mind around it with all the facts, how could she expect people to guess?

"How are ya, doll?" Dave's gravelly greeting made her smile. Not many people appreciated that term anymore, but with Dave it was both shtick and a true endearment.

She explained the phone situation. "I just wanted you to know I won't be reachable for a while."

"We need to cover one point."

"One that we've covered before?"

"The no-nudity clause, yeah whatever. But the extra strictures . . ."

Even with a no-nudity clause in the contract, there were myriad battles. The specifics in hers were spelled out in inches covered and inches revealed. Alec's films could be brutal and always had chemistry, but so far he hadn't stripped for the cameras, and she didn't intend to either.

He said, "They reward cooperation."

"Dave . . ."

"Just seeing how hard you got hit on the head, doll."

"Not that hard."

He sighed. "Okay, but you're killin' me."

"You're a tough guy."

"I'm a pussycat."

She laughed. "Your secret is mine."

The next calls were like talking through a mouthful of gauze. Nobody recognized her growing desperation—until Cameron came and took one look.

"That bad?"

She turned from the window. "I wonder if anyone knows me."

"You're too good an actor."

Was her whole life just one part after another? Ultimate optimist for her parents, daring adventurer with Uncle Rob, a performing doll, indomitable star. Was she so able *to become* that she hadn't learned *to be*? Her truest sense of self had come when she hadn't known who she was.

At least with Cameron she didn't have to pretend. From that first evening on the beach she'd done and said exactly what she meant, and he'd responded accordingly. But that was ending now, this island interlude drawing to a close. "My uncle's being transferred to a nursing facility in Palo Alto."

"When?"

"In the morning."

He joined her at the window. "The police might need you to identify Malakua."

"Then they'd better hurry."

"Gentry." He took hold of her arms. "I don't think he acted alone."

"What do you mean?"

"Grover Malakua's a hired thug with no personal motive, and frankly, he's not smart enough to formulate a plan. That's why they couldn't prove motive in the vehicular homicide charge."

"Then—"

"I don't think it's some kook you've picked up. And I don't think it's random."

Not random? Then someone she knew was . . .

He drew her close. "I don't mean to scare you. But if you go back—"

"You think they'll follow?"

"I'm not sure they're here. You could have brought this with you."

She dropped her forehead against his collarbone. "I have to go on with my life." The life someone wanted to end. "What am I supposed to do? Hide?"

"You could try not wearing a bull's-eye."

She raised her face. "And what? Teach kindergarten?"

"I have fond memories of—"

She shoved his chest. "I have to believe God will—"

"Open your eyes." He gripped her shoulders. "Do you think your uncle expected to lose his leg?"

"He expected to lose his life."

"Gentry . . ."

She shook her head. "It's not your problem."

"Yeah? Well, I'm falling in love with you."

"You told me."

"What am I supposed to do with that?"

The warmth of his hands flowed down her arms. His claim was nothing new. Others had said so after one date. Hundreds shouted it without having met. But his face told her he hadn't anticipated or intended it. His mouth told her he meant it.

She rested her hands on his chest. "Maybe there's a way to bring it back with us."

"Back is where everything else is." The grim look had returned.

Everything else. Their different realities. "Who called you this morning?"

"Myra."

"Your wife?"

"That never happened."

She raised her brows.

He sighed. "I thought we made a promise and she broke it. But she never made it."

Gentry frowned. What did that mean?

"Her psychiatrist said she was not able to commit. She'd spoken empty words. That what was supposed to happen never did." He swallowed. "No covenant, no two becoming one."

He rested his forearms on her shoulders. "Only no one told me. I thought it was real."

She touched his lips. "It was to you."

He kissed her fingertips. "This is real."

Stranger things had happened. She raised her face. "Then it'll find a way."

⌣

Winding through the lush and loamy ferns, palms, and guavas, Nica breathed the scents that identified each variety as easily as their appearance. Okelani had taught her that recognition, but the plants revealed themselves to any who sought. Little puffs of red powder rose from her footsteps as the bouquet of her own yard beckoned.

She had hoped to find Kai and Gentry home. Instead, a big man sat in a heap against the sliding door as she emerged from the path. Unkempt and haggard, he glared as she approached. Not unusual. Many of those who came were strung out, belligerent, used to ridicule and rejection.

She walked up and stood above him. "Can I help you?"

He rose up like Behemoth, a great brown eruption. On the massive arm that hooked her neck, a dragon writhed. His hot breath scorched her, and her heart pumped a single word into her mind. *Malice.*

THIRTY

Cameron's phone vibrated between them like a rude imp set on destroying every tender moment. Gentry's lashes swept up, her rain-forest eyes misty, her lips warm. If it was Myra calling, he'd know she had fixed him with a camera implant while he slept. He'd lacerate every inch of skin until he gouged it out.

But it wasn't Myra on the ID. It was . . . Gentry. He sent her a sharp look, let her go, and answered. "Pierce."

"Your sistah *ma-ke*, brah, less you hear me."

His heart stopped. Every sinew in his body pulled taut. Nothing moved through his vocal cords, but he hadn't been told to speak, only listen or Nica was dead.

"Got one beeg knife at her troat."

He felt the blade on his own windpipe. "Talk."

"You know who dis?"

"I have a guess. What do you want?"

"Off da island."

He expelled a breath. "How am I supposed to—" Nica's squeal sent liquid ice through his legs. A coppery whiff of blood cloyed his mind. "Stop!" His stomach clenched hard as a fist. He didn't voice his doubt again. Instead his brain raced through the possibilities. "You want a boat?"

"No boat. One plane."

"You'd never get through airport security. There's an APB . . ."

"You get da cops, dis rabbit dead."

Wherever they were, one slice of his blade . . . "A boat could take you—"

"Da boat make one trap. Want one plane. Get to da mainland."

His thoughts spun. "You'd need a sizable jet." Like Denny's.

"Den get one." Malakua had to be desperate to take a hostage. He must have burned all his bridges, and going commando into the jungle wasn't his style. TJ had described a lazy thug, but he must know Gentry could tie him to attempted murder and assault.

"Let me think." Even with Denny's jet, they'd never slip Malakua through Lihue security. What other possibilities . . . Princeville? In an emergency, Denny could land a jet at the privately owned Princeville Heliport. No tower. No FAA. The APB would have covered all egress from the island, but he could get around that. Maybe. "I might be able to bring a jet into HPV."

"Do it. Kanakanui's *wahine* go wit me."

"No." Cameron clenched the phone.

Across the line Nica gasped.

Rage erupted. "Let her go. I'll be your hostage."

Malakua laughed. "You one *lolo* buggah."

"Listen to me. She's never left the island—"

"I'll go." Gentry grabbed the phone from his hand.

Startled, he struggled to get it back, but she spoke to Malakua.

"It's me you wanted anyway, not Nica."

No voice emerged from the cell. Malakua must be balancing his options. Which would get him more? Cameron clenched his teeth. No way was he letting either of them—

"Kay den. Trade one sistah for one girlfriend. Get da buggah plane to da heliport. No cop. I see one cop, I cut dis *wahine*."

Cameron said, "Wait," as Gentry said, "Okay."

The line went dead. He could dial it back, but Malakua wouldn't listen. Neither would Gentry.

Her jaw was set. "It's my fault. If I'd gone to the police, none of this would have blown up as it has."

But he understood now why she hadn't. "It's not your fault, Gentry. I won't let you—"

"It's not up to you. You came here to keep Nica from getting hurt. That's what we're doing."

Nica's fear lodged in his chest. He remembered her in his arms, her small frame rolled up and rocking as he'd whispered uselessly, *"They're coming back. I promise."* He hadn't kept that promise. But he'd kept Nica, when she could have been swept away. Conventional wisdom said call the police. But he knew too well how a situation could go bad. And he'd depended on others before.

Gentry dropped her hand. "Do what he said, Kai."

"Your uncle won't—"

"Know? You can't tell him."

His heart pounded. "Gentry . . ."

"Malakua has no control at the destination without a hostage he can handle." She swallowed. "I'm too well-known for him to do something stupid."

"He tried to kill you."

"For someone else in a supposed accident. He'd be stupid to try anything now. He wants to disappear."

"This isn't a movie."

"But I can play it." Determination fixed her gaze. She would do it. But he couldn't let her. He'd call the—

Panic squeezed his throat. An image flashed through his mind so powerfully his heart lost its rhythm; Nica swept away, submerged in a crimson-hued tide. Never once had he experienced visions. Intuition, gut reaction, but nothing like this.

If the police surrounded them, cornered Malakua, how would the man react? There were no highly trained SWAT snipers, no official negotiators on Kauai. The time it would take to alert and transport such personnel would terrorize Nica. And if his vision was real, either collaterally or intentionally she would be lost. Instinct told him this was no fluke of terror in his mind. He'd been warned. His best hope was to end it as quickly as possible.

TJ should be able to clear the tiny private airport for an emergency situation. Malakua said no cops, but calling TJ wasn't the same as calling the police. He had a personal stake, and Malakua had even named him. "Brace yourself, brah," Cameron said into the phone. "Malakua's got Nica."

He hadn't expected an explosion. Like the sea drawing out from the shore to become a tsunami, TJ gathered his fury in silence.

"He wants off the island. He's agreed to exchange her for Gentry and a ride on Denny's plane."

"Going kill dat moke."

Cameron checked his watch. "He must have grabbed her on the path from Okelani's. They had hula classes this morning."

"Where—"

"I think she's home. I heard the cat." Its wrecked vocal cords were unmistakable. At least for the moment, she was in her own space. If they flushed them out, her anxiety would rise exponentially.

"I'm going—"

"TJ, we'll lose her if we try anything stupid. I had . . . I saw something." He described the vision and trusted TJ's heritage to accommodate it. "I wouldn't make this up." The crimson waves that carried her away had not tasted of salt.

"*What* den?"

"I need you to get access to the Princeville heliport for an emergency situation. I'll call you with timing after I talk to Denny."

Denny serviced the six main islands with his charter jet. From any in the string, it was a short hop over. But if he was on the mainland, he'd be six hours away. Too long for Nica's fragile psyche. They'd have to involve the police.

So that was the test. If his decision was wrong . . .

His call connected. *God.* Rang again. *Please.* His thoughts were already known, but he mouthed them anyway. *Let him be close.* With the third ring, he freed the prayer. *Amama.*

Denny's voice. "Hey, Kai."

"Denny, where are you?"

"Nawiliwili Harbor."

Same island. Minutes away. Shame and relief purged his doubt. *Mahalo ke Akua.*

"Denny, I've got trouble." As he spoke, he realized he'd be asking his friend to transport a fugitive and put his own life in danger. But then another possibility occurred. Denny's jet, but . . .

Cameron swallowed hard. He hadn't kept up the hours for his license, and it had been years since he'd piloted anything across the ocean. He pushed that small concern behind the greater ones.

"What trouble?"

He told Denny about Nica and Malakua's demand. He told him Gentry's part. As she'd said, the danger lay at the destination. If Malakua intended to disappear, he'd have to keep Gentry and Denny from revealing his location. Either immobilize—or silence them.

Cameron clenched his jaw. Not gonna happen. He had to be there to control the situation. Somehow.

"You'd have to bring her in to Princeville. Then let me fly her out."

Gentry's gaze shot to his face. He'd taken them by surprise, but the thought started to feel right. *"Trade one sistah for one girlfriend."* No way, buggah. I keep them both.

"It might take some balancing with the tower," Denny said. "I'll phone you an ETA."

He swallowed a lump as hard as a stone. "Denny . . ."

"You'd do it for me, Kai."

He pocketed his phone and began the wait. How long before he heard, before Nica—

Gentry touched his arm.

"I'm guessing he'll wait at Nica's. He'll want a space he can control, and the fewer moves he makes the less attention he draws. If the police close in, he's holding the wild card. He knows I won't risk her. I just wish . . ."

"Could someone check on her? Someone nonthreatening. Like Okelani?"

His respiration increased. Someone to reassure Nica, let her know she wasn't alone. Okelani might be the perfect choice. Who could suspect an old blind woman?

He locked on to Gentry's gaze. "And we'd learn for sure if they're there."

He called Okelani and told her what had happened. "I just need to know she's okay." He roughed his hand through his hair and shut his eyes. She wouldn't be. She didn't understand cruelty. A damaged butterfly broke her heart.

"You know, Kai. *Ke Akua* wen handle dis."

He had to hope. "I know, Tūtū."

"How much time we got?"

Denny needed to get to the airport, fuel, file a flight plan and receive clearance, and then take off, circle, and land. "An hour, maybe two."

"Kay den. You do your part; I do mine."

He slid the phone into his pocket.

Gentry took his hands. "I have one question." Her voice shook. "Can you fly a jet?"

⌒

Pressed down by dread, Nica breathed the sharp, acidic odor of the man hunkered down beside her. The cut on her neck stung where the knife had pressed in, but he no longer held it there. It lay on the table like a totem of violence waiting to be taken up and revered.

She had never smelled her own fear. She'd smelled others'. She knew the scent of despair and long-suffering. The poignant smell of death. But her fear had startled her with its piquant immediacy. Its particular scent lasted only as long as she thought Kai might come for her and die.

Then it subsided beneath the malodorous thickening of the air, a scent that held whispers of ignorance and brutality. Death didn't scare her. Evil did. Cruelty without cause. Banal violence. The man's fingertips felt like the leaves of a rubber plant when he ran them down her cheek.

A quiver of loathing passed through her.

"You one little rabbit." He felt her hair. "Nevah skin one rabbit before."

She closed her eyes and found the face she needed. Blood ran from the four-inch thorns pressed into his head, from slaps and buffets, spittle and insults. He held out his hand. *Come, Nica. Walk with me.*

Blood transferred from his palm to hers as their hands clasped. He hadn't shown her his physical suffering before. She'd seen his sorrow, his compassion, even his grim acceptance of a final rejection, a soul turning its face even in death. But today he was Iesū the man, scourged and pierced.

The rubber-plant fingers slid down her neck, across the cut. "Poor little rabbit."

Her breath caught. His hand moved again.

Wait with me, beloved. Wait and pray. Together they knelt. He hunched over the stone. *Father, if it be possible let this cup pass from me.*

She didn't find it strange that he was already crucified, yet praying for the ordeal to be averted. They were outside time, no before and after. She pressed into him, her side to his, her hands on the chalky stone, his arms pearled with rosy sweat. A scent of olives and night. A nightingale impressed its song. She'd never heard one but knew it now, a melody piercingly sweet that leapt across the stars and slid like moonglow over the night.

She startled at the rap on the sliding door and opened her eyes to shuttered daylight. The man had closed the bamboo screens, but one buckled where it had snagged on a cactus. Like a candle flame illuminating the shadows was the face she glimpsed in the half-moon gap. She found her voice. "It's Okelani. If I don't answer, she'll know something's wrong."

The irony of her statement passed over him like fog. Wouldn't she want someone to know something was wrong? Why inform him of the possibility? But he snatched up his knife and peeked out, saw the walking stick Okelani had used to maneuver the path, the milk in her eyes. He snorted, and motioned for her to answer the knock.

While he stood off to the side, knife ready, Nica raised the screen and slid open the door. "Tūtū, *aloha*." She kissed her cheek. He stood too close to risk a whisper, but she hoped her fear had come through. Okelani could hear a change in the wind.

"Bring you dis." Okelani raised a Ziploc bag of muffins so hot they'd steamed the plastic like fog. "Mo bettah share. Grind too much you come *momona*." She patted Nica's waist with a laugh, but there was more than mirth in it.

As Nica reached for the muffins, she saw a trace of blood in the lines of her palm. Transfixed, she stared for stretched seconds, then the bag was pressed in.

"*Na Iᶜhowa ʻoe e hoʻomaikaʻi mai, ā e mālama mai.*" The Lord bless you and keep you. Okelani's smile always held ancient *kapu* secrets, but now it told only one thing. She knew.

Nica took the bag and kissed her again. "Don't worry. I won't get fat." Her fingers shook in Okelani's for a moment, then they parted.

"*Mahalo*, Tūtū." As the man snatched the muffins, she watched the old woman turn away and pretend to be blind.

THIRTY-ONE

Gentry had left Cameron in the hall while she said good-bye to her uncle. His grim face would have triggered Uncle Rob's instincts, while she was schooled to portray what she had to. She hated to deceive, but this was one situation the truth would not help. "Since they haven't apprehended the dragon man, Cameron thinks I should leave now. He's arranged a flight." Somewhat accurate at least.

Settled back in the bed, Uncle Rob nodded. "I trust his judgment." That statement would haunt him if things went badly, and again she felt a pang of conscience.

"I do too." Knowing he'd be in the plane with her and the dragon man lessened her fear. Except that he'd be flying it—disconcerting at best.

Her uncle looked fatigued, but the haunted aspect had passed. He'd be leaving in the morning himself, and she was one less detail for him to worry about. "Will you be all right?"

He smiled bleakly. "Believe it or not, yes." He sighed. "I'm sorry for earlier."

"For letting me see?" She squeezed his hand. "Since when have we not shared an ascent?"

"It's not your baggage."

"You've carried my pack plenty of times."

He shook his head. "Not for quite a few years now."

"No expiration on paybacks." She owed him so much.

He searched her face. "Are you okay?"

She gulped back the sudden tears. "I will be. We both will."

Taking her angst for the concern it appeared, he said, "This summit's going to take a while."

She sniffed. "Expect a few switchbacks."

"Alternate routes."

"A storm or two."

He almost crushed her fingers. "Your father's a lucky man."

She let the tears drop. "I'm the lucky one. I have you both." She kissed his cheek and went out before she broke down and told him everything.

Cameron said nothing until they were in the truck in the parking lot. Then he turned. "This isn't right. He trusted me to keep you out of harm."

"We don't have a choice."

"I keep thinking we must."

He said that, but she knew that every passing minute his concern for Nica ate at him. "What do you call the biggest, most damaging wave?"

His eyes narrowed. "A cruncher."

"That's what's coming. What are we going to do?"

"Smart thing is to bail."

She held his gaze. They were, neither of them, bailers.

He cupped the back of her neck. "We're gonna climb it. A big S right down the barrel."

⌒

Denny's call came as they were en route to Princeville. "I'm cleared for takeoff."

For the thousandth time Cameron wondered if this could possibly be right. "I'll see you shortly." He hung up and called Gentry's number.

Malakua said, "You got da plane?"

"It's on its way."

"No cop."

"No cops."

Malakua ended the call. Cameron pocketed the phone. He could feel the suck of the water rushing into the wave. A moment too early; a moment too late and they'd suffer the full and deadly force.

Though the Princeville heliport mostly serviced helicopter tours, it had a single runway surrounded by cane fields and pastures. He hoped it was in decent condition; it was all he and Denny would have to work with. Cameron turned off the highway into the minimal lot and saw TJ's truck.

He screeched to a stop and accosted him. "What are you doing here? He said no cops."

TJ climbed out. Dressed in T-shirt, shorts, and slippers, he looked innocuous, but Malakua knew him. "I'm here for Nica, brah. When you go."

Cameron eased up. TJ was right. If he got on the plane with Gentry, Nica would need someone. "Yeah, okay." He looked into the building. "What did you tell them?"

"Someone threaten Gentry Fox. We going get her out."

Close enough. "Any sign of Malakua?"

He shook his head.

"Okay." He led Gentry into the terminal where the tour director met them with a stern mien.

"I've alerted the pilot that's out and delayed the next tour, but that's all the space I can make." He looked at Gentry. "Very sorry for all this, Ms. Fox."

Gentry nodded. "Thank you for helping."

"Could you sign this for my daughter?" He held out an index card.

"Why don't you give me her name and address, and I'll send her a signed picture."

"Great." He wrote the info on the card and handed it over. "Things haven't gone too smoothly for you here, but I hope you'll come back to Kauai. Take a tour." He smiled.

She returned it grimly, sliding the card into her pocket. Her tension seemed appropriate to being threatened off the island. Not far from the truth, except they were taking the threat aboard.

Cameron said, "There's a big guy coming with a young woman. Let them through, all right?"

The man nodded, and Cameron led Gentry out to the windy tarmac. Her hair flew around her face as he searched the sky for Denny's Cessna Citation X. No sight or sound of it yet, but it wouldn't be long. From Lihue he would circle out to make a new approach into Princeville.

TJ sweated. He had one focus in this, to hold Nica after the storm. Cameron turned that thought over. It was about time someone realized how special she was. Or maybe she'd waited for TJ all along.

At the first sound of the jet, he threaded Gentry's fingers into his. Why did it feel like betrayal to let her do this? She leaned in, curling her other hand around his arm, but he couldn't tell whether she was needing or providing comfort. Still no sign of Malakua and Monica.

But as the jet touched down, braked hard, and screamed to a stop at the far end of the runway, the tour director came outside, pale faced. Malakua walked behind him with a seven-inch blade at Nica's ribs. Her fear washed over him like a toxic flood.

Malakua glared at TJ. "I wen say no cop."

Cameron spread his hands. "He's here for Nica. Unarmed." He prayed.

"Take off da shirt."

TJ stripped his T-shirt, showing only skin and muscle and cold fury.

"On da ground." At TJ's resistance, Malakua put a choke hold on Nica and raised the knife.

"Get down," Cameron hissed through gritted teeth. If TJ charged, she'd be cut. The waves churned in the back of his mind.

TJ lowered himself to the pavement as the jet turned, the whistle of its engines becoming a whine against the buffeting of the wind.

Malakua barked in Nica's ear. "Trow him da rope." He seemed to weave on his feet. Was he jacked on something?

She pulled a thin cord from the tote on her shoulder. Cameron caught it. Nylon clothesline from her carport.

"Tie him up." Malakua sounded thick-tongued.

Not waiting to be told twice, Cameron tied TJ's hands behind his back.

"Now him." Malakua jutted his heavy jaw at the pale tour director.

Nica tossed him another rope. Cameron tied the hands of the man whose daughter would get Gentry's autograph. The jet taxied to the near end of the runway and stopped. Without knowing how soon he'd take off again, Denny brought it down to the compressors.

"Now you tie him," Malakua hollered at Gentry as he gestured at Cameron.

"I can't." She raised her chin, pure Rachel Bach standing against the union workers who wanted to crush her. "He's piloting the jet."

Malakua shook his head. "No way, buggah."

Denny opened the door and lowered the stairs. When he started to descend, Malakua shouted, "Stop." Denny froze on the third stair and spread his hands.

Cameron hollered over the jet's idle, "I'm flying you out. That's the condition. Danny's had too many hours in the air. They won't clear him for takeoff."

Malakua faltered. His best chance of leaving the island lay before him, and he knew it. But his mind seemed stalled. He shook himself and said, "Take off da shirt."

Cameron looked down. His T-shirt was tight enough to reveal a holster bulge if there'd been one, but he pulled it off and hung it over his shoulder.

"Pockets."

He took out his truck keys and dropped them on the tarmac. Denny would need them. He palmed his wallet and pulled the pockets inside out. "I'm clean." Not for the first time he wished he wasn't. Maybe he should have had the police there in the cane. If not for that crazy vision, he would have covered every angle. But that didn't matter now.

Malakua shook himself. "Den tie her." He jutted his chin at Gentry.

Cameron balked. "She's here voluntarily."

"Tie her, or I cut."

Nica gasped in the grip that tightened on her neck. Red waves rushed behind his eyes. Rage shook his hands when Gentry held hers out, a seemingly submissive move that allowed for hands in front. He tied before Malakua could suggest otherwise, but apologized with his eyes. A dip of her lashes absolved him.

"You! Down here." Weaving again, Malakua motioned Denny forward.

Denny joined them, went through the shirts-off, empty-pockets drill to prove himself unarmed, and came to a rest on the pavement next to TJ. Malakua didn't order Denny tied, either because of his angelic looks, a lapse in focus, or no more rope in Nica's tote. Malakua yanked the bag off and shouldered it himself.

"Over here," he barked at Gentry.

Cameron tensed. A flicker of fear crossed her face, but she played the scene. When she got close, Malakua pushed Nica aside. In that second, Cameron almost leaped. But Malakua got his arm around Gentry's neck, the knife aimed at her ribs.

Cameron's temples throbbed with tight restraint as he caught his sister and searched her soul. "Did he touch you?" In a more violating way than a knife at her throat.

She shook her head, but there was a blankness to her expression he didn't like.

"On da plane." Malakua jerked his head.

With a final glance at TJ and Denny, Cameron boarded the Cessna and stood at the open cockpit. Malakua followed Gentry up the stairs, knife positioned to do deadly damage, though killing her no longer seemed his priority. As Gentry said, he worked by stealth for others. Those others seemed to have deserted him, and what mattered now was saving his neck.

He pushed Gentry into the recliner just behind the small galley counter and plopped into the other. Hands tied, Gentry managed her seat belt and sat erect. Knife in hand, Malakua stayed free to lunge if either of them tried something. Cameron wished Denny could have stowed a gun somehow, but with Malakua's clear line of sight to the pilot's seat, this would have to simply play out. Cameron drew up the stairs and shut the jet door, sealing them in. They'd fly in executive comfort and style—if he could get them off the ground. He ran a peremptory flight check and started the engines. The lights flickered and air-conditioning paused. He checked the hydraulic pumps for the brakes in case he had to abort takeoff, adjusted flaps for lift at a lower speed. No more excuses.

"Go," Malakua ordered. "Get dis buggah in da air."

"I have to notify Lihue we're taking off. Colliding with an airliner won't work for anyone."

Malakua grunted. Cameron kept it short and sweet. Getting the go-ahead, he pressed back in his seat, wondering where he'd left his mind. Like Luke Skywalker, he closed his eyes and pushed the doubts away. But the force that impressed on him was one he'd openly questioned.

Okay, Lord. If you're in this, make it happen.

He revved the engines and started the plane moving. Near one end of the single strip of pavement they reached V–1. No error lights. The noise and thrust increased. V–2 by mid-runway. More thrust and the exhilarating and terrifying physics of flight. No stopping now. The nose came up. V-R. On wings of angels they found open sky. He breathed, but this was only the start.

Cameron glanced in the mirror that showed him the richly appointed cabin and the passengers seated there. Island turbulence bobbled Malakua in his seat, but he seemed unperturbed. With the knife still clenched in one hand, he grabbed a muffin out of the tote and stuffed it into his mouth. Gentry sat stoically, believing.

Cameron returned his focus to the controls and the vista. Still climbing, he brought up the landing gear and managed a bumpy patch of air. The shoreline passed beneath, and they were over the water. In thirty minutes the Citation could climb forty-three thousand feet to transatlantic-crossing altitude. He could take her up to fifty-one and soar above other air traffic as soon as—

They hit a wicked pocket of turbulence. The air chopped; the plane bucked. In this kind of wind, piloting the midsized Cessna was like taming a mustang. He forgot the two behind him, forgot everything but what he'd learned too long ago. He imagined Denny in his place and subconsciously adjusted as he'd seen him do. Still climbing, the bucking increased.

"Kai?" Gentry sounded strained.

"Just some rough air. Stay buckled." He fought another buffeting. Sweat slicked his palms. His jaw ached from clenching. Once he got over the prevailing winds . . . Even as he thought it, the air calmed, and his grip on the yoke softened.

Sweat beaded his temples as he reminded himself that passenger jets were stable. Denny's Citation X was powered by two Rolls-Royce turbofan engines. Its highly swept, one-piece supercritical wing reduced drag for efficient transonic flight. This baby wanted to soar.

Easing forward with the yoke, he leveled out slightly, but a roar behind sent his heart to his throat. Malakua reared up. Gentry had gotten her hands free, and Malakua didn't like it. The brute lunged. With hardly time to think, Cameron raised the aileron on the right wing, lowering its counterpart on the left. They banked sharply.

Malakua flew into the galley counter and landed hard on the floor. The knife skittered into the cockpit, but Cameron was fighting the adverse yaw of his extreme tilt with the opposite aileron and a little rudder, doing all he could to prevent a roll.

Gentry unbuckled and lunged for the knife.

"Don't!" Cameron hollered. "We're too rough." He fought to get it back on the level in the buffeting winds. The jet canted and dipped.

She fell against the copilot's seat and hung on. Malakua rolled unconscious into the galley cabinet, spit and soggy crumbs sticking to his gelatinous neck. If he hadn't been bleary already, that manuever might not have been enough.

As the plane to settled, he said, "Okay, tie him."

Gentry crouched. She pulled one massive arm back, then the other, and used the rope with which she'd been loosely tied. Her knots were merciless.

"Buckle in."

She groped until she found her phone in Malakua's pocket, then dropped into the co-pilot's seat.

He turned. "You okay?"

She looked a little green. "What wrong with Malakua?"

"I'm guessing the muffins."

"The muffins?"

"Smell it? Kava kava. Causes a nice euphoric high that turns into a powerful soporific. Okelani's an herbalist. What do you bet she provided his snack?"

Kava kava, momentum, and just maybe prayer had done the trick. The air smoothed as they reached cruising altitude, soaring over the blue expanse of ocean. He suddenly felt as though he could fly forever. But it was time to return Denny's toy.

THIRTY-TWO

Bumping and weaving in the copilot's seat, Gentry watched the white-ruffled golden shore give way to the fringe of green that became trees. Cameron had radioed their request for landing, and she checked her seat belt as the island came into focus beneath them. *He took it up*—her hands tightened on the armrests—*he can take it down.*

The Hanalei Valley spread like a jeweled plain in hues of emerald. Before it lay the one narrow runway surrounded by cane fields. Flimsy clouds whipped across the windows. The jet jumped. Her hands clenched.

The noise rose as the engines resisted the speed of their descent. Flaps on the wings came up. They dropped and rocked. She glanced back as Malakua rolled side to side on the floor, unaware of his changed circumstances. They dipped again, tore through some ragged wisps of cloud, and lined up with the runway.

She gasped. "Kai."

"I see it."

Directly ahead stretched a rainbow from the ground to the sky like a ribbon poured from the clouds. The stripes of light bridging heaven and earth caused a pang in her chest so sharp it hurt. The ground rose up, the single runway connecting them to the rainbow, fading but still visible.

Her hands softened on the armrests. The wheels touched down, rose up, and settled. Pressure pushed her into the seat as the brakes, flaps, and God's will brought them to a stop. The jet released a long sigh. Euphoric without one bit of kava kava, she snapped off her belt as Cameron left his seat, and they embraced so tightly she couldn't breathe. She didn't need to.

She crushed his ribs, laughing against his chest. Sheer relief made her giddy. "You did it!"

"I think I had some help."

"And we're down, safe and alive!" That much was sinking in.

He rubbed her shoulders. "You were more afraid of my part than Malakua's."

"Duh."

"You didn't think I could do it?"

"You didn't think you could."

He cocked his head. "That obvious?" At her look, he shrugged. "Has been a while."

"*Now* you tell me."

"Want to do it again?"

She slapped her palms to his chest. "No!"

He laughed. "So now we're in for a different ride."

"What?"

"Didn't you notice the police cars and press vans?"

"No. Where. . . ?" She looked out the window. "I didn't see anything but the rainbow." She drew a shaky breath as reality settled hard. "I wish we were back in the air."

He squeezed her hand. "You'll be fine."

She glanced at Malakua. "Are we in trouble?"

"I don't know."

She caught both his hands. "If we are, don't worry. I've got a rich uncle."

"Yeah. One who'll rather skin my hide than save it."

"I'll tell him it was my idea."

"Valiant, but worthless gesture." He glanced at Malakua, moaning softly on the floor, then reached for the door. "Ready?"

"I guess."

"Aw, come on. At's one bombora wave." He leaned back. "Unless you're bailing."

"What?" She narrowed her eyes. "Bring it on."

She descended the stairs he'd lowered to the tarmac. No one seeing these pictures would miss their rapport, and she wasn't sure she cared.

As she and Cameron desended the stairs into the crowd, the police cut through and boarded the plane to arrest Malakua. She looked for contempt in the faces around her but saw only excitement. Darla was right that her stock had jumped. What surprised her was how well Cameron played it. Complex and moody, transparent and opaque, he made a compelling leading man.

The police had already questioned TJ and Nica, the heliport tour director, and Denny Bridges. She settled into a chair in the small waiting area and crossed her legs, drawing every eye. If she could use her influence to get them all through this, she would.

"By the way." She held up her phone. "I recovered this. Officers Bender and Severt might like to know." She reminded them of the burglary they'd failed to take seriously and Malakua's involvement in the "accident" that injured her uncle and her. Suddenly they wanted to listen.

Aware of the fact that they'd attempted to transport a fugitive and probably broken other regulations and laws, she asked, "Should we secure lawyers?"

The pink and paunchy chief of police cleared his throat. "Ms. Fox, we understand the difficulties you've faced in your short time on Kauai. I need your statements, but I don't believe charges will be filed at this time." He sent a stern look to TJ. "Beyond a departmental inquiry."

"Officer Kanakanui has worked hard to resolve my situation from the start. His decisions today saved lives. I'll be happy to testify on his behalf before any board of inquiry." And she'd play it for all she was worth.

The chief's face softened. If he was wise, he'd avoid the public-relations headaches she could cause him. She didn't want to subvert the law, but they had all acted with good conscience.

He pushed up to his feet. "I don't think that'll be necessary. The press seems to think it's a holiday and you're all heroes. Ms. Fox, do you suppose you might stay out of the news for the rest of your stay?"

She refused to consider any other scenario. "I'm leaving in the morning with my uncle."

He half smiled. "Hate to see you go."

"I might be back."

He gave a short laugh. "Fair warning."

Cameron stood up. "Are we finished?"

"I think we can call it a day."

As the chief and his officers left, Nica hugged Cameron. They stood a long time before he said, "Are you all right?"

She nodded.

"You're sure nothing happened."

"I don't know. I wasn't there."

They shared a look Gentry couldn't interpret.

Nica said, "It's all right now."

Gentry hugged her. "I'm so sorry."

"For standing in my place?"

"For getting you into it all."

Nica tipped her head. "Never hesitate to entertain strangers—who might be angels in disguise."

"If there's an angel here, it's Okelani." Gentry could hardly keep from laughing when she pictured Malakua weaving on his feet.

"It was your idea to call her," Cameron said.

"Well." She shrugged one shoulder. "I listen."

That had been divine inspiration. She had no idea Okelani would use herbal skills, only that she might comfort Nica and make Malakua watch his step. But God was infinitely creative.

TJ came back in. "Da chief relieve me of duty for da week."

"Sorry, brah."

315

He shrugged and hung his arm around Nica. "Maybe fish some."

Nica rested her hand on his chest. "TJ'll take me home, Kai."

"I figured." He leaned in and kissed her cheek. "I'll be over later."

Watching them walk out, Gentry frowned. "What did Nica mean when she said she wasn't there?"

"When she's upset, she . . . goes away in her head. She says Jesus is there. He walks and talks with her." His jaw tensed. "That's where she went the day our parents died."

"Oh." She'd never heard anything like that, but Nica was different from anyone else she'd known.

"Ready to face your uncle?"

Dread settled. "He'll have heard."

"No doubt."

The crowd in the small front lot barraged them with questions, but she didn't sense meanspiritedness. Maybe some of their previous attitude had been hers. If she looked for enemies, she'd find them. If she looked for friends . . .

"Gentry, will you and Cameron Pierce be seeing more of each other?"

"We both have busy schedules." Separate lives. "Besides I'm leaving with my uncle in the morning." She didn't know Cameron's plans. Thrown together under intense circumstances, bonds were inevitable, but whether they had staying power, she couldn't say. Certainly not to the world.

A microphone swept up to Cameron's mouth. "Did you ever think you'd spend this kind of time with Gentry Fox?"

He formed a sideways smile. "I planned it."

Uh-oh.

"Of course, I didn't know who she was." He moved steadily forward. "My sister asked my help for a stranger with amnesia."

"Are you planning more time?"

He pressed the remote on the truck, swept his gaze over the reporters, then landed on hers. "I'd be crazy not to."

The press loved it. He must still be riding the high of not having crashed and burned.

"Are you more than friends? Do you want to be?"

His smile told nothing and everything.

"What's been the best part?"

"The best part," he paused, "was seeing Gentry wrestle a giant centipede and win."

She shook her head as he exaggerated one of her shakier moments. What was he doing? He pulled open the truck door. She slipped inside.

"Are you in love with her?"

"Isn't everyone?" The door closed.

Her mouth hung slack as he rounded the hood and got in.

"What was that?"

"What was what?"

"Your interview."

He backed out of the lot and started down the highway. "Thought you'd appreciate having the pressure off you for once."

"Yes, but . . ."

"I gave them what they wanted. Besides, there's nothing like facts to limit speculation."

"Facts?"

He slid her a glance. "What wasn't true?"

She stammered, "That whole centipede thing."

"I said it the way I saw it." He smiled. "That's what's bugging you?"

She shook her head. "I'm not— You took me by surprise. If they think we're together— We could have played the bodyguard card."

"Uh-huh." He slowed for a rusty pickup with surfboards in the bed.

She rested her head back and closed her eyes. "Was it this morning we went surfing?"

"A year or two ago. You pack a lot into your days."

"Me?" She laughed. "You're the one with the secret skills package."

"You mean piloting a jet or carving a wave?"

"Both." She rolled her head to look at him. He was still riding the high. "You've mastered air and water. What about earth?"

"I think you're the terrain expert."

"And fire?"

He bent his wrist over the steering wheel and stared straight ahead. "Oh, I still get burned."

Rob wondered if rage would be what killed him. Living with Allegra he'd learned to bottle tight everything that approximated anger. Now that control was shattered. Pain triggered fury; fear triggered rage. It came up through him with such violence as Cameron and Gentry walked into the room that he wanted to strike. Gentry had lied to his face, not by what she'd said, but by what she hadn't.

She leaned down and kissed his cheek. "I know what you're thinking."

"Not even close." His voice scratched through his fury.

She lowered her face. "Uncle Rob, I'm sorry."

"Sorry?" he rasped. "Sorry?" His hands shook, hands that had taken hers and led her into places, into experiences she would never have known without him. "I jumped in that water." He sucked air into his lungs, reliving the treacherous plunge, the pain, the cold, the terror. "I lost my leg trying to keep you from getting hurt."

She blanched. Beside her Cameron tensed.

Rob didn't stop. He couldn't. "I thought you knew what you meant to me. That you've been the daughter I never had. That . . ." His arms trembled, his chest quaked with pent-up fury.

He fired his gaze at Cameron. "And you. You gambled with my niece—"

Gentry shook her head. "That's not how it was."

He burned holes through Cameron's face. "What kind of man

pretends to care for a woman he's willing to lose?"

"Uncle R—"

"Stop, Gentry." Cameron put a hand to her arm. "Let him have his say."

Hard breaths hammered Rob's chest. "Her life wasn't yours to risk."

Cameron nodded. "You're right."

"It was my decision." Gentry's voice pleaded, but there was an edge to it, an edge he knew too well. Her decision to stretch for that pinnacle, to leap that crevice, scale that face. It was in her to do what she'd done, but he'd waited helplessly while she did it.

For the first time he hadn't been there at the other end of the rope. It wasn't his encouragement making her strong. She was drawing from her own depths. And God's.

"I'm sorry I frightened you, Uncle Rob, but I could not let someone else be hurt because of me." Guilt spoke, but only faintly. When Gentry mapped her course, she held it. She had risked herself in place of a woman she hardly knew, but that was the spirit that would carry her forward while he fell farther and farther behind. That, not anger, was breaking his heart, and he wondered what—if anything—could ever make it whole again.

⌒

Allegra shook with disgust. Flimsy, narrow walls closed her in, the filthy curtain over the small aluminum window admitting a dingy moonlight. Packed into the tiny space, the smell of her brothers' and sisters' sweaty bodies filled the discarded air she breathed. Not enough to go around. Never enough.

Squalid. She'd learned that word and applied it.

Ignorant. That applied to the rest of them. Not her. No matter how many times they told her she was stupid. She knew things they couldn't begin to grasp. Daddy said she was trash and she'd always be trash, but she knew better. She was different. She dared to dream.

Allegra shuddered into wakefulness out of the illusions of Allison Carter, with her cracker accent, her filth and rags. With everything she'd learned, studied, and perfected, every step she'd taken, every goal accomplished, she'd buried that girl and created Allegra Delaney.

Perfect, well-bred Allegra. But inside, she was still trash.

THIRTY-THREE

In the hall outside Rob's hospital room, Cameron breathed in the antiseptic air and expelled his tension. He'd ridden the emotional roller coaster since waking with Gentry in his arms; Myra's call, surfing, Bette. Then Malakua's threats, the gut-aching fear for Nica and Gentry.

They needed normalcy, but what constituted normal for Gentry Fox? She might leave the island, but this wasn't over. Malakua hadn't acted on his own. He was more sure of that than ever. On the tarmac, he'd looked for signs of rage, fixation, or enmity. By all appearances, Gentry was nothing but a tool for his escape. Malakua was not the source of malice Okelani had sensed.

He took out his phone and called the chief of police. When they questioned Malakua, they needed to learn who hired him to cause the accident. Was it the same person who'd hired Bette Walden to make Gentry's life miserable? Maybe Bette's inability to dig up any real dirt had forced her client to more desperate measures.

Bette had said *she.* He didn't think it was Troy's mother. She'd get nothing with Gentry dead. So who stood to gain? Gentry's friend and partner Helen Bastente? Envy could be a deadly incentive.

Gentry came out after a few minutes alone with her uncle. She looked as ragged at the edges as he felt. He took her into his arms, this woman Hollywood would make a star. But he had no expectations. Maybe years from now he'd watch her and remember when. The thought caused such an ache, he lowered his mouth to hers.

Sharp heels rapping the floor brought him up. Bette Walden stopped a few paces away. "It appears my client was mistaken about the photos. I came to tell you I've wiped them off my Palm Pilot and deleted the e-mail."

Covering her backside.

Gentry drew herself up. "Do you still plan to follow me around looking for dirt?"

"There's no reason for me to continue. I've confirmed Troy's state of mind, and—whatever part your relationship played in his confusion—he's changed his story." She tugged her purse strap up her sloping shoulder, and added, with a hint of mockery, "It appears I was right about one thing, though." She spun and walked away.

So he hadn't been entirely professional. He also hadn't been retained. Whatever work he'd done for Gentry, he'd done as a friend. He'd done it because she reached up inside and found the part of him that could still care.

Gentry released a breath. "That's one less thing to worry about."

"Bette might be stepping down, but not necessarily the one who hired her. And that person may also have hired Malakua."

She closed her eyes with a sigh.

"I'm sorry. But I'm not convinced this is over." He leaned against the wall. "Are they still transferring your uncle in the morning?"

"Yes. He needs to be fitted with a prosthesis and receive specialized therapy on the mainland. They'll also have the appropriate psychological counseling."

"He was understandably angry."

"I know." They started down the hall.

"How would you feel about flying back with Denny and me?"

She stopped walking, her expression puzzled and skeptical. "Why?"

"It might be safer for both of you. Until we know who's out there."

She flushed. "I could still endanger Uncle Rob?"

"Your plans are no secret." She'd even told the press.

"I don't believe this." She clenched her jaw as belief sank in. "Then we have to go tonight, and we have to take Uncle Rob."

"What?"

"If someone's planned another accident, Uncle Rob can't be on the plane either. No one can."

"He'll need a medical transport."

She shook her head. "A medical professional." She stopped abruptly. "Paul. He's a nurse and therapist. He's strong enough to lift and assist Uncle Rob. He'll know what to bring; he's worked with him almost exclusively."

Cameron expelled a breath. She was indomitable—and probably right. "Okay. How do we find this nurse?"

She took out her phone, paged down, and said, "Here."

"You have his phone number?"

"He gave it to me. In case I had questions."

"Uh-huh."

She called the man she seemed to think so highly of, explained the situation, and told him, "My uncle will compensate you for your time." She laughed at whatever he said. "I'm sure we can do better than that."

When she hung up, Cameron cocked his head and assessed her. "Better than what?"

She gave him a secret smile and slid her phone into her pocket. "Should you talk to Denny?"

He frowned. "Yeah, okay." Then he hooked his hand behind her head and kissed her. Just so she knew.

He called Denny on the way to Nica's, ran the request by him. "We'll pay the charter fee."

"Sure." Denny said. "I'll catch a nap and meet you at HPV at eight. Be about right for a clandestine takeoff, and an ETA after the five A.M. noise curfews."

"Perfect." He hung up. "We're on."

⌒

Nica's spam musubi had to be one of the worst things she'd ever tasted. But looking across the table to TJ and Cameron, Gentry guessed they didn't agree. TJ licked a smear of seaweed from his fingers and closed his eyes in blissful surfeit. "So how you going swipe da uncle from da hospital?"

Gentry smiled. "We're not swiping him. Paul's got the discharge papers. The transfer was already in the protocol; we're just modifying the schedule."

"And the transportation." Cameron dabbed with his napkin. "Break da mout."

TJ jutted his chin. "You grind so much you come *momona*."

"Wouldn't talk, brah."

TJ patted his belly. "Dis pure beef."

"I saw that pure beef lying on the pavement."

"Watch da mout." TJ slapped the back of Cameron's head.

Cameron came up laughing. "Like some da kine hot dog roast, the three of you—"

TJ shoved his chair back. "Going take you apart."

Gentry shared a glance with Nica as the other two wrestled. Too much had happened for them to need words. She would miss her so much. Okelani carried a teapot to the table and ordered the boys to stop. They let go and straightened up.

Cameron nodded at the pot. "What's in there, Tūtū? No kava kava, I hope."

"*Liliko'i*. Passion fruit blossom for celebrate *hana aloha*. Da love magic."

His gaze came across the table, and Gentry met it. Once they left this island, she wasn't sure any *hana aloha* could survive. But she'd have this moment, this place in her heart.

And now it was time to go. Cameron made TJ promise to call with whatever they learned from Malakua. He hugged his sister and his adopted grandma.

Gentry hugged TJ. "Thank you for risking so much."

"No problem."

She hugged Okelani, who put a hand-tied lei of leaves around her neck with a kiss. "Ti, for keep da evil spirit away."

"*Mahalo*. For everything." She knew the old woman could see what was in her heart, see it all with eyes of faith and love. "*Aloha*, Okelani."

Next Nica squeezed her. "Promise you'll come back."

"I warned the police I might."

Nica laughed and put a lei of white orchids around her neck. She kissed her cheek. "*Aloha*."

Tears sprang to Gentry's eyes. "I don't know how to thank you." Though she would think of a way.

"Come see me soon. Make Kai bring you."

They drove to the heliport in silence, her throat too thick to risk words. But as they crossed the tarmac to the jet, she found her voice. "Denny can fly in the dark?"

Cameron squeezed her hand. "Honey, Denny can fly in his sleep."

The last time she'd climbed the stairs, Grover Malakua had a knife at her back. This time it was Cameron's hand guiding her. The ambulance had delivered Uncle Rob, and he was set up in one of the central, front-facing recliners. Paul's smile encouraged her. Things were going to be fine.

Cameron stowed their luggage in the interior bins, then ushered her to the recliner next to her uncle's. "I think I'll start the flight in the cockpit with Denny, if that's okay."

She nodded. "Sure. Of course." She turned when he was halfway to the front. "But Denny's flying, right?"

Cameron spread his hands. "I did okay." When she didn't answer, he rolled his head to the side. "Denny's flying."

"Good. I'm exhausted." She settled in across the aisle beside her uncle.

He was watching her with what looked like pride and amusement. She shrugged. "I've had enough adventure, okay?"

THIRTY-FOUR

At 4:30 A.M. to his body, 7:30 West Coast time, Cameron dragged into his house. Gentry and Paul had disembarked in San Jose and had gone with Rob by ambulance to the medical facility. Paul would fly back on his next charter, but a day or so on the mainland had him jazzed. After landing at the San Luis County Airport, Denny had gone home to his three parrots and one blue-and-gold macaw.

Cameron rubbed his face. Gentry, Rob, and Paul had slept all the way in, but he'd stayed up with Denny even though he hadn't napped beforehand. Now his muscles ached, his head spun. He needed sleep.

But as he went inside, Myra stood up. She wore a miniskirt and Lycra top. Her face in the morning light looked intriguing and full of attitude, none of which he was prepared to deal with.

Not asking how she'd gotten in, he raised a hand. "Whatever you have to say, keep it. I'm too tired to be nice." She couldn't have known he'd been up all night, but she had a knack for choosing his weakest times. He turned for the stairs.

"Where is she?"

He climbed.

"It won't work, you know."

He paused.

"You'll crush the life from her, the same as you did me."

He closed his eyes. Dead on his feet, he didn't risk speaking. He'd spent the last four years wondering what he'd done. Now she confirmed what he knew. He loved too hard.

He climbed the last five stairs, went in and closed the door to his bedroom. The bed had been violated. The covers tousled, the pillows indented and scented with Myra's perfume. She'd slept there. How long she'd been in his house, he didn't know and didn't care. He gripped the sheets and yanked them from the mattress.

After shoving the bedding into his hamper, he brought his hands to his face and smelled her. He'd been awake twenty-four hours, but he didn't drop into the stripped bed. He went in to shower. The hot flow washed away her scent, but not her words.

He hadn't been obsessive or jealous. What she'd disdained was his desire to be together, his wanting to be one. He knew how easily people could be lost. If that meant he'd loved her too hard, crushed the life from her, then it couldn't be helped. He didn't know any other way to be.

With the water beating on his back, he almost fell asleep on his feet. He needed coffee. He shut off the water, toweled dry, and pulled on a clean pair of shorts. Then he went down to face Myra.

She followed him into the kitchen. As he ground beans and French-pressed a pot of Kona special reserve, he noted several mugs with soggy tea bags and a couple used plates.

"How long have you been here?"

"Since we talked."

Roughly as long as he'd been awake. "Why?"

"I wanted to be here when you came back."

"In case I brought Gentry?" He filled his cup.

"I saw your interview."

He drew the coffee into his mouth and held it there to absorb.

"You lied."

He eyed her over the rim.

"You're not in love with her, or you wouldn't be letting her go."

"What makes you think I am?"

She smiled, the knowing glint in her stormy eyes. "I know you,

Cameron. You want to settle in and batten down the hatches." She clicked her nails on the table. "You don't want anyone to know what you've got, or something might take it away. Just like the storm took your parents."

In their five years together, he hadn't known to keep his hopes and fears to himself.

"You can't do that with Gentry Fox. She belongs to everyone, every fan who fantasizes."

He looked away.

Myra stood and came to him. She covered his hands on the mug. "You know all this." She slid the mug from his hands and set it on the counter. "You just don't like to give up."

Taking his hand, she walked him out of the kitchen and up the stairs. He stood stupidly, while she took fresh sheets from the linen closet and made the bed. Two years older, she had on rare occasions mothered him. If his brain wasn't mush, he'd order her out, but the things she'd said were wounding something inside, something he might have called hope.

She folded the navy blue coverlet back. "There. Climb in. Your eyes look like Frankenstein."

No doubt. He got into the bed, prepared to roll out if she tried to join him.

She knew better. "Get some rest. I'll be downstairs."

Ordinarily that would have killed any chance of sleep. This time it didn't.

∽

Having settled Uncle Rob into the health facility where he'd rehabilitate over the next weeks, Gentry prepared to go home. Denny had offered to fly her to the San Luis County Regional airport, where he housed his jet and where Cameron would deplane. But she had needed to see her uncle settled.

Now she waited at the San Jose airport for a flight into LAX. On the flight from Kauai, she'd slept like a baby in the recliner next to Uncle Rob, but it would feel good to get home. She kept her head down as she waited, reading the novel she'd bought from the rack and hoping no one would gasp out her name and alert the crowd.

Unlike the locals on Kauai, Californians knew their celebrities. No place in the nation packed people into the theaters like the West Coast. Gentry understood her obligation to them, but still she hoped her overnight flight and surreptitious arrival had thrown off the press. She hadn't intended to lie, but Cameron's fears had altered her announced plans. They couldn't hold that against her.

"Excuse me."

With a sigh, she looked up to the woman standing over her.

"Is that your little girl?"

Gentry followed her finger to a crying toddler a few feet away and said, "No." But then she worried until a young, harried woman rushed back and swiped up the child. Their eyes met and the woman stopped short.

"Oh. You're—"

"Please. Don't say it."

The girl shoved the toddler to her hip and dug through the diaper bag. "Can you sign something?"

Now the other woman had sharpened her gaze. "Oh. Gentry—"

Gentry shot her a pleading glance.

"Sorry."

The young mother thrust a disposable diaper and a Sharpie at her. "It's permanent ink. I have to label all her stuff for daycare." She jiggled the baby to make her stop crying. "Hush, Jillie. That's Gentry Fox."

Several heads came up. So much for the novel. The time before her flight would not be spent reading. Shortly before boarding, she escaped to the rest room. Though a couple diehards waited outside her stall, she took out her phone and called Cameron, just to make sure he and Denny had made it in all right.

She took the phone down and checked the number she'd dialed when a woman with a British accent answered. "Hello?"

"I'm . . . I was looking for Cameron Pierce."

"He's in bed. Can I help you?"

She hadn't imagined him with a housekeeper. *She* had no house-keeper. "Is this. . . ? Who is this?"

"It's Myra, Gentry. I don't know if he's mentioned me."

Right. The marriage that never happened. "I just wanted to make sure he got in all right."

"He's fine. A little ragged, but he'll be fine."

"Okay. Thanks." She hung up, certain that the girls outside her stall had hung on every word. Now they would listen to her pee, because she had a plane to catch and even Hollywood actors' bladders got full.

⌒

Cameron woke with a hung-over feeling he hadn't experienced since college. He wasn't a good daytime sleeper even when he needed it. It worked against his chemistry. And he had a terrible feeling he hadn't dreamed Myra.

For a long time he'd hoped and believed she would show up and do exactly what she was doing, that they could pick up where they'd left off and all the things she'd said and done would turn out to be false. At first he'd avoided all her haunts, afraid he'd see her; then he'd haunted them, afraid he wouldn't. He knew now that she'd left town, left the country, actually—had gone back to London.

And each year without her had thickened his skin until no one but Nica could touch anything soft inside. Gentry had changed that. She had cracked the shell and left him vulnerable. He sat up on the edge of the bed and rubbed his face.

Myra was a living, breathing cliché. The thought that he'd found someone special, even spectacular, had kindled a desire in her to have back what she hadn't wanted before. Her apology had been the one thing she knew would catch him unprepared. He forked his hair back with his fingers and stood up.

The sooner this was done the better. A relationship with Gentry might be impossible, but whatever Myra had in mind would be deadly. He went down the stairs to the patio, where she browsed a magazine in her miniskirt, with bare, tanned legs waxed smooth as marble.

She squinted up. "Get some sleep?"

He sat down on the edge of the planter and rested his forearms on his knees. "What are you doing, Myra?"

"You want the big picture, then?"

"With a broad brush."

"I need your help. You're in the helping-damsels mode, aren't you?"

He swallowed his retort. "I thought you were upset. You apologized."

"Yes, well, you'll expect that when you hear."

"Hear what?"

"What I need."

He leaned back and gripped the nape of his neck. "Let's have it."

"I want you to get my son back."

He fixed her with a stare. "Your son."

"He's with my sister."

He shook his head. "If you know that . . ."

"I can't get him. I terminated my parental rights."

"So you thought I'd just kidnap him?"

Her rain-hued gaze met his. "You never terminated yours."

With anyone but Myra his reaction would be shock and dismay. Because she was capable of lying even to herself with incredible finesse, he reserved any emotional response. "First, I don't believe you have a son. That would be an act of self-sacrifice. And his being mine is a stretch, even for you."

She walked into the house and snatched her purse from the

counter. From her wallet she took a photograph of herself in the indisputable act of giving birth. "I had quite an easy time of it, actually."

His chest tightened. He handed back the picture, not sure he wanted to hear more. "Where does your sister fit in?" He hadn't seen Mary since the wedding. He'd considered their relationship unnaturally distant, but it was just another idiosyncrasy of Myra's that fascinated him. Her self-possession, her independence.

"It was a surrogacy of sorts. I'd no desire to be a mother, and she'd no ability."

He shook his head. "I'm not getting this."

"Why do you think I needed out? You'd have wanted the family thing if you knew. I didn't. But it didn't seem right to throw it away when Mary had such a need. Believe it or not, it was an act of kindness." She could be so horribly convincing.

"You're saying you gave your baby to your sister and now you want him back?"

"He's yours, Cameron. He looks just like you."

His breath made a slow escape and didn't want to come back.

"So you see." She stooped down beside him. "I can give you more than Gentry Fox. I can give you back your son."

He knew better than to believe her. She'd say anything.

"Would you like to see him? He sends photos to Auntie Myra."

"No." He stood up. "I need you to leave."

"You think I'm lying."

"I don't think anything. I just want you to go."

"Cameron."

"Don't." He raised a hand to silence her. "Just go."

She shouldered her purse and walked into the house, paused to leave something at the counter, then disappeared through the kitchen doorway. He stood long minutes on the patio, then went inside and looked at the photograph of a dark-haired little boy. He went into the garage, hoisted his board into the truck bed, and drove to the shore.

Curt licked the blood from his lip, then ran his tongue over his teeth. They might be loose in the sockets, but none had fallen out. He felt an unholy relief at that. He spit, squeezed open his eyes, and rolled his face off the pavement. Pain speared his side.

He tried to move without breathing, to breathe without moving. If he didn't move soon, someone would see him. He couldn't stand that. No one was going to look at him with pity. And he didn't want any questions.

He dragged himself to his knees, spit more blood, but guessed it came from his mouth and not deeper inside. If they'd wanted to cause permanent damage, they could have. This was a warning, an incentive. He pulled himself up by the car door, eased onto the seat, and gingerly slid one leg, then the other under the wheel and onto the pedals.

They hadn't messed up his car; that was good. Slowly he raised a hand and tipped the rearview mirror. He swore, then swore again. It would take days, maybe weeks for the cuts and swelling to leave his face.

"Pathetic. You look pathetic." He wiped the water running from one eye, sniffed through his swelling nose. "Just look . . . how can . . ." He dropped his head back against the rest, eyed himself, and swore again. "You are the sorriest excuse . . ."

Blood trickled from his lip. He had to get cleaned up before anyone saw what a pathetic— *Wait a minute. Wait.* He looked again in the mirror. Maybe pathetic was exactly what he needed. He almost smiled, but his brutalized lips stopped him. Could he get some mileage from this pain and humiliation?

He'd slammed the car into park when they dragged him out. Now he put it back into drive, went through the intersection and turned at the next. Twenty-five minutes later he pulled into the driveway. Ten to one she'd let him in. His attackers had increased his odds dramatically.

He rang the bell and waited, braced himself on one arm, head down. It was only half feigned.

When the door opened, her expression said it all. "Curt?"

He groaned softly. "Hard to tell."

She reached for him. "What happened?"

He pressed a hand to his side. "Three guys . . ."

He bent and took so long before continuing that she said, "Here. Come in."

The pain shot through his side when he lowered his arm, but he exulted. More than ever, he needed what she had.

She led him inside. "Come here to the sink. Let me clean you up. We'll call the police."

He startled. "It won't help."

"What?" They'd reached the powder room sink. She started a stream of water and took a rolled facecloth from the basket.

"I shouldn't have come here. I didn't think."

She dabbed the cloth on his lip, his cheek. "What kind of trouble are you in?"

"I'm not involving you." He gasped when she pressed the cold, wet cloth to his swollen eye.

"Do you know who did this?"

He moaned as she worked the cloth over his face. "I was supposed to pay back an investment, but the deal didn't close. Whole thing fell through, but by then I'd reinvested the original monies. Three of the partners were okay with that. One went ballistic."

"He did this?" She lowered the cloth and looked into his face. Her compassion hurt worse than the blows. He hadn't expected the hollow way it hit him.

"His goons. Listen." He winced, once again holding a hand to his side. "He's foreign. He's not touchable. Got some kind of diplomatic immunity."

"You still have to call the police. People can't—"

He rested a hand on her arm. "It'll only be worse if I do."

She took a step back. "This isn't drugs or something . . ."

He looked hurt. "You think I'd be involved in that?" Real pain found his face. "I saw what heroin did to my mom, my sister." Truth added purity. "Can you really think I'd touch that?"

She rested her hand on his arm. "I just don't understand. Why would someone—"

"I should've known he was crazy. One of the guys warned me. Those Arabs don't . . . think the way we do."

"Curt, you have to—"

"I've said too much. I shouldn't have come here." He ran his blood-streaked hands under the water. "I must have been dazed. Forget—"

"Forget it?" She caught his wrist.

"Allegra, this was a warning. If I don't have his money by tomorrow . . ." He pulled free and swore. "I shouldn't have come here." He backed out of the powder room, turned for the front door.

"Curt, stop."

Again he let the pain show—and the fear. "This isn't how I do business. Please don't think—"

She took both his hands. "How much do you need?"

He shook his head. "Two hundred grand. Maybe I could put him off with half that, but everything I have is tied up." He winced. "One deal feeds another. Sometimes things are flush and sometimes they're strapped. It's just timing, but he wouldn't see that. He thinks I cheated him." He swallowed hard. "Babe, please let go."

"And what if you don't have his money tomorrow?"

He looked away. "I don't know."

"Come with me." She walked him into a study just past the powder room. From the desk she took a checkbook.

"Babe, no." Excitement shot through him like adrenaline, chased by an unfamiliar emotion he'd have to call shame. He was shaky. He hadn't been beaten in a long time.

"I can't do the full amount without transferring funds. But I can give you half."

"No."

"Until you're flush again." She looked up.

"This isn't why I came here. It's not how I wanted—" His voice broke. He braced both arms on the desk. "I wanted to see you, but not . . ."

She came around the desk and handed him the check.

"Allegra."

She cupped his shoulder. "I'm sorry."

"Sorry? I'm the one . . ." He shook his head. "I must've—"

"It's not you, Curt. It's me."

He straightened slowly and shook his head again. "No, babe, you're everything to me." To be able to write a check for a hundred grand without even blinking.

"If this doesn't satisfy him, tell me."

He drew himself up. "You know how that makes me feel? I want to take care of *you*." Her smile held depths of sadness he couldn't fathom. What was happening? He didn't want to see that. "Allegra."

"Not now. Go take care of business."

He swallowed. "Can I . . . kiss you?"

Tears sparkled in her eyes as she shook her head.

He took a step back. "Okay."

Outside the door, he slid the check into his pocket, limped to his car, and pulled out of her driveway. Leaving the house behind, he ignored the splits and smiled.

THIRTY-FIVE

Cameron buried himself in work. He didn't want to think, didn't want to feel anything, only to drive toward a goal. Myra called, but he didn't answer. Nica called, but he wouldn't have been able to keep it from her, so he didn't answer that either. Gentry had phoned that first day according to his call history, but it wasn't on his missed calls, so Myra must have answered. He couldn't begin to deal with that.

He pulled his truck up to the gym where a supposed accident victim worked out. He'd thought his BS meter finely tuned enough to sift anything. He'd been wrong. With Myra there were no limits, no depths. The boy could be his, could be anyone's.

He carried his workout tote into the gym, purchased a guest pass, changed clothes, and hit the weight room. His mark was incredibly fit for all the pain and suffering he was claiming in his suit. He angled the camera in his tote to catch the guy's activity.

Breaking a sweat, he followed the man's workout circuit with his own, noted the weight levels on the machines before adjusting them. No way this guy'd had a major car accident with back injuries a month ago. He'd nail him.

Pain gripped his stomach, rage like acid burning him. He had dared to think, dared to hope his life could be restored. Like there was any chance. Like hope . . . ever . . . kept . . . its . . . promise. He shoved the bar up and hooked it, then rolled out and sat up.

He'd seen what he needed to, caught enough on film. Ordinarily he'd have showered, maybe engaged the guy in conversation. Instead he grabbed his bag, returned the locker key, and got out of there.

Denny had been gone the last three times Cameron went over, but this time his hunter green Miata was in the driveway, dripping from a recent scrub-down.

He went to the door and banged. With a curious expression, Denny opened the screen door. "All you had to do was huff and puff. You'd have brought it right down."

He probably had put more into it than necessary. "Busy?"

Denny raised the can of Armor All and a rag. "Just a little spit and polish."

They walked out together to the car. Denny tossed him the towel draped over the bucket. "Want to dry her off?"

Cameron carefully swabbed the water from the paint as Denny sprayed and rubbed the inside panel of the passenger door. "Taking Megan cruising tonight," he said.

"Megan?"

"The waitress from the diner? Black hair. Dimples."

Cameron nodded. "Sure."

"She's got a dog that loves to drive."

"Is he licensed?"

Denny laughed. "Didn't stop me turning over the jet to you."

"Did I thank you?"

"A hundred times and counting." He gave the armrest a final rub and looked up. "So what was that big-bad-wolf thing?"

"If you had to lay your life down on one answer, what would you guess?"

He sobered. "Myra?"

Cameron's throat tightened. Denny was waiting for God to show him the right woman, one chosen to complete Denny Bridges in this life—unlike his good friend who'd jumped at the most intriguing woman he'd encountered without consulting, maybe even resisting, that divine counsel.

He told him the situation—everything Myra had said, her possible motivation, her obvious fixation on Gentry. Then, watching Denny's features shift from concern to shock, he said, "It doesn't matter whether he's my son or not. Three and a half years after the fact, Mary and Tom are his parents. And she thinks I'll just walk in there and tear him away."

Denny blew out his breath. "I'm sorry, man. I know I counseled you to try everything to save your marriage."

"I never had a choice." Cameron shook his head. "I think it's possible she has no conscience."

Denny shook and folded the rag. "What are you going to do?"

Myra was right that he didn't let go, that he held on until his arms were pried loose. The pain spread from his stomach to his throat. "Terminate my parental rights." He hadn't decided that until this moment. Maybe the thought had come from Denny, or the One who guided his life with perfect certainty. "That way he's free and clear. Myra can't get at him."

"There's no going back."

He nodded. "I know." But for the first time in too long he felt the hand of God.

⌐

In the hot, cramped studio office, Gentry put her signature on the contract. The ink on the page determined the next five months if all went according to schedule. Most of the other parts were cast, and they'd begin shooting in the next few weeks. Still dazed by everything that had happened, she left the office, feeling a little empty and a lot less excited than she'd expected.

"Hey, doll. Don't I get a kiss?"

Smiling, she leaned over and kissed Dave's cheek. "Thank you."

"It's a sweet deal."

"You're amazing." He deserved credit, especially for protecting her limits.

"You'll rock 'em."

She shrugged. "It's a good script."

"It's made for you."

"Hope that doesn't mean I'm typecast." Another scrappy female in a situation too big for her. It hit a little too close to home.

She looked forward to sinking into the character, learning the lines. Once the cast gathered and the cameras rolled, the magic would happen. That was so much more to her than the contract, although she needed the income. *Steel* had provided a nice chunk after the renegotiations, but she'd been forced to get serious about her wardrobe and move into an apartment of her own. The one she'd shared with Helen had no security and, well, too much tension.

"You seem a little pensive. You over that shock on the island, or should you see someone?"

Good question. Since her return, she'd spent too much time looking over her shoulder. Bette Walden had quit following her, but had someone taken her place? With the ever-present paparazzi, it was impossible to tell whether someone with darker intentions than smearing her lurked in the shadows. In the middle of the night, she'd wake with a jolt, wondering who had hired Malakua. "I'm fine, Dave. Don't worry."

"If you say so." He patted her shoulder. "You're a tough duck."

Right. She told him good-bye and headed for her car in the studio lot. A quiet afternoon reading over the script with a nice, cold—

"Gentry!" Helen came out a side door.

She stopped and waited for her to catch up. "Well?"

Helen grabbed her hands. "I got it."

"Molly?"

Helen nodded, her face flushing to the pale roots of her hair. "I got Molly."

Gentry threw out her arms and hugged her. When she'd seen the part for the secondary character who served as a foil for her own intrepid Eva Thorne, she'd lobbied hard for Helen to at least get a reading. Helen had done the rest.

"Congratulations." Gentry gave her another squeeze.

"I can hardly believe it." Helen's cheeks were infused with rose, excitement shining in her eyes.

"Believe it." Gentry set her back. "So what about the troupe?"

"I won't be nearly as tied up here as you are."

"It's still too much to do both by yourself."

Helen turned. "Do you want to come back?"

Not what she'd meant. She shook her head. "I was thinking of Troy."

Helen widened her eyes. "You think he would? He hasn't been part of it since . . ."

"I know. But I won't be there, and I bet he misses it. Talk to him."

Helen nodded uncertainly. "You don't want to?"

"Do it, or talk to him?"

Helen shrugged. "I know he misses you."

Gentry swallowed the sudden ache. "I miss him too. He's a great kid. I'm just not sure where his head is."

Helen looked down. "Can we go somewhere?"

"The studio has a cafeteria." Anywhere else she'd be ducking fans and paparazzi. "This way." They changed course, and she said, "It'll be great working with you, Helen."

Helen nodded, but her agreement seemed strained. Maybe their friendship had been irreparably torn. The lot they crossed smelled of oil and smog, and she quashed a sudden longing for balmy trade winds and fresh, clean rain. Gentry slid her card into the cafeteria door and pulled it open.

They went through the beverage line and got a table away from the few other people in the room. Helen had sounded serious and seemed uncomfortable.

Gentry sipped her iced tea. "The part's perfect for you. I hope they won't change your look too much."

"They can do whatever they want. I'm just glad to be working." Helen raised her diet 7-Up, then set it down without drinking. She looked up. The honest Helen she'd known would tell her right now that she didn't want to chum it up on the set, that their friendship—

"I need to tell you something, and I'm not sure how."

There'd been a time when neither of them would have hesitated to share her deepest thoughts. Gentry felt the pang of loss. How many friends would this world of competition and success cost her? "Would it help if we lay on the floor and kicked off our shoes?"

Helen laughed. "Only if we had our pajamas on and pillows to throw."

"You want to hit me?"

Helen paled, the pink leaving her face white enough to show the soft freckles along her cheekbones. "I already have." She sat back in her chair. "I feel terrible."

Gentry held her breath. Now that it came to it, she was not sure she could hear what Helen had to say.

After a couple false starts, she said, "Everything always works for you. People find you so interesting, so incredible. You landed Rachel Bach without even trying, and it all got so big and important. It seemed that even God would give you whatever you wanted."

Helen must not have read the papers lately. Gentry rubbed the drops from her glass. "I've revised that assumption."

Helen shook her head. "When Troy told me what was going on, you seemed like such a hypocrite, like I'd never known you at all."

Her chest ached. "You didn't even wonder whether it was true?"

"I would have, but when you landed Rachel Bach, I wondered what you'd been willing to do for it; I mean . . . Gentry, you must hate me so much."

Hate wasn't what she felt, just a pale desolation.

"He said your relationship had evolved and . . ."

"You gave the tabloids the pictures? My stage kiss with Troy?"

Helen gripped her hands together. "I wanted it to be true so that I wasn't what it felt like I'd become. I even hired a detective to prove—"

"Bette Walden?"

Helen raised her teary eyes and nodded. "If she proved it, then I'd done a good thing, the right thing. She told me she'd been abused and shared my fervor for the truth. She worked for next to nothing."

Gentry started to shake. "You wanted me killed?"

"What?" The color left Helen's face. "No. Of course not."

"You didn't hire Grover Malakua to push me over the falls?"

Helen's hands fell to her lap. Her mouth hung slack. Her turquoise eyes hollowed. "Gentry, I'm sure you can't believe me after everything I just said . . ." Tears broke free and trickled down her cheeks. "But I never . . ."

Gentry closed her eyes and pressed her fingertips to the sockets. Helen wasn't a good enough actor to fake that reaction, and why bring it up at all if she'd done something so heinous and illegal? She'd hurt and betrayed her, but it was crazy to think she could have orchestrated an accident on Kauai when she hadn't even known about the trip. "I believe you."

Cameron must have been wrong. Malakua had acted alone. Maybe he'd meant to kidnap her for ransom the way he'd taken Nica. Only, she'd fallen. She still didn't remember what had happened above the falls, but that made more sense than someone wanting her dead. Now they had him, and it was over.

"I'm so sorry." Helen rubbed her fingers under her nose.

All those months of ridicule and accusations, all the doubts that would never truly be erased. She tried to put herself in Helen's place. Could she have done the same if Troy had come to her with stories about Helen? She shook her head. But then, she hadn't spent years in Helen's shadow. She understood now how it must have rankled. *"Even God would give you whatever you wanted."*

Not true. But he had given more than she deserved. He had saved Uncle Rob. He had saved her. More than that, he'd saved her soul for all eternity. Was she the hypocrite Helen had thought her? Or did she owe a debt of forgiveness she could never repay?

The pain of betrayal still stung, but she reached across the table and gripped Helen's hand with the *aloha* she'd been shown, the divine grace she'd received. The tightness in her throat released, and she said, "I forgive you."

"That's enough for today." Paul called the session to a halt.

Rob had offered him a personal retainer to stay on through the process, and Paul had surprised him by obtaining a leave from the hospital on Kauai and accepting. Exhausted from therapy, leg throbbing, Rob lowered himself into the wheelchair. "Hard to see much improvement."

"Yet." Was Paul laying aside his usual tart remarks because he sensed the emotional fragility Rob was trying hard not to show?

He had dreamed about Allegra, dreamed that she came and sat on the bed and said, "Here, let me fix that." Then she'd stretched out his leg like a telescope, matched up his feet and said, "Perfect."

Even as she'd said it, he'd thought, *No. Perfection is a summit I haven't reached.* He'd thought he could but knew better now. He wished he could tell her.

But Gentry had told her what happened, and she hadn't come—he guessed because she couldn't bear it. He didn't blame her. She'd had so little substance to fall back on, her self-esteem as fragile as thin blown glass. Her image, her social position, her quest for ageless beauty—none of it had given her the stability she'd longed for. Not when it could be lost, or taken from her.

For a while he'd been her pride, his success her elixir. When he came to faith and revised his priorities, she'd been shocked. She wanted the glitz and glamour. He shook his head. The real shame was that inside she had substance, determination, intelligence. If only she valued the person he'd fallen in love with.

Paul backed him through the doors and took the outside walkway to the building that housed his room. The sunshine reflecting off the sidewalk made him squint. Sprinklers *churk-churk-churk*ed beside him, keeping the lawn green.

"Won't be long before you're walking this path." Paul's voice was strong and confident.

Rob nodded. "If you say so."

"Won't give you a day's peace until you do. So don't think you can shirk it."

"Ah. So it is you. For a minute there I thought you'd been body snatched."

THIRTY-SIX

As soon as he woke, Cameron picked up the phone. He shouldn't have let it go so long, but he'd been hit by a wave he hadn't seen coming, plunged to the ocean floor, desperately hoping he'd have breath enough to come back up. When Gentry answered, he realized she could have been the breath of hope he needed.

"Aloha."

"Cameron?" Her voice sank in and warmed him. How had he gone three weeks without hearing it? Their parting had been brief and harried with the ambulance waiting to transport her uncle. Then Myra's tidal wave had plunged him into silence.

"Sorry I didn't get back to you before."

"Oh. I just wanted to make sure you'd gotten in all right. Myra told me you were fine."

Right. Just before she sucked the air from his lungs. "I need to explain."

"No, you don't." She'd meant to sound sincere, but a hint of hurt came through. "We're back in real life."

"Gentry, can we meet somewhere?"

Her silence lasted a beat too long.

"If you'd rather not—"

"We're starting production soon. It would have to be today or tomorrow."

He thought fast. "Santa Barbara?" Roughly ninety miles for each of them. "Or I can come to L.A."

"Santa Barbara would be better. Stearn's Wharf, end of the pier?"

"When?"

"A couple hours?"

His heart hammered. "Good. I'll see you there."

Myra had proven beyond doubt their irreconcilable differences. In marrying her, he had stepped outside God's will, ignored the check in his spirit, ridden when he should have bailed, and only now risen from the fetal roll on the ocean floor. In severing ties with the boy who might be his son, he prayed the Lord would recognize the sacrifice and forgive his rebellion.

When he'd pulled Nica back the day their parents died, he'd pitted himself against the One who took away. He saw that now. It wasn't that he thought God didn't intervene; it was that he didn't want the intervention. He wanted control. Every wave he'd carved, he'd rubbed in God's face. The very skill God had given him, he'd used to strike back.

But just as the sea took, it also gave. In its embrace he felt renewed, strengthened, alive. Ever mindful of its power, he'd entered again and again. And now he knew the wave was *ke Akua's*. God had allowed the anger and defiance and carried him safely again and again until he could recognize the authority that gave life grace. And in that he found hope and promise.

Gentry was standing at the end of the pier, talking with an old fisherman, when he arrived. The floppy hat and sunglasses did little to conceal her magic, and he wondered how he had ever not recognized her and if there'd ever be a time that seeing her didn't feel like a gift and a miracle.

The sea scent surrounded them, the waves slapping the shell-encrusted piles. Sunshine illuminated each azure peak and ripple—*ke Akua* showing off. The cool breeze ruffled the brim of Gentry's hat as she turned. Her glasses superimposed his face over her eyes. If he kissed her cheek, he'd find her mouth. If he kissed her mouth . . .

"Don't let me stop you," the old guy said, adjusting his poles.

Cameron sent him a glance as she slipped off her glasses and hung them in the neck of her sleeveless hooded shirt. Her Kauaian-forest eyes assessed him with courage and caution. His jaw clenched with restraint, but it was useless. He reached behind her head and kissed her. She tasted like hope, memories, and dreams.

He pressed his forehead to hers. "I wasn't going to do that."

"And yet you do."

"I overestimate my powers of resistance." He rested his hand on the back of her neck. "I ought to admit I have none."

She raised her chin. "So admit it."

He risked another encounter with the lips of a star. "I've missed you."

She huffed. He couldn't blame her. The words were empty after his long silence.

"Gentry." He caught her shoulders and turned her away from a couple strolling near. He didn't want to be interrupted by fans or fanatics. "Myra was there when I got home. I was dog tired and went to bed. I don't know what she told you—"

"It doesn't matter."

"It matters to me." He ran his gaze over every one of her features, then sank back into her eyes.

"She only said what I told you. That she was there and you were fine." She slid her gaze away.

"She didn't mention my son?" His voice grated.

Her mouth fell open. "You never said—"

"I didn't know." He ran a hand over his beard and shot a look at the old fisherman who seemed fixed on the sea. "You'd have to know Myra to understand."

"Okay."

"I met her at the Haleiwa Surfing Championship the only time I won it all. She was covering the event for a British sports station. She had a potent sort of energy; I was feeling cocky. We hooked up for an evening that showed me everything I needed to know but was too stubborn to see." Memories flooded in, all the things he should have realized long before he did. "There's such a fine line between self-confident and self-absorbed. Ambitious and driven. Uninhibited and remorseless."

He shook his head. "I liked her strength, her independence. She didn't need anyone, yet six weeks later we were married. I have no idea why. The novelty, maybe, or a joke. Took me five years to get the punch line. And then it wasn't funny."

Gentry touched his hand. "You don't have to do this, Cameron."

"Yes, I do." He closed her hand in his. "It was a poor excuse for a marriage. I wanted an intimacy she scorned. She wanted a place with the broadcast elite. As hard as I tried to make my dream happen, she tried harder for hers." He locked his gaze on Gentry's. "She went to extraordinary lengths. She described them to me the night she decided to leave."

Gentry reflected his pain.

"Even with that, if I'd known the real reason she wanted out—"

Gentry's phone rang. She let out a breath. "That's Darla."

He swallowed. "Go ahead."

"She can wait."

When the ring stopped, he gathered himself. "Myra left because she intended to give the baby to her sister."

Gentry searched his face. "You didn't know?"

"She saw no advantage in telling me until now."

"Oh, Kai . . ."

The phone rang again. Darla's ring.

"Take it," he said.

Gentry dragged the phone from her shirt pocket. "Darla, what is it?" Sharper than he'd heard her with her publicist before. "Seen what?" She looked up at him while she listened, then pressed her fingers to her eyes and sighed. "In Santa Barbara. With Cameron." She nodded at the next part, even though Darla couldn't see her, then said, "Okay, I'll talk to you later." She hung up and stuffed the phone back into her pocket, then looked up. "Cameron, I'm so sorry."

He frowned. "Must be bad if I'm Cameron again."

She took his hand. "They know. It's in today's gossip mags."

For a minute nothing registered. Then he got it. She'd warned him. She had said they would find all his dirt, that he didn't know how bad it could be. He'd known Myra was a wild card, but he hadn't known about his son. *If* he was his son. He'd instructed his lawyer to proceed with that assumption. He'd expected the notice of termination to arrive at Mary and Tom's with no fanfare, but Myra, it seemed, had other ideas.

He straightened. "Let's see how bad it is."

She tugged him back. "We can't just walk up to some newsstand together. Darla's spitting bullets that we're out here at all."

He tipped his head back. "Does it ever stop? How can you live this way?"

"At least no one's trying to kill me."

It hit him that he'd left her unprotected all this time. Not that it was his responsibility; he'd only agreed to watch out for her until they apprehended Malakua. But if it hadn't been for Myra, he'd have stayed closer to the situation. "How do you know?"

"Helen was the one who gave the tabloids the pictures. She hired Bette to prove me a hypocrite, but no one to knock me off a cliff. Malakua must have acted on his own."

That didn't feel right, but he would follow up with TJ to make sure. Right now he had something else to deal with. "Wait here, and I'll round up the tabloids."

"Good." She glanced at the fisherman. "He can use them to wrap his fish."

He turned to the salty guy. "Mind keeping an eye on her while I make a run for something?"

"Have to be blind or stupid to take my eyes off that one."

Why did that sound more like advice than agreement? He had to walk awhile to find a newsstand, but when he did, his and Gentry's pictures were front and center with Myra's angry cameo framed in the lower right on one, second page of another. The shots were not flattering; the words were worse. *Fox Lover Rejects Kid. When given the chance to raise his own son, Cameron Pierce terminated his parental rights. "He doesn't want anything interfering with his hot romance." Ex-wife tells all.*

Her other quotes were equally disturbing. *"Unhealthy attachment to his sister. Obsessive and clingy."*

The second paper's headline read, *Lover or Stalker? Is Gentry Safe?* But the worst one: *Gentry Forces Choice; Your Kid or Me.* Gentry, looking sexy on the beach after surfing, split the page with the little boy who could be his. Hurt flooded in. She'd given them pictures of her son. All the emotion he'd blocked with doubt and denial smothered him when he looked into that face. He'd lost his child—and thought he'd felt the hand of God.

The girl in the stand had drawn a bead on him. She scratched her studded nose when he pulled the bills from his wallet. He didn't hand her plastic with his name on it, but it didn't matter. She said, "You're him, right? Gentry's new squeeze?"

"How many people buy these things?"

"Lots. Lots more read the headlines and pretend not to. Can you sign this for me?" She reached over and grabbed the one that showed him and Gentry in a clutch, probably in the hallway at the hospital.

"I hate to disappoint you, but none of it's true."

She shrugged. "It'd still be cool."

He looked her in the face. "I'm sorry. I can't."

She frowned. "It's just your stupid name."

Just his name. He took the papers and walked away as she muttered, "Jerkwad."

Not good. The past three weeks, she had ridden the anticipation, gearing up for the new project, but as Cameron returned, she bolstered herself for another blow, the one that showed too clearly on his face.

He said, "Gentry, I'm sorry," at the same time she said, "I'm so sorry, Kai."

She anchored herself in his gaze, no longer the perilous, deep-ocean blue, but the warm, twilight blue of their night under the stars. She'd been too worked up to notice at the time, but it had sunk into her subconscious and came back now so clearly it hurt. The verdant scent of the forest, the insistent voice of the water, and stars—oh, the stars. The sky had been deep and close at once, enfolding them with promise as Cameron told her she was in the shelter of God's wings. She held on to that now, knowing by his face she'd need it.

People had begun to collect on the pier but mostly congregated near the Harbor Restaurant or the Trading Company. She and Cameron perched on the huge, weathered gray log that formed a bench at the far end of the pier. A pure white gull cried overhead, winging out over the still, blue water of the bay.

He laid the first paper in her lap, and she read every word of the story. Then the next and the next. Had Myra any idea how vile she sounded? And what was with her being "forced" to give up her newborn son? She didn't blame Cameron directly, rather the pressures of an untenable marriage. Now stronger, wiser, all she'd wanted was her child back, and a chance for reconciliation.

Cameron shook his head. "I can't tell if she's lying to herself or just everyone else, but that's the last thing she wants."

Then came the worst. Gentry read how she'd supposedly laid down the ultimatum, *"It's him or me."* She stood in wet T-shirt and bikini, looking demanding and risqué. The face of the little boy who shared the page broke her heart.

She looked up at Cameron, staring out over the water, wishing, maybe, they were back across it where he could rewind the last month and not involve himself with the mysterious woman who'd dragged herself into his life.

He dropped his gaze to the hands folded loosely between his legs. "Is this going to hurt Kevin?"

She felt his grief as his voice grated over the child's name. She tried to imagine the little boy tucked safely away where no one would see or recognize him. But the British paparazzi had driven Princess

Diana to her death. What were the chances no one would try to question or photograph the child and his family—when he'd already made front page?

She sighed. "It might."

Cameron shook his head. "I remember the day my life got ripped apart. I thought I'd avoided that for him. I wanted to."

"Would you be the man you are, Kai, if the things in your life hadn't happened?"

"The obsessive, clingy, unhealthy man I am?"

"Consider the source."

He rubbed his hand over his face. "She's powerful. And vindictive."

"God's powerful. And redemptive."

He stood up and took a step to the bare edge of the pier. "I can't keep him safe."

"Give it to the One who can. Ask, Kai. Set the prayer free, and I promise God will catch it."

When he didn't answer, she stood up and stuffed the papers into the trash can. As much as she dreaded what was in store for her, she'd take it all to let Cameron and his son walk away. And then it hit her that this was how it would always be. As long as her name attracted attention, she'd be dragging anyone she cared about into her spotlight. And suddenly none of it seemed worth it.

He reached over and took her hand. "Let's get out of here."

She kept her hat flopped down all the way to Cameron's truck. This one was a midnight blue with no sea turtle decals but plenty of room for a surfboard in the bed. They got in and drove down the length of the pier and the ramp, past the dolphin fountain at State Street.

She didn't ask where they were going. It didn't matter.

After a while he glanced over. "You said you're starting production on a new movie?"

She nodded. "In three days."

"With the guy Darla got excited about?"

"Alec Warner. He's established himself a solid, serious actor—"

"Who appeals to the female audience."

"He does that."

"Good script?"

She crossed her ankle over her knee. "It's tight writing, well-drawn characters. Makes my work easier."

"Work? You make it look easy."

"You make surfing look easy."

He slid her a smile. "You haven't seen me surf."

She leaned her head back, thinking of that morning in the water with him. It had provided that insulting photo and been followed by their altercation with Malakua, but the morning itself had been magical. "Do you still compete?"

"No. It's a young man's sport. And the prize turned brass."

"If you hadn't won, would Myra have gone out with you?"

"Not a chance. Second best might as well have not shown up."

"Who was second?"

"I have no idea. It was never about the other competitors. Only the wave."

"But for Myra it's all about the other competitors."

His jaw hardened. "We've been apart four years. Until she got wind of you, I hadn't heard a word."

She closed her eyes. If not for her, Cameron's face would not be splashed across the tabloids with Myra's hateful accusations. He wouldn't even know he'd lost his son. "But why? If she hated the marriage . . ."

"Because I didn't. I loved coming home to her, loved our discussions, our excursions. I loved watching her work. I loved . . . her. She can't stand that I might get over it."

"That's wrong."

"It's Myra. If she gets replaced, especially by someone incredible, then she's not the best anymore. She'll do anything to stay on top."

Gentry stared out the window, watching the miles pass by. She understood devotion to excellence and could see herself striving for the apex of her art, her industry, just as she and Uncle Rob had ascended the peaks. The lure not just of excellence but ascendence. Could she become like Myra, sacrificing everything to get to the top, then finding hateful ways to stay there—no matter who got hurt?

She shook herself. "Where are we going?"

"My house."

"What about my car?"

"I'll get you back."

"The press will have your address."

He slid her a glance. "Can you play it?"

"What exactly?"

"Whatever."

She released a short laugh. "Cameron . . ."

"It doesn't matter what we do or don't do. They're going to write anything they feel like."

"So what are you saying?"

"That I'm not going to let Myra or the press or anyone else dictate today or tomorrow or ever." He gave his attention back to the road.

Was he really so tough? Or was he hurting more than he wanted to show—and asking her to share it? She swallowed the lump in her throat and settled in for the drive.

THIRTY-SEVEN

Cameron's Pismo Beach house was gray wood with white trim, a modest two-story with an ocean view and a seemingly paparazzi-free driveway. She glanced quickly around. "So far, so good. But beware of long shots."

"So you'd rather I not sweep you back and kiss you breathless?"

His saying it brought the blush to her cheeks, but he headed for the door without noticing. She heard that kind of bravado all the time, but from Cameron Pierce it was different. He didn't boast; he meant the things he said.

A staircase rose to the right of the foyer, a front room opened to the left. It seemed oddly appointed until she realized there were gaps where other furniture had stood. Four years, and he hadn't rearranged what was left? Some of the shelves on the wall held books, but others were bare. No decorative items except for one photo of Nica and Okelani at some kind of festival with flowers in their hair and leis around their necks. Nails in the wall showed where pictures had hung, but now displayed only wispy, gray cobwebs.

He touched her arm. "Want some lunch?"

"Sure." She followed him into the kitchen, equally Spartan; a wrought-iron tree that held mugs, a butcher block with a couple knives, and a clay pot that once housed plant life. Cameron hadn't washed his breakfast dishes or the pans and plate from the night before.

"Sorry for the mess." He opened the dishwasher, half filled with a few days' worth.

He must not have planned on company until the press sent them scurrying for cover. "This is nothing after Helen. That girl could pile up dishes."

He shoved the dirty pans into the bottom rack. "I take it you've spoken."

Their single conversation sat in her mind like the hole where a tooth used to be, no longer bloody, just pulpy and tender. "She read for a part in *Just Illusions*. We'll be working together."

"You arrange that?"

"Only the audition. She did the rest."

He slipped a bowl and several mugs into the top rack, then closed the dishwasher, looking quickly for anything he might have missed.

"Don't worry about it, Kai. Your place is fine."

He shoved his hands into the pockets of his Dockers to halt their frenetic activity.

She went to the refrigerator and opened the door. In a movie, it would have had nothing but beer bottles and condiments, but Cameron's had a half package of spinach wraps, deli turkey, and Havarti in one drawer, baby greens and tomatoes in another. She set those on the counter and fished a bottle of Dijon from the door. "Plates?"

He got them.

"Knife?"

He slid one from the block. "I was going to do that."

"I'm impressed you have fresh and wholesome food. And I'm hungry." She thinly sliced a tomato—his knife was sharp—and layered the wraps.

He filled two glasses with ice water from a filtered tap, set them on the table in the nook, and pulled a chair from the desk to make two places.

Gentry glanced over her shoulder. "I thought we could sit outside. The arid thing you have going with the urns is interesting." Tall pots outside the French doors to the patio held withered reminders of past life, similar to the gaping holes inside.

He opened the door. "Pismo Beach is not Hanalei."

"Evidently." She followed him through. "Was it quick or did they suffer?"

"To be honest, I didn't notice."

"Nica would weep."

"She would, definitely."

Gentry handed him his plate. The plants were so dead they'd all but mummified over several seasons, she guessed. The soil had stretched away from the pot sides, forming an airy moat around each barren isle. But plant fibers were strikingly resilient, if you didn't mind brown and dusty, and might last indefinitely.

Cameron tucked his chin. "Depressing, isn't it?"

Not nearly as much as the patchy living room. She sat down on the stone bench between the urns.

Standing beside her, he raised one foot to the bench and made a table of his thigh. "I had a patio set . . ."

"This is fine. Are you offering thanks or should I?"

His brow furrowed, but he said, "*Mahalo, ke Akua*, for the food I was going to make for Gentry. And . . . please straighten out the mess we're in." He didn't go on aloud, but his eyes pressed shut, and she added prayers for his little boy and the whole ugly situation.

It looked like a desert island she'd landed on this time, but she imagined the pots springing into bloom with the first drops of rain. And maybe something good could still come from it all. He sat down beside her, and they ate in the companionable silence of two people who'd skipped the small talk. Stomach full, she drew her knees up and leaned against him. "So why am I here?"

"I don't know." He looked around. "I didn't realize the place was so . . . bleak." He broke a brittle stem that might once have been geraniums.

She followed his gaze over the dead urns, the windblown leaves huddled against the foundation, a fringe of weary rhododendrons growing along the edge of the narrow yard. They could have stopped anywhere along the beautiful coastline, but he'd wanted her in his home, unprepared as it was to impress a guest.

She turned back to him. "What is it, Kai?"

His throat worked. "She was sitting out here reading magazines. She told me about Kevin like it was no more than something she'd read."

Gentry released a slow breath.

"Not his name, though. I learned that from the lawyers." He shook his head. "I didn't give her a chance to say much, but still, you'd think she'd use his name. Instead she called him her son, my son, as though he were some object that belonged to us."

"Distancing is probably normal when you give up an infant."

"He was a bargaining chip. Her ace up the sleeve. It was her *sister* she wanted me to take him from, as though she'd just parked him there for a while."

Gentry allowed his words to sink in. The whole morning had been a shock—learning he had a son, reading the hateful articles. Who would do that to him?

He clenched his fists. "She's Nica's opposite. She takes where Nica gives, hurts where Nica helps. Nica feels everything, but Myra . . ."

"What did you think when you married her?"

He hunched over. "That she never looked back. Never feared loss."

"You can't lose what you don't care about."

"I'd been caring for Nica so long I thought someone so strong would . . ." He rested his face in his hand. "I thought she'd ripped everything out already. Then this."

"I can't imagine."

"I keep trying to stay ahead of the crest, because once the curtain drops . . ."

"It's okay to hurt."

He pressed both hands to his face. Gentry held his shoulders as he wept.

"I'd have raised him without her, if she didn't want a family. I don't know how I'd have managed it exactly, but I wouldn't have tossed him away like something irrelevant. What will he think when he learns I gave up the chance to change that?"

"What you did was heroic. Maybe someday you can meet him and explain. But right now you've left his life intact."

He groaned. "I tried."

"He's three and a half. He won't be reading the tabloids or know why people want his picture. His parents will shield him."

Cameron nodded. "So what now?"

"Well, for starters . . ." She swung her legs down and stood. "The plants have to go." She grabbed hold of the stems and pulled the withered root block and solid, crusted soil from the nearest urn. "Where's the garbage?"

"In the garage." Nonplussed for only a moment, he stood, uprooted the other two urns, and led the way through the back door into the cramped garage, where they deposited their loads into the large plastic trash receptacle. He turned. "Now what?"

"The living room. Definitely the living room."

When they'd arranged the tan ultrasuede sofa and brown leather chair with a couple end tables and the lamp, she surveyed the room. "Let's go shopping."

"Can we?"

"As you said, they'll print what they want to."

At one shop in Pismo Beach, they collected a table lamp and a glass sculpture of Orcas cresting. Guessing that the empty spots had been filled with items Myra considered hers, Gentry insisted he choose things that appealed to him, offering minimal comment only when pressed. She smiled at the four-foot teakwood surfboard he chose for the blank wall. Her only contribution was a frame for the photo of Kevin that Myra had left on the counter.

He picked another like it and said, "For a picture of you."

"Are you asking for my autograph?"

He shook his head. "Just your smile. And those rain-forest eyes."

Strolling back to the truck Cameron made one more purchase. A potted palm.

Gentry gave him a skeptical look. "Tell me you're not feeling sadistic."

He smiled, hoisting the palm to his hip.

As they'd shopped, she'd signed whatever people held out. Now, arms full, she wasn't approached, though their activity drew plenty of curious glances and photographs. She didn't care. She felt as free as Jade, with nothing more troublesome than a blank slate.

Back at the house they arranged the items that reflected Cameron's personality and filled the empty spaces. He stepped back and circled her shoulders with his arm. "Thanks."

She nodded. "I know what it's like to have gaps."

He turned. "Have you remembered—"

"No. But, Cameron, I don't care. Uncle Rob and I are moving forward, putting all that behind us. Life is too short to waste it looking back."

He raised her chin. "Myra said the same thing. Only, she left destruction in her wake."

She covered his hand with hers. "You're stronger than any destruction she can wreak."

"Gentry." He brought his other hand behind her neck.

"You don't have to do that."

"What?"

"Grab on to keep me from slipping away."

His hand softened. "I didn't realize—"

"I'm not going anywhere."

His mouth parted. "I'm a little raw."

"Understandable."

"Clingy, unhealthy . . ."

"Whatever."

He pulled her tight. "I love too hard."

"Okay."

He shook his head. "I shouldn't have brought you here. It's too . . . close."

"Please don't push me away."

His voice rasped. "Even if I don't, there are too many ways to lose you."

She rested her fingers on his ropy forearm. "Is that a chance you're willing to take?"

⌒

Curt stood outside the rehab facility. Nice place. Hot meals. Private rooms. People to help a cripple get around. An accident could happen, but wouldn't. Not here. He needed the niece to muddy the waters. But information would be priceless.

A young woman dressed in floral scrubs came out of the joint, end-of-shift weariness across her fair, elfin features, pale, downy hair pulled into a ponytail clipped into a scatter at the back of her head. He leaned against the tree, hands in the pockets of his slacks, silk shirt open at the neck just far enough to look alluring but not crass. If Brad Pitt could pull off forty-something, Curtis Blanchard would hold his own at thirty-nine.

She glanced, glanced again. He'd known she would. He drew a slow smile, the kind that said, aha, caught you looking. She blushed, continuing down the short walk toward the parking lot. He fell into step.

"Long day?"

She nodded. "They're all long. Twelve-hour shifts."

"Why do I think you could use a drink?"

"I don't know." She kept walking, but a lot of the pink had stayed in her cheeks.

"My name's Curt."

"I don't go drinking with strange men."

He laughed. "What makes you think I'm strange?"

"I mean stranger . . . men." She faltered. "Men I don't know."

"Then how do you get to know them?"

She reached a '98 Mustang that had been driven hard, probably before she bought it. "Why were you standing there staring?"

"I doubt it's the first time you've had that effect."

"At the building, I mean."

"My dad's in there." *Oh, smooth. Hadn't even planned that.*

"Then why didn't you go in?" She drew out her keys, complete with pepper spray and whistle.

"He's doesn't acknowledge me. We haven't talked in years." There it was, blooming in her face like a rose—sympathy. What a beautiful sight.

She hesitated. "Why not?"

"I was a wild oat he planted unexpectedly." He shrugged. "Now he pretends I don't exist." Truth always rang true. So what if he'd applied it to the wrong man.

"Then why are you here?"

He looked back at the building. "That's what I was asking myself." He shoved his hands into his pockets. "Sorry I bothered you."

"Wait."

He turned back.

"I guess a drink's okay."

He eyed her up and down. "Do they feed you dinner when you work twelve hours?"

"I could get it in the cafeteria if I wanted, but why would I? You know?"

He nodded. "Why don't I follow you to your favorite restaurant and pick up the tab?"

Her mouth formed a V-shaped smile. "Okay. Except . . ." She looked down. "I don't want to go in this."

"Go home and change. Tell me where to meet you."

She pressed her palm to the side of her head. "You sure?"

"Sure. Beats standing outside wondering why it hurts that my old man lost his leg, when he wouldn't care if I died in my sleep."

Her brow pinched just enough to show she understood. "Fanny and Alexander's on Emerson? They've got live music."

He smiled. "My kind of place." Though the music was probably the kind kids her age got off on. The thought surprised him, along with the realization that he'd rather spend the evening with Allegra. But that was the point after all. And to get what he wanted, he could baby-sit.

~

The new cleaning woman had just left, but Allegra crouched on hands and knees and scrubbed the shower floor. It didn't look dirty, didn't smell dirty, but it felt dirty. She rocked back on her knees when the phone rang, her teeth gritting with each invasive tone. She wanted to ignore it completely, but she pushed up. It could be Rob, or news of Rob.

"Hello?"

"Darling, you have to meet us at the club for cocktails." Lorraine's voice was shrill. "It's simply cruel to keep us in the dark."

Allegra winced. They wanted to hear about the mystery man who'd whisked her off to Hawaii. Was it romantic? Was he wonderful? Was she going to make an end of it with poor Rob now that he was maimed? And then she'd break down and tell them how she'd been too cowardly to face him. How she longed to be a comfort, but things had gone so wrong. Curt's words echoed. *"Let him start over with dignity."*

Sometimes she thought Curt must be reading her mind. Could he know how she'd hoped for that very thing when she remade herself? She'd left behind Allison Carter and created Allegra Delaney. Diction tapes to lose her cracker accent, deportment lessons from the movies where glittering stars walked like queens. Personal grooming from magazines, and all the rest from watching people everywhere.

Then she'd met Rob. Anyone who'd known her before would say she'd married his money. And maybe she had. But it wasn't his money she'd fallen in love with.

"No, I'm sorry, I can't," she told Lorraine on the phone. "I have a date."

"My, my, my. Well, one of these days, you *have* to let us meet him."

"I'll try, but with his being away so much on business, he guards our time jealously. I'm sure you understand."

"Of course, darling. But Bev's claiming he's imaginary."

He was. Tonight at least. She hadn't heard from Curt since she'd given him the check, and for that she was intensely grateful. Seeing him filled her with the deep self-loathing she had striven to escape. And yet underneath it all, she deserved him.

⌣

Rob greeted the nurse's aid Nicki the next morning as always, but her response this time was resistant, almost hostile. He rose from the bed, gripping the walker and balancing precariously. At first he'd had to account for the lack of bone and muscle that his mind still thought was there. Now the missing weight was overcompensated by the prosthesis. Sooner or later he'd train his brain to recognize this as his body.

Nicki glowered as she escorted him to physical therapy. He thought he could make it down there alone, but they hadn't declared him stable. Wise in more ways than one. So she was stuck with the job whether she liked it or not—poor girl. Maybe his stump repulsed her. She was too young to realize how temporary physical appearance was.

"Big plans for the weekend?" He glanced her way.

"Not really."

"Weather's going to be nice. Good for sailing." He enjoyed watching the boats in the marina outside his window. "You like sailing?"

"Not really."

He nodded. "Have I . . . offended you?"

She looked momentarily concerned. With what he paid for this facility, his complaint might cause her trouble.

"No." She bit the side of her lip.

"Good. Well, thanks for the escort. Have a nice day." He passed through the automatic doors she activated with a big square button on the wall, to the torture chamber where Paul, personal trainer and royal thorn, awaited him.

THIRTY-EIGHT

Phone to her ear, Gentry drew up her knees and curled into the corner of the couch beneath the trailer window. Cameron no longer barked "Pierce" when she called. It was sometimes "Hey," sometimes *"Aloha"*, but usually he just started talking with "I was just thinking about you" or "I'm glad you called; I had this idea."

This time she heard "Just a second." Some quick keyboard typing, then he was back. "Hi."

"Am I interrupting?"

"It can wait."

Knowing his sharp focus, she appreciated those words every time. "I won't keep you. I just wondered, would you like to come down for a shoot?"

"Ducks?"

"No."

"Rabbits?"

"Definitely not." These past three weeks, they'd made up for the silence of the first three, talking every night and more than once during the day. But she hadn't seen him since fixing up his place—which the tabloids had trumpeted as their setting-up house.

With the ensuing barrage of calls from people willing to pay for interviews, pictures, anything he had to give them, he'd unlisted his number. One guy had perched outside for days with a camera aimed at his bedroom. *"It's sick, Gentry."* But every time she went to her trailer after a long day on the set, he'd be on her voicemail. It amazed her how much she treasured that.

"When?"

"Thursday?"

"Any love scenes?"

"No. But . . . everything's got energy now, all the scenes we shoot together." Her cinematic synergy with Alec would hopefully translate to the screen, but asking Kai to come watch was risky. If their relationship was going to progress, he'd have to deal with that element of her craft, but she was acutely aware that, after Myra's infidelity, he might not want to.

"I could cause interference."

She smiled. "You could." She wasn't at all sure she could relate to Alec with Cameron there. Maybe she needed to see that as well.

"What time?"

She gave him the details and promised him a pass at the gate if she wasn't able to meet him there.

"Can I take you out after?"

"How do you look in a bag?"

"My best."

She laughed. "We'll see."

"How's Rob?"

"He sounded good last time we talked." Her heart warmed. "He told me about your visit."

"I was up that way for business. Stopped in on the way home."

"He said he hasn't enjoyed a conversation so much in a long time."

"It was illuminating."

She heard the smile in his voice. "Oh?"

"Let's see, there was the blue-hair phase—"

"That was an accident."

"The tomboy years, the girlie years . . ."

"Tell me you did not spend the whole time talking about me."

"We covered the Giants, the 49ers, and his book. I agreed to be a resource for the technical aspects of investigation, but I have to say his character's intriguing."

"He let you see it?" Her uncle's gimpy detective story might never see the light of day, but then you never knew; she was starring with Alec Warner. "How did he look? It's killing me that I can't get up there."

"The graft seems to have taken. Pretty remarkable, their reconnecting the blood supply from one part to the other."

She loved that he wasn't squeamish about the injury—that he and Rob could talk, that he would care to. "So, Thursday?"

"Yeah. All right. I'll be there."

And that he never acted starstruck. She especially loved that.

Curt stalked down the sidewalk, the San Francisco night life enticing but not drawing him in. Too irascible to be charming, he'd left Nicki and her nubile friends at the last club. He hadn't anticipated this long a recuperation, or Rob requiring a second surgery because the stump hadn't healed properly, leaving bones and blood vessels exposed.

He shriveled inside to think of them hacking out a flap of muscle from the guy's chest cavity and attaching it to the stump, but Nicki gave him enough details to gag a horse. She assumed he wanted to know—poor grieving son. After what they'd done to Robert Fox, he'd be putting him out of his misery.

He had tried to call Allegra so many times, reached her once, but she'd said she couldn't talk. She hadn't asked about the hundred grand. He hadn't asked about Rob, but according to Nicki, Allegra hadn't been to see him. That was good.

In case the little blond nurses' aide could do math, he'd lied about his age, told her he was twenty-nine, not thirty-nine. He'd forbidden her to tell Rob or anyone at the center anything about him. "It'd only piss him off."

But she'd told him plenty. How brave and kind his poor *dad* had seemed, always praying and reading religious stuff. *"And he won't even speak to his son? What a hypocrite."* But he was sick of spending time with her, and time in any sense was becoming his enemy.

Even with Allegra's donation, the noose had tightened on his throat. Assuming he'd have her and the money long before this, he'd taken risks. If the wrong people found out, he was dead meat. But he wouldn't let that happen. No way. His heart beat faster. He was stayin' alive, stayin' alive.

◡

Shooting the scene with Cameron on the set was going to be as big a challenge as she'd expected. It scared her how much it mattered what he thought, how much she cared what he felt. She had introduced him to most of the cast and crew involved in the day's shoot and to Helen, who didn't have call sheets for any scenes, but who'd come anyway—as she did every day—to support her friend. Gentry suspected she was also still trying to see what it was that made Gentry Fox.

She wished she could transfer the magic, blow it over her friend like fairy dust so Helen could fly too. But Helen had to find her own happy thought to make her character come alive. Not that she wasn't trying; she tried too hard, and the scenes between them had been disjointed at best. By the third or fourth cut, she usually settled in, but by then everyone was edgy. She wished they could find the easy rapport they'd had doing improv with the troupe. She would talk to her tonight. No, not tonight with Cameron there. Her heart fluttered.

Lord, help me focus. She wanted to do her best, not just for his sake but for everyone's. What had she been thinking? She closed her eyes and cleared her mind.

"It's a drag, isn't it?" Alec whispered. "Having him here."

She answered without opening her eyes. "I asked him here."

"You're as crazy as Eva."

"Eva's not crazy. She's right. And you're about to find that out." She opened her eyes as Eva Thorne.

"First team," the assistant director called as their stand-ins exited the set, lights and camera having been positioned.

They took their places—Alec inside the tent; she, poised to stalk in.

"Three bells!" Quiet on the set.

"Background." The extras started milling around behind and passed by the tent.

"Picture's up." Then came the call: "Roll sound. Roll camera. Mark it. And . . . action."

She tossed open the flap. The whole side of the tent was open, but no one would know because that was the camera's position.

Matt Cargill looked up from the crate that held maps and compass. "This better be good."

"Not a word I'd apply to anything here."

He hunkered back on his heels. "Eva—"

"Why won't you listen? I know what's happening."

The camera came in tight. Her expression, then his. Their tension crackled.

"You want to break something big. Fine. I know the hunger."

"Hunger? I'm talking real hunger, starvation."

"Tell me something I don't know."

She crossed her arms. "Okay." She laid out her suspicions with the steely assurance Eva took into every battle. The fact than Matt Cargill had snubbed her at the UN banquet only helped her dig her heels in.

"Wai-wai-wait." He spread his hands. "You're telling me, you know this? You have proof?"

She let her steady gaze lie for her. She knew it, but without him she couldn't get close enough to prove it. She allowed a flicker for the camera to show the audience her duplicity, another shift to show her despair over what she'd seen. They'd go with her because she cared enough to risk it all.

Would he? Could Matt Cargill get past his ego and admit he'd been wrong about her and the information that had strained their professional relationship and eroded the feelings they both worked hard to deny?

He stood slowly. "You realize where this takes us if you're wrong."

Her chin came up just enough to savor the victory. It wasn't hers alone. It was every face that haunted her sleep, every child who might not see tomorrow. "I'm not wrong."

Locked gaze, enough heat to show his decision wasn't strictly professional, the tension of resistance and . . .

"Cut." Seconds later the director called, "Print."

Alec raised his brows with the hint of a sardonic smile. "First take. I think you found your muse."

Gentry shook herself. She'd forgotten Cameron was there. He belonged to Gentry's world, or Jade's. Eva had her own troubles. But she smiled with confidence and satisfaction. She didn't need the director to tell her they'd nailed it. She felt it.

She and Alec were released while they set up the next scene with second team. He walked with her to where Cameron stood beside Helen, who was giving him the lowdown on cinematic lingo and protocol. Alec had been in his trailer when she'd brought Cameron onto the set, but she introduced them now.

As they shook hands and exchanged greetings, she had a sense of disassociation, of clashing with her alter ego, Eva. Helen picked up on her odd mental state and sent her a quizzical look. Then Cameron grounded her with a glance of his own, and she came fully back. "Hungry? There's a snack cart."

It was different seeing what Gentry did, live and in person. He tried to imagine what it would look like as a movie, but it was all in pieces; Gentry going in and out of the scene, someone taking her place while cameras and microphones were adjusted, watching her slip in and out of character.

She was harder as Eva, a little jaded, with a hint of Northeastern accent. And she was right that her scenes with Alec were energized. They'd reached the end of today's shoot without kissing, but it wouldn't be long. Alec Warner and Gentry Fox would pretend they were other people and kiss. With Troy she'd said, *"It only looks real."* But she wouldn't get away with a dip and turn this time. There'd be hands and lips and tongue . . .

His throat squeezed. The director outlined a few things for tomorrow while Gentry, Alec, and four others nodded. Then Alec pushed her hair aside and kissed the back of her neck. "Ciao."

She left them and headed over, murmuring, "Sorry."

"For . . ."

"That."

"What was it?"

"A tease. He knew you were watching. It's . . . He didn't mean anything."

But he recognized her fluster. "Does it bother you?"

"Let me grab my call sheet." She took the pages handed her by the person distributing them, then rejoined him. "It hasn't bothered me to this point because I haven't had someone who . . . mattered. Who it might matter to."

"To whom it might matter, if you really want to beat it to death."

She shot him a glance. "The last person I was serious about bailed at the mention of Hollywood." She led the way to a trailer at the edge of the set. "He'd have been horrified if I kissed Alec or anyone else."

What was she saying? That he shouldn't mind it?

She pulled open the door. "I need to get this makeup off."

He hesitated, but she held the door for him to come in. She sat down at a dressing table and slathered her face and neck with cream. The energy of her day radiated from her like steam and made it hard to breathe in the cramped space.

He crossed his arms. "When you kiss him, you have to feel something, or it's not believable."

She pulled thick, soft tissues from a box. "Eva feels something. It's about what she feels in that circumstance."

He tried to get his mind around that.

She swabbed her cheeks. "I wanted you to see that it's a job. A production. So that when the movie comes out—"

"I know what he'll feel."

"He's a professional, Kai."

"Yeah, I saw. He left his signature."

She shook her head, but the argument was lame. He knew exactly what had gone down. The back of the neck was a lot more than a brush on the cheek.

"When do you kiss him?"

"Tomorrow."

"I want to be there."

"Kai . . ." She dropped her hands to the tabletop and looked at him in the mirror. "No."

"I'm not allowed?"

She snatched another handful of tissues and rubbed the rest of the cream from her forehead and hairline. "I can't do it with you there."

"Why? If it doesn't mean anything."

She threw the tissues into the trash and turned. "Eva will kiss Matt."

"Then why—" He wanted to say he could take it, that he had to, that if he didn't ride this wave, he didn't know if he could catch the next. But the truth was it would bury him.

She dabbed her face one last time and stood up more Jade than Gentry or Eva Thorne. She took his hands. "Do you still want to go out?"

"No." He brought her fingers to his lips. "I want to go away."

She closed her eyes and lowered her chin. He drew her into his arms, pressed his lips to her hair. He wanted to lift it and kiss her neck, but that spot was tainted. Would he feel that way about her mouth tomorrow?

She looked up at him. "I knew this would be hard. But we need to know. If it's not something you can live with . . ."

Was it? Myra seemed a lifetime ago, but it had been a lifetime's worth of hard lessons. "I realize it's your profession, but . . . I've been there."

"I know." She searched his face. As the pent-up energy seeped off, her shoulders softened. "Will you come home with me? I make a mean lobster salad."

He couldn't seem to go a day without talking to her, hardly managed an hour without her in his thoughts. When she looked like that, asked like that, did she think he'd say no? "Okay."

He followed her off the set and past another, leaving worlds behind. He had taken a taxi from the airport, so he had no truck in which to transport her. But this was her turf. She stopped at her pearl beige Honda Prelude in the back parking lot. Nice, but he guessed it was intentionally understated.

She pressed the keyless entry. "They'll be waiting outside the gate. Driving out together could stir things up again."

"I can catch a cab."

She considered a moment, then said, "Get in."

Though they were photographed and followed, it surprised him how passé the attention seemed. It would be bigger news if she fell for her leading man.

His ordeal with the press had run its course, and one day he'd realized no one was out there hassling him. He would handle it if this sparked more speculation about him and Gentry as long as his son was kept out of it. Myra's ploy had been vicious but short-lived since Tom and Mary had kept Kevin safely tucked away. And now it was old news. They had thanked him profusely for not making their lives a battle. But life basically was a battle. You just couldn't always see the enemy.

Gentry's apartment was loaded with personal touches, and he saw by contrast how the blankness of his home must have screamed at her. Didn't take an investigator to realize she liked scents; candles, soaps—the clear glycerin kind—a bowl of potpourri in the kitchen. The place was clean but not fastidious. She liked novels; a wide variety, multiple genres and time periods. Movies: film noir to *The Passion of the Christ*, a floor-to-ceiling shelf arranged alphabetically.

"Are you required to buy every movie ever made?"

"It's a reference library. If a director says play it like Julie Andrews as Maria Von Trapp, I have something to study."

"Do you?"

"Of course." She went into the kitchen and pulled out vegetables and a package of precooked lobster. "In that cabinet you can get the pot for the pasta."

He found it and filled it with water, got the package of tricolor bowties from the pantry, and set it beside the stove. "I can chop."

She handed him a knife, and they worked together on the cutting board—artichoke hearts, tomatoes, three kinds of olives, capers, and green onions. No one would know she'd spent the day being a star. She tucked a strand of hair behind her ear, and he pictured her on Kauai in the salt waves at sunrise. A mermaid. A magical sojourner from another realm. A realm both deadly and beautiful.

"What?" she asked without looking.

He moved the hair off her neck and kissed the place Alec had found. Her breath caught. He turned her face and kissed her mouth. "I love you." She raised her lashes to reveal the teal green depths, and he sank in, drowning. "It started that night with the centipede and hasn't stopped. I think about you all the time. I tell myself, Cameron, you love too hard. You'll crush the life from her."

She set down her knife. "You don't love too hard. You're just in a world that's made love cheap."

"Nothing about you is cheap." He stroked her arms.

"Then you're not mad?"

He cupped her shoulders. "I won't like what happens tomorrow; I'll hate it."

"Kai, I promise you—"

He kissed her, deeply and slowly. "I'll hate it, but if that's the price . . ." He breathed the musky scent of her hair. "I'll pay it."

"Why?"

"Because you weren't the only one lost." He stroked a tendril of hair off her forehead, remembering it damp and muddy. She'd forgotten who she was, had staggered out of the wild, bruised and bewildered. But at least she'd known she didn't have the answers. He'd thought he did. He swallowed the emotion that threatened to silence him. "I need to stop fighting."

She circled his waist with her arms. "I love you, Kai."

And with that he came in from the sea.

THIRTY-NINE

With no other lights on, Gentry lit the candles around her living room. Pillars on trays with polished stones, purple Zen votives, a four-wick pillar on a wrought-iron stand, a hanging, stained-glass oil candle in the corner. She caught his amused expression when she sat and faced him on the futon and drew her knees to her chest. "What?"

"Now I know what my house is missing."

"You have a fireplace." She held his eyes, drinking in the whole of their experience to this point and anticipating. She wasn't fearing for her life or her sanity; he wasn't wrestling his past. They were linked in the moment in a way she'd never experienced with anyone. And he was right; it had started in the mountains of Hanalei beside the stream where the forest met the stars.

She rested her chin on her knees. "What are you thinking?"

"That I want to make love to you."

"To me or the myth?"

"There's only you. That's all there's ever been. I let you believe the other because I didn't want you to know what I really felt."

He slid his hand down her calf and clasped her heel, sending warmth through her like a tonic, loosening her joints and sparking her heart into quick, erratic flights.

His eyes deepened, drawing her in and holding her under. "If you hadn't had your mountaintop experience, would we?"

"Probably. If you weren't a missionary's son?"

"Grandson. My parents were hedonists." At her raised brows, he smiled. "Well, what do I know? I was six." He slid his fingers over her feet.

She bit her lip at the exquisite sensation almost too much to bear. Were feet off limits?

"I just have this sense of their enjoying everything." He rubbed the arches of each foot. "That's what I wanted. A soul mate."

"Doesn't everyone?"

He shook his head. "No."

He didn't have to elaborate.

"Gentry." He clasped her ankles. "Did you mean it?"

She straightened. "I will never tell you something I don't mean. I need to be real with you."

"You are real. Too real." He swallowed. "When I saw you on the shore that first night, I thought, what did Nica get me into this time?"

She smiled. "I thought, who does this guy think he is?"

"I've never been so thankful for Nica."

"I'm still wondering who this guy thinks he is." She squealed as he lunged in and assaulted her ribs.

They tumbled off the futon, and he kissed her on the floor. Then he drew back. "I admire the talent God's given you. If you believe you're supposed to use it, then I'll deal with the parts I don't like. But when all is said and done—"

Her phone rang. Comical how many times they were interrupted by the communication her uncle had helped to perfect. "It's my mother. If I don't answer she'll leave a forty-minute message." She stretched up for the phone on the end table.

Cameron sat up and pulled her back down, and she leaned against him as her mother asked all about the film project. "Is it as good as you'd hoped? And what about that Alec Warner? I can't tell you how many people want to know."

"He's a talented actor, Mom." She tried not to speak too glowingly, but Alec's skills did complimented hers. She looked at Cameron and clipped her answers. "Yes. Yes. Mostly. I don't know yet." She sucked in her upper lip when it got too personal. "Mom . . ."

"Anyway, honey, the reason I called is to tell you Uncle Rob's going home."

"What? When?"

"Tomorrow. We're having a little bash Saturday, and I was hoping you could fly up."

"Of course. Oh, that's great!" She covered the receiver and told Cameron, then went back to her mom. "I'll be there." She asked with her eyebrows and he nodded. "With a friend."

Her mother said, "I don't know if Aunt Allegra's out of town again. She's not answering, but I think she'd like to be included."

Sure. She hadn't been there for him in the crisis, but she wouldn't want to miss the party. Gentry shook her head. "I'll try her."

"Would you? One less thing for me to worry about."

Between the scandal, Dad's heart surgery, and the disastrous trip to Kauai, Mom had worried more than any other time in her life. But Uncle Rob was going home, and that was worth celebrating. She hung up and settled back into Cameron's arms. "You were wrong. Hope does keep its promise."

"Then I hope I'm wrong every day for the rest of my life."

⌒

Once again the night shadows closed in as all the doubts and regrets pressed close enough to suffocate. It had been days since she answered the phone, a week at least since she'd left the house, and then only to grab a carton of milk for her morning muesli. In the impartial bathroom light Allegra looked into the mirror, and an old woman looked back. What she'd feared for years had overtaken her.

The phone's shrill cries hardly registered. Why would Curt not stop calling? Didn't he see what she saw? Her teeth were flawlessly capped, figure undimpled, skin tight and supple, breasts enhanced.

Nails buffed, hair coifed, yet it was the eyes of a hag that looked out at her. She had turned half a century, but it may as well be a hundred. How had she thought she could cheat time? Believed she could deceive fate?

Exhaustion clung like rags to her flesh. Gentry might be the actress getting all the acclaim, but her talent hardly compared. When Gentry Fox walked off the set she stopped pretending. Allegra Delaney-Fox never rested, never ceased playing her part. Oh, she was weary.

She'd been running so long, trying so hard to prove her daddy wrong, to prove she was worth something. And she had been, to the man who'd loved her. But when he had told her that all the things she'd done were worthless, that he'd found what mattered and wanted to start over, she'd walked away. She could not remake herself again. It was already killing her.

Curt banged on the door. "Allegra, I know you're in there." His cuts had healed, the bruises faded. He was not there to play on her sympathies; he had to reestablish their relationship now that Rob was going home. What good was it if she wouldn't turn to sympathetic Curt in her sorrow? He'd get nothing. Zilch. And then it would all catch up, and he'd be the dead one.

If only things had worked the first time. He wasn't cruel, never meant the guy to suffer. Should have been over quick, a simple accident. But he'd depended on someone else. Big mistake. This time he'd do it right. Besides, who would want to go on as a cripple? Robert Fox would thank him—if he could. But right now, he had to work on the other end. "Allegra." He sang her name. "Open up. I need to talk to you."

The door swung inward, and there she was. He'd never known anyone so elegant. The way she moved, the way she spoke. She almost wasn't real. After Nicki, it was more obvious than ever. Allegra was a crystal goblet; Nicki a to-go cup.

He held out the extravagant bouquet, no tacky black balloons or over-the-hill cards. He liked her age. He liked how good she made him feel. How safe. She was class. He leaned in and kissed her throat. "Happy birthday, babe."

"Curt, what . . ."

"I wanted it to be a diamond choker. But I already owe you. It didn't seem right until I can pay back . . . Anyway, I hope you like the flowers."

She took the bouquet. "They're beautiful."

"Went with a white theme. Classy, not flashy. Just like you. Perfect."

Why did she look as though he'd lost his mind? Couldn't she tell he meant it? Emotion flooded his voice. "I miss you." Exactly the right tone, but the sentiment hit too close. He used her indecision to walk in and close the door behind.

She put the roses and lilies and other pure white flowers he'd ordered to make his point into a vase with a tassel tied around the neck. She filled it with water and admired the effect. Gracious, but not exactly overwhelmed. "Thank you, Curt."

"No party?"

Her smile was forced. "No."

"Birthdays are meant to be celebrated. Especially when you're lovelier every day."

"Curt . . ."

"Don't ask me to leave. I know I disappointed you, but . . ." He spread his hands.

"You didn't disappoint me. It's my own—I can't go on with it, that's all."

He sat down on the grand piano bench, determined to talk her out of that viewpoint. He could too. He had to. "Please, can we talk about it?"

She smoothed a lacy thing under the piano lamp. "I don't know what there is to say."

"Then let me talk and you listen. Because I have so much to say I can't keep it in." He'd find the words, the perfect words to bring her back, rekindle the romance. It was there; he just had to make her see.

⌒

Cameron halved a California grapefruit from the fruit drawer and put to boil two of the brown eggs from the carton in Gentry's refrigerator. He was naturally a deep sleeper and early riser, but concerns had assailed him all night; primal fears for her safety and personal fears for his own.

Having met Helen, he agreed that she was not the mastermind behind the accident on Kauai. She and Bette Walden had paired up for an envy-driven assault on Gentry's character, but neither had the resources or imagination to plan a fatal accident. So maybe Gentry was right that Malakua had seen a chance to make a buck and flubbed it. Maybe when they'd asked for directions off the beaten path, he'd told them about a place where he planned to snatch her. Uncle Rob would pay ransom or else his niece was *ma-ke*. Malakua had proved that M.O. with Nica.

Cameron started coffee in the espresso machine. No better explanation had come from Kauai PD. The chief had ordered them mum, and since TJ's position was tenuous, he wouldn't say what, if anything, the interrogation had revealed. Maybe it really was over. He could thank God for that, and had.

What had mostly kept him awake was his own soul-searching. What was he willing to risk? Nothing he valued was inviolable, no matter how hard he held on. Nica's emotional frailty had brought out his natural protectiveness accentuated by their childhood trauma. If he'd trusted God, she might have developed strength of her own. Or had she, and he hadn't noticed?

He'd brought that same zealous caretaking to Myra, who despised him for it. She had proved to be a riptide he'd barely survived. Now Gentry was asking him to trust her in ways that looked so similar to Myra's infidelity it sickened him. He rubbed a hand over his face.

An actor with Gentry's potential would be cast in bigger and bigger projects, her charisma attracting all the Alec Warners in the industry. He knew how it worked, the short-lived marriages and side romances of the stars. If he was this gone after knowing her a couple months, why should he expect it to be different for anyone else? He'd be setting himself up for another train wreck. And yet . . .

Listening to her hopes last night had shown him the intense faith she brought to her work. She believed she could make a difference, be a witness, a part of the body of believers in Hollywood—incongruous as that seemed.

Her childlike faith reminded him of Nica's. But Nica wasn't on the way to stardom. As Gentry's credits amassed, would hope be enough to ward off the temptations, the pride, the weight of fame? What would their relationship look like from the shadow of her glow?

Did he want his life to stay as it had been the last few weeks, scavengers circling, her private life made public, her public life displayed? Did he want the world to watch her making out with Hollywood studs and believe what they saw? She made it believable, made it all so believable. And as Myra said, she belonged to everyone. They paid for the rights to her.

Add to that the way she triggered envy and malice. Maybe it was her goodness people couldn't stand. But how many times would her reputation be trashed, her life endangered? Those were the things he'd told her he'd live with last night in the candlelight, but he braced himself now on the counter and felt utterly vulnerable. It wasn't humanly possible.

Gentry came down the hall. He'd hoped to see her tousled and sleepy-eyed, but she'd showered and dressed and looked professional. This was her world, not his island.

She came to him, laid her hand over his and read his thoughts. "Have you come to your senses?"

He lifted his arm and moved her into the cage he'd formed with the counter. Scary how proximity wiped out reason. All the thoughts that had loomed large last night, insurmountable this morning, disappeared into the depths of her gaze. He'd entered the tunnel, and this wave might peel forever. The question was, could the faith he'd inherited be enough?

"I'm not going into this blind. I know how it feels to fail." He half smiled. "Maybe you should be the one concerned."

"I dreamed last night it was you in the cave, only there was no ledge. You were lying underwater, and I breathed air into your lungs. But then I had no more, and you breathed it back to me."

A song came to mind about only needing the air that he breathed and to love her. He smiled. Maybe it was as simple as that.

⌒

After dropping Cameron at the airport, Gentry pulled into the studio lot an hour before her first call time. She climbed out of the car and rolled the tension from her shoulders. He hadn't asked again to be there, either because she'd said no or because he'd thought it through.

She read over her call sheets once more to know exactly where to be, when. The critical scene wasn't until later. She had one with Helen, several action packed with Alec, and then, inevitably, the part would come where Eva and Matt succumbed.

Alec joked around as they prepared for that scene, relaxing her, the less-seasoned actor. But after the scenes they'd played already, her head was there. It scared her how deeply she stayed in character. She was Eva, and Eva wanted Matt Cargill. As the camera rolled, every bit of that wanting passed between them. Inside, her spirit deflated while the kiss went on, her head tipped back, his hand gripping her ribs, his thumb brushing the base of her breast. *Not in the script!*

But Eva wanted Matt. She imagined him undressing her. The camera rolled. Again the brush of his thumb. Heat coursed through her. Tears burned behind her eyelids, then went away because Eva was in control. Her eyes opened. Her mouth closed. Leave him wanting more. Let him wish he hadn't made her feel small. Back off. Hold eye contact.

"Cut."

Please, God.

"Print."

She drew a jagged breath and walked out of the tent.

A minute later Alec joined her. "Gentry."

She turned. "I need you to stick to the script."

He spread his hands. "I did."

"The script said kiss."

"Didn't you hear? Ron's still raving. Talk about on-screen chemistry."

"It said *kiss*, Alec. Not feel me up." Compared to other such scenes, it was nothing. But all she could think was what if Kai had been there? Then she recalled the word "Print" and realized he would be.

"We were awesome."

She wanted to say it was Eva and Matt. But it had also been them.

He cocked his head. "It doesn't always work, you know."

She knew. But that was the first kiss of the movie. It was supposed to build from there. "Alec—"

"I hardly touched you."

But she'd responded. She was more angry about that.

Alec turned her around and rubbed her shoulders. "The first time's hardest, and we nailed it, take one."

"If we hadn't, I'd have slugged you. Don't do it again."

"I played the scene, Gentry. It's how Matt is."

Had it rung as hollow when she explained it to Cameron?

"And Eva's no ingénue."

He was right. They'd given the scene exactly what it called for. She'd known it all the while the cameras rolled. She stepped away. "I'm taking a walk."

There was only one more scene for them and she'd be done for the day. She had to keep her head straight. And she did. But by the time she got home, it had settled into a hard ache. She showered and tried to eat. She went to her room and thought about sleeping. Then she picked up the phone and called Cameron. At the sound of his voice, she started to cry.

"Hey. What is it?"

"You were right, it's—I can't—it's Eva, but it's me too."

A hard silence, then, "Okay."

She gave way to the broken sobs.

He expelled his breath. "This is worse than when you first saw Malakua. I hate that you're so far away."

She sniffed. "I wasn't just saying what I said. I really thought it was different. It's not as though I haven't kissed someone before. I was almost engaged two years ago."

"Let me deal with one blow at a time, okay?"

She'd been pacing frenetically. Now she dropped to the bed and lay back. "I've been kissed on almost every stage I've played."

"Not in *Steel*."

"Yes, I was. Right near the end, when we reconciled."

"Oh. Right. I blocked that part. So why is it bothering you now?"

She could not believe he was discussing it so calmly. Of course, she couldn't see if he was shredding his pillow or defoliating the palm. "I don't know. I mean, it was more than I've done for the camera. But . . . I . . . Kai, I have to finish the movie. If I breach my contract, I'll never work in the industry again. They could sue me. I—"

"Gentry. No one's telling you to break your contract."

She drew a calming breath. "I didn't want you to have to deal with this, and here I've called and told you everything."

"Have you?"

Her stomach clenched as she realized why she'd gotten so upset. "Kai, they want more next time. The first kiss was such a *success*, they're heating up the next."

"Can they do that?"

"My contract says no nudity. Nothing between the sheets, though they're discussing implied activity." Her throat ached. "Beyond that, there's quite a lot of room for interpretation. And it's real to the story, to the characters."

His hurt carried over the miles and smothered her.

"I shouldn't have called you. I should have just told you not to watch it."

"Then why did you?"

"Because I couldn't see you tomorrow and hide it." Now he'd say he wasn't coming. Like Daniel he'd say she asked too much.

His voice roughened. "That's the best thing you've said all night."

What? She forked the hair back from her forehead and stared at the ceiling as the truth sank in. "It's because of you that it hurts. Because of what we wanted and didn't do. Because of who I am with you. I don't want anyone else spoiling that."

His breath got choppy.

"I don't know what to do."

He didn't speak.

Oh, Lord, I've ruined everything. "I hurt you, Kai. I'm so sorry."

"You haven't hurt me." His voice was thick with emotion. "You're healing something that's been broken a long time."

When they hung up, she went to the bathroom and washed her face, then looked into the mirror. No one would cast her in a Jane Austin movie where nothing more untoward than brittle words were employed. Not after Rachel Bach and Eva Thorne. They'd found what they wanted in her, the brash and vulnerable woman her counterparts wanted to break and possess. And each time they'd want more.

Whether or not what she and Cameron had was real and lasting, she had a choice to make. Had she been called for such a time as this? Like Esther, had God placed her where she was for his own purpose? And how much had Esther, in becoming wife and queen to the pagan king, compromised?

Cameron got into his truck, drove to the shore, pulled off his shoes and walked across the firm, damp sand to the edge of the cold surf. The water rushed in and lapped his feet and ankles, churning as his emotions churned, surging and falling. A heritage of belief wasn't enough. He knew it with aching clarity. He had to make it his.

Gentry's tears had opened and washed the wounds of Myra's betrayal. He might have preferred not to hear it at all, but the fact that she couldn't hide it meant more to him than anything. Now he needed the strength to deal with it. The sobs came. *Akua. No. Iesū.* The God-man who knew all the pain and betrayal of the world.

Standing in the sea, the ground shifting and sucking under his feet, the water tugging against his calves as he called on Jesus, he understood the lure that had almost carried Nica away. Such love and forgiveness. Such power and grace. Who would pull him back?

He wasn't aware of stepping out of the waves or walking to his truck, didn't know which way he drove home. He got out in the driveway, walked to the front door; almost didn't see her.

"Cameron."

The voice set his teeth on edge, but amazingly no anger came through in his own. "What are you doing here?"

Myra wrapped her arms around her knees, a huddled form, rocking slightly in the dark. Apropos that the bulb was out on the porch since he'd been in the dark with her from day one. He sat down, wary and wounded, no idea what wickedness she might still intend.

But when she spoke it was surprisingly honest. "I never wanted to be married. But Mary did and so I had to."

"What are you talking about?" His tone was weary.

"It was always Mary. Not just with Mum and Dad, but with *everyone.* It was as though she sucked up all the attention, all the good feelings in the world. I had to fight just to be noticed. 'Don't interrupt, Myra, your sister's talking.'" She spread her hands. "'Take this to your sister; do that for your sister.'"

The bitterness shouldn't surprise him, though she'd never discussed it before. He'd thought their lack of relationship strange, but

Myra had used it to mock his closeness to Nica, and he'd been unsure enough to wonder.

"No one ever saw me. It was always, 'Oh, you're Mary's sister,' or 'You're the other Blakeney girl.' They didn't even give me my own name, just rearranged the letters of hers. How wrong is that?"

He tried to remember if she'd ever talked about her childhood. But that would have fallen into "looking back"—a taboo that gave this conversation an eerie unfamiliarity.

"Her wedding was *the event*. I was maid of honor so that I could witness firsthand how *perfect* she was." The words poured out of her as never before, words that meant something, told him something. "So I had to make mine even better. And there you were. You looked at me as though I was the most interesting, amazing person you'd ever known."

She had been. In a way.

"It had taken Tom a year to ask Mary, but after one month, you wanted to marry me."

Two months later they had. And now he knew why. Mary had a husband, so Myra needed one.

"I wasn't a good wife." She sniffed. "I know I hurt you."

His throat tightened.

"But when I realized I was pregnant, I had my chance. I could do what Mary never would. I could have a baby I didn't want and give it to her. And every day she would look at the child she loved and know he was mine. I had won."

She'd taken away his son to best her sister. He shook his head.

"Cameron, hurting you is my only regret. I wish . . . I could turn back time."

"And not leave?" A ghost of a voice.

"And not marry you."

He stared out into the night. "We finally agree."

389

FORTY

Since Aunt Allegra had not responded to her calls, Gentry had the taxi stop there before going on to her uncle's. The patio community had immaculate upkeep, something her aunt would require. No uncut grass, no scraggly shrubs. She rang the bell and heard the chimes tone inside. If there was any chance of bringing her aunt to Uncle Rob's homecoming, she had to try.

Allegra opened the door, surprise melting into a smooth smile. "Gentry."

"Can I come in a minute?"

"Of course. Would you like some sun tea? The pitcher's on the porch."

"I have the taxi waiting."

"Oh. Yes." She glanced at the cab. "Is . . . something wrong?"

Could she seriously ask that when so much was wrong? Were they all masters of denial? "I'm sorry to barge in on you like this. I know we haven't talked in too long."

A gracious tilt of her head. "Our situation has been awkward for you."

She didn't say "You chose your allegiance," but she might have. She motioned Gentry to sit and perched on a yellow chintz wing chair like an elegant and content matron. But Gentry always sensed something fragile behind her aunt's poise, a molecular tension that might all fly apart if she lost her temper or said a cross word. They might all be better for it if she did.

"I don't know if you got Mom's message that Uncle Rob is coming home."

She dropped her gaze and nodded.

"I wanted to tell you personally how much he'd appreciate it if you came for the celebration."

"Celebration?" She looked stunned. "He's . . . handicapped."

Gentry smiled. "Have you ever known anything to handicap Uncle Rob?"

"But, isn't he . . ."

"Lonely?" Way more direct than she'd ever been. "Yes. He misses you so much. He doesn't want to burden you, but if you could just come and see him."

"I'm sure he'd rather I didn't."

"How can you think that?"

"He wanted a new beginning, even before the accident." She looked away, and her composure slipped a little. "I don't want to start over. I can't. Whatever you and he experienced—"

"He knows he didn't handle that well. Aunt Allegra, he can live without his leg. He doesn't want to live without you."

Again emotion moved over her face. "He hasn't said so."

"He's afraid you'll be horrified." In the vein of honesty she'd begun, she continued. "He knows how perfect you want things."

"Me?" She looked as though that was something absurd.

"Anyway, I'm going there now. Will you come? Please?"

"Gentry, I . . ." The fissures in her composure widened. "It's more complicated than that."

"Just welcome him home. Wish him well." *Please, Lord, soften her heart.* She sent a flurry of prayers that whatever was blinding her would be broken.

At last Aunt Allegra drew herself up. "All right. I'll take my own car."

She might change her mind and not go through with it, but Gentry smiled and stood. "Okay. Thanks."

⌒

Rob sighed. The party had not been his idea. Julie and his brother were making a big deal of what was only the next step. Since he lived alone, he'd needed to demonstrate adequate stability and endurance. His strength had returned slowly, as Kauai had been fertile ground for systemic invasion.

Spiritual invasion as well—of the darkest and brightest kinds. Since his conversion, he'd filled his head with knowledge, but his heart had remained stubborn, his pride unshaken. He understood now why David had been chased into the desert, his life threatened, his dignity destroyed, his virtue questioned; deserted by his friends, hunted by his enemies. In that extremity he'd poured out his heart to God and learned God's. Only then was he fit to govern in God's name.

Rob turned and continued around the pool. The artificial leg, including knee unit and terminal device, was microcomputer controlled. It was a sign of healing that he'd not only learned to use it but had studied in depth its components and manufacture. Step by step he moved down the length of the tiled deck. Walking took ten to forty percent more energy with a below-the-knee amputation. An above-the-knee prosthesis, such as his, required sixty to a hundred percent more. Something could certainly be done to improve that.

A shadow spread across the tiles. He looked up, expecting Brendan, who hadn't quite gotten around his hale, younger brother being a gimp. But it was Cameron Pierce who met him poolside. He hadn't seen him since their visit weeks ago. They shook hands.

Cameron cocked his head. "No cane or anything?"

"Remarkable units they have these days. Might make some improvements before I take Gentry up another peak, though." He glanced around. "Is she here?"

"She will be. I drove separately."

"Gives us a chance to catch up." He shifted his weight to the artificial limb. "Anything new on the attack?"

Cameron shrugged. "I'm out of the loop. Should've grilled Malakua myself when I had the chance, but he'd passed out and I was flying a jet."

Rob cracked a smile. "Understandable. But I wish we had some answers."

"Gentry's convinced it's over, that Malakua had a scheme that went wrong."

"What do you think?"

"I hope she's right." His expression lacked certainty.

"So tell me the truth. Are you here in my honor, or to steal time with my niece?"

"Your honor, definitely." Cameron had as good a deadpan as he'd seen. "And I'm not stealing. She deigns to entertain me."

"Ah." Rob nodded. "Then this is your lucky day."

Gentry strode in through the gate, and he felt a surge of pride at the effect it had on the young man. There was a time he'd been that smitten. But he was learning to let go. Allegra's silence these last two months had been as numbing as the deafening roar of the falls in the cave. It was time to stop lying to himself.

Gentry's approach was as physical an experience as the rush of a monster wave building, the wobbly sensation in his stomach hardening into sheer anticipation. Last night's conversations had left him winded. After Myra had gone, he'd called Nica and talked for hours. He'd told her everything, especially how he'd walked into the ocean and surrendered. Her tears had been a second salt bath.

'I've longed for you to know him, Kai.'

The strange thing was that he had, at once. As though he'd been away but not forgotten. It had enabled him to hear Myra without a bitter heart. He'd also told Nica about Gentry, and she'd cried some more, happy and sad and confused.

"I don't want you hurt again."

"It's different now. And, Nica? Ku'u ka luhi." *Be freed from cares.* *"You can let go."* They both could.

Gentry stopped, mouth agape, eyes aglow before her uncle. "You're walking." She hadn't seen his transition from wheelchair to walker to cane. Cameron had only seen him twice, but it had given him points of reference. To her it must look miraculous, but to Rob it had been constant, hard work.

Her uncle's eyes crinkled. "I'm not ready for Everest yet."

She hugged him. "Neither am I." Then she turned.

How long before he'd breathe normally under the sweep of her gaze? Other people had gathered around the pool, friends and neighbors, it seemed. No one looked shocked to see Gentry Fox, though more than one had a puppy-longing-for-a-pat expression. He probably did too.

She smiled. "Hi." No physical contact, but so much could be communicated with two little letters.

"Hi." The same back to her.

"Have you met my parents?"

He hadn't.

"Then come on." She inclined her head, listed over onto one foot, and glided toward the house. Did she think her uncle, or anyone there, missed the energy between them? But he let her take the lead with her family.

The woman rearranging chafing dishes on the buffet gave him a glimpse of Gentry thirty years from now. She'd never be anything but easy on the eyes if they happened to grow old together. The energy surged.

He'd gone into it artlessly with Myra and come out scarred. But as he'd stood calf deep in the surf, arms extended, face to the stars, he'd known at last that he wasn't in this alone.

"Mom, this is Cameron." Gentry turned with an enigmatic smile. "My mother, Julie."

He extended his hand. "Pleased to meet you."

She sandwiched it with both of hers. "You were a great help to Gentry—no matter what the papers say. She has a knack for finding good people."

"Thank you."

"You're taller than you looked in the pictures."

"That's what happens when the camera's aimed up from the ground through the bushes."

She clicked her tongue. "Thank goodness that business is over."

Right.

"What can I get you to drink?"

After accepting their icy cold glasses, Gentry handed him his and turned. "Here's my dad, Brendan."

Similar to Rob, without the robust physique, he had a slight slump to the shoulders, and a slack, bulging stomach that was more slack muscle than fat.

"This is Cameron Pierce, Dad."

"Ah. Nice work out there, finding Rob and looking out for Gentry. Could have been tricky, but she's got a lucky star."

So lucky people defamed and tormented and tried to kill her. Had Mom and Pop tuned in lately?

Brendan glanced at his wife. "Remember the time she got lost at Mount Rushmore? Thought she'd march right up and have a closer look at those big chins and noses."

"Colossal nostrils," Gentry murmured.

Her mother nodded. "Uncle Rob decided the child was naturally inclined to mountain climbing."

Her dad said, "And the time she and Rob had that close call with the lightning."

"Truly enlightening," Gentry breathed.

"Anyone else would have been toast. Not our girl. Lightning bolts out of nowhere. Not a cloud in the sky. Nothing but a foot-deep crevice to shelter in. And she's unscathed. Now, that's a lucky star."

Cameron nodded. "A lot of people consider her just that."

Brendan Fox laughed at the switch in context. "Exactly." He squeezed Gentry's shoulders.

She excused herself. "Cameron, let me show you Uncle Rob's museum."

Museum? He followed her into a room that did indeed resemble a museum; items on the walls with plaques describing them, tables with what looked like working models or prototypes in a wide variety of fields. The room didn't come off as self-aggrandizing, more like an avid model-builder's showcase or a collector's collection. These were the cool things he'd made; wanna see how they worked?

"What do you think of my parents?"

"They're . . . positive."

She laughed so hard she snorted soda up her nose and made her eyes water.

Cameron handed over a napkin. "Must be where you get your optimistic attitude."

She dabbed her eyes. "If you only knew."

He held her glass while she blew her nose. "They think highly of you."

She cleared her throat of the residual soda-snort effects. "Too highly."

"Is that why they named you Gentry?"

She raised her brows. "My mother abhors common names. My sisters are Tapestry and Giselle. As something of a pet to all of them, I'm glad I didn't get Princess or Queenie."

"Now, there's a thought."

"Don't you dare. I'm already Doll to Dave."

"Who's Dave?"

"Dave Brock, my agent."

"Am I worried?"

She laughed. "Only if you're threatened by gruff, growly, grand-father types."

"Hmm." He brushed her hand with his fingers.

She sobered. "I wasn't sure you'd come."

"I told you I would."

"Before everything I told you."

He set their glasses on a display table—seriously *kapu* in a real museum—but he needed contact. He took her hands in his and said soberly, "I couldn't let Rob down."

She searched his face. "I kept it simple with Mom and Dad in case that's the only reason you came."

Had she really thought he'd walk away? No wonder she'd kept the introductions impersonal.

"It's better if they don't have their expectations raised. They're not sure what to do with disappointment." She shook her head. "They put a bright face on the whole thing with Daniel. Dad said it was a good thing he showed his colors before I got too attached. Mom called it a sign of greater things to come. But I think it hurt them more than me."

"Daniel's the almost fiancé?"

She nodded.

"What happened?"

"*Steel.*" Her forced detachment suggested it hadn't been as easy a separation as she wanted him to think.

"You've given up a lot to pursue your passion."

"Thank you for putting it that way. It's been called selfish and sinful."

He admired her withholding attribution but suspected her short-sighted Daniel had made the remarks, a wound only someone who mattered could inflict. Couldn't the man tell she wanted to honor God?

"I believed the opportunity came straight from heaven, that I was called for a purpose, like Esther, to use my talent to make a difference. He thought it was a temptation from hell."

"What do you think now?"

"It's both."

Her honesty floored him again. After the mirage that was Myra, Gentry was almost too transparent. How could anyone doubt her authenticity? "Every opportunity has pitfalls. You have to work with what you're given."

She looked into his face. "Can you really say that? After last night?"

"Especially after last night." He told her about standing in the ocean and giving up the fight. Talking to Myra. To Nica. "I almost called, but I knew I'd see you today."

"You told me on Kauai you wished I wasn't a film star."

He nodded. "It would be easier."

"But you're not making me choose."

As if he could. "No, I'm not." He didn't presume to know what path her life should take. Besides, no one with her talent and momentum would give it up. Not after the battles she'd survived.

Her lucky star hadn't neared its zenith.

⌒

Allegra hit the brakes when she noticed the person at the curb. She powered down the window as he came around. "I can't talk, Curt. I'm late already."

"Late?" He held a bottle of wine.

"For a party. Welcoming Rob home." She didn't know what he would make of that; probably he'd want to go inside and talk it over.

But he did a slow nod. "Good. I think that's important. There's no need for animosity. We're all adults."

It astonished her how little she cared what he thought, and how inane his remark sounded. It was as though she'd been in a deep fog and suddenly broken out. "I really have to go."

"Yeah. Okay. I'll see you later."

In answer she powered the window up and eased onto the street. She didn't know what impelled her. Maybe nothing more than it was expected. But as she drove to Rob's house—her house—where she hadn't stepped foot for almost two years, something crumbled inside.

This would end it once he knew. Then she'd be free to let go. Of everything.

Cars lined the street. Rob had so many friends; her friends, too, by association. Not the gaggle of discontents she'd picked up at the patio community, but people who had looked at her and Rob with envy and longing. The perfect couple. She parked and checked herself in the mirror. Except for the ancient eyes, she looked passable.

Inside that face there used to be someone who wanted to make it, who believed she could; someone who'd refused to follow the pattern of ignorance and booze. Inside there had been dreams and gumption, confidence and hope. Step by step she had remade herself into someone worthy.

Now her steps had undone it all, as with the filth on her wedding gown that she had dreamed. There was a certain relief that came with the thought of coming clean. An easing of the tensions that had strung her tight for so long. The moment while drowning in which you simply breathe.

Light-headed from days without food, she let herself into the house—smile set, carriage regal, though inside she was shaking. Pleasantries dropped from her lips as she glided through the assembly and outside to the pool. And then she saw Rob, standing strong and tall. No broken, needing man, but one who'd made his new beginning.

FORTY-ONE

Curt seethed. After Allegra drove off without another look, he had cocked back and fired the wine across the street, smashing the bottle on the opposite driveway. Who did she think she was, treating him in that condescending manner? He'd nearly pulled the door off his new Dodge Charger.

Okay, so she had to make a show of it at the party. He understood. He was reasonable. In fact, he needed her to be cordial, to keep any suspicion off her and reflectively off him. He didn't want any talk of divorce. Not anymore. Things had gone past that now. He needed it all.

But Allegra had dismissed him as though he were nothing. What if she went back with her husband? His foot jerked off the accelerator. Could she?

Maybe that was why she'd been so terse. He got cold. All the way through. He'd put too much time in. She had to pay off—or he was a dead man. If she changed her mind, thought she could dis him that way . . .

He swung the car around, the ESP system keeping it from skidding loose. Where was it the husband lived? He'd checked it out a while back, imagined living there with the grieving widow. Oh yeah. He remembered. He'd have a look, make sure it wasn't a private party, the one-on-one kind.

If it was wild enough, he'd give himself an invitation. He'd love to see Allegra's face when he walked in. If there was enough of a crowd . . . and if there wasn't, he had to know.

～

She walked out to the deck, looking so poised and natural Rob thought for a moment he'd concocted her from equal parts fatigue and longing. If he wasn't medication free, he'd think he was hallucinating. But the tugging inside of knotted hope was too painful to be imaginary.

"Allegra."

"Welcome home, Rob." Her voice belied the silken calm of her expression.

"Thank you." He made no attempt at hiding his emotion as he extended his hand.

She laid her palm atop. "Are you . . . in pain?"

Oh yes. He covered her hand with his other. "Tired. Julie means well, but I'm way over my tolerance."

"Why don't you sit?"

He could, but the up and down was too awkward to manage each time someone greeted him, and to sit while his guests bent over him felt . . . humiliating. *I hear you, Lord.* "Would you help me?"

A flicker of fear went through her eyes into his heart.

"Just be close in case I lose my balance."

"All right."

"Let's get out of the thick of it." Their favorite spot in the yard had been the iron bench by the fountain pond. Maybe she'd sit with him; maybe she wouldn't. He pushed away the hurt of every day she hadn't called, hadn't come. She was there now. It might be his only chance to say what he had to.

A co-worker on the satellite GPS project was on the bench, chatting with one of the neighbors. She noticed his graceless trajectory and stood up. "Getting back to work anytime soon, Fox?"

"Been working. It's all done in my head."

"It's been done in your head since I met you." She grinned.

"Lots of people agree." He waited until the two women wandered off, then positioned himself before the bench. He should have grabbed a cane for up and down.

Allegra took his arm. She'd never been nurturing. Sweet and beautiful, intelligent and classy, but not motherly in any way, as though tying her tubes had severed the instinct. He landed on the bench without embarrassment, God satisfied for the moment with the humble state of his soul. "Will you sit?"

She did, dismay etching her features.

"I'm sorry if this . . ." He waved a hand over the artificial limb, clothed in Dockers.

She shook her head. "It's not that."

If his injury wasn't causing her discomfort, there was so much more it could be. For two years he'd met her financial needs and begged her to reconsider. If she would change *her* mind, see things *his* way, they could go on. The depth and ugliness of his pride sickened him. He wouldn't blame her if she'd come to finally break it off.

"Rob—"

"May I tell you something first?"

She nodded.

"Through all this, I've realized a few things. First, that it might be impossible for you to see me this way." The smallest pucker between her brows was all the response he got. "And I understand that. But mostly I need your forgiveness for being a hardheaded, self-righteous dope. For not listening, not understanding, expecting you to jump in where I was without . . ." He spread his hands and dropped them in his lap. "Anyway, can you forgive me, Allegra?"

She looked shocked and dismayed, more transparent than he'd ever seen her. "Rob, I . . ." She started, then turned with a gasp, staring hard across the pool. She half rose, stifling a cry, and collapsed.

At her Aunt's soft cry, Gentry turned from her conversation with Paul. She rushed over as Uncle Rob barely kept her aunt from striking the ground. Paul and Cameron reached them at the same time, easing her onto the lawn.

Others crowded around. "Should we call 911?"

Gentry chewed her lip. She'd never known her aunt to faint. Maybe something physical had kept her from attending Uncle Rob, but Paul said, "I think she's all right. She's breathing normally."

Bruce Watson, a neighbor who was an osteopath, felt her pulse and agreed. "Probably stress or anxiety, or the sun. Let's get her inside. You okay, Rob?"

Her uncle nodded, but he looked grayer than she'd seen him yet. What had happened? She'd been glad Aunt Allegra had actually come, but maybe a public venue wasn't the best place for restored communications.

Cameron lifted her aunt, and Uncle Rob suggested the chaise in the atrium just off the pool deck.

Uncle Rob's legs jerked when he walked, as though he couldn't quite get the rhythm he'd managed before. She ached for him, for them both. People should go home. She scanned the crowd for her mother to make the suggestion, then jerked with a bolt of recognition.

Where had she seen that man? Her mind rushed with images— bamboo bar, Malakua coming over to say he had something mo bettah, the blond man on the stool, looking over his shoulder, watching them, his expression hard, not curious or alluring.

"Uncle Rob, who's that man?" she whispered in his ear.

"What?"

"That blond man." But already the guy was sliding through the crowd.

They reached the couch, and Cameron laid Allegra on her side. The doctor stooped beside her as her eyes fluttered open.

Gentry grabbed Cameron's arm and tugged him aside. "I saw the man with Malakua."

"What?"

"Out at the pool."

Clasping her wrist, he pulled her through the friends and neighbors who had closed in. "Where?"

She searched the deck and patio. "He's not here."

They rushed around the side of the house as a car rounded the block. All she saw was the back quarter panel. A glimpse of orange. No license plate. Her heart hammered. Her temples pulsed. Again she felt the brush of malice.

Cameron turned, his expression the sharp intensity of that first night. "Talk to me."

"I recognized his face, and then I remembered seeing it before. At the bar in Hanalei. He watched over his shoulder when Malakua told us about an out-of-the-way trail. At the end of our discussion, Malakua went back over to sit with him."

"Describe him. Everything you can remember."

"About your height. Maybe forty. Blond. Blue eyes. Muscular. Tan. A pronounced Adam's apple." It was fading. She could picture him, but no distinctive details.

"Can you draw him?"

"No. I'm terrible." She pressed her fingers to her forehead. "What would he be doing here?"

Cameron drew a slow breath and released it. "Good question."

"Do you think he followed me?"

"It's possible. But why choose a public scene?"

She'd already asked herself all of that. "If he's a stalker, maybe he gets off on the risk. Mingling with my family as though he's one of us." Could he have followed her to Kauai, hired Malakua to snatch her?

He scowled. "What was he doing when you saw him?"

"Standing there, staring. But so was everyone else, watching you carry my aunt."

"Did he know you recognized him?"

"He must have, to run off like that."

She pressed her hands to her head. Why was this happening? She had dared to believe it was over. She'd convinced herself. Just like Mom and Dad, fluffing whipped cream over charred pie.

Cameron hooked an arm around her shoulders. "Why don't you go in with your family."

"What are you going to do?"

"Ask around. See if anyone recognized him."

She dug her nails into her palms. She should be worrying about her aunt, helping Uncle Rob, not wondering whether she'd drawn some psycho into the family fold.

"Hey." He raised her chin. "We'll handle this."

She gathered herself and nodded, then stretched up and kissed his mouth. "Thank you."

"And now she expects me to think."

"I'll be inside." Their hands drifted apart.

Using the description Gentry had given, Cameron tried to find someone who could identify Malakua's companion. A few people had noticed him. "Yes," one woman said. "He had a gold chain on his neck, the flat, shiny kind that catches the sunlight. And he was real tan."

"Do you know him?"

She shook her head. "Never seen him before."

Same story all around until he questioned the doctor's wife, Sandra. "I can't say for sure, but I think I saw him with Allegra once. Outside her place." Her mouth pulled down sternly.

Cameron pondered that. Was the guy a legitimate guest after all?

Sandra leaned in. "Don't take this for anything more than it is, but Allegra was very evasive."

Aha. That turned all the wheels she'd meant it to, but what did that have to do with Gentry? Had he gotten close to the aunt for information? About Gentry's trip to Kauai? Maybe Allegra could identify him when she recovered from her shock. He hoped amnesia didn't run in the family.

At Julie and Brendan's suggestion, the guests dispersed. Cameron wasn't sure he'd questioned all of them, but Sandra's lead was a start, if Allegra was up to answering. He knew little beyond what he'd observed, her elegant entrance and Rob's aching reception. It had cut close to his own experience.

The sun was hot on the empty deck and cast a shimmery net across the floor of the pool. Discarded glasses and plates cluttered the tables, and chairs stood away as though abruptly abandoned—as indeed they'd been. Every setting told a tale.

He took out his phone and called TJ. "I don't care what the chief told you, brah. I need to know what Malakua said." His tone had enough bite to penetrate TJ's silence.

"Say some *haole* wen hire him get dem lost. Make happen one accident."

"Who?"

"No name. Da cell got cancel."

"Got a description?"

"*Haole*. Blond. Built like. Blue eye. So wazzup, bruddah?"

Cameron shielded the sun from his eyes and looked over the pool area. "Gentry saw him—the guy who was with Malakua."

"Got one name?"

"No. But I intend to."

Gentry met him at the door when he went in, strain gathering her brow. "Mom and Dad never saw him. I haven't asked my aunt and uncle. They wanted to be alone."

"Is she all right?"

"The doctor thought so. She always looks cool and poised, but I think she's pretty high-strung."

He noted the closed doors of the sunroom. "The doctor's wife said she saw the guy once before with your aunt."

Gentry rolled her eyes. "Sandra's a walking tabloid. She's seen Elvis."

That deflated him, but he shrugged. "Then it's suspect, but not irrelevant. We need to talk to your aunt."

"I don't know, Cameron. I convinced her to come see Uncle Rob, and it's the first chance they've had to deal with their situation. I don't want mine to get in the way."

"I don't think Rob would agree. He wants answers as badly as I do. Have you remembered anywhere else you might have seen him?"

She furrowed her brow. "Nothing to do with the troupe or the studio. I can't picture him at any other parties or events. But I see him clearly at the bamboo bar. I would have recognized him then, if I'd seen him before."

"But you know he's the one you saw."

"The recognition shocked my recollection."

He nodded. "TJ matched your description. Malakua said a *haole* hired him to cause an accident."

She sagged against the wall. "Then it wasn't money he wanted. He really wanted me dead."

He rubbed her shoulders. "The longer we wait, the farther he gets."

She chewed her upper lip.

"Hey." He put his finger there.

"Stop damaging the body I'm guarding."

Her lip slipped free, and he caught it between his just as her mother's heels clicked across the marble tile.

"Oh."

So much for keeping it simple.

⌒

In the sunroom, alone with his wife, Rob watched Allegra struggle. He'd never seen her overwrought, but now she sat on the lounge, wringing her hands.

"I don't understand." Her voice broke. "Why are you doing this?"

"I'm only saying I'm sorry. I wish . . . I'd been wiser. Kinder."

"Stop it!" She buried her face in her hands.

How could that upset her? What was he doing wrong? He dropped his chin. *Lord.*

She stood up and paced. He didn't remind her that Bruce had just warned her against abrupt movements. Fear kicked in again. Had she been diagnosed with cancer? Become addicted to pain killers? What had happened while he was nursing his righteous anger? "Allegra—"

"That's not my name."

What?

"I'm not Allegra Delaney. My name is Allison Carter. Or was before I changed it."

His jaw slackened. "Allison . . ."

"I'm telling you this so you'll understand the rest."

His thigh started to throb. The phantom-limb pain had decreased in frequency and intensity, but the stump had been fatigued. He should rub the muscle but didn't.

"I grew up in Arkansas, one of five. Had no mama I ever knew."

Rob's mind reeled. Who was this person? She didn't look or sound like Allegra. And Arkansas? She had told him Connecticut. Why lie about where she'd been born?

"From the day Mama ran off, my father told me I was trash."

His spirit plunged.

"He said only trash comes from trash, and no book learning or fancy dreams would change what I am." Her face pinched with the memory of the cruel words. "But I didn't believe him. I was going to be someone. I was worth something."

He surged with pride for what she'd accomplished, just combating such viciousness.

Her hands fell listlessly to her sides. "I was wrong."

"No." The word jumped out. "Allegra—"

"Please. You don't know what I've come to say."

"There's nothing you could say that would make you worthless."

She raised her brows wearily. "Because you believe the illusion.

From the moment I met you, my only goal was to measure up. To be worthy of Robert Fox and the life you'd given me."

His chest caved. Had he been so insufferable? His pride so overweening? Here was God's judgment, his crime against his wife.

"It took everything I had, but I managed. I fixed every imperfection, improved every asset." She gave a bleak laugh. "And then you found God. You wanted to start over, a whole new beginning." Her features twisted. "But I'd already done that, was still doing it. Being good enough for you was killing me. How could I ever be—" She covered her face and sobbed.

He groped to his feet, limped over to her.

"Don't touch me!"

Her brittle cry froze his arms in the air. All he wanted was to comfort her.

"While you were on Kauai with Gentry, I was at Waikiki with someone else. His name is Curt. We had an affair."

His arms sank to his sides. His mind reeled with this added offense. He'd driven her to another man? In his stiff-necked arrogance, he'd been blind to her struggle. In all their years together, and the ones apart, had he wondered what demons compelled her obsessions? His compliments had reinforced her compulsions until he'd yanked even that from her.

Lord. His voice rasped. "I'm sorry."

"What?" The word came on a breath.

If he hadn't almost died in the cave, hadn't faced down the demons of his own; if he hadn't fought these last months against debilitating loneliness, crippling despair, his reaction might have been different. He might have felt wronged, violated. Instead he felt achingly illuminated.

His hands shook. His throat cleaved. "I'm asking again. Allegra, can you forgive me?"

She sank onto the lounge. "You haven't heard me."

"Yes. Yes, I have. Probably for the first time, I've really heard you."

She stared into his face. "I had an affair."

He nodded. "I know." Pain shot up his leg, circled his lower back and resided there. "Now I want you to hear me. Can you listen?"

"I always hear you, Rob."

"I love you. That's the first thing I want you to know."

Her face paled. Was she going to faint again?

"Whatever you've done—what we've done—we'll find a way through it." He shook his head. "I never meant for you to try so hard to be someone you're not." None of his inventions compared to her creation of a complete, altered self. "For every way I've made you feel inadequate, please forgive me."

She stared as though he spoke a foreign language, and he supposed he did. He wished he could get down on his knees as when he'd proposed to her. Instead he took her hands and raised her to his level. "The last thing I want you to know is I love you. Allegra Delaney or Allison Carter. Wherever you're from; whatever you've done, you're my wife."

Her whole body shook. "I can't . . . you can't mean it."

He took her into his arms, breaking all over again. Two years his pride had kept him from holding her. No more. "I mean it."

FORTY-TWO

"Uncle Rob?" Gentry tapped the door. Cameron had waited as long as she could expect him to. The door slid open.

"What is it, Gentry?" Her uncle looked exhausted, yet somehow light.

"We need to talk to Aunt Allegra."

He glanced behind her to Cameron. "Can it wait?"

Cameron shook his head. "Gentry saw Malakua's partner."

"What? Where?"

"Here. At the party."

He looked from her to Cameron and back. "Did you call the police?"

She shook her head. "Someone thought Aunt Allegra might know him."

A shadow crossed his face, and she prayed this would not cause them more heartache. He rotated back on the artificial leg. Her aunt had clearly been crying, her sphinxlike calm shattered. Yet there was something transcendent in her grief as well.

"What's wrong?"

Gentry went to her. "I saw someone who might be involved in what happened to us on Kauai. Sandra thought you might know him. He's blond, fortyish, muscular."

Her aunt sank down onto the lounge. "Curt."

Cameron came up beside her, his focus tangible. "Curt who?"

"Blanchard." Her aunt's tone was barren. "I saw him come in. That's what . . . It shocked me to see him here."

"He came to see you?" Cameron asked.

Her gaze locked with Uncle Rob's. "He couldn't be involved with what happened. We were on Oahu."

Aunt Allegra and that man?

"Whose idea was it?" Cameron probed.

"His."

Cameron squatted down to eye level. "It's a quick hop. Were you together the whole time?"

Gentry stared at her aunt, unable, unwilling, to believe . . .

"Except the first day. He'd arranged a spa for me."

Gentry felt punched. Some guy had arranged a spa for Allegra on Oahu? Had he then arranged an accident for her? Or Uncle Rob. She looked up at him, expecting rage and hurt, but his expression was not recognizable as either.

Cameron stood up. "Gentry saw him in a bar with the man who pushed her over the falls. Do you know any reason why he'd want to hurt her?"

"It wasn't me." Gentry started to shake. "It was Uncle Rob."

Cameron turned. His concern for her had blocked him making that transition, but it only made sense. What would he gain by her death? It was money he wanted after all, just not hers.

Aunt Allegra looked as though she might faint again. She shook her head, murmuring, "He wouldn't . . ."

"You're worth more surviving me than divorcing me." Uncle Rob had caught her thought. "He went for it all."

Aunt Allegra made a soft mew and dropped her face into her hands. "It's my fault. Your leg, your . . ."

Uncle Rob dropped awkwardly to the lounge and encircled her in his arm. He eyed Cameron directly. "You've got the name. Is there anything else?"

Cameron stood. "We'll work with that."

Gentry wanted to shout. Her hands coiled into fists. Cameron grabbed her arm and tugged her out, closing the door behind them, but fury gripped her. "All this time I blamed myself."

"Then you know how she feels."

His comment caught her in the windpipe. How clearly she'd drawn the line between her aunt and uncle. How quickly she'd judged. But Cameron, who'd been in Uncle Rob's place, who could identify so closely, hadn't. This was not the cynical man she'd first met. And his compassion stilled her rage. "Yes." She nodded. "I do."

Allegra had never been real to her. Most of her interaction with Uncle Rob was off and away on their adventures, and she hadn't wondered how her aunt felt about it. She'd assumed Uncle Rob had invited her, and Aunt Allegra refused. But maybe she'd never felt included. Maybe she'd been lonely. A million maybes. Who was she to throw stones at mistakes made?

He threaded her fingers with his. "I'll call the police. You might want to fill your parents in before the uniforms arrive."

Gentry nodded. *Remember the guy who tried to kill me? Guess what. There's another. The good thing is he was after Uncle Rob. I just got in the way.* She found her mother consolidating the food trays.

"We have so much left. I expected people to stay longer and eat more."

"You can offer some to the police when they arrive."

Her mother spun. "That isn't funny. We've had enough— You're serious?"

As a heart attack. But we don't talk about that. "The man responsible for our accident on Kauai was here at the party."

"I thought they'd arrested him."

"That was the one who actually pushed."

Her mother's hands dropped. "Oh my."

I'm sorry life isn't as nice as you want it to be.

She felt a sudden surge of compassion and realized maybe Mom had to gloss over things in order to cope. Maybe both her parents did. Dad had a bum deal with his ticker, and they could have grown paranoid and bitter. Was their alternative so wrong?

With a rush of warmth and love, she hugged her. "It'll be okay. Aunt Allegra knows who he is." And they'd all help her deal with that. Somehow.

~

Stupid. How could she remember him? Hadn't she hit her head, gotten amnesia? All the news stories said she couldn't remember. But Gentry Fox had looked at him with stark recognition. Didn't take a genius to see that. Curt swerved around the corner to his house. How long before they called the cops?

He had to get out, get out fast, but he was zilch on ready cash. He slammed to a stop in his driveway, ran inside, and stuffed a bag with things he'd need. Except he mostly needed money. His cards were maxed, and if he tried to use them he'd be flagged.

There had to be something, somewhere. He searched his closet, his drawers. Maybe he'd stashed some cash. But he hadn't. If he drained one more cent from the Ponzi account, he could kiss himself good-bye. But if they connected him to Malakua, he'd be going down for hard time, and he'd rather be dead. Anyway, it was Saturday and he couldn't get at it.

And then he thought of Allegra and her drawer. She'd written a check, but he'd also seen a band of cash. Might not be that other hundred grand she'd offered, but he'd be grateful for whatever. He grabbed his bag and threw it into the car, drove to Allegra's, and used the key he'd copied in Hawaii.

He'd be in and out so fast. Except the drawer was empty, and the flashing red light on the alarm box showed he'd triggered something silent. Swearing, he started to slam the drawer, then saw the little snub nose revolver in the back. He grabbed it along with the loads and ran out the door into his idling car. He wished now he'd bought something less recognizable. As much as he hated the thought, he'd have to ditch it for another. But first he needed miles under his tires. And a plan.

⌐

After Gentry's parents had gone to bed, Cameron squeezed after her through the little hall window onto a section of roof between two peaks. "And what motivated you to explore this particular exit?"

She pointed up with the most questionably innocent expression he'd ever seen. "The stars, of course."

"Uh-huh."

"You heard my parents. I was a born naturalist." She settled down between the peaks, reclining against one, feet up on the opposite.

"So you never snuck out here to—"

"Tell secrets? Sure. Helen and I planned our lives right here."

"To be alone with someone your parents didn't know you were with?"

He'd packed an overnight bag in case the party went long but hadn't anticipated perching on the roof outside the spare bedroom of her parents' house.

"Mom caught a pretty good view of things. I doubt she's in the dark any longer."

"I didn't mean me."

Gentry stretched out her defined legs and crossed her ankles.

"What I mean is, would that window be perhaps a rite of passage for all the men in your life?"

She stared up into the night sky awash with sparkles and moonlight spilling from a strip of cloud. "This is as close as I could get to that night in the Hanalei Mountains."

A balmy warmth washed over him. He'd felt unburdened last night, open for the first time in years to wonder and happenstance. Now side by side with Gentry, so close not even their fears separated them, he felt it again. "That was some night."

"Do you think everyone knows the moment they fell in love?"

"I doubt it."

She closed her eyes. "Mine was when you said those Hawaiian words, that I was in the shelter of his wings. I knew you were promising your protection as well."

"I just wanted you to shut up and go to sleep."

"You knew exactly what to say to soothe my fears."

"You were furious with me the next morning."

"True. When you woke me, and then at the pool—I could not believe you still suspected me."

"It's my nature to doubt and question."

"When you suggested I was having an affair with my uncle, I wanted to drown you."

"I didn't know he was your uncle." He slipped his arm under her neck and wrapped her shoulders. "And I deal with the darker sides of people everyday."

She sighed. "I cannot believe my aunt and that . . ."

"Curt Blanchard's a predator. He looks for marks like your aunt—alone, wounded, wealthy."

"And he tries to kill their loved ones?"

"He got Malakua to do the dirty work, so he probably hasn't killed before."

She frowned. "Will they get him?"

He pulled her tighter. "Search area's a little bigger than Kauai, but he'll leave a trail. Everyone does. It's just a matter of reading the clues."

"Spoken like a sleuth. How did you get into fraud investigation?"

An innocent question, but it went deeper than she knew. "After our parents were lost, I invented a zillion alternate scenarios. They were spies on a mission so secret everyone had to believe they were dead. Or they'd been kidnapped for some brilliant knowledge only they had. I worked out myriad ways they could have been sneaked off the island, the most obvious that the boat had not gone down, but merely kept going. I studied people's faces to see who knew the truth, who'd been ordered to keep us from guessing, who might break if I applied the right pressure."

"No wonder your teachers were challenged."

"I got good at spotting lies, even those that had nothing to do with my parents' secret mission. Everyone had something to hide; some did it better than others. Some made it a career. I started reading about all the ways people cheated."

"Because you felt cheated?"

He considered that. "Maybe. I studied criminology and specialized in fraudulent schemes, worked for an insurance company when Myra and I married, then branched out on my own and started getting government work."

She turned slightly. "Have you found your parents?"

A smile touched his mouth. "Not yet."

"Nica told me she doesn't go into the water because it's their grave."

Nica was right. It was only when he uncovered something wholly unbelievable that he still allowed himself to wonder. "They never recovered the bodies."

"Kai . . ."

"I know. But I don't let go easily." Except for his son. He'd let go before he had a chance to hold on. For Kevin's sake—and his own. "Consider that fair warning." His gaze slid to her mouth.

"It might be harder than you think to make this work."

Her call last night had shown him that. He pulled her tighter, in case doubt wormed in between them. "But see, I believe in the impossible."

"That from the man who scoffed at hope?"

"Well, God showed me once and for all that I'm not uncovering his scam. He's no fraud. He's the only real thing there is. That and what I feel for you."

Her mouth was soft under his. He had a flash of Alec doing the same, and it ached somewhere deep.

She touched his face. "You're the only man I've brought out here."

Again that tropical warmth. "Not even Dan?"

"Unless the house was on fire, Daniel would never shimmy through a window. It would feel disreputable."

"I have a hard time seeing you together."

"I was a new believer, voracious, and he knew so much. I'm grateful for the things he taught me. We just had . . . different views. Irreconcilable views."

"Does it hurt?"

"A little . . . that he didn't believe me." Her gaze ran over his face like warm, misty rain. "He doesn't think God puts a call on women's lives. Only their husbands have that right."

"Then he hasn't seen your work. If that's not God-given talent I don't know what is."

She sighed. "He won't watch a Hollywood movie."

"There's a lot of junk out there."

She nodded. "That's why it matters. It's shaping our culture, and if every believer bails, if all the moral voices walk away, what check will there be for the realm of darkness? Who will shine, as Nica said, the Shekina glory?"

Her passion rang in his ears. He didn't like to think of her in that realm, but he knew now that *everyone* had a call on their lives. He drew and released a slow breath. "If anyone has the strength and courage to do that, it's you."

"Can you stand it?"

He brushed her lips with his. "I'm not going anywhere."

⌒

Buoyed by the weekend spent with Cameron and her family, Gentry held her ground in the meeting before Monday's shoot. "Sexual tension is secondary for this character. The audience has seen the sparks, but does the movie jump the shark if Eva cares more about the thousands of starving people stranded by war than having an affair with her colleague?" They had all—including her—made the assumption that Matt and Eva would behave that way, but why? If she and Cameron could resist their intense attraction, why couldn't her screen identity do the same?

"Why dilute the reason we all chose this script? Its moral call to global responsibility and personal sacrifice; that's what makes it work, what makes Eva work." She only dared speak because it was true. She would not compromise the project after she had agreed to take it on, but it had all come clear as she'd needed it to.

Because of Friday's kiss, the director wanted to shift from the original tensions to Eva's relationship with Matt Cargill. Alec wanted it too. Ultimately the director made the call, and if he said play up the relationship, that was where they'd go. But the producer was an issues devotee. He chose projects with meat. He might, just might, agree with her, and Dwight had to consider that.

She thought of Cameron standing in the sea, surrendering to a will beyond his, as he'd described his encounter with the living God. Dwight Spellman might not realize his control was secondary, but she appealed to that higher power.

"All right, today we shoot it straight." He speared her with a glance. "I better see the fire for your cause that I saw Friday with Alec."

She nodded, not even a smile of victory, and played the scenes with all she had. By the end of the day, exhaustion hit hard. She had focused so intensely, she hardly heard Alec when he invited her over for drinks.

"Hey. You can forget the starving kids now." He chucked her chin.

She smiled. "Sorry. I have a lot on my mind."

"Like keeping as far from me as possible."

"It's not personal, Alec."

"You are an enigma." He ran his fingers down her arm. "Come over for a drink. All the cast'll be there." He must have read her reluctance. "It's not like I'm getting you alone. *Matt* would get you alone."

"You mean Eva."

He smiled.

"I think I'll just—"

"You ought to rub elbows, Gentry. It's how you get known, considered for the next one. As much as your screen performance, your ability to fit in to the cast and your hunger for the life matters."

Was she hungry for the life? She had played a crusader today, someone who couldn't turn her back on misery. Those scenes would speak to the world. Did she have to play a game to earn the chance for more?

"Dwight'll be there. He's watching you closely, measuring your potential. He pulls weight."

She rested her hands on her hips. "Free career counseling?"

He gave her the hundred-watt smile.

She didn't want to banter. "I'm just tired."

He turned her around and rubbed her shoulders, lowered his mouth to her ear. "They're bandying your name for the co-lead in *Vanished*."

She spun. "How do you know?"

"I'm the other lead. *If* they come through on the contract." He tugged the braid that hung over her shoulder. "You ought to come over. Let your hair down. They know you're professional. They want to see if you're real."

"Is any of this real?"

"It is to the ones shelling out the money."

She had meant what she said to Cameron about being a presence in the industry. To do that she'd have to carefully consider each and every project. She had dodged a bullet by keeping the script straight this time. Did she want to play beside Alec again? "Tell me about *Vanished*."

"Come over and I'll show you the script."

"I don't want to compromise Eva by reading someone else now." She avoided overlapping projects that could dilute her character.

"It's perfect for you."

Just that easily, the lure was there, working in her like a sugar high. She had felt her power today. When they wrapped *Just Illusions*, would she go right into an even bigger production? How many people got that chance? And what might she do with it? "Okay. Give me directions."

"Why don't you follow me?"

She'd have liked to go home and shower, change clothes, unwind. Instead she'd go directly, but she wouldn't stay long. "All right."

Intent on following Alec's Lexus SC, she left the studio without even a glance at the paparazzi at the gate.

In Okelani's kitchen, Nica lifted a platter of teriyaki skewers and froze. Icy paws crept up her spine, claws nicking her skin. She looked to see if Okelani had felt it, but she was calmly wrapping paper-thin strips of raw ahi in limu seaweed. TJ stood silently in the corner.

"Here." She handed him the teriyaki platter. "Put this on the table. I'll be back in just a second."

She ducked out the door and ran up the path to her house. Wary after Malakua, she crept to her back door and then around to her front. No one. Yet the urgency intensified. *Kai?* She circled back.

There was no one in the garden but TJ, who must have followed her up. "Got one feeling?"

"Someone needs help. But there's no one here." She closed herself into her arms. "I need to call Kai."

"Your bruddah plenny *akamai*. He be okay."

Yes, Kai was smart, and strong, and he'd told her she could let go. But the claws clung to her spine. "Something's wrong."

TJ took her hand. "Come back."

She looked around again. Was someone there in the dark needing help? Maybe TJ's uniform kept him or her from coming out, but since no one did, she followed TJ back to Okelani's. When she stepped in the door, her *tūtū* looked up and said, "Malice."

FORTY-THREE

The party was not raucous or licentious. Yet. Alec had a low-key manner that his guests imitated, though she didn't have to look hard to find that mood enhancements beyond alcohol were available. She didn't know if Alec was a recreational or serious user, or if he only had it available for those who were, or if they'd brought their own.

Tonight he seemed intent on squiring her and maybe sparking some fling-between-leads gossip. Her resistance to escalating their on-screen relationship had probably stung, and she doubted he'd experienced that before. She and Cameron had not agreed to anything exclusive, but they'd established it in the Hanalei Mountains and under the falls. She couldn't picture Alec diving under to save her finding a corpse.

He handed her a tumbler of ice and booze from the bartender.

"What is it?"

"Amaretto sour. Liquid candy."

She took a sip. It tasted like SweeTarts. "I'm not big on liquor." Especially a drink handed to her in an uncontrolled environment where date rape drugs or other dope could easily be added.

"Then just carry it so you don't stand out." His tutoring seemed sincere. He had broken through with his last two movies, was levels above her but still proving himself. "Mingle awhile; then I'll grab the script, and we can read."

"Okay." He would have some say in whether she got an official reading, but until she saw the script she wouldn't even hope.

He sauntered off to dazzle his guests. As she sampled the veal and asiago nachos, Helen came up and took her arm. "I *have* to talk to you."

It had been a long time since they'd shared that tone of secrets. Since her confession, Helen had fluctuated between solicitous and defensive, and Gentry took her wavering moods in stride. She crunched the last of the chip as they ducked into a game room, where a few diehards were playing electronic pinball and other virtual-arcade machines Alec had there.

"Are you ready for this?"

The puckish look in Helen's face was so familiar, Gentry laughed. "Tell me."

"Dwight's next movie, *Vanished*?"

Her heart sank.

Helen leaned in and whispered, "I'm reading."

"For the lead?"

"Co-lead."

Gentry squeezed her arms. "Who told you?"

Helen's brow puckered. "I really can't say. Oh, Gentry, I would."

"Who cares!" She shook her. "I'm so excited, Helen. It could be a break."

"A *big* break."

Gentry hugged her. "Thank you for telling me."

"It's not—You can't say anything. I just wondered . . . I didn't know if you'd heard anything."

"About you reading?"

"About you."

Ah. She should have seen that coming. Helen was not above play-ing the sympathy card. *Don't mess me up again.* "I'm not sure I want to go into something right away."

"It's with Alec."

"For sure?"

Helen shrugged. "He sounded sure." She put her hand to her mouth.

Gentry laughed. "Aha. So da leading man iss your source. Verry interestinc."

Helen flushed. "Do not breathe a word. We just . . . hit it off the other night, and he wants me to read."

An amazing lightness filled her. "I'm really happy for you. It'll be great." They hugged and parted so Helen could go find others to keep her secret.

Gentry moved out into the great room, awed by God's providence, how clearly he'd protected her. She didn't need to see the script to know this opportunity was not his will and Alec was not her mentor—talented actor that he was.

On her way toward the door, she chatted with Dwight. He set his empty highball on a tray and said, "Just out of curiosity, did you ever remember what happened on Kauai?"

"Everything but my plunge over the falls. And I don't mind losing that."

He shook his head. "Bad karma. What were you in your last life?"

She shrugged. "I think this is the only one I get."

He eyed her a minute. "Then let me make it better. I'm looking for . . ."

Alec swooped in and circled her waist. "No business at my parties." He spun her away—before Dwight usurped his role as career genie? "Have you tried the speckled eggs?"

"I haven't."

"Caviar." He held up a deviled egg sprinkled with black and orange fish eggs.

"Thanks." She ate it in three bites, hungrier than she'd realized.

"Now," he said, "I'm convinced the party can proceed without me." He leaned close. "Let's . . ."

She slipped free. "I'm not really up for reading, Alec. We have an early call time tomorrow. I think I'll go home."

He cocked his head and studied her. "You're serious?"

She smiled. "See you tomorrow."

As soon as her car had been disarmed, unlocked, and the door opened, Curt slipped out from the bushes and pressed the gun to Gentry's ribs. "No noise," he hissed in her ear, though the music from the house would hide her cries. The thought tripped his brain for a second. In a weird way, it seemed everything he'd done had been leading to this, and he supposed it had—that wild oat that kept trying to bloom where it was planted.

"I'm sliding in first; you're coming with me."

She stiffened as voices broke out, a door opened, and music escaped.

"Don't even think about it." With her practically in his lap, Curt slid under the wheel and pulled Gentry inside without budging the gun from her ribs. Her heart beat against his hand. Her scent filled his nostrils, along with the vanilla freshener in her car and his own sweat.

"Pull the door closed and start the engine." He jabbed the weapon for emphasis.

He had verified the studio where she was shooting her current film with a female paparazzo outside the gate, then followed Gentry to the party. His stolen car sat on a side street, where he'd leave it now that she was providing transportation. He had snuck up to the house on foot, prepared to wait, but she hadn't kept him long.

When the engine caught, he said, "Go."

She clenched her jaw. "Where?"

"Just drive."

She pulled out. He didn't know the city. He'd choose their course as it came. Still aiming the gun, he slid fully into his seat. "Where's your purse?"

With her left hand on the wheel, she pulled a leather money clip from her jeans pocket.

"That's it? No makeup or stuff?"

"The studio does my makeup."

Her ID was the only plastic in the slot. "Where are your credit cards?"

"I don't carry them to work."

He rifled the cash in her clip. "Fourteen bucks? That's it?"

"Not much of a target, am I?" She slid him a glare. "I don't know where you're from, Curt, but this is L.A."

"You know who I am?"

"You're the scum who cost my uncle his leg."

He swallowed. "I didn't mean for that to happen. If things had gone right—"

"He'd only be dead?"

"Yeah. Instead of messed up and wishing he was."

Her mouth fell open; then she shook her head. "You don't know my uncle."

The respect and love in her voice choked him. Was that why Allegra wouldn't let go? He'd seen her sitting there mesmerized by the gimp. Her old-man husband. "Shut up and drive."

After less than a block, she said, "This didn't work very well for your partner, you know."

"Yeah, well, he was stupid. I'm not."

"My mistake."

"Shut up." He hated wise-mouthed chicks. That was one thing about Allegra. She never said a mean word, never made him feel . . . He squashed that thought. "You got credit cards at home?"

Her silence answered for her.

"Go get them."

She drove out of the posh neighborhood into something urban middle class, then slowed.

"What are you doing?"

"Turning."

"You live in here? These apartments? Big star like you?"

"I've done one movie. TV appearances. A theater troupe for troubled kids. Did you think I lived in Bel-Air?"

Maybe her publicity had outshone her income. Didn't matter. She was the tool, not the prize.

There was parking underneath, but she hesitated before entering, probably thinking what a bad idea it was. "Go on. And don't do anything stupid. I've got nothing to lose." He didn't want to admit the truth of that.

Hers was the first place they'd look if this went south. No way he could control an apartment building. But he needed cash. She pulled into a numbered slot and turned off the engine.

"We're gonna walk close. Like lovers." He gripped her and slid out the driver's door again. They walked to the elevator. The doors slid open, saving them entering the security code.

An attractive woman with long cornrow braids looked them up and down as she stepped out. He slid his spare hand across Gentry's abdomen just under the edge of her shirt and murmured into her neck, "Nothing to lose."

The woman raised her brows, going by. They had the elevator to themselves all the way to her floor. She unlocked her door. "I don't have any drugs."

"I look like I use?"

"Just thought I'd save you tossing the place."

"I'm no junkie." Winning was his drug, getting what he deserved, what should have been his from the start. Was that so much to ask? Was it too much to have a mother who didn't blame him for the sperm donor running off? Too cheap to abort and too gutless to leave him in a trash can, she'd preferred to torment him every day with his worthless presence in this world.

He pressed in behind Gentry. "What are you, a nun? Got enough candles for a convent." He let go and she moved away. He looked her up and down. She didn't look like Allegra; too strong, too natural. Too young. "Got a phone?"

She slipped a super-thin flip phone out of her pocket with a condescending look. He'd wipe that smirk off her face.

"Call your uncle. Tell him I'll take fifteen million for you. I got an offshore account he can dump it in."

⌣

Running the beach with his halogen flashlight, Cameron dug out the ringing phone without losing stride. He'd expected Gentry, but it wasn't. "Hey, Nica."

"You're all right."

"I'm fine. What's up?"

"Where's Gentry?"

"L.A." His heart was at a healthy elevation, but her next words froze it.

"I think she's in danger."

It hit him like a wave from behind. He plunged down, spinning and rolling, a stiff, fetal curl of fear. "Why?"

"I feel it. Okelani senses malice. I'm praying for angels, Kai."

He disconnected and rang Gentry. She would pick up and tell him about her day. The worst thing would be Alec putting on the moves. He had tried to reach her before he went out to run, gotten no answer, and assumed she was out with friends or something. She had no obligation to talk to him every night, but as the phone went to message, he said, "Gentry, call me."

He'd been buried in work all day, only coming up to get his run. He hadn't received any supernatural message, no visions. But he had the awful urge now to drive the four hours to Gentry and see her safe and sound.

He imagined her face. *What are you doing here?*

"Loving too hard."

"Lord," he whispered, hearing Nica's prayer—their mother's prayer—in his mind. "Set angels beside her, before and behind her, above and below her." His mother had prayed that for them each night, and each night he'd said, "I don't need them." Even then he'd felt self-sufficient.

Now he wished he could call on legions of supernatural beings. And, as Nica had reminded him, he could. "Lord." He rang Gentry again, left another message. "I love you. Call."

~

"He'll keep calling." Gentry clutched the phone. "He expects to talk to me."

"Too bad."

Uncle Rob had been pivotal in developing modern communications, but he could still choose not to answer his phone, and hadn't. She imagined him with Aunt Allegra, talking through their painful situation, his niece the last thing on his mind.

Her message, *"Uncle Rob, please call,"* had been followed immediately by Cameron's attempts to reach her, but if they didn't talk, he might not actually panic, not assume Curt Blanchard was holding her for fifteen mil.

Hyped up and trying to look cool, Curt inspected the room. Imagining him with her aunt repulsed her.

"He'll call the police. He knows I saw you." And if officers came knocking, at gunpoint she'd say anything Curt told her to. "They're already looking for you."

He turned. "Which is why I need money."

She crossed her arms. "Do you even have a plan?"

He scowled. "Yeah. Keep you until I get the money."

"That could take a while. If I don't show up on the set, they'll know something's wrong."

"You'll call in sick."

"Sick? Do you know what it costs to miss a day of production? It doesn't matter if I'm delirious. I show up for the shoot."

"Well, maybe you caught the plague." At her disdainful look he said, "It was a joke."

"Oh. Thanks for clarifying."

In two strides he'd grabbed her shirt and shoved the gun under her chin. "You think you're so smart? Think you're so tough?"

A fleck of spittle landed on her cheek. She flinched. Her heart hammered in her ears.

"Think about this. If the cops come and surround this building, maybe I can't get out, but I can cut you. I can rape you. I can kill you." He pulled her almost to his face. "Until I get what I want, I have complete control."

His breath smelled citrusy. The cold muzzle of the gun dug into her neck. She counted each throb of her pulse. Eyes closed, she gathered herself as she would to face a ledge or precipice, and freed a prayer.

He let go. "Get your credit cards. We're moving on."

Nothing was certain. Nica and Okelani were thousands of miles away. How could they sense malice directed at Gentry or anyone else? Not reaching her one evening did not mean anything had happened—except she'd recognized Curt Blanchard, and he'd seen her make the connection. Cameron clenched his fists. He should never have let her go home alone.

But he had work and she had work. They lived hundreds of miles apart, and they'd identified Rob as the target. Nica knew nothing about that. He hadn't told her about Curt, hadn't told her any of the recent developments. Her warning came out of nowhere, but he'd never found her intuition groundless. And Okelani . . .

None of that would convince LAPD to go knock on Gentry Fox's door.

He checked his watch. 10:30. Hardly curfew in L.A. She could be out with the cast, one party or another. Plenty of places she could be, things she could be doing. He paced his living room, praying for a call. *"I went out; everything's fine."* Maybe the shoot had gone badly, or well. Maybe she'd clicked with Alec, or gone out with Helen. A million possible scenarios. Yet his gut told him Nica was right.

He would look like a paranoid, possessive freak showing up at her door. Did he care? He slipped his Glock into the shoulder holster, threw a jacket over, and went out.

Denny didn't answer the door. His Miata was not in the garage. Cameron pressed his speed-dial number. *Come on.* They had lined up before when he needed him, but this time Denny didn't answer.

Cameron closed his eyes and pressed the number again. *Answer.*

"Yeah, Kai. What's up?"

"Where are you?"

"Hula Moons."

Maui. Halfway across the Pacific. He groaned.

"Need something?"

"No, man. Enjoy your dinner." He hung up. He'd have to do this himself. Was he crazy to drive all that way with nothing more than Nica's warning? What if Gentry was home but not taking his calls? What if she wasn't alone?

He clenched his fists. Better to know. She didn't owe him anything. But if she was in trouble . . .

⌣

Rob would remember these last three days as long as his mind could hold them. He and Allegra, talking as they'd never talked before, tears and secrets held too long, the whole world going by without them. No phone calls, no business, no interruptions. Little by little she'd come to believe he didn't hate or blame her. Little by little he'd explained how that was possible. For the first time, she'd looked as though his faith might not be the threat he'd led her to believe it was. Perhaps she'd find her way there as well.

But there was one thing still before them. He said, "Are you sure?"

Seated on the settee in the master suite they'd shared until two years ago, she nodded.

They had both slept in the house, but not together. Trust was fragile, and building back the threads would take time. Their actions had left a permanent reminder they could not ignore. His hands shook as he unfastened the baggy Dockers and let them drop in front of the woman he'd married twenty-nine years ago.

Fitted into the cup of the artificial limb, his stump might repulse her. And because the confidence man, her lover, had been the one to cause his accident, her guilt could be destructive.

She swallowed. "Does it hurt?"

"When I'm up too long, or off it too long. Sometimes I wake up and don't remember the rest isn't there. Sometimes it's the rest that hurts."

Tears streamed. Her mouth worked, but no words came.

He lowered himself to the end of the bed, detached the prosthesis and set it aside. He could hardly make himself look up, but when he did, Allegra didn't look away. They sat there a long time. Then he said, "Would you want to sleep in here tonight?"

She dropped to her knees and laid her head on his thigh. "Yes," she said, her tears soaking his scars. "I would."

FORTY-FOUR

Cameron knocked on Gentry's door. He had slipped through the security doors with a group of partiers, but at 2:30 in the morning most of the building was quiet. A hint of music seeped from somewhere; a wall sconce fluttered across the hall. His own breathing was louder than either. No sound came from behind Gentry's door. If she was sleeping, she'd be confused and frightened by the knocking, more so by his next move. He took the lock pick from his wallet.

The click of the lock seemed magnified. He slid his Glock from the holster before easing the door open. No security chain. If she was inside, he'd talk to her about that. Even with the coded entrances, she should be more careful.

Candle scent surrounded him as he recalled the room's layout from the wonderful evening he'd spent there. He lit the tiny flashlight on his key chain and sent the beam around the main room and kitchen, then started down the hall to Gentry's room.

He crept carefully, making no noise that could startle her. The door stood open. No sound of breathing. No sense or scent of her. He turned on the light, fear and disappointment hitting him in the gut. He turned back and lit up the kitchen and living room, revealing arched doorways and alcoves, but the rooms lacked the magic she'd made with candlelight and, most of all, her presence.

There was no sign of struggle. No forced entry. But he was careful not to touch anything just in case. 2:45. Where would she be? He holstered his Glock, opened the desk drawer in the kitchen, and found an address book. It was filled with names, some he might recognize, most he'd never heard.

He flipped through the pages and realized he hardly knew her. When they were alone together, it seemed as though he did, as though he always had. But he'd had nothing more than a glimpse. When she'd called the other night, had she been telling him she liked Alec's kiss? Was that what had upset her? That she'd felt something with Alec? He ran her wording through his head. *"You were right. It's Eva, but it's me too."*

Had today's shoot developed a heat between them that neither wanted to end? He'd felt it, her potent presence. The mind-numbing, visceral, awakening power of her gaze. Alec's back-of-the-neck kiss had not been teasing. He wanted her, wanted her to want him. Alec had opportunity and motive.

Cameron clenched his jaw. He thought of holding Gentry on her parents' roof. Did she turn it on for whatever man she was with? *"I've been kissed on every stage I've played."* Jealousy like nothing he'd ever known shot fire through his veins.

Myra's betrayal had dumbfounded and disenchanted him. But he'd never wanted to go after the men she'd been with the way he wanted to go now and rip into Alec Warner. Because he was part of her passion? The acting she loved, the thing that made her "come alive." He burned. What Myra had not accomplished in five years with her multiple infidelities, Gentry achieved now. He tossed the book into the drawer.

What was he doing? He didn't belong here. He'd been stupid to come. He turned off the kitchen light, plunged the hallway back into darkness. He reached for the switch to extinguish the living room lights, but caught sight of a strip of paper on the carpet.

He picked it up and read the single word. *Help.*

His heart hammered. He closed the note into his fist, his ego crashing in. He had let his mind go the other way, because he couldn't think of her with the man who'd hired someone to kill her. The single word stripped away his doubts and jealousies and focused his mind. Whatever it took, he'd get Gentry the help she'd called for.

⌒

After withdrawing all the cash he could get from her bank and credit cards at several ATMs—and freezing all her accounts in the process—Curt had secured a fleabag room in a part of town Gentry had never seen in the four years she'd lived there. It was the kind of place where they didn't ask questions when a man half dragged a woman out of the car and shoved her through the door.

She shouldn't have angered him. He'd seemed absurd as her aunt's lover, but her indignation had made her foolish. This was no spitting contest. He jerked her through the small, dingy space and tossed her onto the bathroom floor. Her chin banged, and she gagged at the sour smell that arose from the yellowed linoleum.

With a knee in her back and the gun to her head, he coiled a phone cord around her wrists and cinched it. "Sit up." He tied the rest of the cord to the brown, corroded plumbing under the sink, then stooped down and raked her with his gaze. "Welcome to the sewer with the rest of us."

She pressed in between the tub and toilet, away from the snake who'd seduced her aunt while Uncle Rob fought for his life, fought because this same piece of trash had ordered them killed. She wanted to rake her nails over his smug face, chop his chiseled chin with her knee.

His gun kept her docile. She didn't walk out on a crumbling shelf, didn't stand tall in a lightning storm. But if one way was blocked, she found another. And when she found it, she'd take it.

"How's it feel?" He slid his fingers over her cheek, down her neck. "Big Hollywood star, every man's dream."

She clenched her teeth when he touched her mouth and willed herself not to bite his fingers to the bone.

"Maybe that's what Uncle likes, hmm? Off alone together on your little adventures."

"You filthy—"

He grabbed hold of her ponytail, brought the gun's barrel to the hollow under her ear. Fear surged through her. Everything she'd done, all that she'd hoped for ended here. Bloody carnage. Headlines. For once she wouldn't care. She'd be gone.

Curt ground his mouth into hers so hard she tasted blood. "Is that how he kisses you? How that cripple kisses you, Allegra?"

Gentry sucked a breath. "I'm not Allegra."

He bent her head back hard and scowled. "Not even close. But Uncle Rob likes you better, doesn't he?"

"Uncle Rob loves his wife."

He smacked her head against the chipped edge of the tub, then let go and stood up. "You're lucky I'm not a violent man."

Sharp stabs of pain shot from the back of her head. Her shoulders burned. The tang of blood seeped into her mouth and warned her not to provoke this "nonviolent man." If he was crazed enough to imagine her Allegra, then he was more than some con after Uncle Rob's money. There was no telling what anger he might work out on her.

He backed out of the bathroom. "I need some sleep."

Through the open door, she watched him empty his pockets, lay her phone and his gun on the table beside him, and then stretch out prone on the bed. Within minutes, his breathing slowed and deepened; he snored. She writhed and tugged against her bonds.

If she screamed would someone hear? Would anyone care? He would gag her—or beat her senseless. Her whole body shook. She couldn't see the watch on the wrist tied behind her, but she knew it was too late for Uncle Rob to return her call. The tiny note she'd left would probably lie inside her door for days, a piece of evidence in a crime bag after the fact.

She sank back against the pipes under the sink and pulled her knees to her chest. Drawing a jagged breath, she fought the tears. The bang on her head felt wet and throbbed. Her arms and shoulders ached. Her lips had swollen. But it could get worse. If Curt thought she was Allegra, or got angry that she wasn't . . . *Lord!* Fear choked her. *Help me.*

Into her mind came the blurred image in the photo that someone had called her strong angel. Cameron claimed she had divine protection; the centipede, the falls, Malakua. Was it true? Was any of it true?

⌒

Closing the door behind the police, Cameron released his breath. The officer who'd recognized him from the tabloids had assumed he had legitimate access to Gentry's place. He never thought he'd be glad for those rags, but it had given his presence and his fears legitimacy, and though he'd furthered the impression that he and Gentry were lovers, he didn't care.

He'd laid out the situation, shown them the note. The officers were treating it as an abduction rather than a missing person, which would have required a delay of days. The lack of disorder indicated that Blanchard had a weapon, probably a gun. Otherwise Gentry would have fought.

All over the city, cops would be on alert for Gentry Fox, for her car, her credit cards. But was it all too little, too late? Fatigue dragged him to the futon. Though he doubted he could, he needed to sleep. It was too intimate to use her bed, too presumptuous. He'd like nothing better than to get caught there, if it meant she was free and able to do so, but he was too realistic to imagine it.

He lay back, assailed by memories of Gentry lighting candles, her eyes laughing, her mouth . . . Fear caught him by the throat. "Jesus," he breathed. He'd carped about Alec kissing her, but darker thoughts assailed him now.

Curt had seduced her aunt. What would make him keep his hands off Gentry Fox? Ransom and leverage were probably the reasons he'd taken her. But this was a man who used sex as a tool. He was already wanted, desperate. If Gentry pushed him, angered him . . .

He clenched his fists. Denny had called her a light in the darkness. Was she so radiant, evil couldn't tolerate her?

He pressed his hand to his face. *Lord. Akua. She's in your hands.* He closed his eyes and saw her flinging off the centipede. He'd believed on the island. Did he believe now?

~~

Gentry cringed against the chipped bathtub, averting her face when Curt came in and relieved himself. His crassness chilled her as she gagged on the sharp odor. He zipped his pants and stood there with an expression she didn't want to see. How desperate must Aunt Allegra have been to fall for the sensuality he exuded?

The frailty she'd seen at Uncle Rob's, the despair in her aunt's face, explained so much—a woman fighting time, faith, and anything too real. Curt Blanchard found and exploited weakness. And while she'd never thought of Aunt Allegra as weak, he'd seen what the rest of them had missed.

She pulled against the cord. Both wrists were raw. She had worked at it throughout the night, whenever she woke from the snatches of sleep that had overcome but not restored her. These were not the gentle knots Cameron had tied when Malakua ordered it. *Kai.* If he knew, nothing would stop him helping her.

But how would he know anything was wrong? Not talking to her one night wouldn't tell him. She twisted her wrist; the cord only dug in. If she had stayed and read with Alec, would she be safe now? If she hadn't left early . . . But she'd followed her conscience. And now this.

She inched away when Curt squatted beside her. Though a handsome man, the smile that found his lips was ugly. She braced herself when he touched the swelling on her lip where his teeth had ground it into hers. Her stomach turned.

"Sleep well?"

She was not playing his game. "I need to use the bathroom."

The corners of his mouth pulled as he experienced the power of her helplessness, her need to ask because she couldn't get up high enough to use the toilet. He could refuse, but he reached under the sink and untied the cord from the pipe.

She imagined head-butting him, but there was hardly room to stand. Her hands were trapped behind her back, and he would clobber her. He took the gun from atop the toilet tank and held the end of the cord like a leash while she struggled to her feet.

She looked him in the face. "I'd like some privacy."

He stepped out and pushed the door almost closed.

Immediately she realized her mistake. How could she undo her jeans? Trembling, she called, "Curt."

He opened the door with a lascivious look. "Need help?"

"I want my hands untied."

"Can't risk it."

"You've got a gun." *You slimy coward.*

He pondered, then turned her around. She gasped with relief when her arms fell to her sides. Her thumb and forefinger felt like frozen sausages. She'd probably crushed the carpal nerves trying to get free. Tears stung, but she would not let him see. She waited until he had walked back out, and then closed the door. There was no escape from the bathroom, no window, no ceiling panel or air vent large enough to slip through, only a rusty fan vent and a cracked light fixture.

When the toilet flushed, he opened the door, gun raised. He motioned her toward the bed.

Her stomach clutched into a fist, but he said, "Call your uncle."

She sat down near the nightstand where he had laid her phone, then opened it and dialed. *Please, Uncle Rob, please.* The phone rang. *Oh, God, please let him answer.*

"Good morning, Gentry."

"Oh, thank God."

Curt snatched the phone from her hand without shifting his aim. "Listen close."

"Who is this? What's going on?" Her uncle's voice carried.

"You know who it is. And it's what's going to happen that matters; what you're going to do, and what I'm going to do if you don't."

She quailed at the look he shot her. What would stop him doing anything? Her muscles tensed. Her hands were free. She could jump him right now. The bullet might go wide, or it might rip through her abdomen, followed by a whole cylinder of cartridges tearing through her. She wasn't that desperate. She prayed he wasn't either.

Curt instructed Uncle Rob to send the money to his offshore account, money he'd been willing to kill for. What would stop him now? She could identify him, testify in court. He must know that. She had to get away. But how?

Hiding her fear had kept her strong, but showing it might lower his guard. She needed a director to tell her which way to take the scene—and then she realized she had one. *Lord, show me how to go over these falls, how to stop this wrong.*

If this were a script, there'd be something she could do. But it wasn't make-believe. It was real. And she could die.

Curt pocketed her phone and picked up the cord. "Lie down." His voice was cold. "Hands over your head."

Her breath stopped. *Fight. Kick the gun from his hand. Run for the door.* But it was bolted and safety chained. He was bigger, stronger. She wouldn't make it out.

"On your face on the floor." He pressed the barrel of the gun to her head.

She dropped to her knees, shaking. He pushed her down, pinned her arms with his knees, his weight on her back. He knotted her hands with the cord. Then he attached the other end to the leg of the bed frame against the wall. The minute he released her, she rolled to her side, but his face was right there.

"A note to the sex goddess. If I want it, I'll take it." He stood.

She pressed her back to the bed frame. It was time to report to the studio. What would they think when she didn't show? Alec might tell them she'd been acting strange. They'd call, send a runner to her apartment, but no one could get in; no one had a key, not even Cameron. How had she thought they would find her note?

She pictured Dwight, tight-lipped and sharp, cursing the money she was costing them. He'd shoot scenes that didn't include her and hadn't been on the call sheets, but that would take time to gather the actors, rearrange the sets. Time and money.

It made her sick to think of Uncle Rob scrambling to meet the demand. Could he come up with so much? He'd done well, but . . . that well?

Curt sat down against the wall, confident that she'd been neutralized. She couldn't do anything he didn't want her to, and he could do anything he wanted.

"So. Tell me about the kid."

She swallowed. "What kid?"

"You know the one."

Then it hit her. "Troy?"

The air-conditioning unit came on with a heavy growl. It hadn't cooled the bathroom, but it chilled her now where she'd sweat a circle at the neck of her cotton tank.

Curt leaned forward. "Tell me how he felt about you."

"He had a crush. He's just a boy."

Curt rested his forearms across his knees. "Why you?"

She shook her head. "I gave him a venue to express his feelings. I guess he got confused."

"He wasn't confused." Curt stood and paced the room. "He wanted to be recognized, appreciated."

"He was." She raised her chin, "I gave him a chance through therapeutic improv to work through his feelings, but also to learn the craft. He knew he had talent. I gave him confidence."

Curt sneered. "You didn't get it. You still don't."

She sighed. "Maybe not. But at least I tried."

Curt's anger gave way. He slid down the wall to the floor and stared at her. He was at least ten years older, probably more, but looked as lost as the kids she'd tried to help. Maybe he was what happened when no one did.

FORTY-FIVE

Cameron woke up in Gentry's apartment, amazed his eyes had even closed. He'd been lured to sleep by an assurance that drained from him now like sweat. He sat up, went down the hall and showered in Gentry's bathroom, surrounded by her scented soaps, candles, and shampoos. Only, her scent was missing.

In the kitchen, he sipped a mug of bitter grocery store coffee and called the police for a status report. The first person he reached was not forthcoming. "Then give me to the person authorized."

The detective in charge of the case came on the line and told him they'd found several overnight withdrawals from Gentry's account from various ATMs. They'd collected video from those locations and plugged them on the map, but she was the only person visible in her own vehicle. In other words, nothing to prove Curt Blanchard's involvement.

He dropped his forehead into his hand. "What can I do to assist the investigation?"

"We're aware of your qualifications and your relationship, Mr. Pierce." Detective Stein's voice had rusty undertones. He didn't like his toes stepped on. "The best you can do is stay calm and available, in case she tries to reach you."

No way he was calm, and available? "I'll be as reachable doing something as not." Gentry had all his numbers in her phone. She could reach him if she got the opportunity. "This isn't just anybody. We're talking Gentry Fox."

"In this department, everyone's case is taken seriously, and we don't know for sure that she's in danger."

"Don't know . . ."

"Mr. Pierce, we're doing all we can to locate Ms. Fox. But what we have right now to indicate foul play is a scrap of paper that could have been part of an errand list."

He expelled a breath. "She was attacked on Kauai. Days ago she recognized the man who ordered it. Now she's missing. How much more do you need?"

"We have competent officers on the search. My partner and I are covering every angle."

"What other angles are there?"

"In the bank security tapes from last night, Gentry Fox appears to be on her own."

Cameron gripped the phone. "The officers who responded agreed Curt was probably armed. He could have stayed out of sight in the car and still had her at gunpoint."

"We are proceeding with that assumption, as you've seen on the news. All units are on alert for her and her possible companion. Trust us to do our job. And don't get sideways of this investigation. We won't look away from the kind of thing you pulled on Kauai."

"Fine." The worst thing he could do was antagonize the detective. "But keep me in the loop."

"That I can do."

Mug in hand, Cameron invaded the living room. He wanted a plan, needed one, but Detective Stein had neutralized him. His glance fell on Gentry's Bible. He sat down in the chair and picked it up. The pages were penciled with dates and comments, personal notes and study notes, and a lot of thoughts with question marks that might have been Daniel's interpretations.

He flipped through the pages where she'd inserted markers, passages she wanted to find easily. It felt like reading her diary, but he was glued to the notes in the margins. Joy poured from her scribbles, as she found new meaning or personal application to phrases and paragraphs. Her words illuminated passages he'd heard but had never taken personally.

A ribbon marked Psalm 64; verses 2 and 3 were highlighted and underlined. *"Hide me from the conspiracy of the wicked, from that noisy crowd of evildoers. They sharpen their tongues like swords and aim their words like deadly arrows."* Beside it she'd written, *Pray for Troy.*

His heart squeezed. Where was she? How was she? Brave, yes, and strong. Spitting mad, he hoped. He couldn't imagine her afraid, broken, violated. And he wouldn't. He pulled out his phone.

‿

The washcloth bound into Gentry's mouth with a lamp cord, would keep her quiet. The cord connecting her wrists to the bed held fast. Curt went out to the motel office to pay up a couple days and keep the manager off his back. But when he ducked into the tight and dingy office, Gentry was on the portable TV with a snapshot of him alongside. It was like a hammer to the head.

How could they know? He'd told Fox to keep silent. Cold fury gripped him. He ducked out before the manager responded to the bell on the door. Swearing all the way to the room, he let himself in, anger forming like a fireball in his gut.

He ripped the cord off and yanked the rag from her mouth. "What did you do?"

She lay there, scared and confused.

"How do they know? The cops. The press."

"I told you I'd be missed."

He shook his head and paced. "I warned him not to talk to anyone."

"It wasn't Uncle Rob. They've been looking for you since the party. What did you expect when you showed up there?"

"Shut up." He hated someone telling him his mistakes, like he didn't know already. She sounded like his mother. "Just shut up." He should have left the gag in. He needed to think, and he couldn't do it with her shrilling in his ears.

He'd remained anonymous through the whole interaction with Malakua and left him to take the heat. He'd pulled all kinds of cons, but he'd never been on the run. What should he do?

He'd planned to leave Gentry in the room once the money was transferred, but now he'd need a hostage. And then what? If he left her alive she could finger him. He swore.

All he'd wanted was Allegra and the life she had. He could have cleared his debts, gotten his neck out of the noose. They could have been happy. But she'd gone back to Rob. He smashed his fist into the other palm.

Gentry jumped. He turned and stared at her. Did she think him a brute? He was no worse than the bighead actor whose house he'd taken her from. No worse than that boyfriend who'd given away his own kid. The investigator. And then it clicked.

He crouched down and grabbed her face. "You told him. How?"

"What are you talking about?"

"Your boyfriend, Cameron Pierce."

"He expected to talk to me last night. I told you he'd wonder."

There it was again, the tone that made him feel stupid, worthless.

He gripped her throat. He could crush her skinny neck, squeeze it as he'd wanted to squeeze his mother's so many times. He felt her fear. She was helpless. *Feel it. Feel what it's like to be small and vulnerable.*

⌒

Allegra stood over Rob's shoulder, an ache deep in the pit of her stomach as he stared at the screen. "I fitted Gentry's phone with a GPS chip and software that enables the satellite to locate her within a two-meter radius. The program isn't officially operational, but from my computer I should get a ping if her phone is turned on."

She squeezed her hands. "I can't believe he'd do this." Had he been so desperate? She remembered the night he'd come to her door, beaten bloody like someone in Gentry's movies, and she still hadn't seen it coming. She felt responsible not only for Gentry's danger, but for letting Curt believe, for allowing too much. "I could talk to him, offer to meet—"

"No."

"If it would help Gentry . . ."

"You're not getting anywhere near him."

"He's not a monster."

Rob looked up, pain darkening his face. Curt had cost him his leg and almost his life. He could have cost Gentry hers and might still. How could she say he wasn't exactly that?

She dropped her face into her hands. "I'm so sorry."

They'd been finding their way, in spite of the crushing guilt. His forgiveness had been so profound, so unexpected. Incomprehensible really, utterly foreign. Tears stung her eyes. "I did this, Rob. I have to find a way to . . ."

"Punish yourself?" Hurt as he was, he turned and took her hands. "You've had enough condemnation, Allegra. Enough."

"But I encouraged him. He believed there was a future."

"He conned you."

She shook her head. "It wasn't like that. There was . . . an emptiness in him too." She looked into the face of the man she loved. "Like finds like."

He clutched her hands to his chest. "Then how do you explain us?"

Her throat squeezed. "I never let you see what was really there."

"You're wrong. And so was your father. Three days isn't enough to undo fifty years of wrong thinking, but if you could see how God—"

They both jumped when his phone rang. Rob pressed Speaker.

"Rob," the caller said, "I think Curt Blanchard's got Gentry."

"I know." Rob sagged in the chair. "He wants fifteen million dollars."

"Fifteen mil?"

Allegra echoed his incredulity. Rob had told her Curt wanted ransom, but not the amount. Not . . .

"Can you do that?"

"It's roughly what I'm worth, after fees and penalties, if I liquidate everything I own, including the house I—we—live in."

She grasped the back of Rob's chair, feeling weak. Had she caused her worst fear, returning to the poverty of her youth? She was terrified, and yet, if it wasn't that Rob would lose it, too, she'd give it all up to be free of her guilt.

"There's got to be another way."

The man sounded adamant, but what other way was there? Rob would do anything for the niece he loved like a daughter, the child she'd denied him. Another weight. These last days had been the most painful and wonderful of her life. Now it was all crashing down.

Rob rubbed his face. "Where are you?"

"Gentry's apartment. I came in last night, but she was gone and hasn't been back."

"If her phone was on, I could locate her."

"GPS?"

"A highly accurate system, but so far her chip's only operational from my computer."

"Do you need a sustained connection?"

"She only has to power on, Cameron, now that I'm watching. Maybe it's time to pray." Rob disconnected and stood like a man whose heart had been torn out and held up for his inspection.

"Who was that?"

He raised his head. "The man who loves her."

She saw the love in Rob's face too. Wounded by her mother's desertion, her father's cruelty, she'd chosen sterility before she ever met Rob, tied the tubes that could have produced life. But her choice had become his loss—if she'd only known.

⌒

Curt released her throat. He hadn't cut off the air, just let her know he could. If that didn't shut her up, he would finish the job. She lay gasping on her side, half crying, half seething. But her anger couldn't touch his. He'd gone beyond anything he'd known before. Something had slipped. A line was crossed.

Holding her throat, he'd felt invincible. Life. Death. Hers. His. Didn't matter. They were nothing. It was all a sham.

He turned her phone on, scanned down to a number, and called.

"Gentry," Cameron Pierce all but hollered.

"Wrong." His own voice sounded cold and distant. "I need papers. ID, birth certificate, social security, and credit cards." The man who'd caused the trouble could fix it now.

"What makes you think I can do that?"

"You deal with fraud. Are you saying you can't come up with a purveyor?"

A pause while he considered that. "I can."

"Get me a name and address. If you try to mess me up, go to the cops again, set a trap, anything, you won't find Gentry alive."

"I want to talk to her."

"No."

"If I don't know she's alive, why should I help you?"

"Because you don't know she's dead."

"No deal."

Curt seethed. "You'd take that chance?"

"Let me talk to her."

Fine. No harm, no foul. Curt put the phone on speaker and crouched down.

"Can you hear me, Gentry?"

"Kai?" Her voice broke.

"Are you all right?"

Her breaths came sharp and quick. Curt felt her fear. He raised the phone. "She's fine."

"I wasn't finished. Gentry—"

Curt hung up and pocketed the phone. He gagged her, checked her bonds, and went out.

~

Cameron called Rob. "Did you get it?"

He heard the smile first. "I'm locating the ping now. Was it you she called?"

"It wasn't Gentry calling; it was Curt."

"What would he call you for?"

"Anonymity. He wants me to help him disappear." Ironic that he'd just shown them where he was.

"Okay, write this down." Rob gave him an intersection and a distance east of that. "This is accurate within three meters—if they don't move."

Cameron hung up and called Detective Stein. He got the station.

"I'm sorry, Detective Stein is not available."

"His partner, then. It's urgent."

"The detectives have been called to a shooting. I'll page, but he'll have to return your call."

And in the meantime, Curt could take Gentry anywhere. The detective had told him not to interfere, but they'd be tied up at the new crime scene. If dispatch sent uniforms, Curt might act on his threat. He'd sounded too calm. As though he had nothing to lose.

Cameron placed another call—to FBI agent Joe Ridder. "Hey, Joe. I need a false ID specialist in L.A."

"This in connection to the missing girl?"

His throat tightened. "Yeah." If helping Curt disappear saved Gentry . . .

"I'll get back to you. Nice work on the Bulger file. Very clean."

"Thanks." Cameron hung up. He checked the loads in his Glock and holstered it. He had his plan.

⌒

As soon as the door closed again behind Curt, Gentry felt the bed frame for anything sharp. She'd cut herself on enough frames to know the possibility. Her fingers found a pointy metal nub that might do it, and she worked her wrists up to that diagonal section and started rubbing the plastic cord. Her wrists burned; her arms throbbed, but this was her chance.

She didn't know where he'd gone this time or how long he'd be. She didn't know if Cameron could or would do what Curt had demanded. She only knew she had to get free.

She wedged her head under the bed to see, then worked the loops harder over the point. It was tiny, and the plastic was much tougher than her skin. But she kept rubbing in spite of the pain.

She had barely marred the cord's surface when the door opened again. She dragged her head out from under and lay still. Curt stopped at the end of the bed, a small paper bag in one hand, her car keys in the other. His gun protruded from his waistband. She gave him a sullen stare as he went past into the bathroom. Minutes later her nostrils were assailed by the sharp odor of hair dye. He was changing his appearance.

She rubbed the cord while the shower ran. Steam added the scents of egg and rust to the chemicals. The air conditioner choked and spewed out blasts of cold air. Her arms shook. She rubbed harder. The water stopped. Had he heard the bed bang the wall? The curtain rings squeaked along the rod.

She heard him moving and forced herself to lie limp and discouraged. With only a ratty towel around his waist, he stepped out and scrutinized her. His wet hair was dark brown. Water drops pearled his muscular chest and shoulders, smooth and bare like a weight lifter's. He'd probably posed before stepping out. She looked away.

"I wouldn't have thought you such a prude. Not with your reputation."

The gag kept her mute, but his assumption rankled. He walked back into the bathroom. Maybe he'd leave again. The plastic coating had started to peel away from the wire inside the cord. If she could snap one strand . . .

But he came out and sat down on the floor across from her. "Hungry? Thought I'd order pizza."

⌒

The shoddy, sixties-style motel looked like the kind where rooms were rented by the hour. Not much activity this early, but amid the forms huddled against the graffiti-covered walls and the heaps of garbage, despair hung thick. Making a slow pass, Cameron saw what looked like Gentry's Honda in the parking lot.

It could have been abandoned after the phone call, but Curt was no pro at covering his tracks. According to the cops, he was nothing more than a petty schemer in over his head. But that didn't mean he wasn't dangerous.

Cameron circled the block. Before ordering the accident on Kauai and now holding Gentry at gunpoint, Curt had no arrests for violent crimes. No rape, no battery, no accidental manslaughter. He was cleaner than Malakua. That only slightly eased the chest-squeezing vise. Anyone could be pushed to violence. Cameron knew that by how much he wanted to hurt the man himself.

He parked across the street beside a Dumpster midway between a pawn shop and rescue mission. The windows of both were as heavily barred as a prison. From that position he could observe the motel, but he got out and walked hunched and slack-hipped to the office. The twenty he passed over the manager's palm refreshed her memory.

"Room seven. He paid cash, hasn't checked out."

Back in his truck, Cameron tried Detective Stein again. His message had been forwarded; the detective wasn't available. Cameron got back in his truck and waited. If Curt was inside and had Gentry with him, it was only a matter of time. As soon as Agent Joe Ridder gave him the name of the false ID specialist, he'd have the means to separate Curt from Gentry. That was all he cared about. Curt was LAPD's problem; Gentry was his.

FORTY-SIX

Curt removed the gag and settled back against the wall. "So what's it like making movies?"

The question, his tone and posture were so ludicrous they struck her dumb. Did he seriously intend to converse as though this were a social occasion? As though one of them wasn't there by force? He'd swung so erratically between rage and calm, she didn't know what to think or how to be, but it was such a relief to have the gag off that she answered the question. "It's difficult."

"How?" His blue eyes looked stark now with the dark brown hair and eyebrows.

"To keep the focus; step outside yourself and play the part."

"That's not hard. I do it every day."

She looked away. What she did was nothing like his cons. She represented the truth in an imaginary scenario. He made real life a lie.

"So is your life perfect now that you're a big celebrity?"

That question proved him certifiable given the situation. "My life's not perfect."

"Everyone screaming and begging for your autograph? Like you're something special, something more than anyone else. Your face in all the papers."

"The lies people tell." She looked him dead in the eye. "And the lengths they'll go to destroy me?"

He rubbed his face. "I didn't want it to be like this." He didn't seem to know where to rest his hands, as though they anticipated already the task before them.

She thought of Uncle Rob lying in the hospital in Kauai, fighting for his life. And of herself with no idea who she was and only a vague sense of fear to tell her something was very wrong. "How did you think it would be, Curt? When you imagined it."

"I didn't." His agitation grew. "I just took the opportunity I got."

"Did you ever think there might be more to it than taking what you want?"

He gave her a cold stare.

"Maybe if you'd thought beyond that, things would have turned out better."

"Beyond it to what?"

"To what you could do for someone else."

He snorted. "When your lunch is whatever you can grab, and a good day is when you break the other guy's nose? Yeah, I'm gonna worry about someone else."

"There's always someone worse off. And someone trying harder. There are people bringing good out of the worst things imaginable."

"Is that what you tell the kids in your troupe? Take this crap and make it good?"

"I tell them God knows the plans he has for them, plans to prosper and not to harm." But harm happened. It happened and happened and happened. Something inside her cracked.

Curt scoffed. "When he shows up with my plan, let me know, cuz so far it's been straight from hell."

"Your plan is the same as everyone's." She sounded like Daniel, so sure of the truth he'd made certain nothing ever tested it.

Curt tossed his head back and feigned a quavery voice. "Salvation through my personal Lord and Savior."

The fracture inside widened. *Out of the depths I call to you. . . .* But did God hear? She had promised Cameron the Lord would answer, but where was he now?

"Problem is, when they handed out personal saviors they skipped me. Maybe you got mine, you with your fairy-tale life." His face darkened dangerously. "You don't know what it's like to wake up starving and bruised and pray your teacher won't notice and call authorities to move you from one hell to another."

"I don't pretend to know what you've been through. But it doesn't give you the right—"

He lunged up and grabbed her. "Don't tell me my rights. You think you know fear? Pain?" He brought his hands to her throat. "Prove it. Show me some therapeutic improv."

∽

He had intended to wait until Joe called with a name. He'd wanted to give LAPD a chance to arrive, but the longer he waited without hearing from the detectives, the more it hurt to think of Gentry in that shabby room with a guy who'd slipped into the zone between conscience and crime. What if stuff happened because he hadn't acted soon enough?

With those thoughts churning, he barely held himself in check. He knew not to interfere with a police operation, but when the dented pizza-delivery car pulled into the lot, Cameron was out of his truck and crossing traffic before he found a reason not to. The motel looked pretty empty. Did he dare hope. . . ? A hundred bucks bought the pizza, the hat, and the room number. They were in there.

As the car pulled out, he placed a 911 call, gave the address for a hostage situation, and hung up. He shouldered the box and approached room seven. Brim lowered, pizza tipped to fill most of the peephole, he knocked and called, "Pizza." Then he slipped his Glock from the holster.

He hadn't planned a showdown, but some instinct outside himself drove him now. The seconds ticked. Had Curt slipped out some other way? He wanted to call out to Gentry. But he waited, head down. *Open the door.*

At last he heard motion. A bolt. A safety chain. Cameron dropped the pizza, brought both hands to his weapon. The door swung open and they were face-to-face, guns raised. Cameron rasped, "Put it down."

Curt took a step backward, another. "You don't want to do this."

"Just give me Gentry. You can walk away."

Curt backed again.

The room looked empty, even the bathroom, but he couldn't see the tub. "Where is she?"

Without breaking eye contact, Curt swung his arm, pointing the muzzle down. Gentry whimpered. Cameron's heart hammered. With the gun on Gentry, all risk factors skewed, as Curt had known they would. Even shot, he could squeeze off a bullet, but he would not risk her.

"Put it down." Curt's voice shook. The tendons stood out in his throat.

Cameron's rigid arms went soft. If Curt hadn't hurt her yet, maybe he wouldn't. If he got what he wanted . . . "Let me see her."

"Drop it." Curt's hand shook. "Drop it or I shoot."

Worked up as he was, he could shoot her by mistake. Cameron swallowed. His breath came in short bursts. "Okay. I'm putting it down." He started to lower the gun.

Sirens sounded in the distance.

"What did you—" Curt swung the gun around.

A flash of motion as Gentry dove for his legs. Curt fired. Cameron launched himself. Another shot went wild. He grabbed Curt's wrist and yelled for Gentry to back off, but she clung to Curt's knees and kept him from kicking loose. Cameron banged the gun out of Curt's hand and took a punch to the temple.

Gentry scooped up the gun and rolled out of the fray. The sirens screamed louder. Curt punched Cameron's ribs. Cameron drove his fist into Curt's face, feeling his index finger crack. Curt grabbed his throat. Cameron broke the hold. They rolled. Curt heaved him off and leveraged another grip on his throat.

Gentry hollered, "Stop."

Curt's grip tightened.

"I'll shoot!"

He couldn't breathe to tell her not to.

Cops burst into the room, grabbed and subdued Curt Blanchard. Cameron rolled to his side and watched Gentry lower Curt's gun to the floor between her knees. Good thing she hadn't tried to shoot. She could have hit either one of them.

He crawled over to her, breathing hard and bleeding from a cut to his shoulder. One of Curt's bullets? She untied the gag hanging around her neck and threw it. He pulled her to his chest, crushed her with his embrace. She was safe; she was whole. He swallowed the lump in his throat and rasped, "Are you through scaring the wits out of me?"

⌒

The medical team had bandaged her wrists and Cameron's grazing, treated the cut on the back of her head, and provided them both a light pain-killer. The detectives had taken her statement, the arduous retelling of everything that had happened. She had enthralled them with no effort at all, signed a sheet of stationery for Detective Stein's daughter; *To Haley, may all your dreams come true.* But she no longer took that for granted.

Her bold confidence had been shattered. The helplessness she'd felt, the fear and pain were now intrinsic. She would never face danger without its shadow. Curt's hands on her throat, his desire to silence, to quench her light. If Cameron hadn't come to the door . . .

They rode the elevator up to her apartment, where Curt had sneered at her candles. He would be there in the glow, their scent eliciting the cloying fear in the back of her throat. She had to purge him, his words, his brutality. The helplessness.

Was it worse because he'd shown her his soul? Because she'd heard the pain behind his accusations? Because no one had stopped his suffering, given him strength and hope when he needed it. She hated feeling compassion for the person who had cracked her spirit. She swept aside a tray of pillar candles and pebbles that clattered to the floor.

Cameron reached out and drew her close. Concern etched his face, and she hated that too. Curt Blanchard had damaged her life, her family. Her soul.

She clenched her jaw. "He had no right."

"No."

"How could he do what he did to Uncle Rob, to me?"

"Lots of messed-up people in the world."

She had cared once, tried to make a difference. "No one can reach them all."

"Doesn't mean we don't try."

She looked up at him. "And be sneered at and targeted?"

He cupped her cheek. "I stop cons like Curt. You change lives. We can only do our parts."

"What difference does it make? We can't stop evil?"

"But we can stand against it."

She clenched her fists. "I felt so helpless." That, more than anything, fueled her rage.

He raised her face and kissed her bruises. She kissed him back ferociously. He responded, engulfing her with his own wanting. They fell to the couch, unable to get close enough. She wanted nothing between them, not even air. Her fingers snagged his hair. She kissed his mouth, sweeter and deeper than any stage kiss. This was real. This was now. All the wanting she'd pretended couldn't touch it. "Make love to me, Kai."

"Gentry."

Her whole body shook. "Tied to the pipes, to the bed, all I could think was he could take everything, even what I want to give you."

"Not like this, in anger."

"Yes, in anger. In rage." She could hardly contain it.

His kiss was soft, his embrace a safe confinement. His palm warmed the back of her neck, in the way he always held on as though she could be lost too easily. He murmured, "I love you. And God knows I want you."

Heat coursed through her. But instead of stoking the fire burning inside, it soothed the awful ache.

His fingers stroked her cheek. "I cherish you." His lips found the hollow of her throat. "And I'll protect you, even from myself."

"But you can't. Life is too precarious. I want . . ."

His mouth silenced her so long the words died away, then he pressed his forehead to hers. "Please. Let me give you this."

She started to cry, haywire emotions crippling her senses. He held her as the rage dissolved.

Her sobs deepened. "Don't let me go."

"I promise."

She wept away her anger, frustration, and fear until the tears were spent. He still held her. She could feel his desire; she'd spoken hers. She'd yearned for his body. But he gave her his soul. And she loved him more than she'd ever thought possible.

Exhaustion hit like a tidal wave. She slept. And woke. He kissed her, and she felt whole.

"Kai," she breathed, thinking of turquoise waters and golden sands, the salt tang and deep-blue mysteries. Fresh tears came, but no anger or fear. "I can't let you go."

"Then don't."

"Have you ever thought you might want to marry me?"

He expelled his breath. "I think it every day. Every hour. I make myself work between thinking it." He touched her lips. "I told you I love too hard. I gave you fair warning."

She ran her fingers over his beard, surprised again how soft it was. Not at all intimidating. "I have to finish *Just Illusions*."

"You're saying this because . . ."

"After that . . ." She gave a single shoulder shrug.

His fingers shook as he traced them over that shoulder. "Are you proposing?"

Everything she felt for him found her eyes; she couldn't hide it.

He half laughed. "You've just carved one bombora wave. You'd better see if you can stand me when nothing worse than a traffic ticket comes your way."

It was impossible to explain the bond they'd formed through crisis. But she knew. It was fire that tempered steel. And whatever came, they'd be stronger for it.

FORTY-SEVEN

Nica rested her hand on her belly and felt the flutter inside. She glanced across the green space to TJ's gaze and shared his wonder at the life they'd made. Kai had been his best man six months ago, and TJ stood now between her brother and Denny in their hand-painted tropical shirts. Although her heart belonged to that silent Hawaiian, this day it swelled with joy for Kai as Gentry came toward them on her father's arm.

Birds of paradise, jasmine, and orchids trailed from her hands against the tea-length, white silk sheath she wore. Jasmine and snow-white orchids crowned her hair. A smile trembled on her lips as she passed her aunt and uncle seated together in the front and took Cameron's arm.

They had kept the time and place secret, but what they were paid for the exclusive wedding photos and interviews would furnish the Hanalei beach house they'd purchased with the rest of Kai's inheritance and some of the earnings from Gentry's last movie as well.

She and TJ would have them close, at least until Gentry accepted another script. After *Just Illusions* the offers were too many, but she could choose carefully and intended to. If the Lord brought her a part she believed in, she would take it on her terms.

Kai had never looked so happy. He wore his hopes as brightly as his shirt. He wanted a baby. She'd known that even before the look of wonder and yearning he'd gotten when he felt her son kick.

"Strong, da love," Okelani said beside her.

Nica smiled, unable to contain the joy. She'd been on the edge of despair, unable to face one more stranger in need. Her throat swelled with emotion. Almost a year to the day since Gentry had staggered into her life, she would now become her sister. Yes, she thought. Strong, the love. *Mahalo*.

And there before her, Cameron's face told the story. Gentry's steps sang the song.

ACKNOWLEDGMENTS

Special thanks to David Ladd for valuable input as this story emerged and, along with Betty and Rick Busekrus, for Hawaiian expertise.

To Bod and Suzie Yunker for the fabulous Kauai condo.

To my mom Jane Francis, daughter Jessica Lovitt, friends Kelly McMullen, Karen Mohler, Doug Hirt, and Mary Davis for prayerful reading and critique.

To my son Trevor for encouragement.

And to my husband Jim for everything.

. . . for God's gifts and his call are irrevocable.
ROMANS 11:29

Be the first *to know*

Want to be the first to know
what's new from
your favorite authors?

Want to know all about
exciting new writers?

Sign up today